THE F
SOLUTION

By

Peter Kitson

www.peterkitson.com

Chapter 1

It was the emergency siren that woke me, wailing and whining… first high pitched then low, piercing my fuggy blanket of sleep. I stirred, shifting my position slightly, wondering why the bed felt unusually hard and the sheets smelt different. Opening my eyes a fraction, I looked up at the ceiling, its once-white plaster yellowed with age, or nicotine, and followed the spidery cracks radiating from the light fitting.

I remembered where I was.

For a moment I rested my forearm across my eyes, postponing the day for a few precious seconds, until I fully awoke, then sat up and leaned against the wooden headboard.

It was a pokey and dull little room, sparsely furnished with a small writing desk and chair in the corner, a basic wardrobe of aged pine, and a rug on the floor that looked Arabic, but was of course just an imitation. Still, however uninspiring, the room was to be my sanctuary, for a few days at least – and I was glad of it.

There it was again, louder and closer now, sounding like an out-of-tune trumpet.

Was it fire, police or ambulance? I'd never heard one in France before. Whichever, it signalled bad news – something I was getting used to after losing my job as a freelance reporter and my girlfriend in one disastrous weekend back in England.

I had just arrived at the hotel in Saint Pierre (a small village I once visited on a family camping holiday as a seven-year-old) to take a break and decide what I was going to do with my life – something I should already have worked out at 35 years of age. Still, a few days walking in the mountains or lying on the beach and something would come to me.

So, which first, beach or –

It sounded again – much louder. So close now it could have been just outside the building. And still I had no idea the emergency was right here in the hotel, and that its repercussions were about to wrench my life onto a different and dangerous track.

I slid to the edge of the bed and gingerly raised myself off the mattress, trying to prevent my dehydrated brain from rattling around inside my skull, and then shuffled over to the mirror for a morning inspection. Hmmm… not good. Ghostly pale skin and bloodshot eyes. I ran my hand over my hair to flatten the bits sticking up and then patted my stomach which, thanks to the football training of my earlier years, was still flat. My yawn was interrupted by a scampering sound outside my room – people running up stairs – voices in French I couldn't understand, the urgent tone indicating something was wrong. I pulled on my clothes, half-stumbling whilst forcing my feet into my trainers, and eventually got to the door and opened it.

And then I saw the ambulance man entering the room of the woman opposite. She must be having the baby now. Another stood in the corridor as if guarding the door, and I asked him, " Is she all right?"

It was a stupid question. Having a baby wasn't an emergency – not a real one anyway. No doubt she would soon emerge, cradling the newborn infant in her arms.

The ambulance man gave me a disapproving look, said something I couldn't understand, and then pushed me back inside my room and pulled the door shut. What was I supposed to do, just wait there? Of course I didn't really know her, but I felt I did. I paced up and down the room like an expectant father.

The sound of shuffling footsteps.

I yanked the door open. The two ambulance men carried out a stretcher, a white sheet covering the face of whoever lay upon it. They struggled down the narrow staircase, the man in front walking backwards, carefully placing his feet, the strain showing on his face. I stood for a moment, confused, refusing to believe it could be the pregnant woman from the room opposite who was being carried out. She had been so full of life – literally – the day before.

I followed them down the stairs and when we got to the reception, the hotel manager stood hunched over, looking at the floor, shuffling from one foot to the other, his hideous left eye swollen like a bullfrog's, weeping continuously. Couldn't he do anything other than just stand there? He was an insipid, shifty little monkey, the sort I imagined gleefully sifting through the underwear of the female guests.

Outside the hotel a group of locals had gathered. They nudged each other, tut-tutting and shaking their heads.

The first ambulance man backed down the three small steps that led out to the square, and then he stumbled, the stretcher tilting to one side, the crowd gasping collectively.

Jesus Christ, hold on to her!

He managed to twist the stretcher back to level, and then he muttered something to his colleague.

The sheet!

It had partially slipped off, showing her face, and I squeezed past to cover her up again. Holding the white material in my hand, I looked down at the waxy, lifeless face, and then knew for sure – it *was* her, and she was dead.

"Monsieur, s'il vous plaît," said the second ambulance man.

I lowered the sheet and looked up at the crowd. Solemn faces. Reverent. Except one – an old lady, grey hair pulled back into a bun, deep-tanned walnut of a face, shabby, loose black dress and cardigan, her hand clasped to her mouth in horror, eyes bursting out of their sockets. She saw me looking and scowled at me before drawing herself upright and giving me a look of pure defiance.

They loaded up the stretcher and moved off slowly – as slow as a hearse – there was no need to hurry now.

With hushed voices the crowd chatted, and out of the corner of my eye I saw the old lady walking alone, diagonally across the square, her head bowed. Then she disappeared into a shop that had baskets of fruit and vegetables outside.

I stood alone, the heat of the sun warming my head and arms, and I felt an unexplainable loss, the intensity of it puzzling me.

Soon the crowd of gawpers began to dissipate, and I stepped back in to the hotel. The manager looked up at me from behind the reception desk, still dabbing his weeping eye with his handkerchief.

"That woman. Would you tell me her name?" I said.

He jumped back.

"Zat is not possible, monsieur!"

"I just wanted to know her name, that's all. I briefly met her yesterday – helped her with her bags." What *he* should have done, the lazy bastard. "It can't hurt to know her name can it? She's dead."

"Not possible!"

Back in my room, slumped on my bed, staring at the ceiling, a voice in my head told me to snap out of it, she was a virtual stranger after all.

The previous afternoon I had seen the pregnant woman struggling up the stairs with a heavy suitcase, and had helped her with it, as anyone would (except, it seems, for the hotel manager). The number on her key indicated she had been given the room opposite mine, and so I unlocked it, went in and put the luggage on the stand in the corner. After trying to speak to her, it was clear she spoke no English, but our eyes met, and for a fleeting moment it was as if we *were* communicating in some way. Beautiful, heavily pregnant, just arrived at a small hotel – it was all strangely biblical – except there was no Joseph and she wasn't wearing a wedding ring – I always checked the third finger left hand of any attractive woman. I gazed at her face for longer than was polite, and eventually left the room, albeit reluctantly. What was it that had drawn me to her? Had it been that open face, radiating a curious mixture of innocence and sadness?

I shifted position on the bed, putting my hands behind my head, my gaze following the line of spidery cracks around the light fitting. No, there was something else about her, something I couldn't work out. She had touched something filed away in the back of my mental filing cabinet, and I was determined to find out what it was.

I stripped off and showered, the warm waters soothing away all remnants of my hangover, but then images of the woman's face flashed before me in the shaving mirror and I nicked my cheek and cursed the hotel manager for refusing to tell me her name. It had been a simple request.

No, zat is not possible, monsieur!
Bullshit!
If he wouldn't tell me I would damned well find out myself.

I dressed and stepped out into the hallway, listening out for the sound of approaching footsteps. Everything seemed calm and peaceful after the morning's excitement, and so I began to make my way down the stairs, stopping six steps from the bottom to check there were no voices coming from the reception, but there were none. I continued to the bottom and walked over to the reception desk, looking like a guest who wanted to ask something. Behind the counter was a door that led to a small office at the back. I peered inside and saw it was empty. Certain there was no one around, I leant over the desk, stretching as far as possible, groping for the registration book. It had to be down there – the manager had got it from under the desk when he checked me in. I touched something and recognised the feel of leather binding, but I couldn't get a grip on it. On tiptoes now, stretching further, almost –

Footsteps!

I pushed myself upright, smoothed the front of my T-shirt and felt my cheeks redden, like a schoolboy caught scrumping apples.

The manager came into view.

"Do you want anything, monsieur?"

Yeah, the name of that woman, you officious little prick.

"Um... yes. Do you have a map of the area? I'd like to do some exploring."

He shuffled his way around to the other side of the reception desk, opened a drawer and pulled out a tourist map.

"No charge, monsieur."

I moved away to the small sofa opposite and the manager gave me a look that said, *I know you're going to be trouble.* Burying my head in the map and running my finger over it, faking intense concentration, I watched from the corner of my eye as the manager opened a drawer, closed it, moved a few papers and then positioned his stapler next to his penholder. He coughed – a dry one at first, then a phlegm shifter, and spat into his handkerchief. Too many Gauloises. He coughed again, his face turning puce, and then he shuffled out of the reception heading towards the restaurant.

He must be going to get a drink, I thought.

Once he was out of sight I sprang to my feet and hurried over to the reception desk, but this time went behind it, still clutching the map in my hand. I bent over to look down on the low shelf, and there was the register, old and dusty looking. After grabbing and lifting it out onto the desk I thumbed through the pages, desperately trying to find the last entry. Yes – there it was! I ran my finger down the column until I saw the name *Danny Avery*, but where was hers – it had to be after mine? Mr and Mrs Ralf... Monsieur Dubarry... Mr and Mrs, what was that – Wan? Something Asian anyway. But she wasn't Asian, and Ralf sounded English or American, and she couldn't have been married to someone of either of those nationalities because she didn't speak the language. In fact she couldn't have been married at all – she hadn't been wearing a ring and there was no husband wandering around grieving.

Footsteps again.

I put the register back on the shelf and hurried around to the front of the desk, still clutching my map, the manager appearing before I made it back to the sofa.

"Um… I was just looking to see if you have anything on the attractions – you know, the historical things to visit in the area."

He looked at me as if looking at an idiot.

"But they are listed on the back of the map, monsieur!"

I turned it over.

"Oh, right. I see now."

I left him looking incredulous at my stupidity and stepped out of the hotel and into the square, the bright sunlight hurting my eyes.

Not registered? She arrives here, heavily pregnant, gets a room, dies, and she isn't even registered. Why? Wasn't there a law that said all guests had to register when they checked into hotels?

The restaurant called the Café de la Place, where I had drunk too many brandies the previous night, was just across the square. It was time for a coffee, and so I took a seat at one of the tables outside. Two minutes later a waiter appeared.

"*Un café, s'il vous plaît.*"

He looked at me as if he was a bulldog and I had taken his bone. I couldn't understand it, this was a tourist area; weren't they supposed to smile and welcome us? We were the people putting cash in their pockets, for Christ's sake – why was I *persona non grata* around here?

It had been the same the night before.

I had gone over to the restaurant for a quick drink, and when I had opened the door, immediately in front of me were a group of men who had been playing petanque in the square when I had arrived at the town. They puffed away on their cigarettes and sipped their pastis, the air thick with the smell of tobacco and the hum of conversation. I stepped inside, closed the door behind me, and suddenly the conversation died, making me feel like a stranger entering a saloon in a spaghetti western. I approached the bar and a stocky man wearing a checked shirt and three day's beard growth turned towards me and glared, refusing to move, blocking my path. My stomach tightened. Seconds passed, although each one felt like an hour. Still the man didn't budge.

"*Excusez-moi,*" I said, trying to keep my voice strong.

Eventually he moved to one side.

"*Une biere, s'il vous plait.*"

The barman looked as friendly as a wasp, but he picked up a glass and began to fill it with cold beer from the tap. The sound of the splashing liquid seemed to be magnified a hundred times and my body was racked with nervous tension. I swallowed hard and shuffled from one foot to the other, trying to look unphased. The barman put the beer down in front of me and I picked it up and made my way over to a table in the corner, as far away from everyone as it was possible to be. Soon the conversation started up again, the old men at the table by the entrance talking with their hands as much as their voices. What the hell was wrong with these people? OK, so there had always been some tension between the French and the English, but did they really hate us that much? Waterloo was a long time ago.

They left me alone, although the man in the checked shirt glared at me occasionally, and then the door opened.

A woman with a boyish haircut entered. She wore dark blue jeans and a waistcoat over a white shirt with rolled up sleeves. The old men looked up.

"Sylvie!"

She kissed each of the men on both cheeks and when she reached the bar five more men greeted her in the same manner. One of them passed her a bottle of Kronenbourg and she took a long suck on the end of it.

She certainly wasn't English.

The woman laughed and joked with the men in the bar, and even the gorilla in the checked shirt smiled from time to time. I carried on sipping my beer and when my glass was half-empty I noticed her laugh whilst looking in my direction. It seemed I was the butt of their humour.

Eventually she walked over to me.

"Hello. I'm Sylvie," she said, in flawless English. "How are things back in England?"

She seemed friendly enough. I stood up and shook her hand.

"Name's Danny. Things in England are fine," I lied.

"It's been a while since I've been there."

"Been a long time since I've been here, but unlike you I never learned the language."

"Well, maybe you'll stay around long enough to learn it this time?"

If that was a come-on it was wasted on me because she wasn't my type.

"So what do you do, Danny?"

I shuffled around in my seat. That was a good question. Was I still a reporter? Maybe. It wasn't something I wanted to discuss at that moment, especially with a stranger.

"Hey, I'm here on holiday – I want to forget about work." Over her shoulder the men at the bar were staring at me and I wondered if one of them was her boyfriend.

"So, what were you doing in London?" I asked.

"Learning English, working in hotels, au pair work, the usual. You're from London too, right?"

"Leyton-Middleton. You know it?"

"Of course I do. The same Leyton-Middleton that are playing Manchester United at the weekend?"

My jaw dropped. "How did you…?"

"There are Manchester United fans all over the world, didn't you know?"

"Well, yes, but… in France?"

"Even here. We get it on satellite TV. You'll watch it with us of course – if you're still here. You'll still be here won't you?"

"Yes."

But I had a damned good reason *not* to watch that particular game; in fact I wanted to forget all about it. We talked about football – she was knowledgeable too – and we drank brandy – not a good idea for my head or my wallet.

At 10.30pm she said, "Well I hope you have a good holiday," shook my hand, and went back over to the bar. A circle of men gathered around her, listening intently to what she had to say, and the stocky, unshaven one cut me a look. He was a mean looking bastard, but I decided he couldn't have been her boyfriend because if he had been he would have hit me by then, after all the time Sylvie had spent chatting to me.

Around that time the brandy had got to me, and I had returned to the hotel on unsteady feet.

The waiter came back with the coffee and banged it down on the table, spilling part of its contents. Service with a grimace. I felt as welcome as a pig in a mosque and a voice in my head told me to leave town and find somewhere more friendly, like Bolivia or Peru. But I told the voice to shut up. I had come here to get a grip on my life, find a new direction, and part of that meant not being pushed around, certainly not by ignorant waiters or nasty little hotel managers.

Zat is not possible, monsieur!

Fuck him. He was hiding something and I was going to find out what.

There wasn't much to go on, but I went over the events again, reliving the ambulance men going down the stairs, how they had almost dropped the woman on the hotel steps, the slipping of the white sheet, and that still beautiful, but lifeless face. Then the expression on the face of... Yes of course! The old woman with the walnut face! She had reacted differently from the other people in the crowd, and when I had noticed the odd look on her face she had given me that defiant expression, as if she had wanted to hide her reaction, but then, when she knew I had seen it, she had thought, *So what are you going to do about it?* Had I read it wrongly?

She had gone into the shop just a few yards farther along the square. I dropped some coins on the table and made my way towards it.

In the baskets outside the shop were various fruits and vegetables. In the window displays were canned items – soups, stews and cassoulets. Green paint was flaking off the door, and when I pushed it open and stepped inside I was hit by the pungent smell of garlic and smoked sausage. The shop was empty, but then I heard footsteps and the old lady entered through the doorway at the back.

"Bonjour, monsieur," she said.

Her broad welcoming smile ceased somewhere between the *"bon"* and the *"jour",* and again she scowled at me, her knotted hands held together in front of her stomach.

I took a step towards her.

"Excuse me, do you speak English?"

Silence…

"Madame."

"Viens!" she shouted.

What did that mean? Was she shouting at me or someone else?

More footsteps, and then a younger woman appeared.

"Danny, how are you?"

It was Sylvie.

"Oh, hi. I'm fine. What are you doing here?"

She put her arm around the old woman's shoulder.

"Not a crime visiting my grandmother is it?"

"Sorry, I didn't know."

The old woman continued to scowl.

"Is the food not good enough for you at the hotel, or do you want something for a picnic?" Sylvie asked.

"Actually, I wanted to ask your grandmother something."

Sylvie visibly stiffened.

I continued, "You probably heard about the woman who died at the hotel yesterday?"

She nodded. "Of course."

"I was there when they carried her out to the ambulance. One of the men carrying the stretcher stumbled and the sheet came away from the woman's face. It's just that… I was trying to find out something about the poor woman, and your grandmother looked as if she might have recognised her. I was wondering if you could…"

"I think you'd better leave."

"Couldn't you just ask?"

"No. Leave please – now."

She was immoveable.

I left the shop and set off back across the square towards the hotel, pausing halfway across to glance behind me. Through the doorway I saw Sylvie and her grandmother waving their arms about in the midst of an animated discussion.

What the hell was that all about? Last night she had been so friendly. Ask her a question about the dead woman and she becomes as mean as the rest of the locals around here.

I lay on the bed in my room trying to work out what was going on. What had caused Sylvie's reaction? Nice one minute, nasty the next. Some women were like that. Take Izzie, my girlfriend, or rather ex-girlfriend. Painfully, I remembered the row we'd had back in England and the way she spat her words at me. *You're a dreamer. You'll never get that job. What do you want it for anyway? I know the truth about you – you're just obsessed with all your political nonsense. Your dad's dead, Danny, so why don't you forget it and lead a normal life like any other 35-year-old? You're pathetic! Move on!"*

The hole those words had burned inside me was still there.

But Sylvie? I remembered the way she had greeted the men in the bar last night, and how she had been with me. She seemed less complicated than Izzie – more at ease generally – certainly not the moody type.

She *knew* something.

It seemed that half the town was acting strangely, especially when I mentioned the dead woman – almost as if there was some sort of conspiracy going on.

I shivered.

No, that was a crazy idea. But if there was a simple explanation for everything, what the hell was it? The need to know the woman's name grew inside me, not just because I had been so drawn to her, but also because everyone seemed to be blocking me from finding out who she was, and the stubborn son-of-a-bitch in me wouldn't let it go.

I decided to go back to the bar that night and ask some more questions.

After a dinner of *magret de canard*, the best duck I had ever tasted, along with half a carafe of house red, I felt ready to take on the whole town.

I crossed the square and entered the Café de la Place.

The air was cleaner than it had been the night before, and it was less crowded. I marched up to the bar and ordered a beer. If the chatter died down at all it wasn't by much – maybe the locals were getting used to me. On my right, leaning against the wall, was the same stocky guy in the checked shirt who had blocked my path the night before. He glanced in my direction, held my gaze for a couple of seconds, and then turned away.

I took my drink over to the table where I had sat the previous night, and waited. The TV was on but the sound was turned off, and a CD was playing of some doleful, male French singer, pouring out his heart. In the corner sat two tourists, fat and round, probably American, cameras still around their necks after a hard day's sightseeing.

Would Sylvie come in tonight? It was just an assumption on my part – she could be doing anything. The bar began to fill and I went over to buy another beer while it was still easy to get – there was no waiter service at night.

Halfway through my second Kronenbourg the door opened and in she walked. Several locals greeted her in the usual way – kisses flying around like sparks in a welding shop, and I stood up to cut her off before she got to the bar.

"Sylvie."

She turned around, her face flat, expressionless.

"I need to talk to you."

No response.

"Why don't you join me?" I gestured towards the table.

Suspicion was written all over her face, but after a few seconds she moved towards the table and took a seat.

"Have I done something to offend you?" I asked.

"Is that it? That's what you want to talk about?"

Still nasty. Better get to the point.

"Sylvie, a woman died in the hotel last night. I met her yesterday – she was very much alive and she seemed to me like a nice person. No one cares who she was or wants to find out. I do – and I will before I leave this place. Your grandmother knows something that could help me. Why won't you ask her – or have you done that already?"

"My grandmother is old. You leave her alone."

"What makes you think I want to do anything to your grandmother? I just want her to speak to me."

"She doesn't know anything. Now leave it, Danny."

"Oh, I think she does and you're trying to cover it up. Why?"

"Rubbish."

She was as immoveable as she had been in the shop.

I changed tack. "We were getting along fine last night – and in the shop today. Right up until I mentioned the woman. Then you changed – turned cold and nasty."

"You've got a male ego problem."

"Sylvie, what's going on?"

She stood up to go and I stood up to stop her, grabbing her arm.

"Let go of me, Danny."

"Just tell me what you know. That's all."

"I don't know anything!"

Strong fingers gripped my throat, pushing me back against the wall. I couldn't move. A punch landed flush on my face and my head snapped back, hitting the wall. My ears buzzed and time slowed, and from somewhere I heard a distant cry of: "*Non!*"

Chapter 2

"Hold still," Sylvie said, holding the wet tissue against my nose. The hotel en-suite bathroom was small and there was barely enough room for both of us to manoeuvre.

"He had no right to do this. Jean-Claude is such an idiot."

"I'd have said something stronger."

She pulled the tissue away – a sopping red mess – and threw it into the toilet.

"Let me look at it," she said.

She moved her face close to mine and while she looked at my nose I looked at hers. It had a neat line, almost too small for her face, like a pixie's. It was pretty cute actually.

"It's stopped bleeding I think."

We moved out of the bathroom and into the bedroom, Sylvie sat on the bed and I took the chair in front of the small desk.

"Sorry you got hit."

"All I did was ask a simple question."

She looked at me as if to say, *Not so simple, actually.*

"Sylvie, it was just a name."

"I'd better go."

"No, wait. You *do* know something, don't you?"

"You're trying to play on my female sympathetic nature."

"I didn't know you had one."

She smiled, stood up and moved towards the door.

"You're alive. I'm going."

"You can't go yet. I mean what if people saw you leaving my room? What would they say?"

"Not what you think."

She opened the door.

"Sylvie?"

She stopped and turned around and I gave her my most doleful puppy-dog look – she owed me something for my pain, didn't she?

"Look, if I tell you will you leave town?"

"Will I want to?"

"No, I don't think you will, and that's what bothers me."

I held her gaze.

"Well?"

Seconds passed and I watched her trying to come to a decision, and then the tension in her face eased as her resistance wilted. She took a deep breath and said:

"OK, here it is. The woman was a nun."

I laughed.

"She couldn't be. Your grandmother told you that? Are you sure your grandmother is…"

"She's as sane as I am," Sylvie snapped. "And she said the woman was a nun."

The idea was preposterous.

"But Sylvie… she was pregnant."

"What?"

I explained how I had met the woman, struggling up the stairs with her suitcase.

"My grandmother never mentioned she was pregnant."

"But she did say she was a nun."

"She was definite about it. Said she couldn't forget her face and that it was very beautiful."

Her grandmother was right about that.

"Doesn't make her a nun," I said.

"My grandmother sometimes delivers vegetables to the convent – she saw her there one time."

Sylvie had more faith in her grandmother's observations than I had, but it wasn't the right time to argue about the old woman's sanity.

"If someone dies like that, where would they take her?" I asked.

"Hospital morgue I expect."

"Can you take me there?"

"Oh, now wait a minute – I don't know about that."

I held my palms open and shrugged my shoulders in the French way.

"It's just a lift to a hospital."

"Look, she's dead. Let her lie in peace. Anyway they won't tell you anything – it'll all be confidential."

"You leave that to me."

After she left I lay on the bed thinking: *A pregnant nun, eh?* A story about a pregnant nun wouldn't shake up the world or rattle the political establishment (something I wanted to do to avenge my father's death), but it was a story, and it would be saleable.

I fell asleep dreaming of the small fortune a scandal sheet might pay me for a salacious story.

At 8.30am the next day I showered and inspected my nose. It was sore to touch, but didn't look broken. I drank coffee, ate a croissant and waited in the hotel reception for Sylvie. At 9.15 she honked the horn of her dark blue Citroën CV 5 van, and I got in and grinned at her, but she continued to frown.

We set off for Nice.

"Well, it makes life exciting, you have to admit," I said.

She glared at me, but said nothing.

Twenty minutes later we arrived at a long cream coloured building that had a definite hospital look to it.

"This is it," she said.

"Is this the only one?"

"I'm sure this is where she would have been brought."

"OK. Let's go."

"Not *me*. I'm staying here."

"What? I need a translator. No point in me going in there without you, how am I going to talk to anyone?"

She looked away from me and out of the side window, letting out a long sigh. Five seconds passed.

"Oh, God. Come on then."

Ten yards away from the entrance my stomach fluttered with excitement – it was like some crazy game. I suppressed the urge to smile and put on a sorrowful expression.

A pretty woman, early thirties, with curly blonde hair and freckles, manned the reception desk.

"Do you speak English?" I asked.

"Yes, a little."

"Oh, good. I wonder if you can help me. I'm looking for my sister. She went missing a year ago and we know she was seen in the South of France."

The woman seemed instantly sympathetic.

"I am sorry to hear that, monsieur, but maybe it is better if you go to the police?"

"Ah, yes, of course it is a matter for the police, but you see we have heard that someone was found dead in a hotel room in Saint Pierre."

I looked at the floor and swallowed.

"Oh, I see," she said.

"Naturally I hope it isn't her, but I must check to be sure… for the sake of the family, you understand?"

"Of course. What is your sister's name?"

"Mary. But that will be of no help to you – we've heard that the woman you found had no name. I mean she had nothing to identify her."

"I see. Please sit down. I will make some enquiries."

We sat on the bench situated against the wall opposite the reception desk.

"You *can* turn it on when you want to," said Sylvie. "Nearly had me in tears."

"Hollywood beckons huh?"

The receptionist made three phone calls, during which she glanced repeatedly in our direction. Was this going to work? God only knows what regulations there are in France about turning up to see dead bodies.

Twenty-five minutes later a short man of Arabic appearance came out to see us. He was wearing green operating theatre clothes.

The receptionist hurried over.

"This is Monsieur Barami. I think he will be able to help you," she said.

"Bonjour. I am Danny Avery and this is Sylvie."

The man offered me his hand.

"Monsieur Avery, I work in the mortuary here in the hospital. The receptionist has told me that you are looking for your sister and that you think a woman who arrived here from Saint Pierre may be her."

"Yes, doctor. We hope not of course, but my sister, Mary, went missing and... well you know, I have to check."

"Can you describe her to me?"

"Well, she is about five foot seven inches..."

"One metre seventy-five," Sylvie said.

"Thank you," I said. "She has light brown hair and blue eyes; she is very attractive. Is the woman from Saint Pierre like that?"

The doctor pinched his chin and thought for a few seconds.

"Does she have any distinguishing er... no. Forget I said that. Maybe you should come with me."

We followed him, weaving our way through cream-walled corridors, which had been scuffed at waist height by trolleys carrying patients – or dead bodies. We descended in a large square cube of a lift with scrubbed aluminium walls on all sides. I looked at Sylvie's face; it was full of unease.

The lift stopped and we stepped out into the corridor, turned left and entered the morgue through swing doors.

"Just one minute, please," said Barami.

He went into an office.

"Danny, you are crazy!" Sylvie whispered.

Five seconds later Barami came back.

"Come this way please."

We entered a cold room. On the left-hand side was a row of what looked like drawers – a kind of giant filing cabinet. I remembered seeing something similar on an American cop show and realised I was looking at a giant refrigerator full of chilled human meat. I looked at Barami and wondered just how anyone could do the job he did.

He pulled out one of the drawers. It glided easily on its well-engineered bearings and came to an abrupt halt when the rails reached the end of their extension. The white plastic body bag looked like a badly stuffed cushion from the 1960s, but there was no swelling in the middle, which had been so noticeable when she had been carried out of her room on the stretcher.

I shivered – not from the cold.

Barami unzipped the end of the bag and pulled back the plastic. He beckoned to me to approach.

"Monsieur, if you please."

I took a step forward, paused, swallowed hard, stepped forward again, and then saw her face – waxy, lifeless, cold, like alabaster – her beauty preserved by death. Again I felt an unexplainable loss weighing down my heart.

"Is it your sister, monsieur?"

As I looked at her I remembered the fleeting moments we had spent together. A nun? Yes, she could have been – she had an ethereal quality, or did death and refrigeration give that to people? But Holy Sisters don't get pregnant. Looking at Barami, and with no need to fake my sadness, I became aware of what I was doing, and suddenly I felt dirty, and that all this was irreverent and sacrilegious – a terrible charade. But I knew I had to continue with it, not only because of the deep shit we would be in if Barami knew we had entered the morgue under false pretences, but also because there really was something suspicious about the woman's death, and I felt it was my duty to get to the bottom of it, for her sake, not just to revive my career.

"No. She's not my sister, but she looks like her in a way." I sighed. "So young and so beautiful. We heard the woman was pregnant and I thought I'd lost a nephew or a niece as well as a sister."

"That is true. I am afraid she died because of complications with the childbirth. These things happen from time to time, but we could have saved her if she had been here in the hospital."

Hospitals. Strange that life should begin and end in the same building.

"Such a tragedy. She looks so beautiful and innocent," I said.

"Well, maybe not so innocent."

"What do you mean? Was there anything suspicious about the death – no wounds were there? You were going to ask me earlier something about distinguishing marks weren't you?"

Barami had the look of a man who had said something he shouldn't.

"Um, well, sort of."

"Sort of?"

He looked uncomfortable.

"I… um. I shouldn't say anything really, but she's dead and she's not your sister. There was something I had never seen before, although Dr Dupont had seen it once – he is the senior doctor in this department. She had her pubic hair shaved into the shape of a cross."

I looked directly at Barami.

"What?"

"We have to look out for anything suspicious, anything that might give us a clue as to how someone died – in case the circumstances are suspicious, and we record everything. It was strange, but Dr Dupont told me he had seen it on an American woman – someone he had examined at his sanatorium. She was crazy, saying all sorts of weird things – obviously paranoid and deluded."

"He owns a sanatorium?"

"We doctors are not always paid as much as you think, and he has a background in psychology, so he has a sanatorium. He thinks it was just a bizarre fashion thing – not something relevant to her death and not worth recording. He's right of course, shaving one's pubic hair like that isn't dangerous, unless you aren't careful with the razor." He looked down, seemingly embarrassed by his own tasteless comment.

It sounded to me like the sort of thing a Hell's Angel biker-chick might do, but this woman was no Hell's Angel.

"What will happen to her?"

"We're keeping her here for now. The police pathologists have taken fingerprint and DNA samples and are trying to find out her identity."

"It's a tragedy, a young woman, pregnant, dying needlessly – two deaths in one. And it is so sad that she has no one to mourn for her. I'm glad it wasn't my sister, but it could so easily have been."

"Do you know for sure that your sister's in France?"

"Er… yes. We had a postcard from her – just after she disappeared."

"So many people go missing each year. It's the way of modern families I am afraid."

"I suppose you're right. Listen, I'd very much like to come back later and see if you've managed to find out who she is. I can't help thinking she has a family out there waiting for her to come home, like we are waiting for my sister, and well… it would be nice to meet them and help in some way, if it were possible."

"You are very kind, monsieur, and I am sorry you have not found your sister, but at the same time I am glad you did not find her here today."

A woman came in wearing a white lab coat, carrying a buff coloured folder. She said something in French, Barami thanked her, and then she left.

"Just one minute, monsieur."

He read something inside the folder and then raised his eyebrows in surprise.

"It seems the police have identified her from the fingerprints. Her name is Virginie Lavelle, from Paris. She was a professional woman."

"A what?"

"She was a prostitute."

Sylvie started the Citroën and we pulled away from the hospital. The car bumped along the badly maintained roads and I sat back in the passenger seat, staring at the floor, remembering Virginie Lavelle's pure face. A prostitute? How could I have been so wrong about her?

Something else struck me: Why did she not have her identity card with her? All French people carried identity cards.

"Sylvie, mind if we stop for a coffee?"

"I've got things to do you know."

I looked at her dolefully again, and she sighed.

"OK. Why not?"

We pulled over in front of a small restaurant and ordered a coffee and a cappuccino.

"Looks like your grandmother was wrong," I said. Sylvie didn't answer. "She was a prostitute, for Christ's sake, not a nun."

"Look, my grandmother may have made a mistake, but she isn't senile, OK? Don't take it out on me because your dead dream girl isn't what you thought she was."

Sylvie was right, I was taking it out on her, but I was pissed off. It appeared that Virginie Lavelle had conned me and I felt stupid. When it came to women my judgement always failed me – Izzie was testament to that. I tried again to reach into my mental filing cabinet to identify what had made me feel so drawn to this nun/prostitute, but whatever it was it stayed out of reach.

Sylvie turned to me, "You have no shame have you?"

I kicked away a small stone that lay by my foot and resisted the urge to goad Sylvie about her grandmother being wrong about Virginie Lavelle being a nun.

"Pubic hair trimmed into a cross – this isn't some French fashion is it?"

She glared at me.

Of course I was also pissed off that this was the end of my story. A pregnant nun was news; a pregnant prostitute was not, although something still smelled like a week-old kipper – particularly the reaction of the hotel manager.

The waiter put our drinks on the table.

A young woman passed by. She was about twenty years of age, tall and slim, and wore a short clinging skirt. She tossed her hair and swung her hips from side to side in the exaggerated manner of a catwalk model. For a few seconds she drew my gaze, and then Sylvie, who seemed equally captivated by the girl's undulating buttocks, raised her eyebrows in appreciation. I thought about Sylvie's short haircut and remembered the masculine clothes she had been wearing when I first met her.

"I see you like looking at pretty girls too. We have something in common."

Sylvie turned to face me, a smile playing on her lips.

"I could see why you were interested in Virginie Lavelle – she was very beautiful. You're not married?"

"No, not my thing. Unfortunately it is my girlfriend's thing – or should that be ex-girlfriend's thing?"

"You don't know?"

"We had a blazing row about the things we always row about: getting married, having kids, settling down, becoming normal, whatever that is. She wants stability – stability equals boredom – boredom equals death. I still want to live. So we had an argument – a big one this time. She walked out – went back to her mother's."

My précis of the events was the version for public consumption, missing out the painful bits.

"So that's why you came here – to think about whether you and your girlfriend should carry on together?"

"Partly."

"Hmmm. Sounds like a good enough reason. How much holiday do you have?"

"Plenty." I shuffled around in my seat. "Look, I don't want to keep you from your work – maybe we should get back. But listen, I really appreciate the lift. Let me buy you a drink tonight to say thank you."

At 9pm, after I had finished my sea bass, I crossed the square and entered the Café de la Place. Sylvie was standing at the bar talking with a group of men, among them the pugilistic Jean-Claude. She came hurrying over to me.

"He's tame tonight, he promised."

I wasn't so sure.

"I'll get you that beer," I said.

"Pierre, deux biere," Sylvie shouted.

It appeared that getting service in the evenings was not a problem for her. We sat down at a table.

"Well, I have to thank you once again for your help today."

No response.

"How were things at the shop?" I asked.

"OK."

Her voice was flat.

"Sylvie, what is it?"

She shifted around in her chair. Before she answered, Pierre arrived with the beers.

"Cheers," I said.

We clinked bottles and each took a sip.

"Well come on, something's up. You can tell me."

"It's my grandmother."

"Is she ill?"

Sylvie shook her head.

"You think she is… suffering mentally?"

As soon as I said it I realised I shouldn't have. Sylvie looked up at me with a pained expression.

"Look, I'm sorry, I shouldn't have been so insensitive."

She folded her arms and then unfolded them, preparing herself to say whatever was on her mind.

Eventually she said, "I asked her again about the woman, Virginie Lavelle, or whatever her name was. My grandmother insisted that she saw her in the convent when she was delivering fruit. I told her she was mistaken, but she wouldn't listen – she got quite angry and upset."

"Sometimes they do. It's just age."

"No, it's not that. She said she knew it was her because they had an argument. My grandmother delivered the vegetables and asked the woman for money – the convent hadn't settled their bill. The girl said it was nothing to do with her and grandmother got angry – she's pretty fiery, as you may have gathered. Apparently the woman gave back as good as she got. My grandmother and a nun, fighting in the convent?" She shook her head in disbelief.

"But we know that isn't true. Are you worried about your grandmother?"

"Wouldn't you be? She was so definite about it. She said it happened on October 9th, so she couldn't forget it. That was the anniversary of my grandfather's death, you see."

I sat back in my chair and thought for a moment. Giving details as precise as that would certainly make her grandmother's version of events sound convincing. No wonder Sylvie was disturbed and confused. I sipped my beer.

"You don't suppose the police have got it wrong do you?" I said.

"Fingerprinting is supposed to be foolproof isn't it?"

"I'm not sure, but if it's ninety-nine per cent accurate maybe this is the other one per cent?"

She shrugged her shoulders. I decided to bring up something that had been niggling me.

"Aren't French people supposed to carry I.D?"

"Sure."

"Then why didn't she have hers with her? She couldn't have lost it just before she died – that would be too convenient. And what about this pubic hair thing?"

"Danny, people have all sorts of ways of amusing themselves."

"But she wasn't alone was she? What about the crazy American in the sanatorium? We could check that out couldn't we? That doctor's name was Dupont wasn't it?"

"We can't go checking out a woman's pubic hair."

"You do want to see if your grandmother is right, or if she's losing her marbles... don't you?"

The next morning I opened the *Yellow Pages* for the Nice area. There were four possibilities. On the third try a woman answered the phone.

"I'm calling to speak to Monsieur Dupont, is he in?"

"Ah, non, monsieur. He will not be in 'ere today. Do you want to leave a message?"

Success!

"No, that's OK. I'll call him another time."

I tore out the page and ran over to the shop.

"Sylvie!" Her grandmother glared at me from behind the fish counter. "I've got it!"

I explained what I had done.

"Danny, this is crazy."

I looked across the room at her grandmother, held my gaze on the old lady for a few seconds, then looked at Sylvie once again before saying softly:

"Wouldn't hurt to make sure though… would it?"

We followed the same road towards Nice that we had taken on the way to the hospital, but this time we took a right turn and headed west, parallel to the coast. We passed through three hamlets and then turned left off the main road down a track. Immediately on our right was the entrance to a chateau. Sylvie stopped the car.

A sign said: *Sanatorium du Soleil.*

It was an imposing building with round towers, like those on a fairytale castle, rising high at each side. At first I thought it was an old medieval chateau, but when I looked harder I saw it was a fake. The stones were cut a little too cleanly and the lines of cement were too perfect. At both sides of the towers high walls ran outwards and to the rear, enclosing the gardens.

Sylvie said, "So what are we going to do now – ask to see the woman with the odd-shaped pubic hair?"

I pointed to a space through the gates at the side of the driveway. "Looks like we can park over there."

We clunked our doors shut, the sound echoing off the trees, and made our way to the entrance, gravel crunching loudly beneath our feet. The bell was situated on the wall beside the studded wooden door. I pushed it, and then steeled myself for my next performance.

Seconds later the heavy door drew open, squeaking loudly, as if in pain.

"Bonjour, madame, monsieur," said the woman.

She wore a crisp white uniform, soft white shoes and heavy makeup.

Her figure was trim – very trim for her age – and her face had a pinched look, obviously the product of a plastic surgeon.

"*Bonjour, madame,*" I said. "I am an American. Do you speak English?"

"Yes."

"Ah, good. 'Fraid my French isn't too good. May we come in?"

Grey stone slabs made up both the floor and the walls of the reception. On the right was a leather couch, art deco style, in cream. In front of me stood an antique desk with thin, ornately carved legs.

The woman took up her position behind the desk.

"How may I help you, monsieur?"

"I am looking for my sister."

"I see. What is her name?"

"Ah, now that is something of which I'm not sure."

The woman looked perplexed.

"Pardon?"

"You see, she left America some time ago and we lost track of her. However, I did find a person she shared an apartment with in Paris who told me my sister had left Paris and got married, but to whom, she didn't know. So I don't know what her name is, you see."

"With no name, I cannot help you, monsieur."

"I wonder if I could see your patients. I am sure I could..."

"Impossible!"

Her reaction reminded me of the hotel manager's when I had asked him for Virginie's name.

"But if I could just..."

"Monsieur, this is a sanatorium, we operate a policy of privacy. Of course we cannot have people wandering around looking at the patients. Impossible."

"Well can I ask if you have any Americans here?"

She drew herself up and lifted her chin.

"No you cannot. Monsieur, I think you had better leave."

"But my sister –"

"I am sorry about your sister, monsieur, but we operate a policy of privacy. Please, you must leave now."

She stood up and made a shooing gesture, and I conceded that my lost sister act wasn't going to work this time.

We got back in the car.

"Well, that was a waste of time," Sylvie said.

I was hoping for a little more support.

"Do you think she's hiding something?" I asked.

"She's protecting the privacy of the patients. Anyway what were you going to do if she had let you see them – walk up to each of them and ask them to remove their knickers?"

Sylvie started the car and we pulled out of the drive. At the main road she indicated to turn right.

"Hold on a minute," I said.

"What now?"

"Just go left a little way."

"Why?"

"Just *do* it, Sylvie."

She turned left.

"OK. Park here."

She pulled over. I got out and darted into the narrow strip of woodland that ran between the road and the garden walls. Sylvie wound down her window.

Dry twigs cracked beneath my feet as I pushed against the narrow tree trunks, testing them for strength until I found one that didn't move with my weight against it. I reached up, grabbed a branch, and then began climbing a tree for the first time in twenty-five years, inching my way up, palms moist with sweat. The branches grew thinner higher up and when I was almost at the top the tree swayed making me cling on like a cat, not moving, until at last the motion stopped and I could turn my head and look over the wall.

There they were, in the gardens, patients in white dressing gowns, wandering around. Two were just thirty yards from the wall, stock still, looking lost. Behind them a man with greasy black hair was moving in an animated fashion, as if he was out of control of his limbs. Another, with a faraway expression, looked up at the sky, and I prayed that I would die before ending up in such a place.

I heard the sound of a vehicle approaching, looked to my right and saw a battered blue van trundling along the road.

Sylvie called out, "Danny, come down for Christ's sake, you'll be seen!"

After the van had passed I climbed down, choking in the cloud of dust it had thrown up. I brushed myself off and got back into the car beside Sylvie.

"So, can we go now?" she asked.

We set off for Saint Pierre and when I described what I had seen Sylvie drove fast, the car swerving left to right around the bends, her hands white knuckled, gripping the wheel.

"It was a crazy idea!" she said, getting all worked up.

Maybe she was right – it had amounted to nothing. Perhaps it was time to give up on finding out anything more about Virginie Lavelle. I had tried, but what else could I do? There would be no scoop for me, and no verification of Sylvie's grandmother's mental health.

We drove back up the hillside. On my right, Saint Pierre sat atop a hill that was shaped like a Christmas pudding. The town's buildings looked like brandy butter melting over the top of it, prevented from sliding to the bottom by a solid grey band: the ancient stone ramparts.

We passed through the stone archway marking the entrance to Saint Pierre and swept around to the left and up a hill, before coming to the small square.

In the hotel I ate a *salade nicoise* for lunch, and then took another walk through the narrow, medieval streets, eventually arriving at the stone walls that separated the convent from the rest of the town. My thoughts turned again to Virginie Lavelle and I pictured her wearing a nun's habit, shrouded, nothing but her face and hands to distinguish her from the other sisters. It was easier to remember her as a nun than a prostitute. Was she my "dream girl", as Sylvie had called her? Was that the reason she had instantly fixated me? Maybe everything that had happened was somehow explainable and she was just some romantic fantasy created to fill the void I had always felt in my relationship with Izzie.

Was Sylvie's grandmother going senile? I saw again the old woman's expression when the sheet had slipped off Virginie's face. It had been one of shock, not horror – I was certain about that. Horror would have been easily explainable under the circumstances, but shock was born of something else. Recognition, perhaps?

A thought struck me.

There was something strange about what Sylvie had been told by her grandmother – or rather what she had *not* been told. Yes, her grandmother had said Virginie was a nun, but what she hadn't mentioned was that she was pregnant. Why? I remembered the mound Virginie's stomach had made of the sheet as she lay on the stretcher. How could Sylvie's grandmother have missed something so obvious? There had to be some explanation. I remembered Virginie climbing the hotel stairs, carrying her suitcase. I had immediately seen she was pregnant, and that was partly why I had rushed to help her, but Sylvie's grandmother had missed it... something so evident.

I walked around in a small circle, looking at the ground, and kicked a small pebble.

And then it struck me.

Of course! Yes – there was an explanation! Sylvie's grandmother had only seen Virginie wearing a nun's habit, loose and baggy, hiding the shape of her body. Maybe Sylvie's grandmother had thought that the woman on the stretcher was just overweight rather than pregnant and that was why she hadn't mentioned it? I ran the theory through my head a few times. It seemed to work.

I looked up at the walls of the convent. How long did people stay in there – forever? It would be an ideal place to hide from the world if you wanted to. Anyone could live there without possessions – no money, no credit cards and of course, no ID. It still didn't explain the pregnancy or the pubic hair – nuns didn't shave their pubic hair into a cross, but at least two people had, and that must be more than pure coincidence. The damned riddle was driving me nuts. Every time I thought I had one end of it sorted out, the other end became unravelled.

I hurried over to Sylvie's grandmother's shop. Sylvie was arranging baguettes on the bread rack.

"I need to talk to you," I said.

"By the look on your face it's got to be about the woman again. Drop it, Danny."

I told Sylvie what I had been thinking about and how my new theory backed up what her grandmother had said.

"And anyway, Sylvie, I just can't believe the woman I met was a prostitute."

"You really are a romantic, aren't you?"

"Well she can't be a nun *and* a prostitute, can she? It would explain why she hadn't got any ID on her. Living all her life in a convent she wouldn't need it."

"So what are you going to do?"

"We're going back to that sanatorium. I want to find the American crazy woman with the cross-shaped pubic hair."

"No! I've done enough."

"But..."

"No, Danny. You can't be serious. You want to chase around trying to find someone you know is crazy because of... It's just stupid!"

"But it would sort out your grandmother's..."

"My grandmother is sane – I have no doubt. Leave me out of it."

"Well at least let me borrow your car?"

Saturday morning. The day of the FA Cup match between Leyton-Middleton and Manchester United. A day that should have been one of the most important of my life. But Izzie had screwed it up for me – or was it Gazza Johnson? I could still hear Eddie Sinclair's words: *Get the fuck out of the country before I cut your balls off!*

But all that was history – to be forgotten about, for now. I had something more immediate to deal with.

I set off in Sylvie's Citroën CV 5 van, bumping and rattling along the roads, a ladder tied to the roof, sticking out in front like a turret on a tank. I held the wheel steady, glanced down at the directions Sylvie had written on a scrap of paper, and thirty-five minutes later stopped the van alongside the sanatorium.

For a moment I contemplated what I was about to do, weighing up the likelihood of ending up in a French jail. Bernstein and Woodward, my two reporting heroes, hadn't given up when they had investigated Watergate. They kept on going until they uncovered the truth. This wasn't Watergate, it wasn't even political, and so would do nothing to avenge my father's death, but there were questions unanswered, and I wasn't going to let it go.

I got out of the van and looked around, checking that no one was watching. Then I untied the rope and lifted the ladder off the roof. The strip of woodland between the road and the wall was narrow, but there were sufficient trees to shield me from anyone in a passing car. I leaned the ladder against the wall and extended it to the correct height, sunlight glinting off its bright aluminium surface. Putting my weight on the second rung, I bounced up and down, testing the firmness of the ground.

I gripped the ladder, swallowed hard, took a deep breath and began to climb. My head popped up above the top of the wall and I looked into the gardens, but there was no one to be seen. My watch said it was still only 9.27am – a lot earlier than the last time I had looked into the gardens. They would be let out later for sure, wouldn't they? It was Saturday – did they follow the same routine at weekends? Better to wait in the car. I descended one step, and then something white moved in the distance. It was a patient. They were coming out.

The figure in the white dressing gown staggered as if drunk, slowly making his way along the path that led from the house, his head bobbing with each step. Another followed, this one taller, walking slowly, almost gracefully. I looked down at the ground in front of me and then to my right where a bush and a small orange tree stood beside each other. Quickly I climbed down the ladder, moved it twenty feet to the right, in line with the bush and the orange tree, ran back to the car, put on the white dressing gown I had taken from my hotel room and scrambled back up to my vantage point.

Fifteen minutes later the gardens were full of patients and I knew it was time to do what I had to do.

Straddling the wall, I hauled up the ladder, lowered it down on the other side, obscuring it behind the bush and the orange tree, and then climbed down into the gardens. There was no turning back now. Stooping for cover, I felt like a member of the SAS dropped behind enemy lines and told myself to calm down and act normal, or at least like one of the patients.

I tilted my head to one side, letting it hang limply, and walked with a stiff left leg. Which way should I go? Towards the house? A patient approached me. Shit. What the hell do I say? Nothing. Pretend to be mute. The man passed beside me, a distant look in his eyes and a broad grin on his face.

"Salut!" he said.

Keep walking – say nothing. I glanced back over my shoulder and saw he had stopped and was looking at me with a puzzled expression.

I breathed heavily. The dressing gown over my clothes was making me feel hot and sweat patches were growing under my arms. I passed another patient – a woman this time, short and dumpy with greasy dark hair and acne spots. She said nothing.

Was she the one? How would I know? I had to speak to them.

Now there were thirty or forty patients in the gardens, some standing in groups, some wandering around on their own. How long had I got? They wouldn't be out here all day. I glanced over my shoulder at the ladder; it seemed a long way away. I had to find this American quickly.

At the bottom of a slope a blonde woman sat alone. She looked younger than the others, different somehow, and I made my way towards her, still walking with my 'stiff' leg. Ten feet away from her I struggled to find the right thing to say. *Hi, are you the woman with the pubes cut into a cross?*

I stopped two paces from her. She continued to stare at the ground, blank expression, eyelids heavy.

I took a step closer and said, "Bonjour."

She didn't move – not one inch. It was as if I didn't exist. Should I give up and just get out of there before someone put me in a straight jacket and locked me up? A tear trickled down the girl's face and splashed onto the grass.

"Hello, are you all right?"

I squatted down next to her and put my hand on her shoulder.

"Do you need any help?"

A stupid question – especially for someone in a nuthouse. No response. There was nothing to be done, it was time to get out. I began to stand up, and then the girl shot out a hand, grabbing mine. I froze.

She raised her head and said, "They don't believe me."

The accent was definitely American.

"Who doesn't?" I asked.

"None of them."

None of them? Didn't Dr Barami from the hospital say the American girl had been locked up because she was paranoid?

"*I* believe you," I said, patting her hand. She looked up at me with a desperate face and her eyes seemed to clear, as if she was managing to focus on me for the first time.

"You do?"

Her hand gripped harder. I nodded.

"Thank God!" she said. "But you can't help me."

"The doctors will."

"But they don't believe me."

"Don't believe what exactly?"

"Anything."

This was going nowhere. I shouldn't have come here, shouldn't have got involved. Time to leave these poor people to their carers.

"I have to go now."

"Will you come back?"

I looked into her eyes – so sad and heavy.

"You'll be OK. Dr Dupont will take care of you."

"No! No!"

She squeezed my hand so hard it hurt.

"It's OK, really."

"They wanted to force me, I wouldn't do it, that's why I'm here – I'm not a whore."

My body stiffened.

"Tell me what you mean. Tell me everything that's happened to you."

"If I tell you, you won't be mad at me?"

"Of course not."

"Dr Dupont always gets angry with me and I have to have an injection."

I began to dislike this Dupont character. What kind of a place was he running here?

"You won't have to have an injection, just tell me what happened to you."

"I refused to do it. The others… They all did it, but it isn't right. It just isn't right."

"What did you refuse to do?"

"Fuck him. I wouldn't do it like the others, I wouldn't. I'm not evil, I'm not."

I tried to stand up but she pulled my arm to stop me.

"Don't leave me."

How could I if what she was saying was true? But she was in a place for the mentally ill; was this all in her head? I looked into her eyes.

"What nationality are you?"
"American."
"What's your name?"
"Tara."
"How old are you?"
"Twenty-eight. Why are you asking all these questions?"

She was sane enough to know her nationality, her name and her age, but that wasn't proof of anything.

I looked up at the house and a nurse stepped out into the garden, ringing a bell. Immediately the patients started to make their way back inside. My God, they were all trained like dogs! I began to panic. What was I to do? I couldn't let her go back in there and face… I didn't know what. As for me, I was already in it up to my neck. Might as well be hung for a sheep as a lamb.

I pulled her up onto her feet, keeping a grip on her arm to steady her.

"Can you walk?"

She nodded. By now most of the patients were halfway to the house with their backs to us, and the nurse had gone back inside. If we were quick we would make it undetected – providing she could get up the ladder.

We arrived at the wall and she began to climb, one rung at a time, agonisingly slowly, eventually reaching the top.

"Sit down on the wall. *Do* it!" I said, praying the drugs hadn't totally screwed up her balance, and then I shot up the ladder as fast as a chimpanzee and straddled the wall.

"Don't move!" I heaved up the ladder and positioned it down on the other side. "OK climb down it, carefully, but be quick."

There was no way she could be quick. She put one foot on the ladder, went to stand up and it slipped. I grabbed her arm, holding her up, and she let out a whimper of fear.

"OK, slowly! Better to take your time than to break your neck." I glanced behind but couldn't see anyone looking at us. "Just feel for the rungs with your feet."

She reached out with a leg and it wavered in the air before finding the rung. A minute later she reached the bottom and I slid down, hitting the ground hard, jolting my ankles and knees. I retracted the extension of the ladder and dragged it along with Tara towards the van, but she stumbled in the undergrowth. I managed to hold her up, but dropped the ladder. A car was coming. Shit!

"*Get down* !"

We ducked behind a tree, pressing ourselves against the trunk until the car had passed by. There was no time to mess about with the ladder so I threw it into the undergrowth, manhandled Tara into the passenger seat, got in beside her and drove off as fast as the wheezy little vehicle could go.

Two minutes later I eased off the pedal, giving the engine some respite. Tara sat in silence, her fear and panic all gone now that she was away from that house of horrors. At least I hoped that was why she was calm. If it was all a delusion on her part, then…

My God! I had just abducted a patient from a mental hospital! Jesus, what the fuck was I doing? I could get years for this! Could I take her back, right now, before it was too late – just drive up to the door and tell them it was a practical joke or something? No, that sour-faced nurse on reception would have me clapped in irons if she could, I was sure of it.

I wouldn't fuck him, like the others.

I looked at the red marks on my wrist where Tara had gripped me. There was no doubt her fear had been real. But if I didn't take her back, what was I going to do with her?

One kilometre further on I pulled the car off the road. Tara's eyes were heavy, like a zombie's, and I wondered what she would be like when the drugs wore off. The lacy collar of her floral nightdress poked up above her white dressing gown. If she were seen in those clothes I'd have some explaining to do.

I drove towards Nice and stopped on the edge of town in front of a clothes shop.

"You have to stay here," I said.

She looked at me blankly.

"Don't move, OK? This won't take long."

I got out, locked my door and then went around to her side, locking her door from the outside. She would be too drugged to work out how to open it.

I ran to the shop and burst through the entrance. Down the left-hand side were shelves full of jeans. What size was she? Izzie was a size twelve. Tara's smaller – size ten. What was that in continental size?

An assistant approached. *"Bonjour, monsieur."*

"Bonjour. I have to buy some jeans for my girlfriend, but I don't know the continental sizes."

"Do you know it in English sizes?"

"Ten."

"Zis way, monsieur." She took me over to the rack of jeans. "Do you think zis is good or do you prefer zis colour?"

"That one. T-shirts?"

"Over here."

She led me to the other side of the shop and I grabbed two T-shirts; one white and one black.

"That's all thanks."

The girl sauntered over to the till and was interrupted by a woman who wanted to ask her a question.

Come on, for Christ's sake! I had visions of Tara fumbling with the car door lock.

The woman got her answer and moved off. I paid for the clothes in cash and ran out of the shop.

The car was directly in front of me, but when I looked at the windscreen there was no sign of her. I span around, desperately trying to spot a woman in a white dressing gown, then ran fifty yards down the road, clutching the T-shirts and jeans, but there was no sign of her. I sprinted back towards the van, passed it, and eventually stopped when I was fifty yards beyond it. Still no sign of her. She couldn't have got any farther, not in her condition, could she? I ran back to the van, clutching the key in my hand, stooped to put it in the lock and… there she was, slumped down low in the seat – asleep.

Thank Christ for that!

Hot and sweaty I got in the van, opened the windows, and set off for Saint Pierre. Five kilometres before the town, I pulled over. The blast of air had cooled me down and woken Tara. Her eyes looked almost normal. Turning off the main road we headed down a track that lead between two hills, then took a right fork to a wooded area, stopping the van amongst the trees.

I handed her the clothes. "Put these on. Go on, you can't stay in that dressing gown." I leaned across her and opened the door. "Change amongst the trees." She got out and trudged through the bushes, out of sight.

Minutes later, my fingers drumming on the steering wheel, she appeared, walking towards me, her T-shirt hanging loosely outside her jeans. She still had on the soft white shoes the sanatorium had provided – with the jeans they looked fine – and she carried her dressing gown and nightshirt draped over one arm.

"How do I look?"

She sounded brighter – the drugs were wearing off.

"Better."

She got back into the van.

"Where to?" she asked.

I had absolutely no idea, but someone in the sanatorium, probably that pinch-faced receptionist, would have called the police by now. I was a wanted man – I was sure of it.

Chapter 3

I started the van and negotiated the track back to the main road, turning left, back towards Nice.

"I'm thirsty," Tara said.

"I'll get you something."

We had passed a garage; we'd be able to get some bottled water there.

They'd be circulating her picture to every policeman in the area. What about the radio and TV? Outraged French people would see our pictures pop up on their screens. They'd be shaking their heads, determined to help catch the Anglo-Saxon kidnapper who had taken a mentally retarded young woman – for what? To demand a ransom for her return, or to gratify his evil sexual desires? My heart thumped and adrenalin pulsed through my veins. But then I told myself I was being silly. Not enough time had elapsed for that yet, and they hadn't got any photographs – not of me anyway.

I glanced at Tara out of the corner of my eye. She was like a ticking time bomb, waiting to explode, but how could I abandon her after what she had told me at the sanatorium?

Need to get a grip. Need to start thinking clearly.

At the garage I threw Tara's white dressing gown and nightshirt into the rubbish bin along with my own dressing gown from the hotel, and bought two one-litre bottles of Evian water – nicely chilled. My mouth had gone dry and we sat in the car sipping them slowly.

It was 11.15am. Sylvie would need her van back. It was impossible to tell her what I had done. If she knew, *she* would be involved in Tara's abduction and I couldn't drop that on her. In any case she might call the police – she hardly knew me.

Tara had to be taken to a place where she wouldn't be seen, where we could talk and she could tell me exactly what had happened to her and what this Dr Dupont guy had been up to. It seemed there was only one option: my hotel room. Would it look suspicious? No, we were in France and men on holiday must get lucky and take women back to their hotel rooms all the time.

We drove back to Saint Pierre with the windows open, the breeze on Tara's face blowing away the remnants of her drug-induced drowsiness. I stopped the van on the hill just short of the square so Sylvie wouldn't see it. I didn't want her to come rushing over.

"You feeling OK?" I asked.

Tara nodded. Her eyes looked quite bright.

"Got to get you into the hotel. You're going to have to pretend to be my girlfriend."

Arms linked, we walked up to the square, which was full of tourists now, so we were unlikely to draw anyone's attention. Tara's legs seemed to be steady. I glanced across towards Sylvie's grandmother's shop; Sylvie was no doubt serving someone inside. We entered the hotel and the manager looked up from behind the reception desk. Thankfully he had covered his hideous eye with a black patch. The sight of it might have unsettled Tara. With the drugs wearing off she might be unstable; they hadn't given them to her for nothing.

I forced a smile.

"Bonjour."

"Bonjour," he replied, glancing at Tara without changing his expression.

The room had been freshly serviced. Tara sat on the bed, let herself fall backwards and lay still, looking up at the ceiling. Was she *really* insane? She didn't look it. Not like some of the people who had been in the sanatorium.

"How are you feeling?" I asked.

"Tired."

"You want to sleep?"

"I need a shower."

"There are fresh towels in the bathroom, help yourself."

She looked directly at me and I got the message.

"Er... I need to go and do something. You take your shower, but please don't leave the room, OK?"

"I'm a prisoner, huh?"

"I will be if someone sees you."

I left the hotel and walked across the square to Sylvie's grandmother's shop. Sylvie was there and when she'd finished serving some cooked meat to a woman with a small child, she asked, "What have you done?"

My God, had she heard something on the radio, already? My body went rigid.

"Er... nothing."

"Doesn't sound like you."

"I had a reality check on the way there. I think you're right – I really should just give up on this, there's probably a simple explanation for all of it."

"What's got into you?"

"Nothing at all – really. Actually I'm just feeling rather stupid. I couldn't find the place on my own, got lost and ended up in the hills somewhere."

She put her hand over her mouth to stifle a laugh.

"And your ladder wasn't tied on the roof too well; it came off going around a bend. It's somewhere in a valley, but where – God only knows."

I pulled out some money and handed it to her.

"For the ladder, sorry."

"What about the van?"

"Oh, that's fine. It's on the hill by the square. You want me to move it somewhere else?"

"Safer if *I* do it. *You* might get lost." She took the keys from my hand. "So what are you going to do now – watch the football at the restaurant?"

I certainly wasn't going to watch *that* match – too painful – and I knew just who *would* be watching it.

"No, I'm going to check out the pretty women around here. You must know the best places to go for that."

"Soon got over Izzie then?"

I didn't answer.

She continued, "Sure, I know some places, but that's my secret. You should stick to the tourists."

"Now there's an idea."

I knocked on the door and Tara opened it once again wearing a white dressing gown, but this time it had the hotel's name embroidered on it.

"You feeling better?"

"Much."

She sat back down on the bed. I walked around it and sat on the chair.

"You know we have to talk," I said.

"You got me out, I'm grateful."

"What you told me in the sanatorium – I need to know more details."

"Why?"

Good question. What had happened to her was not necessarily any of my business – even if I had rescued her.

"What you told me in there, was it true?"

"What did I tell you?"

She didn't remember? Why? The drugs? Or had I taken someone from the sanatorium who was so damaged that she had no memory?

"About the doctor – Dr Dupont – trying to sleep with you."

"What? Are you crazy?"

She's asking me if *I'm* crazy?

"You said he wanted to... the exact word you used was *fuck* – you said he wanted to fuck you."

"No, I didn't!"

She was agitated. I had to keep her calm; without her drugs who knows what she might do.

"Look, there's no need to talk about all this yet, but you did want me to get you out of the sanatorium, didn't you?"

"Of course."

"Because I'm beginning to wonder if I've done something seriously wrong."

"You haven't. Don't worry."

"*Don't worry?* Probably half the police in the area are looking for you right at this moment and I'm the guy they think abducted you, and you say, 'Don't worry'. I don't want to end up in prison for the rest of my life. Who are you anyway? If you won't talk to me about Dr Dupont and what you said in the gardens you can at least tell me why you were there in the first place."

"Why don't you tell me why *you* were there in the first place?"

"What?"

Obviously paranoid – that's what the doctor at the hospital had said, and he was right. Christ – what a mistake I had made. I had to get her back to the sanatorium.

"Look, Tara, I think this is all wrong. You'd be better off back with the doctors – they can help you."

"Don't need any help."

"I think you do." I stood up.

"You take me back there and I'll scream the place down – I'll tell them you abducted me and tried to rape me."

"Now hold on minute – I haven't touched you."

She glared at me and I knew she wasn't joking. Then, as if flicking a switch, she turned off her intensity.

"You know what? I think I'm hungry. Let's get something to eat," she said.

Her sudden change of mood unnerved me.

"I'll call room service."

"No. I need fresh air, and I'm in the mood for a pizza."

"They don't do pizza here."

"Not here, Pizza Roma, in the town."

"You know this town?"

"Sure." She got up off the bed and walked towards the door.

I stood up.

"Hold on, for Christ's sake, we can't go out there, we'll be seen!"

Ignoring me, she opened the door and stepped out into the corridor.

"Well at least take off that dressing gown and put some clothes on!"

We walked along the narrow streets shaded from the sun by tall buildings and, despite the infinite blue sky, I felt as if a black, doom-laden cloud was descending upon me. I stared into the faces of passers-by, looking for any hint of recognition in their eyes, but saw nothing. Fortunately the restaurant, Pizza Roma, was dimly lit inside, presumably to create an intimate atmosphere.

Throughout the meal I kept my elbow on the table and a hand in front of my face. Tara ate a pepperoni pizza, then tiramisu, and followed it with two cappuccinos. It appeared they had not fed her too well in the sanatorium. I took the four seasons pizza, ate only half of it and skipped dessert. There was too much on my mind to think about eating.

After I had paid the bill we left the restaurant.

I followed Tara along the street like a puppy dog, feeling controlled by her and irritated, unable to decide if she were insane or not. Had she *really* suffered in the sanatorium, or had she told a pack of lies to make me get her out of there? The insane could be manipulative, couldn't they?

Hearing a car engine behind me, I looked over my shoulder and almost tripped over the cobbles.

It was the police!

I grabbed Tara and dragged her towards a shop window.

"Hey!" she shouted.

"Shut up."

I held her close, as if we were two holidaymakers window-shopping. She tried to struggle and I strengthened my grip on her. The police car edged along the narrow street and I squeezed her against the shop window, hiding our faces. She turned to look at them.

"Look away for Christ's sake!" I whispered.

The car drew alongside. I held her still and smelt the hotel's complimentary herbal shampoo in her hair. After what seemed like an eternity they passed by and I relaxed my grip, taking half a step away from her. She narrowed her eyebrows and with one swift movement stepped towards me, punching me hard in the solar plexus, knocking the air from my lungs in one great *Huuuuuhhh*. I doubled up and a sick feeling spread outwards from my chest and onwards through my entire body.

Insane? She needed locking up all right!

"What the fuck was that?"

"Keep your goddam hands to yourself!"

A family of tourists walked by, disapproval written on their faces, the mother putting a protective arm around her young son.

"For Christ's sake, Tara, I'm trying to save you – for the second time! The police are going to be looking for you. You want to go back to the sanatorium?"

Please say yes!

"Just keep your hands to yourself," she repeated, fists clenched, body trembling from… what? Fear or anger?

"Let's get back to the hotel."

I opened the minibar and took out a bottle of Kronenbourg.

"You want something?"

No response. She lay back on the bed and by the time I was halfway through my beer she had fallen asleep.

I sat on the floor, leaning back against the wall, jumbled thoughts running through my head. A week ago I had been in England, in the middle of all kinds of shit with Izzie and that Rottweiler, Eddy Sinclair. Coming to France was supposed to get me away from it all – give me time to reflect and think about what to do with the rest of my life. All I had done was leave one hysterical woman in England and end up in a hotel bedroom with another – one who punches me in the stomach when I try to save her. It was the second time someone had hit me since arriving in France. If only I'd walked out of my hotel room five minutes later, or earlier, I never would have bumped into Virginie Lavelle, and I'd be doing… well I didn't know what, but not this.

Saint Pierre wasn't the most relaxing of places – the locals were as hostile as insects. Why? I still didn't get it. It was a tourist place, they couldn't be like that to visitors – we were the ones who gave them their livelihood. So why was I being singled out for the treatment? And what was the hotel manager hiding, apart from that hideous eye behind his patch? Was Virginie Lavelle a nun? Sylvie's grandmother was adamant that she was. How come the police said she was a Parisian prostitute? In any event what was she doing with her pubic hair shaved into a cross? I wondered if Tara had hers shaped that way. If I asked her she'd give me more than a punch in the stomach, I was sure of that. Just how violent was she without her drugs?

I looked at my watch. It was 4.03pm; France was one hour ahead of England, so the Manchester United against Leyton-Middleton football match would be under way by now – Sylvie was probably watching it on the satellite TV in the Café de la Place. In my mind I saw Eddie Sinclair's grinning face and wanted to punch it. My guts twisted. The mistakes of years ago come back to haunt you, sometimes when you least expect it, and I suddenly realised that everything that had happened in the last week could be traced back to one event twenty years earlier, when I had failed to go to the aid of Gazza Johnson. Gazza – bloody – Johnson.

Well, *I hadn't* stood by when something had looked suspicious about Virginie Lavelle's death, and I *had* acted when this crazy American wanted me to rescue her from… what? Probably nothing – just the demons in her head, but at least I had answered her cry for…

I fell asleep.

I awoke to the sound of gentle sobbing, rubbed my eyes and sat up. It was 9.30pm. Tara lay on the bed in the foetal position, her hands in front of her face. Did she have anything to cry about or did crazy women cry for no reason? I suppressed the urge to console her, fearing that if I touched her she might turn violent again.

Standing up, I went to the minibar, took out two bottles of Evian water and offered her one. She reached out with a trembling hand and took it from me. I sat back down on the floor, leant against the wall and took a sip.

"Thanks for getting me out of there," she said.

Still remembering the punch and not feeling friendly, I didn't respond.

"Sorry. I've been a bit rough on you, haven't I?"

"I can handle it."

"It's difficult to trust people." She sniffed. "Why were you there, you never said?"

Neither had she.

"Someone I knew died. I was trying to get some information, that's all."

"They died in the sanatorium?"

"No. Look, it's a long story, something that right now I wish I hadn't got involved with."

She sniffed again.

"I'm sorry to hear about your friend."

"Thanks."

Was Virginie Lavelle a friend? She had felt like a friend. I stood up, went into the bathroom and came back with some toilet paper.

"Here."

She blew her nose.

"Look, I hate to bring this up, but I feel I have to. They were giving you drugs, right?"

She nodded.

"Do you need them?"

"No, not at all."

I wasn't convinced.

"You tell me you don't want to go back but if the sanatorium's where you can get help, well then that's where you should be."

"There's no help for me there."

What was that supposed to mean? Not that I *could* take her back without her consent of course. If she carried out her threat to report me for rape I would be locked up in a French cell for God knows how long. Why hadn't she been afraid of the police? Had she no perception of the situation we were in, or was it just that she knew it was *my* ass on the line not hers? The police wouldn't do anything to *her*, she was crazy – not responsible for her actions – running away from institutions was what crazy people did. But I was an abductor...

I changed the subject.

"Pizza Roma. You knew it. How come?"

"I lived in Saint Pierre for a year before being sent to the sanatorium."

Jesus! I had been wandering around the town in broad daylight with her and she was practically a local – we could have been spotted at any moment!

"For God's sake why didn't you say something? We can't go out of this room, you'll be seen and I'll be locked up."

She chuckled.

Laughing all the way to the gallows – totally nuts and bloody dangerous.

"Nobody knows me here. You see... I'm a *nun*."

"What?"

Chapter 4

This was too much of a coincidence. Virginie Lavelle a nun and now Tara telling me she was one too? She had to be the least nun-like person I knew. Locked up in a sanatorium, telling me a doctor tried to force himself upon her, then denying it, and punching me in the stomach when I tried to shield her from the police. Oh, yeah, she's the Virgin Mary all right.

"Pardon my scepticism, but if you're a nun what were you doing locked up in a nuthouse?"

She didn't answer.

"OK. Well how about this one: Does Dr Dupont know you're a nun?"

"Of course."

"Yet he still wanted you to… fuck him – to use your words."

"I never said that."

"Yes, you did, Tara. I can assure you I have full control over *my* faculties and that's exactly what you told me. Or was that just something you said to manipulate me into getting you out of there?"

"No. Look, I'm grateful for what you did, but some things are best left alone. This is one of them."

"You want me to drop it just like that? I commit a criminal act to rescue you from some fate – probably all in your head – and you just want me to forget about it, act as if it never happened? I'm in deep shit because of you. The police are probably looking for me. You owe me an explanation."

"The police won't be looking for you."

"Why?"

"They just won't be, that's all. Don't make this any harder for me."

"Harder for *you*?"

She was a selfish bitch too.

"I'll be out of your way tomorrow."

That was good news, but I still wanted some answers.

"Tell me why the police won't be looking for me."

"Because some others got out recently and one of them was run over and killed. There was a big fuss and they threatened to close the place down. They're not going to tell the police they've lost another one, are they?"

That made sense – if it was true. Then it struck me: if she really was a nun she might have met Virginie Lavelle.

"Do you know Virginie Lavelle?"

"No, never heard of her."

So much for that idea. If Tara was a nun and didn't know Virginie Lavelle, then maybe Virginie was a prostitute after all. On the other hand Tara not recognising the name could mean that Tara wasn't a nun and Virginie Lavelle might still have been. The riddle remained.

"Are you going back to the convent tomorrow?"

She laughed.

"What's so funny? Whatever you've done they'll forgive you won't they? Aren't Christians big on forgiveness?"

"Yeah, but I'm not."

"So *you* won't forgive *them*? Why? You telling me the Mother Superior put you in the nuthouse? What happened, they prayed for you and it didn't work?"

"There was nothing to pray for."

"So what's to forgive? Come on, Tara – you owe me!"

"Danny, if I owe you anything it's not to get you mixed up in something you'd be better off keeping out of."

"So there *is* something. What's going on in that convent?"

"Nothing."

"OK."

I stood up.

"Where are you going?"

"I'm going to knock on the convent door and tell them you're here. Ask them to look after you. They'll be glad to see you, I'm sure."

I moved towards the door.

"No! Danny, don't!"

She looked petrified.

"What are you afraid of? You tell me you haven't done anything wrong, so why are you so afraid? After all it's just a convent, right?"

"Danny, leave it, *please!*"

"Don't think I can."

"Just keep as far away as possible."

"Too late. I'm already mixed up in whatever it is. I told you, a friend of mine died; something about all this stinks, and it looks like it all leads back to that damned convent, the convent that scares you shitless for some reason. I'm going there to find out what's been going on."

I moved towards the door again.

"No, wait. It's not safe."

"Now why would a convent not be safe?"

"You'd never believe me."

"Try me."

She began telling me the most fantastic story I'd ever heard, pure fantasy, and a little perverted. She was right; I didn't believe her. She really would have been better off in that sanatorium. It was obvious that she needed the drugs they'd given her – probably to help her with her hallucinations, and if she had been a nun and it was the Mother Superior who had sent her to the sanatorium, then it had been the right thing to do. Perhaps it wouldn't be a good idea to take Tara back to the convent; she needed mental, not spiritual help. The sanatorium would be better. If she carried out her threat to say I'd abducted her and tried to rape her, would they believe her or me? After listening to her spout off her fantasy I knew she had a dangerous and wild imagination – the doctors would know that too – they would believe me. I could just say I found her wandering along the road.

She finished her story and I looked at her with pity – she was certainly damaged, but how much and why was for the psychiatrists to determine.

"Well, that's quite a story, Tara."

"Is that *all* you're going to say?"

She sat up, straight as an arrow, her eyebrows drawing together, the skin at the top of her nose wrinkling – it was the same look she had given me just before punching me in the solar plexus.

"You don't believe me do you?"

"Sure I do."

"Bullshit!"

"Look, you've had a stressful time over the last few hours. Maybe you should get some rest."

And while she was sleeping I could plan how to get her back to the sanatorium.

"Sleep? I don't need any fucking sleep – I need someone to believe me!"

Her eyes filled with tears, but she wasn't just upset, she was boiling mad too.

"OK, OK, I believe you," I said, trying to placate her.

"The fuck you do. Right. What day is it?"

"Saturday."

"Perfect. You want to take me to the convent – no problem. Better than that, I'm gonna take *you!* But not now, later. Tonight."

Chapter 5

Breaking in again. If it turned out I wasn't meant to be a reporter there was a career waiting for me as a cat burglar. Climbing the walls of a convent accompanied by a mad woman was not my way of spending a Saturday night, but Tara was determined to show me something. Her story was fanciful rubbish of course, but the word 'nun' kept popping up in whatever it was I had become involved in, and so I agreed to go with her, partly because I was curious to find out exactly what went on inside those forbidding convent walls, and partly because I think she would've had a fit – literally – if I'd refused. It wasn't until we arrived at the place where the convent wall butted up to the town's ramparts, that I began to regret my decision.

There was no moon in the darkness above, thank God, just millions of stars, like glitter sprinkled on black velvet. The night air was perfectly still except for the sound of distant laughter coming from people dining late outside the restaurants in the town. I glanced at my watch. It was 11.30pm – the exact time Tara had said we needed to be at the wall.

"Er…Tara, are you sure you are up to this? I mean, these walls are high – this could be dangerous," I said.

"I was a gymnast in high school. Piece of cake – as long as I'm not full of drugs that is. Follow me – if you can."

Tara mapped out her hand and footholds, then began to scale the wall. When she got to the top she turned around and looked down at me, seemingly unperturbed by the drop on the other side.

"Come on," she whispered.

My palms were sweating. I put the fingers of my right hand into a crack in the wall.

Tara said, "No, not there. Here. Look. Use this crack, and the stone jutting out over there."

I followed her instructions.

"Down there to your left – that's where you put your foot."

It took me twice as long as Tara to get up, but I got there eventually, breathing heavily, and then made the mistake of looking down on the other side of the wall at the ground falling away almost vertically.

"Shit!" I said, my head spinning, my stomach feeling weak. "You've got a good head for heights, right?"

She grinned at me.

"Not really, but I spent hundreds of hours on the balance beam doing back flips and pirouettes, so I figure I'll manage to walk along the top of this without falling."

"Wish I had your confidence."

We made our way along the wall and I tried not to look to my right. With each step I paused slightly, making sure my foot was securely planted before transferring my weight onto it.

To my left were the convent gardens – shadowy shapes of olive and cypress trees, along with beds of flowers, the colours not apparent under the night sky, but the ordered layout indicating the gardens were fastidiously kept.

Tara took ten steps then turned to watch me follow her.

"This is madness," I said, "Where are we going?"

"Just follow me."

Glancing to my right, my stomach turned over and over like a tumble dryer and for a moment I closed my eyes.

"Look at the wall, for Christ's sake, or you'll fall!" she said.

"Tara, this is dangerous. We should go back."

"No chance! You wanted to know what's going on in here, so come on, follow me."

"Look, I believe you, OK?"

"The hell you do – but you will. If I don't prove to you that I'm not mad, I promise I'll go back to the sanatorium – and I won't say anything about you helping me get out. Deal?"

The offer was a good one. All I had to do was play along a little longer, hope and pray we weren't caught, and then she would be off my hands forever.

"Deal."

We made our way farther along the wall, past some buildings with closed window shutters, no shafts of candlelight or nuns to be seen. Then we passed an internal wall butting up at ninety degrees to the ramparts.

"See that?" she said, pointing. "Divides the convent off from the inner sanctum."

"Inner sanctum?"

"Only trusted nuns are allowed in this section. I was one of them."

"So what did you get when you became a trusty – extra food rations, or did you get to pray longer?"

"You'll see."

"How much farther?"

"That building up ahead." She looked at her watch. "We need to get a move on."

She set off again.

Standing with my weight on my left leg, I stretched out my right, lightly touching a stone on top of the wall, began to move forwards, and then… it gave way, the piece of granite falling into blackness, my foot pushing down into thin air.

"Ahhh!"

I went down on my left knee and clung on, desperately trying to stop myself from toppling over the ramparts. Looking down to my right, my head filled with dizziness, and I sucked in a gulp of air.

Tara grabbed the back of my shirt.

"Be quiet!" she said. "Don't die on me yet, I need you."

"Thanks. I'll try to keep alive a bit longer. Wouldn't want to upset your plans." I placed my foot back on the wall and eased myself up. "I'm OK. Let's get on with it."

We continued until we came alongside the top of a building. Tara stopped and turned to me.

"We've got to get onto that roof."

The gap between the building and the walls upon which we stood was no more than four feet, but the ground had fallen away sharply, making the drop to the left of us much greater than I had at first realised.

"Are you sure the roof is safe?"

"No."

"Oh, Christ!"

"I'll jump over first, I'm lighter." She sprang across like a gazelle, landing lightly, perfectly balanced, and the roof held. "OK. Now you."

Oh, shit, I shouldn't be doing this.

"Come on, we're running out of time!" Tara said.

I took some deep breaths and prepared myself, lowering my body into a 'get set' position, then swallowed hard.

Got to do it now.

I jumped.

My feet landed heavily. One of the tiles cracked. I felt myself overbalancing backwards and Tara grabbed my left arm to hold me steady. My right arm wind-milled and I teetered on the edge of the roof. Step back and I was dead. Tara yanked my left arm and somehow my balance recovered.

I moved my feet and part of the broken tile slipped off the roof. I held my breath, waiting for the sound of it hitting something below, followed by our inevitable detection – but there was nothing. The tile must have hit something soft, some bushes perhaps.

"Come on, we're nearly there," Tara said.

The slope on the roof was shallow and we walked around the edge of it to the other side of the building. Tara pointed at a skylight.

"There. That's where we're going, through that."

We clambered up to it. Fortunately it was not locked and it lifted away easily.

"I'll go first," she said.

"You know where this leads?"

"Of *course* I do."

She lowered herself part way through and seemed to be standing on something solid, her head sticking up through the roof. Then she ducked down and I followed her in. Like her, my feet came into contact with something solid and I had to bend at the knees to duck my head inside.

"Can you see?" she asked.

"Not well."

My nostrils filled with the smell of old wood and dust. A few seconds later, my eyes adjusted to the dimness and I saw we were standing on a stack of long wooden bench seats – church pews.

"Climb down carefully," Tara said.

I followed her, slowly shifting my weight, making certain the pews didn't topple.

At the far end of the loft was a door and we made our way over to it. Tara said, "Be careful. When I open this door you mustn't make a sound. There may be people below."

"How much farther have we got to go?"

"No farther. We're there. Just watch... and don't make a sound."

She slowly turned the handle and eased the door back, inch by inch, in case it started to creak. Thankfully it didn't. Through the doorway stone steps lead down to a gallery, made visible by a faint glow coming from within the building. We crouched low, made our way down the steps and squatted on the planked wooden floor at the bottom, Tara pressing her left forefinger to her lips, indicating that I should say nothing.

I raised my head a fraction to look over the railings. The gallery went all the way around the inside of what looked like some kind of baronial hall, and on the opposite side were steps leading down to it. Below us were simple wooden chairs laid out in rows across the room – four rows of ten chairs. At the end of the hall to my right was an altar with an effigy of Jesus on the cross; twenty or thirty candles burning brightly at its base, throwing warm light against the wall behind. In front of the cross was a large, ornate silver bowl, and six feet in front of the altar stood an oblong table covered by a white cloth.

"What are we supposed to be seeing?" I whispered.

Tara looked at her watch; for some reason the time seemed to be important. I glanced at mine. It was 11.56pm.

"Patience."

Ten seconds later I heard the clunking sound of a heavy latch being lifted. A side door swung open and then, in total silence, a procession of nuns filed into the room, their black habits swishing as they moved, each of them taking up position on one of the forty chairs. Two minutes later every seat was taken. To the left of the altar, next to a wooden door with wrought iron studs, stood an older nun, short and tubby, with a large crucifix hanging from around her neck.

Silence.

"Is this *it*?" I whispered. "Have you brought me here to witness a prayer meeting?"

She glared at me.

Two long minutes passed and still nothing happened – except for the circulation in my legs cutting off and my right leg going numb.

Midnight.

The sound of a latch again. The door to the left of the altar, where the older nun stood, swung open, and there was a shuffling sound as all the nuns stood up. Light shone through the doorway. The old nun standing beside the entrance bowed her head. Someone was entering the room. At first all I could see was a hand, holding a candelabra – three candles burning brightly. Then the figure came in – a man dressed in flowing white robes, long black hair parted down the middle, a black beard. He took up his position in front of the altar and stood looking at the room full of nuns, the candelabra lighting up his face, his eyes startlingly blue. In his other hand he held a small book, presumably a Bible.

"My God, it's Jesus Christ," I whispered.

"That's the High Priest. You haven't seen anything yet."

The nuns remained still, their heads bowed. The High Priest began chanting some words in Latin – presumably some kind of prayer, and when it was finished, in unison, the nuns said, "Amen."

He bowed his head and for a full minute there was complete silence. No one moved. Eventually he glanced across at the older nun and she walked across the room to stand in front of him, holding out a piece of paper the size of a postcard. The High Priest opened his Bible, held it out in the palms of his hands, and the nun placed the piece of paper on it. He glanced down at it and then slowly closed the Bible, pressing it between the pages. Then he turned and put the Bible on the altar, looked up at the effigy of Jesus on the cross, crossed himself and bowed his head. Without turning around, with a voice that was deep and resonant and filled the room, he said simply, "Sister Ruth."

A nun from the third row back walked slowly towards the altar, and when she was directly behind the High Priest she got down on her knees. The High Priest dipped his hand into the silver bowl, turned, and with his finger drew a cross on her forehead, water trickling down the side of her face. He uttered more words in Latin and then turned again to face the altar. The older nun and another from the front row moved to stand either side of Sister Ruth. Then Sister Ruth stood up and shuffled backwards until she was against the edge of the oblong table, the two nuns helped her up onto the edge of it, and she lay back. They lifted her habit, pulling it up above her waist and she parted her pale legs and drew back her knees.

The High Priest moved his hands rhythmically between his legs and then turned to approach the table where Sister Ruth lay. The two nuns each took one of her hands and looked down at her face, their backs to the High Priest. He gripped the nun's legs, pulling her slightly towards him, then lifted his robe and entered her, thrusting fast, like a Jack Russell terrier.

Thirty seconds later he grunted in an unholy manner and it was all over. He pulled himself out, let his robes fall and turned to face the altar once more. The two nuns helped Sister Ruth off the table and then they all returned to their places.

All was back to the way it had been minutes earlier.

Picking up his candelabra, The High Priest exited the room. The studded wooden door closed behind him with a gentle thud, and the nuns filed out of the side exit, leaving the hall silent and empty.

Slack-jawed, I gazed into space for a few seconds and then said:

"What the fuck was that?"

"So, am I mad?"

"This whole thing is mad, but no, you're not. I guess I owe you an apology."

"Well, thank God someone believes me at last." She looked relieved. "Come on, we'd better get out of here."

"Hang on a minute. Jesus has left his Bible, and that note he was given – it's down there on the altar."

"Leave it. We should get out of here."

"I want to see what it said, and anyway, no one'll ever believe what we've seen – we need something to take as evidence."

"No, it's dangerous!"

"Won't take a minute."

I took off my shoes and in a semi-crouched position hurried around the balcony and down the steps to the hall. I hurried over to the altar and paused for a second to look up at the effigy of Jesus on the cross. The likeness was uncanny – it could have been the High Priest up there.

Grabbing the Bible, I ran back up the stairs to an anxious-looking Tara.

"OK, let's get out of here."

I helped myself to a beer from the minibar. "Want something?" I asked.

"Got another one of those?"

I handed her the last bottle of Kronenbourg and then slumped to the floor. Tara climbed onto the bed.

"Guess I don't have to go back to the sanatorium," she said.

"Sorry I doubted you, but you have to admit, who wouldn't have?"

"I'm glad you saw it – I needed someone to. I've been called insane so much I was beginning to believe it."

"So tell me again, who is that guy? You told me before, but the whole thing sounded so crazy I wasn't really listening."

"I don't know who he is, they just call him the High Priest."

"How the hell did he manage to get into the convent – I mean it's supposed to be women only, right?"

"He has some kind of hold over the Mother Superior. She says he's the *Second Coming*."

"You don't believe that shit, do you?"

"No, I don't. Look, I was just travelling through Europe like thousands of Americans do. My mom was a child of the Sixties and it kind of rubbed off on me – I was just searching for something, you know, the way kids do. I did some drugs and then got into religion and just thought maybe that was 'the way', you know? Down here I joined the convent and my rebelliousness evaporated. I prayed and did my chores day after day, and for a while the church was my guiding light, my compass – the thing that gave me direction. The nuns were pleased with me and made me a trusty – which meant they allowed me into the back part of the convent, where we've just been. Actually I wasn't just allowed there, I was kept there – amongst the other trusties. Turned out we trusties were 'chosen'."

"Chosen for what?"

"Chosen to join with the High Priest in preparing for the '*new world*' – after Armageddon."

"You what? What does that mean, exactly?"

"It means we were to have the children of the High Priest – children of the Son of God, if you like – a pure new race of people – the 'chosen' ones."

"This is incredible. You were to have the High Priest's child? You didn't?"

"No I didn't. I may have been gullible, but I'm not stupid. I wasn't going to lie down on a table and get fucked by some priest – no way. When I saw what I was supposed to do I knew it was time to get the hell out of there."

"So you left?"

"Come on, Danny, people who start running secret cults don't let their followers just walk out. They earmarked me for some religious training. Brainwashing more like. I wasn't going to have that, so I began to plan my escape – that's how I found out where the skylight was. But before I ran away the High Priest and the Mother Superior got suspicious and drugged me. Next thing I know I'm in the sanatorium."

"Didn't you raise the alarm when you got there?"

"Of course I did, but the convent had already told the sanatorium I was ranting and raving about sacrilegious things and sexual stuff, and that they had rescued me from the streets and had tried to help me, but couldn't. So when I told them what was happening in the convent the doctors just thought I was as crazy as the convent had said I was. I got angry – they thought I was dangerous – so they drugged me up. There was nothing I could do, until you came and got me out."

"So when you were talking about not letting someone fuck you, you meant the High Priest, not Dr Dupont?"

She nodded.

"Makes sense now."

"Well I'm glad you're clear. So now maybe you'll tell me why you were in the grounds of the sanatorium in the first place?"

"I'm a reporter... or *was*."

I told her about Virginie Lavelle and how I had tried to find out more about her – whether she was a nun or a prostitute.

"But how come you ended up looking for me?" Tara asked.

"The doctor in the morgue told me Virginie had her pubic hair shaved into the shape of a cross, and that Dr Dupont had seen the same thing on an American patient in his sanatorium. So I came looking for the girl with the cruciform pubes. But you told me you didn't know anyone called Virginie Lavelle."

"She would have been a nun all right."

"So… you have yours shaved into a cross?"

"We *all* did. The High Priest said we had to. He tried to make out the sex thing was the will of God and it was all OK if we did it 'under the cross', so to speak. It would mean we were doing it in *His* name."

"So how come you don't know anyone called Virginie?"

"No one uses their own names in the convent. I was Sister Amelia."

So it seemed that Virginie Lavelle was a nun after all, but this didn't explain why she was in the hotel. Maybe she had come to her senses and had been running away – trying to keep her soon-to-be-born child away from the High Priest. But if she had been running away why would she have stopped just a few hundred yards from the convent, and why did the police think she was a Parisian prostitute?

"Well, Mr Reporter. Now that you know the story, what are you going to do about it?"

"I don't know yet"

"But you *are* going to write the story?"

"Well, yes, I'm going to have to, but I've got to sit and think about this."

I was still stunned by what I had seen, unable to take it in, as if I was floating around in a bad dream.

"What's to think about?"

"I just need to work out exactly what we've got here."

"I'll tell you what we've got. We've got some pervert who's wheedled his way into a convent posing as the Son of God, fucking all the nuns, trying to create a master race. What else do you want?"

"Yeah, I know we've got that, but we haven't got the whole story yet."

"He's fucking the nuns, for Christ's sake, and he had me locked up!"

"I know, but it was Dupont who kept you in the sanatorium. Is *he* in on it too?"

"I don't know, maybe, maybe not."

"We need to find out."

"Are you telling me this is not a story?"

"No, of course not. It's one hell of a story. I can make shit-loads of money out of this."

She gave me a sharp look.

"OK, *we* can make shit-loads of money out of this. I just want to make sure we get everything before we sell the story. After this gets out the world's press will be on to it and we'll be just one of the pack, and if Dupont is in on it he's going to run."

"What else do we need to know, apart from finding out about Dupont?"

"Well, for one thing we could do with finding out who this High Priest guy really is – his background – he sounded American."

"He is. Accent sounds Californian to me."

"Right. We just have to think of a way of finding out more about him."

"Do you know there are kids in there?" Tara said.

"What?"

"Kids. Some of the nuns have had babies already."

I sat upright.

"Shit! Why didn't you say?"

The thought of innocent babies being brainwashed and brought up in some unnatural way sent a sickening shudder through my body.

"We've got to work fast. We can't afford to muck around with this story long – those babies might be being mistreated in some way." I stood up and paced the room. "This is like looking for a needle in a haystack. How the hell do you find out about a man whose name you don't know? We don't even know where he's from, except that he's an American."

"You could start with my uncle."

"What?"

"You could start with my uncle – Uncle Jim. He's in the CIA."

"Now you're kidding me, right?"

"No, I'm not. You've got the Bible – it's got fingerprints on it. We could start with that. Anyway, it's time I visited home."

"Tara, I can't go traipsing around the world. I'm a failed ex-reporter. I'm so broke I could pass for a monk."

"Just bring your notebook and pen. Leave the rest to me."

Chapter 6

Train journeys. I had never liked them. I always hated the incessant tuh-tum-tee-tum, the gentle swaying of the carriage, and the on-board 'catering', which inspired me to fundamentalist anorexia. But French trains were better – no stains on the seats, passable food and smiling staff, making the journey from Nice to Paris bearable. The French countryside sped past my window in a blur.

I looked across the carriage at Tara. Her head was buried in the *International Herald Tribune* as she caught up with what was happening in the world.

"My God, I can't believe this," she said, holding the paper closer, concentrating on every sentence of whatever story she was reading. After being removed from the world for over a year, watching her synchronise with it was like watching someone who had just awakened from a coma. I thought about what she had been through – the indoctrination at the convent, the peer pressure to fall in with the other trusties (she had been strong enough to resist and I respected her for that). Then being drugged and held against her will in the sanatorium; coming through all that unscathed would be difficult for anyone.

Tara put down her newspaper.

"How come you're an *ex*-reporter?"

Did I want to get into this right now? "Because twenty years ago I stood by and did nothing when someone was in trouble."

I chuckled to myself, and turned to look out of the window.

"You don't sound too upset about it."

"It wasn't as serious a thing as I'm making it sound, but I think that's the honest answer to your question."

"Well, now you've got a story that'll put your reporting career back on track – it was your lucky day when you met me."

She was right – the story was going to get me back in the reporting business. And if Tara hadn't taken me to the convent and shown me what was really going on in there I would still be wondering what to do with my life.

"Look at that," she said, pointing to a large country house nesting amongst the trees on top of a hill. She drank in the view, then sighed and sat back in her seat, and I could sense her imagining life in such a place, wrapping herself up in her thought, as if it were a warm blanket. "What a great place to spend one's life."

She surprised me – I had her down as a city dweller.

"You wouldn't rather party in Paris?"

She looked at me as if I had insulted her. Then she smiled and in a husky voice said, "Darling, you are right. How could I live without champagne?"

I coloured up, and then remembered she had told me her mother was a hippy and that Tara had been travelling in Europe, trying to 'find' herself. She was not some spoiled little rich girl who lived for parties, flitting across Europe with the changing seasons. Curiously she had told me that if I could get her to Paris she would get us to the States, and I wondered if her uncle in the CIA was going to organise tickets for us. She had called him before we left Saint Pierre.

"We could have flown from Nice," I said.

"Not without a passport. There'll be one waiting for me when we get to Paris."

Ah, that explained the phone call. Having an uncle in the CIA was a handy thing.

We reached Paris and I used most of my depleted reserves of cash to pay for a cab to the American Consulate. The driver pulled over to the kerb.

"Wait here," Tara said.

"With the meter running? That'll cost a fortune, I'm nearly out of money."

"Just relax."

She slammed the door shut. Tara obviously had no experience of bureaucracy – you didn't just walk into a government building and pick up a passport, she could be waiting for hours in there. The driver turned to me with a quizzical look on his face and I held out my hands and shrugged my shoulders. He seemed to understand, but still the meter ran up. My foot tapped involuntarily, my stomach began to knot and I reached into my pocket pulling out my remainder of my euros.

I counted my money and deducted the amount on the meter. I was thirteen euros short – and that wasn't including anything for tips. How was I going to get out of this? If I got out now the driver would probably call the police. If I sat there waiting for Tara for God knows how much longer, possibly hours, I would be in deeper shit and arrested for sure.

"Monsieur, it is not possible for me to wait here. The traffic is very bad. I am blocking the road."

I wiped the perspiration from my upper lip and looked across at the building. Should I get out now, pay him what I could and tell him I had made an innocent mistake? He didn't look like a man of compassion. Maybe I could give him my watch? It wasn't worth much, but it would cover the shortfall. It seemed like I had no choice.

"Er… I think perhaps it's better if I get out here."

Something caught my eye. It was Tara, striding towards the taxi, a smile on her face.

"Ah, she is back now!"

The knot in my stomach loosened, but I still had no idea how I was going to pay the driver. Tara opened the door and climbed in.

"Got it," she said, holding up the passport.

How the hell had she done it so quickly? I wished I had an uncle in the CIA.

"Great," I said, in a voice devoid of any enthusiasm. "But I think we need to get out here. I –"

"American Express Office please."

"Tara –"

"Relax. Leave things to me. American Express Office," she repeated.

The taxi driver moved off into the stream of traffic without looking in his mirror. A white van honked furiously behind us and the taxi driver uttered something I couldn't understand. Minutes later Tara jumped out as we pulled up outside the American Express Office.

I sat looking at the meter wondering what French jails were like. The taxi driver rested his elbow against his door and supported his head on his hand. The silence was awkward. Tara's 'Leave things to me', comment had done nothing to ease my discomfort and I was dreading the moment of reckoning when the taxi ride ended.

I shuffled around in my seat and then, mercifully, Tara returned – she had no idea of the trouble we were in.

"Charles De Gaulle Airport," she said.

The taxi moved off. I leaned over to her and whispered, "Tara, for Christ's sake, I haven't got enough money! We're already thirty-two euros short of what's on the meter. We've got to get out!"

She was unmoved. For a moment I was reminded of Izzie and the countless arguments we had had over money. *But it was a bargain, Danny. I just had to buy it. It was in the sale!*

Tara tutted, shook her head, put her hand in her pocket and pulled out a thick wad of cash.

"Like I said, leave it to me."

Oh, how I wished I had an Uncle Jim.

At the airport Tara paid for the tickets.

"OK. So now it's time I got some more clothes," she said. "You might want to get yourself a coffee."

I ordered a cappuccino at a restaurant in the terminal building and twenty minutes later she approached wearing a new pair of tight white jeans, trainers and a skin-tight white top. She had put on some make-up – when I saw her, my mouth fell open.

"Hi there. Managed to get some other things as well." She held up a carrier bag.

"Quite a makeover."

"Thanks. Come on."

"There's no rush, the flight's not going for another hour."

"Yes, but there's no point in sitting out here. Better to make full use of the tickets."

She led me along the concourse, turning right into the lounge reserved for first class passengers. Just how high up in the CIA was Uncle Jim, or did everyone in the CIA travel at the front of the plane?

After a comfortable thirty minutes we boarded the plane and sank into our enormous seats. Within seconds a hostess with a big smile and bright red lipstick gave us each a glass of champagne. This was definitely the way to travel.

Once we had levelled out in the cruise we dined on *filet de boeuf* and drank a full-bodied burgundy. Feeling full and a little light-headed, I reclined my seat and Tara did the same.

I glanced across at her.

"Tara, this is amazing. I'm afraid I'm strictly a second class traveller. Your Uncle Jim is quite a guy."

"You got me out of the sanatorium – I owe you one. Anyway we're partners now; I want half the money for the story. Let's just hope Uncle Jim can find out something about the High Priest."

She seemed to have forgotten the trauma she had been through.

"You're enjoying this aren't you?"

"Yeah. It's exciting. I think I understand why you became a reporter."

"I've a confession to make – I was never much of a reporter."

"Why do you say that?"

"Because all I ever managed to do was become a small-time freelance reporter for a local newspaper. I just went to sports games – soccer and cricket mostly – and wrote about what happened. Not very exciting."

"So you became a reporter because you're a sports nut?"

"No."

"So why then?"

"It's a long story."

"It's a nine-hour flight."

She held my gaze waiting for an answer.

I hadn't talked about my father's death for a long time – not since I had first met Izzie, and even after twenty years the subject was raw, like an open wound. Tara didn't know it, but she was asking me to talk about the one thing that had shaped my life more than any other, and my cheeks reddened. And yet, though she was little more than a stranger to me, I felt comfortable with her, trusted her. She was direct and seemingly without guile.

"When I was a kid we lived in a flat over my parent's little convenience store. It wasn't exactly Wal-Mart and we didn't make much money. We owned the small paddock next to it as well, which we rented out to a businessman called Arnold Mullet, who wanted it for his daughters' two ponies. I used to watch Aimee and Nicola riding. They put up some jumps and they were pretty good.

"But Arnold Mullet was a slob of a man and my dad didn't like him because he was always late with the rent and we needed every penny of it. I remember when I played football I never had boots that fitted. Mum bought me a pair a size too big so I would grow into them, and then I would have to keep them until they pinched. Anyway, Dad had an idea. Leyton-Middleton —"

"Where?"

"That's the name of the town where I grew up. It was expanding fast, and if we could get permission to build on the paddock we could sell it to a builder and make some money. That land was going to save us, except we never got permission to build, just some bullshit excuses, time after time. Dad gave Arnold Mullet a hard time when he came into the shop. You see, Arnold was on the council, but he said he had nothing to do with the planning committee. Times got harder. They put up the rates."

"The what?"

"It's what we called the local property tax back then. Dad got desperate. We used to eat stale bread and food from the shop that was past its sell-by date. Then Arnold Mullet came over and offered to buy the paddock. He said he was worried Dad would sell it and his daughters would have nowhere to ride. We didn't need to think long about it. Dad took the money and for a while his depression lifted, then something happened to tip him over the edge.

"We were having breakfast in the flat over the shop one morning. I had the radio on and Dad told me to turn it off for a second. I wanted it on and was pissed off when Dad hit the off button. When the music was turned off I heard the sound of diesel engines and Dad rushed to look out of the window. 'Bastards, bastards!' he shouted, and then he fell to the floor clutching his chest. Mum shouted for me to call an ambulance, but his pain seemed to go as fast as it had come and he told me not to bother. He was a stubborn man and he hated doctors. When I looked out of the window I saw diggers levelling the ground ready to build. Arnold Mullet had got himself on the planning committee and had made himself a fat profit out of my Dad's paddock."

"My God, that's terrible."

"Dad never recovered from it. Some months later I took him for a walk, which was difficult for him, but he needed to take some exercise, and we walked past a pub. Arnold's maroon Bentley was in the car park and he came out of the pub, more red-faced than usual, with two of his cronies holding him up. Dad went mad calling him a cheat and the scum-of-the-earth – I had to hold him back from lunging at him. Arnold told Dad he was a sad loser and then he drove off in his big car with a smug smile on his face. I got Dad home and later that night he had a massive heart attack and died."

"I'm sorry to hear that. It must have been a terrible time for you."

"That bastard killed my father as sure as if he'd put a gun against his head and pulled the trigger. He made my life harder too, and my mother's. I was just fifteen, but I vowed to get even with him. Trouble was the fat old slob wasn't too healthy and he died a couple of years later and I felt cheated out of my revenge."

"How was your mother through all this?"

"She died five years after my dad. Not bitter – she was too kind and soft to be bitter – just sad and lonely."

"Oh, Danny."

Tara reached over and squeezed my hand.

"I got wise to politicians, and I wanted to strike against the system in some way, like Bernstein and Woodward, the reporters who uncovered the Watergate scandal and brought down President Nixon. I wondered if I could do the same – the power of the pen is mightier than the sword, and all that. Pretty noble ideals, huh?

"I never got to bring any politicians down. I just reported on sports events, and I don't think I did that too well. Like I said, I got the sack just before coming over to France. I was supposed to be in Saint Pierre re-evaluating my life, trying to decide what to do next, and then I got mixed up with all this."

We met each other's gaze and I felt totally connected to her.

"That's a sad story," she said. "But I'm glad you got the sack. If you hadn't I'd probably still be drugged up in that sanatorium." She patted my hand. "You're *my* hero anyway."

She smiled at me and warmth flowed through my body. I reached out and touched her arm, then withdrew my hand, feeling embarrassed. But then she took my hand in hers and squeezed it, holding on for a second longer than perhaps she should have.

Chapter 7

Florida – not far from Naples. In our hire car, we turned down a narrow road that led through some trees. Any minute now we were sure to come across Tara's mother's tumbledown shack, no doubt with a yard full of broken down trucks, and a visiting alligator picking at the garbage.

"Turn here," Tara said.

I turned right again and fifty yards down a driveway stopped in front of an imposing pair of wrought iron gates. A mean looking man dressed in black, a Stetson on his head and a rifle his hand, stepped out in front of us. He raised his gun, holding it away from his body and diagonally across his chest, giving us a piercing are-you-looking-for-trouble kind of stare. I slammed the car into reverse.

Tara grabbed my arm. "Wait!"

I froze for an instant.. Tara wound down her window and stuck her head out. The man in black smiled, stepped to one side, pushed a button on the gatepost and the gates swung open.

"He's the guard. It's OK," Tara said.

The guard? Hippies in shacks don't have guards.

"Danny, drive on. It's fine."

I closed my mouth and drove through the gateway, the guard touching the barrel of his rifle to the brim of his hat in a kind of salute.

Thirty yards through the gates I stopped the car to let a dozen luminous pink flamingos move out of the way, and then we rounded a bend, my eyes widening in wonder at the sight before me. At the end of a lawn, so lush and perfectly trimmed it seemed unnatural, stood a pink mansion built in the style of a Greek temple with four fluted columns in the centre. In front of it were cypress trees, tall, slim and evenly spaced, and a swimming pool, the sunlight glistening off the surface of the water.

"You live here and your mum's a hippy?"

Tara nodded.

"I should have gone into the hippy business myself."

I drove up to the side of the house, turned off the engine and got out.

"Tara! Where the hell have you been?"

I looked behind me and saw a tall, slim woman with long dark hair and mahogany skin.

"Hi, Mom."

"If you're gonna take off you might at least call once in a while. Jesus Christ, there are phones everywhere aren't there? Even email, for God's sake."

Tara walked over, kissed her mother on the cheek and hugged her, but she didn't hug back.

"Mom, this is Danny. Danny, this is my mom, Isobel."

"Hi," I said.

She looked at me suspiciously, then said:

"I suppose I better organise you some food."

She led the way to an airy room with tall, arched windows and a floor of unusually large black and white tiles, like an oversized chessboard. Isobel gestured for me to sit down on one of the wicker sofas, and then, as if by magic, a man in a white waiter's jacket appeared.

"Neil, bring us some tea." She interrupted herself then turned to me and said, "You do like tea I suppose?"

"Tea would be fine, thanks."

She sat very correctly; neck long, head balanced, back straight, like someone who practises yoga.

"So, Tara, now that you're home what are you going to do?"

"Aren't you going to ask where I've been?"

"I'm not sure I want to know. You're back now and I'm glad about that, although heaven knows what you said to Jim. He's arriving tonight. He sounded in a real flap."

"I'm not here for long. We've got something to do back in Europe."

"In Europe? Beautifully vague as ever," Isobel said.

The tea arrived and then the clock struck.

"Ah, it's time for my swim. You'll excuse me." She got up and appeared to flow rather than walk across the tiled floor and out of the room.

"She doesn't like me does she?" I said.

"She doesn't much like anyone I bring back. She's a little protective."

We drank our tea and then toured the endless rooms on the ground floor – a library, a music room, various drawing rooms and a dining room with a long, Italian looking glass-topped table with sixteen chairs around it.

"Dinner will be in here tonight," Tara said.

We went out into the garden – a perfectly flat carpet of grass, coiffured to perfection, not a trace of brown earth to be seen anywhere amongst the green healthy blades.

"You don't have any flowers?" I asked.

"No. Mother was into minimalism when she designed the house. She keeps her flowers at the main house."

"You mean this *isn't* the main house?"

She laughed and said:

"This is a kind of weekend house. We use it in the winter mostly. New York State gets pretty cold then."

"Tara, I've got to ask you, what does your father do?"

She looked down at the floor.

"Now there's a question."

"Look, tell me it's none of my business, but you say your mum's a hippy and I can't see how a hippy got to be so wealthy. Is she in the music business or in films? But then she would be famous and I would know her, and I don't recognise her. Should I?"

"My grandfather made the money. Newspapers, property and ranching. He knew Mom and Uncle Jim hadn't any interest in the business and would probably run it into the ground, so he sold everything before he died and put it in trust for them. He's buried in the family crypt along with Grandma at the main house."

"How big's the house up in New York State?"

"Twenty-nine bedrooms."

"That's a lot of dusting."

"Yeah, but it's handy when you want to have a few friends stop over."

Jet lag hit me like a shot of Valium and I went to my room to sleep.

After what seemed like minutes, but was actually several hours, I was awakened by the sound of knuckle knocking on wood.

"Danny! Come on, wake up. Mom says Uncle Jim's here."

It was time to see if Uncle Jim could do his stuff.

I showered, put on some fresh clothes and joined Tara at the top of the stairs. She was wearing a long, tight red dress with a plunging neckline and I saw her face fully made up for the first time – the sight of her clearing from my head any remnants of sleep left after my shower.

We descended the stairs.

"Hey, Tara, where the hell have you been!"

Uncle Jim threw open his arms showing his barrel chest – like a wrestler's. He was square jawed like a cartoon cowboy, and his grin was lopsided. He hugged Tara, resting his chin on her shoulder, swinging her around, the folds of skin on the back of his thick neck showing beneath the bristles of his crew cut.

Tara escaped his bear hug.

"This is Danny," she said.

The smile disappeared from his face.

"Hello, Danny."

His welcome was about as friendly as the one I received on my first night in Saint Pierre, and when we shook hands he came menacingly close and I sensed he wanted me to feel the power in his grip.

"Well, let's all sit," said Isabel.

The servant, who had brought in the tea earlier, now arrived with a bowl of vegetable consommé, which he served in white china bowls with a gold design that resembled a family crest.

"So, how was Europe?" Uncle Jim asked enthusiastically.

Tara told him about her time in London and Paris, but left out everything about the convent and sanatorium.

"Well it's great to have you back," he said.

"I'm not staying."

"Jesus, Tara, you only just got here. Haven't you got it out of your system yet?"

"There's something I need to do. Actually… I need your help."

He paused, holding his spoon steady in front of his mouth.

"Sure, whatever I can do just let me know. Always ready to help my favourite niece." He slurped his soup.

"I'm your *only* niece."

"Still my favourite!" He laughed and slapped his thigh. "How did you two meet anyway?"

"Danny and I met in the South of France. He... helped me out of a tight spot – did me a favour. So now I'd like to do him a favour in return, or rather I'd like *you* to, on my behalf."

Uncle Jim's eyebrows drew closer together.

"What would you like me to do exactly?"

"Run a check on somebody."

"Who?"

"That's what we want to find out."

She told him I was an investigative reporter working on a story and needed to find out more about someone – an American.

"Tara, I can't use government resources to go looking things up for just anyone."

"Danny isn't just anyone, and I owe him a favour."

"Why?"

"Can't tell you that."

"Can't or won't?"

"Amounts to the same thing. Look, Uncle Jim..." She tilted her head to one side, gave him her soft-soap smile and put her hand on his shoulder. "You did say you'd do *anything* to help..."

He wilted like a flower under the desert sun.

"Well... OK... just this once." He turned to face me. "Just remember this is strictly a one-off."

"Absolutely, and I thank you for your help," I said.

He shot back, "Wait 'til you get it."

Before going to bed, Tara handed Uncle Jim the Bible in a plastic bag.

"The man we want to check out has his fingerprints all over this."

"A *Bible*? Just what are you getting mixed up in?"

"Oh, Uncle Jim! I'm not getting mixed up in anything. I told you Danny is working on a story that's all."

The next morning Tara and I toured Naples. Uncle Jim had already left the house.

"You think he'll do it?" I asked.

"Hey, I'm his favourite niece, remember?"

I hoped she was right, but if he was going to do it he had to do it quickly – I was worried about the babies in the convent. The sooner we finished our story the sooner we could get them away from the influence of the High Priest.

At the house we played tennis, swam and sat out in the sun, and then Tara took me into the music room.

"You play?" I asked, nodding towards the piano.

"Yep."

She sat down on the stool, began to play 'Fields of Barley'. Her voice was pure, and the hairs on the back of my neck stood up. I hadn't heard anyone sing that song so well since Eva Cassidy.

Later, by the pool, I asked, "Tara, when's your Uncle Jim coming back?"

She dangled her feet in the water. "Tonight. Relax. He'll have tracked him down. We'll know who this High Priest guy is in a few hours. Uncle Jim always comes through."

I heard the sound of footsteps – leather-soled shoes on paving stones, and I looked up.

"Uncle Jim!" Tara said. "You're early."

She jumped up and ran over to him, leaving wet footprints on the terrace, and then she kissed him on the cheek.

"Looks like you two have been enjoying yourselves. Hello, Danny."

His tone changed whenever he spoke to me.

Tara said, "We were just wondering how you got on. Danny's anxious to get back to writing his story."

Uncle Jim cleared his throat. "Well, I'm sorry to have to tell you that we couldn't find anything. Sorry, Tara, sorry, Danny."

He shrugged his shoulders, like a Frenchman almost.

"But you did test it for fingerprints?" Tara asked.

"Dusted the whole thing, scanned through the pages, found lots of prints, but none we had on record. Nothing I can do to help you, sorry."

"But the guy's American and I don't believe you haven't got a record of him somewhere. This guy can't have been out of prison all his life, I just don't believe it," Tara said.

He looked at me. "Can't help you, Danny, I'm sorry."

The hell he was. He looked about as keen to help me as I was to wrestle an alligator.

Isabel came out onto the terrace.

"Tara, what's the problem?"

"It's me, I failed her," Uncle Jim said.

"You didn't fail me, Uncle Jim. That's not fair. I failed to help Danny – it was silly of me to make the assumption."

Uncle Jim turned to me.

"So anyway, Danny, what will you do now, go back to Europe to continue with your story?"

"Yes, but thanks for trying."

"That's the spirit. I know you investigative journalists are a persistent bunch." He turned to Tara. "Honey, how'd you like to come and spend some time with me and your Aunt Phyllis? We'd love to have you over, and little Mary is five now and doing well on the piano. She'd love to see you and maybe you could help her with her lessons. What do you say?"

"Can't. I'd love to see Aunt Phyllis, and Mary, but a debt's a debt and I owe Danny a favour, so I'll be going back to Europe with him."

Uncle Jim looked shocked.

"Tara, you've been away for Christ knows how long. You can't be serious about leaving again. Isabel, tell her."

"Tara's a grown woman now, Jim. She can do what she likes. If she wants to go travelling around what can I do?"

"For Christ's sake Isabel – this is your daughter! It's one thing applying your love-and-peace, let-it-all-hang-out philosophy to yourself, but not to Tara, for God's sake. You're supposed to give her some guidance."

"Jesus Christ, you sound just like Daddy when he tried to stop me going to see the Rolling Stones."

Uncle Jim's face swelled up, red and angry looking.

"Yeah, well times have changed and the world's a dangerous place, and you can't just let her go running around the world chasing after the leader of some cult – she could get hurt!"

Isabel looked just as angry.

"Don't tell me how to bring up my own daughter!"

"Shut up a minute!" Tara said. "I'm here, and I don't appreciate you talking about me as if I wasn't."

Uncle Jim took a softer line. "Now honey, we're only trying to do what's best."

"And I don't appreciate you lying to me, Uncle Jim."

"What?"

"Who told you the man Danny was investigating was the leader of a cult?"

"Er... why, you did. Or was it Danny? Yes, *you* mentioned something, didn't you Danny?"

"No, I didn't. I'd remember," I said. "We've hardly spoken since we met."

I enjoyed that.

"Uncle Jim, stop holding out on us – you know something don't you?"

His face was pinched.

"Uncle Jim! Tell us! It's important!"

We waited for him to speak. He tilted his head back slightly and eventually said, "The only thing that's important is that you stay here, where you're safe."

"No! You don't get to control me like that! I'm going to Europe and that's final – whether you like it or not!"

"Tara, it's not safe!"

"I'm going! Are you going to help or not?"

Silence.

"Well?"

No answer.

"As you like. Come on, Danny, let's eat in town tonight."

I stood up.

"Isabel, stop her. For once in your life, do the normal thing!"

"It's out of my hands. She's a grown woman and I don't have the right."

Tara looked at me. "There's a flight tomorrow morning," she said. "Let's take it."

I followed her out of the house feeling disturbed by Uncle Jim's insistence that what we were doing was not safe. What did he know?

On the way to Miami Airport the next morning, I tried to work out what we would do when we got back to France. We still had to find out more about the High Priest before we went to the papers, but I couldn't think how to do it. In the meantime there was the sanatorium to look into – maybe we could find out how Dr Dupont fitted into the scheme of things.

After dropping off the car at the Alamo office and taking the free bus to the terminal, I loaded our bags on a trolley and Tara bought the tickets.

"Breakfast?" she said.

We had left the house earlier than necessary – Tara was still seething with Uncle Jim and hadn't wanted to bump into him – so we had two hours to kill.

"Why not," I said.

Bacon, eggs and pancakes – delicious. Tara folded her newspaper, sipped her coffee and said, "You know we really ought to…"

I looked up from my paper. She was staring over my shoulder. I turned around. Someone was approaching us wearing a crash helmet and green and white racing leathers with 'Kawasaki' written on them in black letters.

"It's Uncle Jim," she said.

Uncle Jim, the CIA man, a biker? Then I noticed the man's barrel–like shape, stretching the leathers to their limits. He took off the helmet and when I saw his red face I knew he was going to make a scene.

"Tara, what the hell are you doing?"

She looked at him defiantly.

"We're going to Europe, like I said."

"Tara, please, think about it. You just can't go messing around in things that might be dangerous… I mean, think about your mother!"

Even I could see that was a stupid and desperate comment.

Tara said, "Don't be so manipulative. She made her views clear last night."

"This is crazy! You sneak out of the house in the middle of the night to run off to Europe… What's this guy got on you?"

"I didn't sneak out of the house. We've got a plane to catch. Now stop wasting your time and leave us alone."

"But… it's dangerous, please leave it."

"Can't do that. Of course, *you* could make matters less dangerous."

"What do you mean?"

"You could tell us what you know. After all, you have to accept now that we're going and nothing you can say'll stop us. If it really is as you say, will you be happy knowing we're going into a dangerous situation without the knowledge that *you* refused to give us? Are you going to be happy about that?"

She had him.

I watched him deflate and then he said, "All right. Let's go somewhere more private. You're travelling at the front of the plane, I take it?"

At the entrance to the first class lounge Tara and I showed our tickets and Uncle Jim flashed his identification and then had a quiet word with the security staff. We found a corner in the lounge and sat down on an L-shaped sofa with a low table in front of it.

"Tara, you'd better get me a drink," Uncle Jim said.

"Bourbon?"

He nodded. She made her way over to the bar and Uncle Jim turned to me.

"You'd better look after her, Danny." His face twisted and his eyes looked menacing. "I'm holding you responsible. Don't know how you got her mixed up with all this, but I never did approve of her boyfriends."

"I'm not her boyfriend. If it's any consolation to you, we're not sleeping together. I helped her, she wants to help me, that's it."

"Good. She's not for you. Maybe I underestimated her taste."

I let the slight go.

Tara returned with the bourbon and sat down.

"So come on then, tell us what you know."

Uncle Jim paused for a few seconds, preparing himself, like a man about to dive into a cold swimming pool.

"All right, all right, but remember you didn't get this from me. A friend of mine in the FBI ran the prints and yes we know who the guy is – or rather we don't."

"You're not making any sense."

"Patience. I'm getting there. The guy calls himself the High Priest. He used to run a small cult from a regular house on a housing development outside LA and had a group of followers who were all nuts – they thought he was the Son of God. There were some complaints from the neighbours who got spooked, so the police got involved and later the Feds – anxious to avoid another Waco/Jim Jones-type affair.

"The cult never did anything illegal, or at least nothing we ever knew about, and we were jumpy about interfering after Waco. We had orders to go gently on these religious types – no shootouts. Seemed like the followers were all pretty normal on the outside – many had successful jobs with big corporations. But then this High Priest guy disappears and goes to England with one of his followers, a guy named Michael Richards, who was a young hotshot scientist working for a corporation called Agrifusion who make fertilisers and crop seeds. With the High Priest gone the cult stopped meeting. We thought we'd washed our hands of them so we just gave a copy of our file to the British authorities and that's the last we heard of it."

"So you don't know who this High Priest really is?" I said.

"No. We never found out his real name and no one knows where he comes from. When he travelled to England we know he used a false passport with the name, John Eugene Hovar – think about it – J E Hovar – Jehovah."

"Spooky," Tara said.

"Spooky's one word for it, but I'd say *dangerous* is more accurate. These religious nuts give me the willies – they're crazy, for all their spouting the 'good word'. So now you tell me how you got the Bible."

"Danny's doing an investigative story into cults. He saw this High Priest guy once and when he walked off leaving his Bible, Danny picked it up, that's all."

"Tara, promise me you'll keep away from this guy, OK?"

"Uncle Jim, I can promise you I shall keep as far away from him as possible."

"There's one more thing. Two of the neighbours who were complaining about him disappeared."

"You don't think he killed them?"

"I don't know what he did. No bodies have been found – yet."

"We'll be careful."

Uncle Jim sat back in his chair. "Well, that'll have to do, I suppose. If you're still hell-bent on helping your friend Danny here, you'd better go to England. I'll speak to a contact I have over there who'll be willing to talk to you, especially if he thinks you've got some information on this High Priest guy."

"If the authorities in the UK knew he was travelling on a false passport why didn't they just arrest him when he arrived?" I asked.

Uncle Jim said, "Sometimes it's better to watch and wait. That way you get to catch all the perpetrators, you know what I mean?"

Tara grabbed my arm. "Danny, come on we've got to change our tickets!"

Chapter 8

Heathrow Airport. We collected our bags, Tara changed some money, and then we caught the Heathrow express train to Paddington. May in England was never hot, but today felt especially cold. Grey clouds blocked out the sun and there was a chill in the air. We took a taxi to Leyton-Middleton and I watched the meter tick over. This was going to be more expensive than Paris and I was totally broke. When we pulled up outside my house the fare had grown to £62.55. Tara handed over the cash and I cringed with embarrassment.

"Forget it," she said. "I'm having the time of my life. Anyway you can pay me back from your half of the money we get for the story if it makes you feel any better."

I stood at the end of the drive looking at my characterless, 1960's box of a house. What a dump. I never had any pretensions about it, but after Tara's Florida mansion it looked even worse.

"I... er... I'm sorry it's not quite what you're used to."

"Danny, what I'm used to right now is a room in a sanatorium, and before that a poky little bare-walled room in a convent. Come on, it's cold. You do have some tea don't you?"

"Long as you take it black."

Then a thought struck me: What if Izzie was in the house? Maybe she had thought things over, realised she couldn't live without me and had moved back in while I was away. What the hell would she say when she saw me entering the house with an attractive young American girl?

I opened the front door, picked up some bills off the floor and stepped inside. No, Izzie couldn't be back – the house was freezing. I turned on the heating.

"I'll show you your room."

"Great. I need to take a shower."

When she had finished I took one, and later made two cups of steaming tea. In the fridge the milk had turned to thick sludge, but I found some powdered stuff in a cupboard.

Tara came down wearing Izzie's dressing gown.

"I found this upstairs, hope it's OK to wear it."

"Why not?"

I handed her the tea and we sipped it in front of the electric fire.

"So do you think your uncle will have made the call to his contact over here yet?" I said.

"Yep."

The phone rang.

"Excuse me."

I picked up the receiver.

"Mr Avery?"

The voice was suave, supercilious, and not one I recognised.

"Yes."

"Name's Cleaver, Alistair Cleaver. Had a call from the States – Jim Reynolds."

I swallowed hard and pressed the phone firmly to my ear.

"Oh, right."

"Good idea if we meet. Tonight?"

"Er... yes. Where?"

"Le Coq D'Or. Know it?"

"Yes."

Only the best restaurants for the Secret Service.

"What time?"

"8.30."

"How will I recognise you?"

"You will. See you later."

The line went dead and I told Tara who it was.

"Jesus, your guys move fast," she said.

Exactly what I was thinking, but there was something else that unnerved me: I didn't remember giving Tara's Uncle Jim my number, and it wasn't in the phone book. I dialled 1471 to find the number from where Cleaver had called and a recorded voice told me it wasn't listed.

Tara moved closer to the fire. "Well, we've got a whole day to kill. How about you showing me around the town?"

"Aren't you tired?"

"If we're going to get back on European time we need to keep awake until late tonight."

My limbs were heavy with tiredness and I didn't know how I was going to keep awake, but maybe the cold English air would help.

"OK. Hope you're ready for the Leyton-Middleton experience. Disney World it ain't."

We took a cab to the shopping centre.

"Fancy a coffee?" I asked.

Tara linked her arm through mine and I led her along the walkway towards a coffee shop. A woman laden with bags rushed out of a shop, almost running straight into us. We jerked to a halt, and when the woman looked up my jaw fell open and my body stiffened.

"Izzie!"

"Didn't take you long to find someone else to mess around," she said.

"What?"

She looked directly at Tara. "I could tell you a lot about him, love. Mind you it'd spoil the fun of watching you find out for yourself."

"Izzie, this is not what you think," I said.

She looked at our linked arms, and I unlinked them.

"Nothing is what it seems with you, is it, Danny?"

She said to Tara, "Hope you don't want kids."

"Izzie, this is crazy. I told you we could talk everything through."

"You think I'm going to listen to you trying to soft-soap me? No thanks. Been there, done that. Oh, I heard you lost your job too. What the hell was I doing wasting my life with a loser like you?" She stood there slowly shaking her head.

My guts tightened.

"I lost my job because I was trying to deal with another one of your stupid hormonal tantrums!"

"Oh, I like that! I'm responsible for your failures, huh? And I thought Eddy Sinclair once said you couldn't string two words together!"

"I never got a chance to 'string two words together'. Because of you I never got in to see the bloody match!"

She looked at Tara again.

"If he's still trying to become a reporter out of some crazy loyalty to his father, I'm afraid he'll always be poor, so I wouldn't marry him, love. Oh, but of course you won't get the chance – he doesn't believe in marriage. Don't suppose he told you that though did he?"

"Izzie, this is –"

"I'll tell you what *this* is. The end of the road, that's what this is. I've enjoyed being away from you, I wouldn't change it for the world." She looked at Tara. "He's all yours love, you're welcome to him. God help you." She turned and walked off.

"Izzie!"

The heat radiated from my cheeks and I watched her disappear around the corner, her shopping bags swinging from side to side as she moved.

"Sorry about that, Tara."

She linked her arm through mine again and calmly said, "Shall we get that coffee now?"

The Rembrandt Café was probably the most pretentiously named dive in all of England, but it was the best the shopping centre had to offer.

We sat in a corner and a blonde-haired waitress with bad acne brought us two cappuccinos. I breathed in deeply.

"God, that woman can be such a stupid bitch!" I fought hard to release the tension in my guts and gradually my anger came under control. "Well, I guess that makes things clear between us. It's definitely over now."

"I'm sorry."

My forehead furrowed.

"Sorry? You've got to be kidding. Can't think what I was doing chained to that nasty old witch for so long."

We held each other's gaze for a moment, and then burst out laughing. I hadn't seen her laugh before. Her face lit up like a firework and I was struck by how perfect her teeth were.

She dabbed the tears from her eyes and said, "So you lost your job because of her hormonal tantrums!"

That set us off again and we shook with laughter. It was several minutes before we came to our senses, both wiping our eyes with our handkerchiefs.

"Oh, boy," she said. "I shouldn't laugh, really." She blew her nose. "But on a serious note, how *did* you lose your job?"

"We had a row, I tried to patch it up and was late getting to a football match."

"That's all?"

"Yeah, but it was the most important game in Leyton-Middleton's history, and if they won it they'd get to play Manchester United in the FA Cup. United, in case you don't know, are probably the biggest football club in the world and a little team like Leyton-Middleton getting to play them – well that's big news."

"And you were the reporter, right?"

"Right. I couldn't get into the ground, I forgot my press pass and it was a full house – they wouldn't let me in. So I sat across the road in a grotty café wondering what the hell to do – Eddy Sinclair was my editor and he was going to kill me. Anyway, the game ended and I saw someone leaving the ground – someone I was at school with called Gazza Johnson who's a reporter now with another paper. I pleaded with him to tell me what had happened at the game and the bastard refused, saying I hadn't helped him twenty years previously when some of the lads sat him on the drinking fountain and gave him an enema."

Tara started laughing again.

"In the end he gave me the story – after I'd paid him £20 and promised I would change it around a bit. I thought I was saved, phoned the story in, and it was printed in that night's edition. Trouble was the bastard had told me a load of rubbish – my story was wrong – even had the wrong goal-scorers in it. Next day I was sacked."

"That's terrible!"

"Yeah. What made it worse was that Leyton-Middleton had won and the next week they *did* play Manchester United, so I missed out on the biggest opportunity of my life. I could have been interviewing Sir Alex Ferguson after the match. Instead I was sitting in a hotel room in the South of France with you."

"You're kidding! Oh, Danny, I'm sorry."

"Not your fault. It was that bloody woman's fault. The one with the hormonal tantrums."

We laughed again.

Back at home, I put some clothes in the washing machine – I was not as helpless as Izzie believed. Tara and I relaxed in front of the TV, a tide of sleep washing over us, and dozed off while watching an old black and white Spencer Tracy movie.

I awoke with a start and glanced at my watch, afraid we had missed our rendezvous.

"Tara, wake up!"

We rushed about upstairs getting ready, Tara went to the bathroom and then the doorbell rang. It was the cab I had booked earlier. I ran down to tell the driver to wait.

"*Tara!*"

I stood at the bottom of the stairs shuffling from foot to foot, and then I saw her – and she looked amazing. The long black dress, simple and elegant, clung to her gentle curves. She descended the stairs, her body moving in a sensual way, and when she reached the bottom I couldn't help but gaze at the shape of her breasts.

"Does this look all right?" she asked, giving me a big sparkly grin.

"You know it does," I said.

The cool night air made Tara's nipples stand up and when we got in the back of the cab I caught the driver sneakily peeking at her in his rear-view mirror. Couldn't blame him for that. The cab moved off.

I forced myself to concentrate on the meeting we were about to have. What exactly did this Alistair Cleaver know about the High Priest? Enough for us to write our story, I hoped. Images of babies in the convent flashed before me, reminding me that we didn't have much time.

The cab turned into the driveway to Le Coq D'Or, the tyres crunching the gravel as we eased our way towards the entrance. A man in a dinner jacket opened the door for Tara – I opened my own. I got out, gazing at the Jacobean building, its stone walls covered in creeping ivy, soft amber lighting glowing through the diamond-patterned leaded windows. I never thought I'd get to eat there in a million years.

Once inside the *maître d'* approached.

"We're meeting a Mr Cleaver," I said.

"Certainly, sir. Please come this way."

We made our way through the dining room, past table upon table of middle-aged men in dark suits with bejewelled women – some far too young for the men they were with. At the far end of the restaurant a man sat at a table alone. He stood up.

"Mr Cleaver, sir, your guests," the *maître d'* said.

Alistair Cleaver wore a pinstriped suit with an oversized, purple silk top-pocket handkerchief. He must have been six–feet–five inches tall and he knew how to use his height. Standing ramrod straight he stretched out his hand.

"I'm Cleaver. You must be Avery."

His grip was firm, but I felt a soft feminine quality to his skin, as if his hands had been regularly manicured.

"And this is?"

"This is Tara Reynolds. She's working with me."

"Ah, yes, you're the niece."

Tara nodded.

"And you're a reporter too?" Cleaver asked.

"More of an assistant, I'd say."

"Yes, quite. I hope you don't mind, but I've taken the liberty of ordering for us. You do like foie gras?"

A man who likes to be in control.

"Er… yes, that'll be fine," I said.

Tara nodded.

"So how's your story coming along?" he asked.

"Fine, thanks."

"Good, good. Always love to read stuff from you investigative types, and an excellent job you do too – public service and all that. How did you come to find out about this High Priest chappie?"

The directness of his manner unnerved me and my body tensed. I was supposed to be asking the questions, not this overbearing, pompous prick. But I needed to humour him.

"I was doing an article on religious cults and we happened to be in Florida where I met Tara's Uncle Jim and asked him if he knew of anyone I should include in the article. He mentioned this High Priest guy. Seems like a good subject to include, wouldn't you say?"

"Oh, yes, absolutely. So what do you know of him up to now?"

"Not much. Just that he used to run a small cult in America."

The foie gras arrived – the waiters serving it with religious reverence, and the sommelier poured the wine for Cleaver to taste. He sniffed the air above the glass and washed the wine around his mouth before declaring it fit to drink.

We began to eat, Alistair chatting to Tara with greasy charm about the various cities he had visited in America. She played her part well, smiling when she should, and when we finished the foie gras he turned to me once more.

"Did you find any of his followers?"

The change in subject was so abrupt that I wondered what he was talking about for a moment. Then it registered.

"Er… no, but it would be very useful if I could. Do you know any?"

"'Fraid not, old boy. I was rather hoping *you* might."

"Why?"

"Dangerous. Bloody dangerous these religious fanatics – not stable. You sure you've not heard anything?"

"No – nothing at all."

"Of course you'd tell me if you had, wouldn't you?"

"Er… yes. I would."

"Please be sure you do, Mr Avery. I'm sure you're a patriot. National security and all that, we can't have religious subversives running around the country upsetting things, can we?"

"No, we can't." This guy was as old-school tie as you could get. "But Jim said, he'd sent you a file on the High Priest. Didn't you keep a watch on him when he came here?"

"He only stayed a short while. Nothing to watch really. Then we lost him. Last we heard he'd given up religion and gone to Sweden."

"Didn't you contact the Swedish authorities about him?"

"Ah, well… er… no. You see we… er… we don't have good intelligence sharing with the Swedes – they've always been a neutral country, you see."

"So you don't know anything?"

"'Bout the same as you old boy, but I have your word you'll let me know if you find anything?"

"I'll make certain you get to know whatever I find out." *Just keep reading the damned papers every morning, you pompous ass.* "Of course, that is if there is anything *to* find out. Doesn't sound to me like there is."

"Quite. Well, you'll have to excuse me; I have another engagement.

You two enjoy your evening. I've ordered the chicken for you, and don't worry about the bill – it's on my account."

He stood up, shook hands with us, gave me a card with his number on it and marched out of the restaurant.

"Jesus Christ," Tara said. "Now what makes you think he's English? I didn't know people like him existed in real life."

"'Fraid they haven't all died out, yet."

"Can you believe that – he just up and left – and he ordered everything for us too."

"Unfortunately, yes, I can."

The waiter brought the chicken, we finished our meal, took coffee in the lounge in front of a roaring log fire, and then I asked for a taxi to take us home.

On the way back Tara said, "I'm sorry, but it looks like Uncle Jim didn't come through after all – well not much anyway."

"Not your fault."

"Why do you think he thought the High Priest went to Sweden?" Tara asked.

"No idea."

We travelled the rest of the journey in silence, Tara paying for the taxi when we arrived outside the house, and me feeling guilty about it. We walked up the drive and I pushed my key into the lock, but before I could turn it the door swung open.

Tara said, "You know I –"

"Shhhh!" I said.

The hairs stood up on the back of my neck, my heart beating as if it was trying to break out of my chest. I listened for the slightest sound, but there was nothing. I stepped inside and listened again. Still no sound. If someone were in house I'd hear them ransacking it, wouldn't I? I needed a weapon – just in case. I opened the drawer in the hall side table and I took out a letter opener. It would do. Should I creep in and surprise them, or rush them like a madman? Maybe it was better to just make a noise and scare them off? They could be drugged up to the eyeballs and armed to the teeth. I turned on the light and coughed loudly. Tara followed me in to the hallway, I slammed the door shut so hard it rattled the house, then opened it again and rang the doorbell. Still there was nothing to be heard.

"They must have gone," I said.

The lounge had been ransacked. Sofas and cushions ripped to shreds, pictures lying on the floor – the backs ripped off them. The TV was turned over and the video smashed. In the kitchen every drawer had been pulled out and the contents tipped over the floor. What little food there had been in the cupboards was scattered around the room; breakfast cereal, canned food, jar of coffee, tea bags. The fridge door was open and so was the oven. I ran upstairs. The bed linen had been ripped off the beds, the contents of the wardrobes strewn everywhere. The filing cabinet in the spare room had been forced open and the files scattered over the floor. Miraculously my laptop computer was still there, still in its case. The window was wide open and I looked outside. Directly below me was the garage roof. Tara came up behind me.

"This must be where they climbed out," I said. "Looks like we might have disturbed them. Thank God they didn't want to fight their way out."

"Oh, Danny, I'm sorry."

"I'd better call the police."

We sat on the sofa waiting for them to arrive.

Tara said, "Is there anything missing?"

"No."

It bothered me. Why did someone break in and not steal anything? The video had been smashed, not taken. Why was it sitting there in pieces alongside the TV? Of course, we might have disturbed them while they were in the spare bedroom, and they could have gone out through the window in a hurry before they saw my computer. But they had *smashed* the video. It didn't make sense.

"Just wait here."

I got up and walked around the house again, checking for anything missing, but as far as I could see everything was there.

"Whoever it was knew what they were doing and what they wanted. If it had just been kids or an opportunist burglar they would have taken the electrical things. There's no sign of where they broke in, no smashed doors or windows – so they must have picked the lock on the front door. And they either had nerves of steel or were able to do it very quickly because the front of the house is lit up by the streetlight and they risked being seen by a neighbour."

I paced the room, the cogs turning in my mind. Something about this felt bad. Then suddenly things clicked into place and chill ran through me.

"What are you thinking?" Tara asked.

I pressed my right forefinger to my lips, gestured to Tara to follow me outside, and led her to the end of the small garden at the back of the house.

"This whole thing – it was a set up!"

"Danny, you're not making sense. What was a set up?"

"Tonight! Look, your Uncle Jim called Cleaver. Cleaver calls me. Where did he get my number? Spooky, right? We arrange to meet him at a swanky restaurant out of town. When we get there *he's* supposed to be giving *us* information about the High Priest – but he gives us nothing – just asks us what *we* know. Then he tells us they know nothing about him, except that he's gone to Sweden of all places, and that he's given up religion – just like that. Very likely! He says they lost track of him, but they don't share intelligence with Sweden because they've always been a neutral country. Bullshit! The guy was putting us off the scent. Then he says if I find out anything I must let *him* know. He's all insistent about it and pulls the patriot number. Must do your duty to queen and country, and all that. But if the guy's given up religion there's nothing for me to find out, is there? How come they supposedly lost track of him? The CIA tells them all about him, and that he's travelling on a false passport and the British Intelligence Service *loses* him? Not very likely. Meanwhile, The High Priest travels to France and they think he's in Sweden? I don't believe it. The Intelligence Service is not *that* stupid."

"Danny, why are we out here? You're not thinking what I think you are thinking... are you?"

"You're damned right I am. That bastard Cleaver wanted to know what we knew about the High Priest – enough to have the house turned over. Don't you think it's a coincidence it got burgled when we were eating dinner with him – not while I was away in France or Florida? Funny how he 'had another engagement' and had to leave early. Strange nothing was taken – but maybe something was *left*."

"You mean a bug? Fuck!"

"Fuck is right. Listen, just act normal while we're inside, OK? Be careful what you say. We've got to let them think everything is fine and we know nothing and are giving up on writing the story."

The police arrived three hours after I called them. They apologised for the delay – manpower shortages, they said – and went through the motions of carrying out an investigation. A fingerprint man dusted the likely places. The whole thing was futile. They gave me a crime number for the insurance company and then left Tara and I to tidy up.

Mindful that Cleaver could be listening, I said, "Well, I suppose there's not much more we can do except put this down to experience. Crime's getting worse everywhere. I guess we may as well go back to France and have a bit of a holiday. We don't have anything like enough information to include the High Priest in the article, so we'll forget him and concentrate on finding some others. Or maybe we should just find something else to write about."

"I guess so," Tara said, playing along.

I felt like I was being watched by a ghost and I shivered.

Unable to face tidying up the house, our bodies heavy with jet lag and desperately in need of sleep, we put my bedroom back together and collapsed onto the mattress, pulling the duvet over our bodies. Two minutes later Tara was asleep and I heard the rhythmic sound of her breathing. My body may have been numb and tired but my mind was jumping around like a cricket. I wanted to get hold of the bastard who had ransacked my house. I wanted to punch Alistair Cleaver's face, and I wanted to know if there was something going on between the British Secret Service and the High Priest. At the same time, try as I might, I couldn't stop thinking about the fact that I was lying in bed next to Tara.

In the morning we put the rest of the house back into some sort of order, took our washing from the tumble-dryer and packed our suitcases.

Tara beckoned for me to follow her outside. At the bottom of the garden she said, "Are you sure we can get a flight?"

"We'll get one. We have to. We've got to get back inside that convent and take a look around – we need this story wrapped up fast."

"But... what do you think we're going to find there?"

My jaw muscles tightened and my lips compressed into a thin line.

"I don't know. I haven't got a damned clue. Something that will tell us what the connection is between the High Priest and Cleaver."

"Danny... are you sure there *is* a connection?"

"What?"

"Well, maybe we're just imagining things – you know, with the Cleaver guy."

"For Christ's sake, Tara! We're not imagining the break-in are we?"

"No, of course not. But maybe it wasn't Cleaver's men. Maybe we just disturbed a burglar. All right, so Cleaver seemed... evasive, but he's in the Secret Service – he's not *supposed* to tell us anything."

"Right! Well there's one way to find out!"

I stomped back into the house and over to my suitcase, turning the combination lock, almost tearing the lid off. I yanked out my jacket and pulled out Cleaver's card from the inside pocket. There wasn't much written on it – just his name and a number. I marched over to the phone and called him; on the third ring he answered.

"It's Danny Avery. I've found something. We need to meet."

"Er... right. Where?"

"There's a service station with a roadside café on the main road between Leyton-Middleton and Highbridge. Be there in an hour."

I slammed the phone down.

I heard Tara behind me and I turned to face her.

"Wow, this is incredible! Just look at this, a full dossier on the guy – he seems dangerous to me."

I held out my empty hands and mimed turning over the pages of a file. Tara realised what I was doing.

"Oh boy!" she said.

"Of course I'm not going to show the whole thing to Cleaver – we'll keep the file hidden under the sofa cushions until we decide what to do with it. I'll just take a couple of things to show him – you know, to make it look like I'm doing my patriotic duty."

I called a minicab and it arrived ten minutes later – a beige Ford Sierra estate with no taxi sign or other obvious markings. The driver, a skinny, wheezy old man with a red face and thinning silver hair, said, "Where to, mate?"

"Down the road, take the first left, and keep taking the first left."

"Eh? We'll go around in a bloody circle."

"Just do it." We set off. "I want you to end up back on this road, but entering it from the other end."

"I could have just –"

"Just do it, please."

We went around the block and then entered my road again.

"Go slowly," I said.

The house came into view and when we were a hundred yards away from it I said, "Stop here – pull over."

"You getting out?" the driver asked.

"No. Just wait here."

"I've got to keep the meter running, you know?"

"Yes, I know that. Just wait here until I tell you. We're going on somewhere else afterwards."

Minutes passed. The cabdriver picked up his newspaper, relaxed back in his seat and flicked through the sports pages.

"You still want to just sit here?" he asked.

"Yes."

"You're the governor."

Later, I looked at my watch. How long had we been there? It seemed like a long time. Was this all in my imagination? Maybe I was getting carried away here. I shuffled around in my seat. Tara looked at me, but said nothing. Two more minutes – long minutes. The driver turned another page of his paper. I peered down the road. Nothing had happened – I had got it wrong. What the hell should we do now? There was no point in going to see Cleaver – we had nothing to show him.

It was time to give up.

"OK, driver, let's move on."

He turned to give me a quizzical look.

"You sure, mate?"

He made a great ceremony of folding his paper, putting the car in first gear and eventually moving off. Then I saw something.

"*Stop!*"

"Oh, Jesus Christ! Make up your mind, mate."

"Pull over again!"

I nudged Tara. A man was crossing the road opposite my house. He was short and stocky, wore a black leather jacket, dark trousers and a black knitted hat on his head.

"You see him?"

"Yes."

"OK, pull away, but go slowly."

"Bloody Nora. I'm stoppin' and startin' like a number nine bus here."

"Slowly please! Whatever you do, don't look at my house, OK?"

We approached the house.

"Tara, get down."

Low in our seats, we looked across to the right.

"Shit!"

The man had the door open already. He put one foot inside the hallway then stared at the Ford Sierra, watching us pass. There was no doubt about it now.

"OK, driver, take us to the roadside café on the road to Highbridge. You know it?"

"The Highwayman Restaurant."

"That's the one."

We drove through the housing estates on the outskirts of Leyton-Middleton, adrenalin pulsing through my body, my fists clenching and unclenching involuntarily.

"What are you going to say to him?" Tara asked.

I hadn't worked that out, but I wanted to wrench his head from his shoulders and use it for football practice. How dare the bastard have my house burgled!

We left the housing estates behind and headed out into open countryside. Two miles along the road we passed a sign saying: *Fuel and Food 200 yards,* and then the cab turned into the parking area in front of the restaurant.

"Wait here, please," I said.

"What? How long for?" the driver asked.

"This won't take long."

I got out of the car and slammed the door shut, Tara following close behind me. I yanked open the door of the restaurant, we stepped inside and paused to look around. There he was, wearing another dark pinstriped suit, but this time the top pocket-handkerchief was yellow silk. He looked uncomfortable and out of place in the Highwayman Restaurant, sipping his coffee at a corner table. It seemed he always sat with his back to the wall – he was a man who needed to.

He looked up and smiled at me as I stormed over to his table. Cleaver held out his hand.

"Avery, good to hear from you so soon."

"Cut the crap, Cleaver. Why did you have my house burgled?"

"What? There must be some..."

"Save it, you supercilious prick! I know it was you and in case you haven't noticed, asshole, I'm not carrying any papers with me, and the ape who's right now tearing my sofa cushions apart isn't going to find jack-shit. Do we understand each other?"

Cleaver retracted his hand, the smile disappeared from his face and he sank back down in his chair.

The restaurant owner looked over.

"Oi, you two ain't gonna cause any trouble are you? You gonna fight you do it outside, right?"

My eyes looked straight into Cleaver's and he looked away at the man behind the counter.

"I'm sure you have no need to worry on that score, there'll be no trouble from me," he said.

I sat down on the chair opposite and Tara sat beside me.

"Tara's uncle said you could help us and I know you can – so you'd better start talking. I want to know about this High Priest guy and why you lied to us last night."

"Look, I'm sorry about last night, but as I told you, we don't know anything about him."

"Bullshit!"

"We don't, I assure you."

"Why did you burgle my house?" I balled my fists and banged them on the table.

"We have to check on these things – for the protection of society. We're the Secret Service. You might have been withholding information from us, that's all."

"Liar!"

"I beg your pardon. Now look here –"

"No, Cleaver, *you* look here. You've got five seconds to start talking and you'd better tell me something interesting, or else I'm going to run the story – tell the whole world what's happening in France right now."

"No, you can't do that!"

"So you do know about France then?"

Cleaver's face fell.

"All right," he said. "What do you know?"

"Fuck what *I* know! What do *you* know? You've already had three of the five seconds."

We held each other's gaze, as if we were playing some teenage game of chicken.

"Four seconds."

He isn't going to tell us anything. Fuck him. We'll run the story with what we have.

"OK, Cleaver. You had your chance."

We stood up.

"No, wait. Wait. I'll tell you, but for Christ's sake this goes no further than us, OK? You've got to promise me you won't run the story; it's a matter of national importance. Do you give me your word?"

"I'll give you my word that if you don't tell me what's going on I'll run the story — that I promise. It's up to you to convince me not to, if this really is a matter of *national importance,* as you put it."

"OK, fair enough. Waiter, bring two more coffees would you," Cleaver said, ordering for us again.

We sat down.

"So, Cleaver, talk."

"I… er. This is all very secret you understand?"

"Get on with it."

"Wait a minute — until the waiter's brought the coffee."

We waited. Two minutes later the man from behind the counter sauntered over and put two cups down on the table.

"OK, Cleaver. Stop stalling."

"All right, but this mustn't go —"

"Oh, for Christ's sake!"

Cleaver took a deep breath, looked down at the tabletop and said, "The High Priest is a genetic freak. Somehow he has an immune system that…"

"What's his name?"

"We don't know?"

"You don't *know?*"

"Look, let me finish, for heaven's sake."

I shut up.

"Like I said, he's a genetic freak. He's got an immune system that works differently in some way. Don't ask me how – I'm not a scientist. I just know that he's never had a cold in his life."

"Is that it? The British Secret Service is interested in the man because he hasn't had a *cold*?"

"Avery, you seem to misunderstand the nature of the Secret Service these days. The cold war is over. We don't go running around like James Bond spying on Russians any more, we do other work – industrial espionage. *Yes,* we are interested in this High Priest fellow because he hasn't had a cold. Do you realise how many productive working days are lost by industry every year because of nothing more than the common cold? Do you know what that costs this country and every other country in the civilised world? Do you know what a cure for the common cold is worth? Think about it man! The pharmaceutical company that gets hold of it will make billions, and so will the government – as long as it's a British company that patents it. That's why we're interested in him, and we're near to getting the cure. We don't need a journalist like you out to make a name for himself to interfere! Do you understand?"

"But I don't get it. You mean the High Priest – the nutcase with the staring blue eyes – is trying to make a cure for the common cold?"

"No, of course not. The man's insane – hell bent on making a master race – he's a cross between Hitler and a born again Christian."

"Aren't you a little worried about that?"

"No."

"Why?"

"Because the High Priest, as he calls himself, is working with a clever young geneticist – a genius in fact – and it's he who's going to get us the cure. And anyway we have an operative there."

"In the convent?"

"Yes. One of the so-called *inner circle*."

Tara and I looked at each other. Could this be true? It sounded plausible. Uncle Jim had said the High Priest left America with one of his followers, a man who worked for a corporation that produced fertilisers and crop seeds. Could it be this was the geneticist? As for the part about industrial espionage, I'd heard the Secret Services did get involved in that these days. Cleaver mentioned the inner circle of nuns – he knew about that – he could have an operative in there. In fact he must have an operative in there, how else would he know the inner circle existed?

"So, Avery, now you know."

I nodded.

"I must again ask for your silence. It is very important that pharmaceutical companies in other countries don't find out about this."

"Which one of ours will get the formula in the end?"

"That's classified. If it got out think what would happen to their share price." He scratched his nose. "So I have your silence, Mr Avery?"

I didn't answer.

He continued, "Look, I know you've put a lot of work into getting a story together, and I sympathise. I'll tell you what I'll do. I'll see to it that you get the exclusive when we break the news. It won't be too long. Testing is in its final stages, so I'm informed."

"You can do that?"

"Well someone's got to report it. I don't see why it shouldn't be you, and after all you should be rewarded for your silence, shouldn't you?"

"How will I know when the work is complete?"

"As soon as the patents are in place I'll contact you."

I weighed it up in my mind. It all sounded believable and it would be an incredible breakthrough with huge ramifications. Definitely the sort of thing that had to be kept quiet. I looked up at Cleaver.

"You know there are babies in the convent?"

"Yes, we do. I can assure you they are being well looked after and will come to no harm. This will all be over soon. Do I have your agreement?"

I looked at Tara. She shrugged as if to say, *why not?*

"OK. It's a deal. Just make sure those babies are taken care of. You don't have long. And make sure we get the exclusive story."

Cleaver stretched out his hand and this time I took it.

A voice behind me said, "Listen, mate, how much longer have I got to wait in the bleedin' cab for you two lovebirds?"

We set off back to Leyton-Middleton.

"So what do we do now?" Tara asked.

"I don't know."

I felt stunned. I had gone in there to have it out with Cleaver and find out what he knew about the High Priest, but what he told me had changed things completely. We couldn't sell our story – not yet anyway. It seemed as though I was back in the same position I had been in when I had first taken myself off to Saint Pierre – an ex-reporter, unemployed, with no direction.

"I'm sorry, Tara. This has all been a waste of time for you."

"You're kidding – I've had the time of my life. We've been chasing around the world like Bonny and Clyde! Well, we haven't robbed any banks – but you know what I mean. It's all been... well, fun." She squeezed my hand. "You know the house is still bugged, we can hardly go back there. *But...* we do have our bags packed... and this cab driver could take us to the airport. I mean... I did interrupt your break down in Saint Pierre and I feel guilty about that. The least I can do to repay you for getting me out of that sanatorium is to accompany you on a proper holiday in the South of France, don't you think? That is if you don't have anything pressing to do. What do you say?"

I grinned so hard I almost pulled a muscle in my cheek.

Chapter 9

We took separate rooms at the Sofitel Hotel in Cannes and on the fourth morning sat at a roadside café, sipping cappuccinos, watching the old men playing petanque in the square by the port. A procession of cars drove by, honking their horns in celebration – someone had just got married. Distracted by what was going on around me, I didn't notice the tall, fair-haired woman pushing a pram on the pavement in front of us. But then she stumbled, a pram wheel slipped off the edge of the kerb and she let out a cry of terror as she struggled to keep the pram upright and her baby inside.

I leapt up to help her and together we steadied the pram, getting all four wheels safely back on the pavement.

"Monsieur, merci! Merci beaucoup!" she said, red-faced.

Then she smiled at me and I looked down at not one but two babies – twins, still sleeping under a blue woollen blanket.

The woman went on her way and when I sat down again Tara said, "You seem to be making a habit of saving damsels in distress."

I shrugged off her comment, but the incident invoked a memory of the ambulance men struggling to right the stretcher as they carried the body of Virginie Lavelle out of the hotel in Saint Pierre, and I was reminded again that I still hadn't got to the bottom of the mystery of the dead nun/prostitute.

And what of the babies in the convent? How much longer would it be before Cleaver had the formula he sought and those babies were taken to safety? Suddenly I felt guilty enjoying myself on the Cote d'Azur. There had to be something I could do to speed things up.

I went back over what had happened since I had first arrived at Saint Pierre and the many questions Cleaver's explanation in the Highwayman Restaurant hadn't answered. Why had I been given such a hostile reception when I arrived? Why was the hotel manager so defensive when I had asked for Virginie Lavelle's name? And why wasn't she registered in the hotel? How involved in all this was Dr Dupont at the sanatorium?

"What are you thinking?" Tara asked.

"Just that there are some things still bothering me. I wouldn't mind another look around Saint Pierre."

I drove our hired Renault along the winding road to the old town – perfect scenery for a landscape artist – thinking that no one would guess a picturesque little place like this could hide such… I groped for the right word, but the only one that came to me was 'evil'.

After entering the town gates, I pulled over to the left of the hill, just short of the square. We got out and walked towards the hotel, stopping just outside it.

"You want to go in?" Tara asked.

I wasn't sure what I wanted to do – maybe just soak up the atmosphere of the place – get a feel for it again. So many things still puzzled me about it. We carried on past the hotel and on our left just up ahead was the shop owned by Sylvie's grandmother with its baskets of vegetables and fruits on display in front of the green-framed windows. The shop door opened and a figure came out carrying a basket of potatoes. It was Sylvie. She put the basket down next to some lettuces, and as she turned around to go back inside she saw us.

"Sylvie!" I said.

Her face stayed blank. No smile. No greeting. The last time I had seen her I had given her back the keys to her van and apologised for losing her ladder. She couldn't be angry with me about that – she hadn't shown any annoyance at the time. We walked over to her and still she didn't smile.

"Sylvie, this is Tara."

They shook hands, then Sylvie looked at me with a cold expression.

"So how come you've come back?"

"Thanks for the welcome."

"Er… well, no, it's just a surprise that's all."

"I just wanted to have another look at the place. After Tara and I met we went off and did a bit of travelling and we never got to explore it all. We're staying in Cannes at the moment."

"Oh, right."

Did I detect a note of relief that we were not staying in Saint Pierre?

"What happened to Virginie Lavelle in the end?" I asked.

"Yes, you were always fascinated to know about her weren't you?"

"Well, it was all a bit strange wasn't it?"

"Yes." She paused before continuing. "They released the body and then buried her a few days ago."

"Where?"

"In the graveyard. Where else do they bury people?"

She nodded to her left. "Down there, end of the street, turn left. I expect you'll be going to take a look at it."

Tara and I followed the road to the end, turned left and after fifty yards came to the graveyard on the north-west side of the town. I scanned the headstones, many of them pitted with age and weather-beaten, despite the mild winter climate in that part of the world, but none of them looked new.

We walked up and down the rows of graves, reading the names, being careful not to tread where we shouldn't, but found nothing. Then I looked across at a row of what could only be described as monuments – great stone edifices, some with statues of angels on top, others with huge stone crosses stretching up towards the heavens. One of them *was* new, with fresh flowers at the feet of the white stone angel who stood with her head bowed and her hands held together in prayer. My feet crunched on the newly raked gravel and then I saw on the plinth in gold letters the name: *Virginie Lavelle*.

"My God," I said, my mouth gaping.

"This is it? Was she wealthy?" Tara asked.

"Not as far as I know."

How had she come to be buried with such an elaborate monument, statue, or whatever you called such a thing? When she had turned up at the hotel she had looked pretty poor to me. Whoever heard of a rich nun? And if *she* hadn't paid for it, who had?

I paused for a moment, remembering her beautiful face and the air of tragedy that had surrounded her when we had met. It seemed that Virginie Lavelle would always be a puzzle to me.

"Come on," I said. "I want to ask Sylvie something."

We returned to the square and approached the shop. When I was three feet from the entrance I saw Sylvie's grandmother inside at the back of the shop, scowling at me through the glass. I stepped forwards, but before my hand grasped the knob, Sylvie opened the door.

"So, Danny, what do you want to ask now? You *do* want to ask something don't you? Or have you come to buy some food?"

She had the knack of making me feel awkward.

"The question's obvious," I said. "Who paid for the gravestone – if that's what you call it?"

"Well that I can't tell you. Maybe it's time you got over her. You've got a nice girlfriend now, why don't you let Virginie Lavelle lie in peace?"

I didn't bother to correct her about the girlfriend remark.

"Is that *can't* or *won't* tell me?"

"Can't."

"How come?"

"Because nobody knows. Someone anonymously ordered and paid for the burial and the monument. Seems like she had a friend somewhere after all – someone with money, although your guess is as good as mine as to who it might be."

We left Sylvie standing in the square, a cold look on her face. When we had first met in the Café de la Place she had been warm and friendly, but now she was like all the other locals. What had I done wrong? Again I remembered the High Priest's piercing blue eyes and wondered, not for the first time, if somehow he had the whole town under his spell. It was a macabre thought.

A cold shiver ran through me.

Had Cleaver told me everything he knew about the High Priest? I racked my brain, trying to think of something that didn't fit in with what he had told us. Everything had a ring of truth to it, and if the geneticist really was developing a miraculous cure that would benefit the world, then I had no choice but to hope that no harm came to the babies and wait for events to take their course. As for the High Priest breeding some kind of master race, if such a thing were possible, surely the Secret Service would be able to stop him. It seemed they did have an operative inside the inner circle monitoring what was going on.

We arrived back at the hotel in Cannes, went to my room and ordered some tea from room service.

Tara said, "You know I should contact my mother – I promised I would. I'll ask the hotel if I can send her an email."

"No need. I'll plug in my laptop – you can do it right here."

I set up the computer on the writing desk, plugged in the modem and tried to get a connection. It whined and whistled, eventually shaking hands with the server, and then a light flashed in the bottom right-hand corner of the screen, telling me I had emails – it had been ages since I had checked them. I clicked on the icon; there were seven messages waiting for me.

Someone knocked on the door. Tara went to open it. It was room service with the tea. She took the tray and poured me a cup while I scanned my messages. Six were from friends – the usual stuff – lists of jokes. But the last one, dated the previous day, I didn't recognise, and was from someone called DT946020@hotmail.com. Was it a virus? There was no attachment so it was unlikely to be.

I clicked on it and read –

> EVER BEEN TAKEN FOR A FOOL?
> DO NOT REPLY.
> WILL ONLY RESPOND TO EMAILS FROM
> INNOCENTFOOL999@HOTMAIL.COM
> IMPERATIVE – ANSWER FROM CYBER CAFÉ ONLY!
> DEEP THROAT.

My heart thumped in my chest.

"Jesus Christ!" I said.

Tara brought over a cup of tea.

"What is it?"

"Look at this."

She read the message.

"What does it mean?"

"Look at the name – *Deep Throat*. Do you know who Deep Throat was?"

She shook her head.

"*Watergate!* The film *Watergate* – it wasn't just a film – it was real life too. Deep Throat was the name of the informer who pointed the two reporters, Bernstein and Woodward, in the right direction to uncover the Watergate scandal – the scandal that led to President Richard Nixon having to resign in disgrace."

"Shit."

"Shit's right. Someone is trying to tell us something. We've been sold a dummy by that bastard, Cleaver!"

"Are you going to reply?"

"Of course I am. I never trusted that son-of-a-bitch in the first place."

"But why do we have to go to a cyber café to reply?"

"I don't know. I… Jesus!" I jumped back from the computer as if I'd been electrocuted. "The computer! It must be bugged in some way – some kind of interception device for my emails!" The cogs of my brain span like crazy. "The bastards who broke into the house left the computer untouched, or so we thought. But it wasn't untouched – they must have done something to it!"

Could they have put an audio bug in it too? I put my finger to my lips, indicating to Tara to be quiet, picked up the computer and then, holding it at arm's length as if it were a bomb, took it into the bathroom, dumped it in the bath and ran the tap. Tara followed me in.

"My God, Danny. What the fuck have we got into here?"

"I don't know, but we'd better reply to Deep Throat and find out."

When I was sure that whatever electronics had been put in my computer were destroyed, I took it out of the bath, dried it off and wrapped it in a carrier bag. Five minutes later we walked out of the hotel with it tucked under my arm and three hundred yards along the road dropped it in a litterbin, relief washing over me. We returned to the hotel and asked the concierge where we could find a cyber café. Ten minutes later were standing outside one.

The place was half full – mostly of young student types – keyboards and mice rattling and clicking over the soft background music, cigarette smoke drifting across the room. After buying two cappuccinos we took a seat at one of the computers.

The first thing to do was set up a hotmail account in the name Deep Throat had given me – the only name he said he would respond to. We chose 'Florida' as the password and a few minutes later were all set up. Now we could go to any cyber café in the world to send and receive emails without fear of anyone accessing our account.

"OK. Let's see what he knows," I said.

I typed an email –

> INNOCENTFOOL REQUESTS ADVICE FROM DEEP THROAT.

Then I clicked on the 'send' button.

"How long do we wait?" Tara asked.

I hadn't got a clue. We could be sitting there for days until we got a reply, but then again, Deep Throat could be waiting right now at a computer anywhere in the world – he might answer immediately.

We sipped our cappuccinos and pretended to be searching for something on the Web. Every few minutes I went into the hotmail account to check for incoming mail, but there was nothing. After an hour we had to concede that wherever Deep Throat was he certainly wasn't staring at his computer waiting for an email from us. We paid for our computer time and left.

Walking along the Croisette, my thoughts returned again to Cleaver. Just what hadn't he told us? Could it be that we were about to uncover a scandal of some kind that linked back to the government? Why else would whoever emailed me call himself Deep Throat – a direct reference to the most famous political scandal of all time?

Perhaps after years struggling to make it as a reporter, losing my job and then coming to France, I was finally getting closer to achieving what I had always wanted: revenge for my father's death. The bitterness that had lurked deep within me for twenty years was fuelling my hunger to get to the bottom of whatever we had stumbled across. I knew it must be something big – why else would the British Secret Service go to the trouble of bugging my house and computer? And if it *was* big and the Secret Service *was* involved... then it would also be dangerous, and although I was prepared to do whatever necessary to uncover the truth, I had no right to expose Tara to the same risks.

"Tara, you know I'm going to get to the bottom of this, one way or another, don't you?"

"I know."

"I don't know what it might involve or how dangerous it might be." She looked puzzled. "What are you saying?"

"I'm saying that it might be better if you went back to Florida – for a while at least."

"What! Are you crazy? I don't give a damn how dangerous it is! Look, I know this might be your chance to do the big-political-scandal-thing and get even for your father's death, but you need to remember you wouldn't be in a position to do it at all if it wasn't for me. Anyway, I have an interest in nailing this High Priest asshole after he got me locked up in that damned sanatorium, right? And what else would I do with my time? I'm having a blast here. We're partners in this, OK? So stop being so damned patronising. When do we check for emails again?"

So much for my attempt at chivalry.

"I don't know. Could be a long wait."

"I don't think so."

"Why?"

"Because if something bad is happening, whoever wants to tell us is likely to be in a hurry. I figure they'll be as keen to tell us as we are to hear it."

It was a good point.

I said, "If they know about whatever this is, and they know about us too, they must be very close to Cleaver. It must be someone working in the same part of the intelligence service. They're not going to contact us from the Secret Service offices – they'd wait until they were either at home, or more likely use a cyber café. Let's try again at seven o'clock tonight."

At 6.55pm we entered the cyber café again. There were no computers available.

"What do we do?" Tara asked.

We bought coffees. Fortunately, by the time we had taken a couple of sips, a tall, thin teenager dressed in black with a silver stud in his nose got up and left, his blue project folders tucked under his arm.

We took our seats and I logged on, praying there was a reply waiting for us. If there wasn't, what could we do? Hanging around Cannes, just waiting, knowing that something bad was going on, was not an option.

We focused on the screen as if our lives depended on it.

"Yes!" We had mail.

I clicked the mouse and together we read –

FOR SECURITY, OPEN ANOTHER ACCOUNT AND EMAIL ME IMMEDIATELY.

"How many accounts have we got to open before he tells us something?" Tara said.

I looked at the time the email was sent.

"He wrote it five minutes ago. He's probably still there waiting for us. We've got to send one back quickly."

I clicked the icons to open a new email account.

Tara said, "What name are you going to choose?"

"Guess it doesn't matter – he'll know it's from us – but let's stick to the Watergate theme."

I mixed up the names of the two Watergate reporters and opened an account in the name of woodsteinwatergate@hotmail.com. Then I sent an email to Deep Throat –

AWAITING YOUR ADVICE.

Almost immediately we got an email back –

CHANGING MY ACCOUNT NAME. WAIT TWO MINUTES.

"Jesus, this could go on forever!" said Tara.

We stared at the screen, oblivious to whatever was going on around us. Two minutes later I clicked the icon and saw I had another email, this time from dtwatergate999. It said –

CHECK OUT THE PHARMACEUTICAL LOBBY.
DEEP THROAT.

Tara said, "What does that mean?"

I emailed back –

EXPLAIN?

We waited. No reply. We ordered two more coffees. Twenty minutes passed.

"I think that's all we're going to get," I said.

"How on earth do we check out the pharmaceutical lobby?"

I had no idea.

We made our way back towards the hotel, stopping outside a fish restaurant at the side of the port.

"Want to eat something here?" I said.

We ordered a bouillabaisse, which was tantalisingly good, and so was the cool, crisp Chablis we drank with it.

Tara said, "Why the hell doesn't he just tell us what the deal is? He can't be worried about security any more, not now we've changed email addresses."

"I don't know, but it was like that in the Watergate film."

"You don't think this is just some nut who has a hard-on for the film do you?"

I shook my head. "He asked us to check out the pharmaceutical lobby. He must know what's really going on in the convent – it would be too much of a coincidence him saying something about pharmaceuticals after Cleaver told us they were about to discover a cure for the common cold."

"You don't know any politicians do you?" Tara asked. I gave her a look and she said, "Silly question."

After dinner we walked back to the hotel, sat in the bar and listened to the pianist singing some Frank Sinatra tunes. *New York New York* didn't sound quite the same when it was sung slightly off key in a heavy French accent.

The next morning I awoke at 6 and lay in bed trying to work out what Deep Throat had been trying to tell us. Tara was right about the clue – it was infuriating. I knew absolutely nothing about the pharmaceutical lobby, and so Deep Throat's email was no help at all. At the same time I was ever-mindful of the fate of the babies in the convent. Time was not on our side, but did Deep Throat know that?

In the restaurant, over a breakfast of croissants with strawberry jam and coffee, an idea came to me.

"I have to make a call," I said. "Come on, let's go for a walk."

"Why?"

"I'd feel more comfortable using a public phone."

We walked to the port and found a phone box. I looked at my watch. It was 9.03am. Perfect. We both squeezed into the box and I dialled the number.

A voice answered.

"*Leyton-Middleton Advertiser*, how may I help you?"

"Colin Moreton, please."

"Who's calling?"

"Andrea, it's me, Danny."

"Danny! What are you doing calling up here? Eddy's going to kill you. What happened with that match report?"

"Some other time, Andrea. I need to talk to Colin, it's important."

"Hang on. I'll see if he's free."

I listened to the awful hold music. Why did people use that stuff? Finally she put me through.

"Good God, Danny Avery. You've got a nerve calling here!"

The glee in Colin's voice told me he was up for some major piss taking.

"Yes, yes. Look, Colin, just save it will you, this is important."

"Oh, yeah? What's this then – a story for me? Don't tell me, the prime minister's the queen's love child, right?"

"For fuck's sake, Colin, just listen will you. You would like to make an easy thousand, wouldn't you?"

The piss taking stopped.

"Go on."

"I'm on to something big. It's political and I need your help."

"Thought you were strictly sports?"

"Colin, shut up, for God's sake, that's all history. What I'm onto is big. It'll shake the foundations – you know what I mean? This is CNN – world news stuff. I mean it, seriously."

"So why do you need me?"

"I could go with it now, but I know there's more. I've got a source connected with the top, but I need to verify some things – double-check some facts."

"Like what?"

"Well, for one thing, how big is the pharmaceutical lobby?"

"If the story's that big I'll need five grand."

"Two."

"Two and a half."

"Done, but I may need to get some information from you for a week or two – until it's ready to roll."

"Well hurry up for fuck's sake. Marlene wants to go on holiday to Mauritius and I've got to pay for it soon."

"So, what about the pharmaceutical lobby?"

"Big. Pharmaceutical companies are some of the biggest in the country; they're always lobbying the government for something, or trying to get political favours – sometimes to get help protecting their markets, or it might be to get a grant to build a factory in a high unemployment area. All big businesses do that sort of thing."

"What about donations to political parties?"

"Tricky. Governments are very sensitive about that sort of thing. They don't want to be seen to be in the pockets of the pharmaceutical companies or any others for that matter."

I couldn't see where all this was going.

"Well, if they can't donate money, how do they get influence?"

"That's easy. You put a load of politicians on the payroll."

"What? You bribe them?"

"Nothing so crude. Give them directorships. The pharmaceutical companies are littered with politicos on their boards. It all looks above board – big companies are encouraged to have a collection of non-executive directors, so they might as well pay politicians as anyone else."

"But the politicians have to declare it."

"Of course. Doesn't stop them influencing things in favour of their employers though does it?"

"So they have political power."

"Any big business with deep pockets has clout with the politicians – all politicians are greedy bastards."

What he said still didn't give me any clues about whatever it was Deep Throat wanted to tell me. I couldn't think what else to ask.

"OK, Colin. Thanks."

"Is that it?"

"I'll be back."

"Well don't forget my fucking two and a half grand, OK?"

"Stay cool. You'll get it. Hang on, give me your mobile number."

I wrote it down and then I hung up. Tara and I stepped out of the phone box and I told her what Colin had said.

"Still don't get it," she said.

"I don't either. All we've confirmed is that the pharmaceutical companies have a lot of political power, but why is that significant in all this?"

"Didn't Cleaver say there was one company that was going to get the formula for the cold cure? It's got to be the one that has the most influence, right?"

"Goes without saying, but Deep Throat said, *Ever been taken for a fool?* Cleaver never told us which company was going to get the formula, so we haven't been fooled about that. There must be something else."

We headed over to the square opposite the port, sat at a table and drank Coke. My forehead furrowed. What the fuck had we missed? There had to be something staring us right in the face – something obvious. I had gone over our meeting with Cleaver so many times I was bored with it. We needed to look in another direction.

I went back over the events since I had first arrived in Saint Pierre, and thought again about the suspicious behaviour of the hotel manager. Why had he reacted so strongly when I asked for Virginie Lavelle's name? Why hadn't she been registered at the hotel? Why had I been given such a hostile reception by the whole town?

"Tara, when you were in the convent, did you know if the High Priest ever left the place?"

"Don't think so, but I wouldn't have known about it if he had. Why?"

"There's something about the town that puzzles me. The first night I got there the locals were not exactly friendly – hostile, I'd say. In fact I've had a lot of hostile receptions recently – your mum and uncle weren't exactly friendly either. It's like I've been wandering around wearing a hat with *idiot* on the front."

Tara laughed.

"Hey, relax. Mom and Uncle Jim are… protective shall we say. It's because I have a trust fund and they think everyone I meet wants to get their hands on it. Kind of insulting really – as if they don't think my charms are enough on their own."

"But that doesn't explain what was going on with the locals up in Saint Pierre – I managed to get my nose punched by one guy."

"What the hell did you do?"

"Nothing. I just wanted some answers – about Virginie Lavelle as it happens."

"So, what are you thinking?"

"Look, I know this sounds far-fetched, but could the High Priest have some kind of hold on the whole town?"

"Kind of like in *The Stepford Wives*, only more sinister – the whole town under some kind of spell. That's weird."

"That's why I wondered if you ever saw him leave the convent."

"Never."

"Funny thing is Sylvie was the only one who was friendly to me, but you saw for yourself how that's changed."

I was exasperated. I wanted to get hold of Deep Throat and shake him, but I knew we wouldn't be able to contact him until early evening. I felt guilty for not doing anything, and frustrated because I didn't know what I *could* do.

At 7pm that night, we entered the cyber café and sat down in front of a computer with a dusty screen and filthy keyboard, and I prayed that Deep Throat was sitting at a similar computer at the other end of cyberspace. If he wasn't I was going to explode.

I logged on and clicked the icon on my inbox. Yes! I had mail.

I opened it and read –

> *CHECK OUT THE DRUG MARKET.*
> *DEEP THROAT.*

"Fuck! More cryptic clues! It's like trying to work out some goddamned crossword puzzle! He's got to give us more than this – we're getting nowhere."

I wrote a reply –

NEED MORE THAN JUST CLUES. PLEASE TELL US WHAT WE ARE SUPPOSED TO FIND OUT.
WOODSTEINWATERGATE

I pressed the send button. We waited.

"Come on, reply for Christ's sake!"

Five minutes later I said, "It's no good. If he was there he would have replied by now."

"What do we do?"

I bit my tongue to stop myself from snapping at her – I was as tight as a piano string. We got up, left the café and sat on the low wall beside the port.

Tara said, "We'll work it out."

"You don't think I'm obsessed do you?"

She looked at me quizzically.

"Don't be silly. We both know something's not right about all this. If the Secret Service is involved, then the government is involved too, and I know you want to avenge what happened to your father. Why shouldn't you? Fathers are important."

"You never mention *your* father. I asked you something about him once and you sidestepped the issue."

Her face coloured and she looked down at the floor. I knew I had touched on something sensitive.

"I can't tell you anything about my father – I don't know who he is."

"You mean your mum never told you?"

"She never knew. Mom was a hippy, right? Grew up in the Sixties. Peace and love and all that. She spent years doped out of her head, sleeping around with anyone who 'had a pleasing aura' as she would say. One of them was my father, but which one is anyone's guess."

The hurt on her face was obvious to see.

"I'm sorry."

I put my arm around her and pulled her towards me.

"I wish I'd had one. I'm mad I didn't, but I'd probably be madder if I'd had one and then had him taken away from me, like yours was."

I squeezed her body against mine and kissed the top of her head.

"Come on. Let's go and eat," I said.

We began walking to the old town.

"Hang on a minute. Let me call Colin. You never know, he might make something of it."

We got into the phone box and I dialled his mobile.

"Colin, it's me."

"Ah, Danny. Don't tell me, you want my account details so you can pay me my two and a half grand."

"Very funny. You need to do a bit more work first. What can you tell me about the drug market?"

"You mean illegal? You want to score some dope or something?"

"No, I mean legal – I think."

"Well, make up your mind."

"Legal."

"I do politics, not economics."

"But they cross over sometimes, right?"

"Suppose so. Danny, just what the fuck is it you want to know?"

I didn't answer – I couldn't answer.

"You *have* got a story, haven't you? 'Cos I'm not going to waste –"

"Yes! I've got a story, OK? Bigger than you can imagine."

"Then fucking well ask me what you want to know."

"OK. How big is the market for drugs in the UK?"

"I don't know, but it's massive of course. Go into any high street chemist – in fact think about how many chemists there are – bloody thousands – all selling drugs. Have you got to have the exact figure?"

Did I need the exact figure? Was that where the clue was?

"Er... no. Well, yes, if you've got it."

"I haven't got it, but I can get it. Give me your number and I'll call you back."

"No, I'll call you."

"Suit yourself. Is that it?"

"Er... yes. That's it for now."

I hung up.

"This is doing my bloody head in!" I shouted.

"Did he say anything useful?" Tara asked.

I shook my head.

"OK. Look, let's forget it for now – give ourselves a night off. We'll pick it up again tomorrow."

At four in the morning I dialled the number for Tara's room.

"Tara!"

"What time is it?" she asked, yawning.

"It's early. There's something I need to ask you."

"What is it?"

"Uncle Jim told us about the scientist who's a follower of the High Priest – the man called, oh, what was it?" I racked my brain. "Michael… Michael something. Roberts? Richards! That was it – Michael Richards."

"What about him?"

"Cleaver said a geneticist was working on the cold cure thing with the High Priest in the convent."

"So?"

"Well, you were in the convent – in the damned inner circle, for Christ's sake. Did you ever see this guy, Michael Richards?"

"No. Can't say I did. Do you think it's important?"

"Well if he isn't in the convent then where is he and how the hell can he be working with the High Priest on a cure for the common cold? We need to get back inside the convent. If there's no sign of him, then everything Cleaver told us is bollocks."

Chapter 10

We decided to break into the convent at midnight, which meant we spent a frustrating day sitting around twiddling our thumbs. I had never wanted a day to pass so quickly. Did Michael Richards exist or was he part of a grand lie cooked up by Cleaver to put us off the scent? The more I thought about it the more convinced I became that he was a fictional character. After all, how could a man stay in a convent without the nuns ever seeing him?

At 7pm, we went back to the cyber café to see if we had any more emails. I clicked on the icons without enthusiasm. Whoever this Deep Throat character was he had given us little to work on up to now, and I had no faith that we would be able to decipher *any* clue he gave us.

I opened my inbox. I had mail. I clicked on it and read –

AFRICA'S PLAGUE.
DEEP THROAT.

I turned to Tara. "That's easy. It's AIDS."
"Do you think they're working on a cure for AIDS?"
"I don't know."
Tara noticed my puzzled expression. "What's up?"
"The clue – it just seems too easy."
"Well, you wanted him to stop being so cryptic."
"Yeah, but this is all *good* news. Why would Deep Throat be trying to warn us about this? What would be the point? OK, we may have been fooled by Cleaver, it's an AIDS cure they're working on not a cure for the common cold, but so what? There would be no reason for Deep Throat to do all this? We've still got to get into that convent and see if we can find this Michael Richards guy."

Standing against the convent walls in Saint Pierre, I looked at my watch – 11.30pm.

"Let's get on with it," I said, reaching into my pocket to take out the small flashlight I had bought that afternoon. I switched it on for a second, making sure it worked. "You're sure the High Priest isn't going to be doing his thing with the nuns tonight?"

"I don't think so. Saturday night is party night," Tara said.

My stomach felt fluttery and nauseous at the thought of walking along that wall again. Tara picked out the same hand and footholds she had used the first time, nimbly climbing to the top of the wall. I watched where she put her hands and feet and breathed in deeply, preparing myself.

Here we go.

She moved off and I followed, telling myself, *don't look down – take it easy – you can make it – stay calm – you've done this before*, but it made no difference; it was no easier the second time around, and yet for Tara it seemed to pose no more problems than it would for the average squirrel.

Minutes later, the thought of leaping across space to get to the roof of the hall sent a wave of terror through me. I desperately tried to resist the urge to look down, but some strange force drew my gaze, and as I peered over the edge a crazy urge to let myself tumble into nothingness gripped me. I closed my eyes, my head swirled, and I told myself, *No! Don't look down! Don't look down!*

"Danny!"

Tara grabbed my arm and I opened my eyes.

"Fuck!"

I steadied myself, feeling the wall with my feet, my arms outstretched like a tightrope walker. Fifteen seconds later my senses returned to normal.

"OK. I'm all right now."

Tara leapt onto the roof of the building.

"Oh, Christ – this has got to be last time I do this!" I said.

I clenched my fists and jumped, landing with a thud, and again a tile cracked under my weight, but this time it didn't slide off the roof.

The hard part was over.

We entered through the skylight, climbed over the pews and

stopped to catch our breath. I took the flashlight out of my pocket and shone it around. Above us were wooden beams thick with dust, giving them a muted khaki colour. Dislodged particles irritated my throat and I struggled to stop myself coughing. I shone the beam to the left and it fell upon a row of simple wooden chairs lined up against the attic wall, similar to those that had been laid out in the great hall during the Saturday night ceremony.

Something moved.

I jumped. Tara saw it too and she gripped my arm. I jerked the light beam towards it and two pinpricks of light close together shone back at me. There was a scurrying sound… and then nothing.

"It was just a mouse," I whispered.

The beam of the flashlight fell upon the wall, and then I saw behind the chairs a small wooden door, brown and dirty looking, no more than two feet high – more of a hatch than a door. The cobwebs in front of it were thick with dust. On the other side of the loft were more rows of chairs and in front of us was the door that led to the gallery of the great hall.

It was time to find this Michael Richards.

We approached the door in front of us and I turned off my flashlight. Tara reached out a hand, lifted the latch and inched the door back. A weak yellow glow cast its light on the stone steps leading down to the gallery and we took off our shoes and made our way down. Steadying myself, I placed a moist hand on the wall to my right and, as I descended, the uneven surface of the stone steps, pitted with age, dug into my feet through my socks.

We reached the gallery, crouched behind the railings and I peered over. The room looked just as before – the rows of chairs perfectly positioned, the effigy of Jesus on the cross standing high and imposing on the altar, its polished silver surface reflecting the candlelight.

"Where do we look now?" I asked.

"I don't know."

"What? You must know the layout of the buildings here."

"Well, yes, but I don't know where this Michael Richards guy hangs out. If I did we wouldn't have to be here."

"What's outside – I mean through the door where we saw the nuns come in for the 'fucking ceremony'?"

"A garden."

"That's it?"

Tara heard the frustration in my voice.

"Of course not – there are buildings as well. For Christ's sake, Danny, if the scientist guy was here when I was, he wasn't wandering around the damned convent for all the nuns to see. How the fuck should I know where to look?"

It seemed we only had two choices: Go through the door that led out into the gardens, hide amongst the trees and look for a likely building, or take the door through which the High Priest had entered the room. In my mind I saw again the hand of the High Priest appearing through the doorway holding the candelabra with its three lit candles, then his blue eyes like cold sapphires, and his long black hair parted down the middle. The man who claimed to be the Son of God had looked to me like the epitome of evil, and the idea of going through that doorway filled me with dread.

Still undecided as to which door to go through, we crouched behind the railings and made our way along the gallery, like two assassins. After we had gone no more than five yards I heard something and froze. Tara bumped into me. I turned to face her and put my finger to my lips. Again I heard something. It was the rattle of a key in a lock, then the lifting of a latch and the ghostly creak of a door. I pressed my face against the railings and looked down into the hall below.

A nun entered, then another. Tara had said the High Priest only did it on Saturdays. I looked at her and she shrugged. We watched and waited for the procession to continue but no one else came in. A minute passed. My watch said it was past midnight already – they should be in the room by now if they were going to get to it. Unable to see what the two nuns were doing, I slowly got on to my knees, then onto my feet and leaned over the railings. There they were, cleaning and polishing the effigy of Jesus on the cross and the big silver bowl that stood on the altar before it. I got back down and whispered to Tara.

"Cleaning at this hour?"

She shrugged. "A nun's work is never done."

There was a lot of silver to clean; this could go on all night and we had to be out of there well before sunrise or we would be seen returning along the convent walls. But the idea of returning to Cannes empty-handed was infuriating.

Then an idea struck me.

I whispered in Tara's ear, "Follow me."

On our hands and knees we made our way back to the stone steps. Staying low, we clambered up, making our way back to the loft.

"Where are we going?" Tara whispered.

"There's no way out down there."

"Yes, but we can't go back – not yet," she said.

"I wasn't going to."

Safely back in the loft, and with the door closed behind us, I turned on my flashlight.

"Help me move those chairs."

I positioned the flashlight on one of the pews so its beam lit up the room and then began moving the chairs away from the wall, exposing the brown wooden hatch.

"You want to go through there?" she asked.

"It's got to lead somewhere."

I approached it and pulled away the cobwebs, brushing their remains off my hands. The wood was riddled with woodworm and on the right-hand side was a handle in the shape of a wrought iron ring with a bolt attaching it to the door. I grabbed it and pulled, but it wouldn't budge. I pulled again, harder, and the handle came off in my hand, the decaying wood too weak to hold it. I put my finger in the hole where the handle had been and felt how rotten the door was. It would be easy to kick it in, but we couldn't do that – the noise would carry to the nuns in the hall.

I gripped the part of the handle that was shaped like a metal bolt and began to force it between the edge of the wooden door and the point where it butted up to the wall, twisting and turning it. Soon there was a crevice and I widened it, wedging the bolt into the gap. I pulled and pushed it in a sawing motion, opening up the space, until thirty seconds later the rotten wood gave up, the door disintegrated and a dozen newly evicted earwigs scattered over the floor.

I took the flashlight and shone its beam through the doorway, but there was nothing to see, just an attic about the same size as the one we were in, but totally empty.

"Does it lead anywhere?" Tara asked.

I pointed the flashlight at the wall opposite, trying to see if there was another door like the one I was looking through, then stretched my head through the opening and pointed the beam along the walls to the left and then right, but there was nothing to see.

"No. Fuck it!"

What he hell were we to do now?"

"Give me that flashlight," Tara said.

She scanned the walls of the attic we were in looking for another doorway, but it was hopeless. Frustrated and angry, I looked back through the hatchway into the dimness of the adjacent loft. And then my eyes grew accustomed to the lack of light.

"Tara! Come here. Turn off the flashlight."

She made her way over and crouched beside me, her shoulder up against mine.

"What?"

"Just wait a second."

We both looked into the blackness – except for me it wasn't so black now.

"Let your eyes get used to the dark."

"What exactly am I…"

"See it?"

"You mean the light shining through the floorboards?"

"Of course I do! Come on, let's take a look."

I clambered through the opening, scraping my back on the wall at the top of the hatchway. Tara followed behind. I stepped towards the light and a sharp pain shot in to my foot, making me jerk it into the air, my face contorting in pain.

"Jesus! Splinters! Be careful where you tread." I reached down and pulled out a shard of wood from my heel.

We edged our way over, and then got down on our stomachs to peer through the gaps in the floorboards.

And then we saw them.

Tara had said they were here in this wretched convent, but I hadn't expected to see them tonight and it was impossible to tell exactly how many there were. The gaps in the floor were small and the planks were thick, restricting my field of vision, but I could see at least six of them.

Six babies in cots. All in a neat line. Seeing them lying there, the progeny of some half-crazed religious nutcase, brought home to me the crazy, evil nature of this High Priest. If there was good going on here, there was evil too, and I didn't know how long I could ignore it.

"Jesus, Tara. We have to do something about this!" I whispered.

I wanted to rush down there and… do what? Gather them up in my arms and run off with them? Whoever was down there with them wasn't about to let me walk out with a whole crèche of babies, and I had no weapon. There was nothing I could do tonight, I reasoned, telling myself they looked healthy and well cared for, and that I would be making a big mistake if in my haste to remove them from the convent I stopped a cure for AIDS being discovered.

I remembered what we had come for, to find Michael Richards, and I placed my palms flat on the floorboards to push myself up, but before I averted my gaze from the room below something moved at the edge of my line of vision.

"Tara, did you see that?"

"What?"

I looked hard trying to make out what was drifting in and out of sight. Five seconds passed and then…

"There! I can see it. It's a clipboard."

It moved to the right and then I saw the man holding it – a man with sandy-coloured hair, wearing a white lab coat.

"I see him now!" Tara whispered.

"It must be him – Michael Richards!"

Who else would be wandering around the inner sanctum of a convent wearing a white lab coat? And if it was Richards he might be working on a cure for AIDS, just as Deep Throat had told us in his last clue. The man jotted something down and stepped to his right, out of sight.

We had found what we had come for. It was time to leave.

Through the night I tossed and turned telling myself the babies would be OK and that we had solved the riddle of the emails. But sleep was still difficult.

After breakfast the next day I said to Tara, "Come with me. There's something I've got to do before we go to the beach."

I led her across the road.

"We're going back to that cyber café, aren't we?' she said. "You're getting to be a regular web surfer."

"Just thought I'd send a quick email to Deep Throat thanking him for the clues and letting him know we've worked it out."

Once in the café, I logged on. We had another email from Deep Throat and judging by the time it was sent we'd only just missed it the night before. I wondered if he'd been waiting for a reply to his earlier email and when we didn't send him one he'd sent us another clue.

I opened and read –

WMD!
    DEEP THROAT

"My God! Tara, look!"
"What does it mean?"
"It means we have been conned. Duped. Fucked with!"
"Why? By who?"
"By everyone! WMD – Weapons of Mass Destruction. Whatever it is they're doing in that damned convent, they sure as fuck aren't making a cure for AIDS."

I typed a reply:

URGENT.
    WE MUST MEET. NOW!
    ADVISE PLACE AND TIME

Deep Throat wouldn't be on line at this time so I logged off the computer and we left the building.

Cure for colds. Bullshit! No wonder that bastard Cleaver ordered my house to be burgled and bugged my computer. MI5, MI6, Secret Service or whatever they were, they were all puppets of politicians – bent conniving, twisting, self-serving bastards. Why had I been so stupid? I, more than anyone, should never have trusted anything Cleaver said.

I marched over towards the phone box beside the port.
"What are we going to do now?" Tara asked.

I flung open the door, grabbed the receiver, rummaged around in my pocket for Cleaver's card and dialled the number. Got to confront the bastard – get him to tell me what was really going on. If he didn't I would blow the whole thing open. Seconds later my ear filled with one continuous tone.

"Fuck!"

"What is it?"

"The line is dead! He must have lines available to set up and close down whenever he wants. Right, that's it. We go to the papers – we sell the story!"

Chapter 11

With paper and pens from an office supply shop, we sat in a restaurant drinking endless cups of coffee, writing down what we knew. First there was the High Priest – we knew what he'd done in the USA before coming to France and the false name under which he had travelled. We knew he had infiltrated the convent and that he was fucking the nuns, getting them pregnant and trying to build a master race, but we didn't know who he really was. And then there was Michael Richards, the scientist who was working with the High Priest, developing weapons of mass destruction to create their own Armageddon, and the British Secret Service who knew what they were doing and allowed them to continue, presumably to steal the secret from them – an insane and dangerous gamble.

Of course we still didn't know whether Virginie Lavelle was a nun or a prostitute, why the locals in Saint Pierre had been so hostile towards me, and what the hotel manager had to do with anything. But those questions seemed unimportant to me now that we knew what was really going on in the convent.

The pieces thrashed around in my head and I tried to start an article several times, each time stopping just a few lines in, tearing up the page and screwing it into a ball.

"This is no good," I said.

"What about Deep Throat? We can use his emails too."

I shook my head and thumped the table.

"Tara. We need more."

"But we must have enough, surely?"

"We haven't got any evidence! The first thing an editor is going to want to know is how we know all this. What are we going to say?"

"We can tell him I was in the convent. We can tell him I was held in the sanatorium."

"We need *proof!* An editor wants to be sure we aren't just a couple of nutcases, or someone with a grudge. You start telling him you were put in a sanatorium, suspected of being a nutcase, and that's exactly what he's going to think you *are*."

"Well, we can print out Deep Throat's emails."

"They don't say anything. Besides, anyone could have set up a hotmail account and written them."

"So what do we do?"

"We've got to get that meeting with Deep Throat. Let's get back to that cyber café."

I clicked on the icon. Nothing. No reply. I looked at my watch – 3.12pm. Too early. Deep Throat only got on line around 7pm our time. Nearly four hours to kill.

We walked around Cannes, up and down the Croisette, until the soles of my feet felt raw, but I couldn't keep still. *Cure for colds.* My hatred for Cleaver festered like an angry boil. Somehow I was going to take him down.

Deep Throat had to talk to us.

At 6.53pm we logged on. I clicked the icon. I had mail – yes!

I opened it –

> NO MEETINGS. TOO DANGEROUS.
> DEEP THROAT.

I replied –

> NOT GOOD ENOUGH.
> IF WHAT YOU SAY IS TRUE WE MUST MEET NOW!
> TOO IMPORTANT TO IGNORE.
> YOU MUST TELL ME EVERYTHING – NO MORE CLUES!

We waited. Every ten seconds I clicked the icon for incoming mail. *Come on, for Christ's sake!* I looked at my watch – 7.29pm. Still no reply.

I wrote another email –

> HELP US!

Again we waited. Still nothing.

Tara took her eyes off the screen and looked at me.

"He's not there is he?"

"Fuck it. If he won't give us any evidence we'll just have to get it ourselves. Come on." I logged off.

Outside the cyber café I looked at my watch – 7.55pm.

"Do you have any money?"

"Sure."

"Come on, run!"

I grabbed her hand and we dodged the shoppers on the pavement, jumping out into the road and back onto the pavement, weaving our way to the end of the street, turning right and then left.

"Danny, where are we going?"

I pulled her into a shop that sold electronic items and paused to get my breath back. *Jesus, I need to get back in shape.*

"Camera. We've got to buy a camera."

At 8.03pm we left the shop with me clutching a red plastic bag containing a digital camera and a pack of batteries.

"We're going back to the convent."

Chapter 12

At the convent walls I looked at my watch – 10.45pm. Earlier than the last two times, but darkness had set in. Driven by anger and the image of Alistair Cleaver's face, this time I went first, and when we reached the gap between the wall and the great hall, I leapt across without hesitation, my nerves steeled by rage.

Once through the skylight and inside the attic, Tara said, "Where to now?"

"We've got to try and get into the room below where we saw the babies. You say that door in the great hall leads to a garden?"

"Yes."

I tried to imagine a plan of the buildings and where we might find an entrance to the place where the babies were. It couldn't be difficult to find. Hopefully we could look for it under the cover of any trees or bushes that might be there.

"OK. Let's try that way," I said.

I briefly turned on the flashlight to get my bearings, then made my way over to the door leading to the gallery. It opened without creaking. Total blackness. No candles burning in the great hall tonight. I turned to Tara and whispered, "Can you make it down these steps without the flashlight on?"

"I think so."

We made our way down to the gallery, and then, convinced no one was down there, I turned on the flashlight and shone the beam over to the other side of the great hall and then down at the doorway that lead out to the garden.

"OK. Let's carry on," I said.

At the opposite side of the gallery we stopped at the top of the stairs. I listened hard again, but heard nothing I shone the beam around the room like a mini searchlight, from right to left. The chairs were laid out in neat rows as before. Then the beam fell upon the altar and the effigy of Jesus on the cross, and for a moment I had the eerie feeling it was watching us.

We began descending the staircase and halfway down I glanced across to my left at the door beside the altar through which the High Priest had entered for the ceremony with the nuns. What lay beyond it was anyone's guess. In my mind I saw the crazy image of the High Priest laying in an oversized manger on soft comfortable straw, eyes closed, face serene, palms clasped together in front of his chest, as if in prayer. I shook my head to dispel the vision and we continued down the stairway.

Reaching the bottom of the steps, I gazed at the door again.

Tara stopped behind me.

"What is it?" she whispered.

"Nothing."

I turned to my right and walked towards the other door that led to the garden.

Tara said, "This part of the garden isn't overlooked by any windows. It'll be OK."

I put my hand on the latch and gripped it, but as I began to lift it, I froze.

"Danny, what's up?"

It was as if I was being drawn in another direction by some kind of magnetic force. I turned and looked at the other door again, wondering exactly what kind of evil lay behind it, and then I realised I had to go through it and find out – I couldn't put it off any longer. A cold shiver ran down my spine. I nodded towards the door.

"We're going through there."

"No, Danny. We can't!"

"We've got to. We've got to get to the root of all this."

"But he's down there, for Christ's sake!"

"So what if he's down there – I hope he is."

"But, Danny, it isn't safe – the guy's dangerous! Weapons of Mass Destruction – remember?"

"I can handle him and a bunch of nuns," I said, puffing out my chest. "Anyway, let him find us – we're going to sell the story and blow the whole thing wide open, so what difference does it make?"

"Yes, but you're forgetting why we're here! We're supposed to be taking pictures – getting evidence. We don't have enough to go on – you said so yourself. If he sees us he's not going to let us snap away with that damned camera and then just walk out of here, is he?"

"We've still got to go through there and check it out – you know it, Tara. If we want evidence the one place we are going to find it is down there."

I took a step towards the door. Tara grabbed my arm, and then saw the look on my face. She seemed to sense her words were wasted.

"OK, OK, but for Christ's sake, let's be careful."

I grabbed the wrought iron latch handle, paused to prepare myself, lifted it and pulled the door towards me, feeling its solid weight. Behind it was a spiral staircase made entirely of stone. The solid blocks of the curved walls had been carefully fashioned, each stone precisely butting up to its neighbour. I took a step forwards and peered down, stretching my neck to look as far around the spiral as I could. Down below on the wall was a glow of some kind, faint, but noticeable. I turned to Tara and pointed to it.

"I see it," she whispered.

Two steps down my bravado was replaced by a feeling of trepidation. My heart thumped and my pulse throbbed in the side of my neck. Another five steps down, around the curve of the stairway, the air grew cooler, and I wiped away a trickle of cold perspiration from my nose, my gaze fixed on the strengthening glow on the walls. I checked behind to make sure Tara was OK and then continued.

Five steps farther down the source of the glow came into view – a capsule-shaped industrial light, high up on the wall, its amber light shining through its protective glass and wire mesh cover. There was a faint humming noise, and a cool breeze kissed my face – obviously some kind of ventilation system, but despite it the air smelled of dampness.

Farther down, the light grew stronger and then I could see the end of the staircase. I knew we were close now; it felt like we were in the lair of a beast, its presence permeating every pore of my body.

I turned to Tara. "I hope to God we're doing the right thing here."

She didn't answer.

At the foot of the stairway a corridor ran across our path, its sides hewn out of the rock like a mineshaft, the floor cobbled with closely-fitting stones. At the end of the corridor to my right was a formidable oak door with wrought iron studs. Along to the left a hidden light source of some kind was casting a glow onto the walls. And then I saw at the far end another wooden door – this one with a large blood-red cross painted on it – and I immediately sensed that beyond it lay the answer to all the things that had been puzzling me.

"Do you see it?" I said.

Tara bent forwards and looked towards the end of the passage, then up at me. She nodded. "What do we do if he comes out?"

I hadn't worked that out.

We made our way along the passage slowly. The light source was coming from the right hand side, but I still couldn't see from where. The humming sound grew stronger, the smell of damp faded, and then on the right I saw frosted glass windows recessed into the wall, stretching down from the roof of the passage to a low brick wall, no more than three feet high. I took three more steps then stopped, listening hard, but heard only the humming of the ventilation system.

Tara was close behind me.

"Keep to the right," I said.

Pressing myself against the rough rock walls so anyone on the other side of the glass wouldn't see my shadow, I inched my way along to the point where the windows started, and then stretched my neck forwards to look through the glass, but the frosting was too strong and all I could see was a crinkly sheet of light. There was a door farther along and I gestured to Tara to get down. We stooped, keeping in front of the low wall, below the level of the glass, and when we reached the door I noticed it had a clear glass panel near the top. I stood up and to look through it.

My jaw dropped.

"What the…?"

Benches, long and wide, stretched away to the far end of the room. Upon them was a jumbled maze of glass tubes, pipes, and bulbous containers, like some modern art masterpiece. Liquids bubbled away, green, orange and purple, with plumes of white steam rising into the air.

I grabbed Tara by the shoulder and pulled her to her feet.

"Look at this!"

It was pure Frankenstein.

"Come on," I said.

I took Tara's right hand in my left and gently turned the handle on the door. We stepped inside and closed it behind us and I wondered where Boris Karlof was. I expected to hear a crack of thunder and see lightening streak down and explode one of the bubbling glass containers.

We made our way to the end of the laboratory and I shifted my attention away from the benches and gazed in horror at a row of cages running across the back wall. Two sad brown eyes stared at me through thin metal bars. The chimp's head drooped like that of a traveller struggling to keep awake on a long train journey. Tara and I approached its cage, but it didn't move.

"My God!" Tara said. "This is disgusting."

We walked along the line of cages looking at the other animals. Brown and white mice, rats, small monkeys, more chimps, like inmates on death row — except there would be no quick end for these poor pathetic creatures. They would be tortured, infected with disease or gassed before suffering some agonising unnatural death. It was like some horrific animal Auschwitz. The sight of it turned my stomach. We walked back along the line of cages and stopped in front of the old chimpanzee. I looked at the eyes — almost human — and the greying muzzle, and I imagined the poor creature pegged out, being sliced open by the vivisectionist's scalpel, its intestines spilling out in a bloody tangle.

"We've got to stop this," I said.

But how?

We couldn't carry them out — we weren't the animal liberation army, and there were only two of us. I reached into my pocket, took out the digital camera and began taking pictures of everything in the room. Then I went over to a small office area near the back wall and tried to open the drawers in the desk, but they were locked. Three filing cabinets stood side by side. I tried pulling them open but they too were locked. Fuck it.

"Help me find —"

"Shhh! Someone's coming!" Tara said.

"Quick – behind the desk!"

We crouched down trying not to breathe. I pictured the door with the blood-red cross, now open, and my mind raced – jumbled panicky thoughts.

A weapon, I need a weapon!

The footsteps grew closer; leather soles on a tiled floor. My stomach tightened and I balled my fists. If I had to fight my way out of there I would – kill or be killed. Would he be violent? A holy man who fucked nuns on a Saturday night might be capable of anything. The footsteps grew louder – he was almost upon us. Tara grabbed my arm, terror written all over her face – and then the footsteps stopped. He was no more than ten feet away. Any closer and he'd see us – the desk was too small to hide behind. Tara's fingers dug into my arm like talons, and my chest thumped.

More footsteps. Shit! There was no point in crouching any more.

Got to get ready to fight.

I grabbed Tara's arm, we stood up and then I froze.

He looked directly at us and let out a gasp. "What the..." He stepped back. "Who are you?"

I looked at the man's pale blue eyes and short blond hair, almost college boy in style. It wasn't The High Priest – it was his disciple, Michael Richards – the crazy bastard who was in the process of developing...what? Probably some lethal chemical cocktail to wipe out most of the world.

Weapons of Mass Destruction.

He stood with a clipboard under his arm, his white lab coat open at the front showing the beginnings of a paunch.

Panic consumed me, but I didn't make a run for it – some crazy sense of indignation made me stand my ground. It was not us who should feel afraid of being caught. It was *he*, Michael Richards, who should be feeling guilty and afraid, because of what *he* had been doing.

"How the hell did you get in here?" he asked.

"You're Michael Richards, aren't you?"

His mouth fell open. For a second he was on the back foot. I scrambled around in my head for the next thing I should say and after a flash of inspiration added, "We're MI6, British Intelligence. This whole convent is surrounded. There's no escape."

He appeared to be unmoved, and I stood tall, looking him directly in the eye, determined not to show any fear. Seconds passed, then the corners of his mouth lifted a fraction, and small lines appeared in the corners of his eyes – the bastard was smiling!

He shook his head slowly.

"No. You're not MI6."

"You're surrounded, there's no way out," I repeated, but still he shook his head. "We know about you and the High Priest and how you met in America and what you are up to here."

He seemed unruffled, and then a terrible thought struck me: *Is he so calm because he knows we'll never get out of here alive?*

He stepped towards us.

"Stay back!" I said, holding up my hand like a policeman stopping traffic.

He stopped advancing and shrugged his shoulders. "You're not MI6. So why don't you tell me who you really are?"

What made him so sure, and why hadn't he cried out or raised the alarm?

"So come on, who are you?" he said.

Obviously we weren't fooling him. We didn't look like agents from MI6, and if we were we'd have our guns pointing in his direction. I sized him up. As dangerous as he was, he wasn't physically big, and although I wasn't a street fighter I was sure I could overpower him if it came to it.

"OK. We're reporters, we know what you're doing and we're about to blow this whole thing wide open."

The smile disappeared from his face. I grabbed Tara's arm and attempted to walk past him. He reached out and put his hand on my shoulder.

"Wait!" he said. I jumped back, balled my fists and met his gaze. "Hold it a minute. You don't know what you are doing."

"We know what *you* are doing."

"No. No you don't."

"Nuns getting fucked on a Saturday night – that do you? Building a master race? Weapons of mass destruction? Believe me, Richards, we know what you two crazy fuckers are doing down here. You're finished. We're putting a stop to it – right now."

"Hold on! You don't know what's going on! You can't print this, not anything about it. Not yet."

Not yet? What did he mean, *not yet?* It was an odd thing to say but I wasn't curious enough to know what he meant by it to hang around and find out. I led Tara around him and he grabbed my arm.

"Wait! For God's sake wait!"

For God's sake. Funny thing for a religious man to say.

He continued, "Ask yourself how I know you aren't MI6."

I did wonder how he knew that, apart from the fact that we didn't have guns.

"So, tell us."

"I know you aren't MI6 because I know who is."

"What the fuck are you talking about?"

"There's an MI6 operative in here already. I know who it is so I know you two are definitely not MI6." He saw the confusion on my face. Then he glanced across at the door to the laboratory, as if he was worried about someone coming in. "Look, come with me a moment."

He took a couple of steps towards another door, at the side of the room. Tara and I stood still and when he glanced behind to see if we were following, he said:

"Come on, you can't stay here – you'll be seen."

There was a voice in my head telling me to get the hell out of there as fast as possible, but I was sure I could handle him, and my desire to get to the bottom of whatever this was overrode the voice.

Tara looked at me with an expression that said: *Whatever you want is OK with me.*

We followed him.

He punched a code into a keypad, opened the door and we stepped through into the next room. Inside, the tangled web of glass tubes and bubbling liquids was just as Frankensteinian as the one we had seen in the other room, but on the far wall were banks of computers, rack-mounted, with green and red flashing lights.

"What the fuck have you got going on down here?" I asked.

"It's not what you think."

"You don't know what I think."

"Take it from me. You have no idea what this is about."

"Then start talking."

"We don't have enough time and it's too dangerous for you to stay here."

"Then you'd better hurry and you better be very convincing, or we're getting out of here and the story's going to be in the press tomorrow."

I stood in an aggressive stance, ready to punch him if he made a move towards us, and when he noticed the look on my face he raised his open palms in a 'calm down' gesture.

"Hey, come on, relax. I haven't raised the alarm, have I?" That was another thing that puzzled me. "I'm not going to try to do anything." I clenched my fists to let him know he'd better not. "You can trust me."

Trust this guy, the High Priest's right-hand man?

"Yeah – like I'd trust a thief with my life savings," I said.

He shook his head and his expression seemed to say: *Just how do I get through to them?*

"Look, I am asking you to trust me. Don't go and print a story about this place – not yet. I know what you think is going on in here, but you're wrong. Things aren't what they seem. You don't know the damage you're going to do if you run with the story, believe me."

"Whatever you're doing, it's fucking evil. We've seen the babies. You and the High Priest are sick weirdoes."

"You think you've got a big story. You haven't. You think this is about Weapons of Mass Destruction – it isn't. It's much bigger than that, but you'll kill your story if you go to the press now. Please trust me. Don't do it."

What could be bigger than WMD?

"If you expect us to just walk out of here with all this shit going on and say nothing then you really are crazy."

"Meet me tomorrow and I'll tell you everything."

I scoffed.

"I promise you, I'll tell you the whole story. If you're not satisfied with what I tell you, then go on and print what you have."

"Yeah, and in the meantime you clear out of here, right?"

"Come on, look around you. You think anyone could dismantle this in twelve hours?"

He was right, that would be impossible, and even if he did we had our photographs so we could print the story no matter what. I was puzzled. In the movies there would have been hundreds of guards in identical uniforms, carrying machine guns, who would take us away to a dungeon where we'd await some fiendish, tortuous death. But he just stood there without trying to raise the alarm and all he was asking for was to meet us the next day to tell us what was really going on. Not exactly the actions of an evil scientist hell-bent on creating a master race.

I looked at Tara. She gave me another, *whatever-you-want-is-OK-with-me* look. There were still things I didn't know. Maybe it would be stupid to go with the story now and risk never getting to the bottom of the things that had gnawed at me for so long?

"Where do you want to meet?"

"There's a café on the road out of Saint Pierre, on the left, do you know it?"

"Grubby looking place?"

"That's the one. Meet me there at 11am."

"If we do, you're going to have to be convincing. If not, I'll be making a call and the story's going to run."

"Don't do that before we've spoken, promise me."

I nodded. "See you at 11am. Now we're getting out of here."

I turned to go.

"Wait. I'll show you how to get out."

My hackles were up. I still didn't trust him. Was he leading us into a trap? We followed him back into the other laboratory and then turned left towards the door leading out of the lab. He opened it and peered into the passageway, checking the coast was clear.

"OK. Quickly," he said, beckoning us with his hand.

We followed him out and I looked to my right at the door with the blood-red cross on it – it was still closed. We turned left and made our way past the spiral staircase and on to the studded oak door at the far end. He turned an iron key in the lock, swung the door open, flicked a switch on the wall and a series of weak amber lights came on, illuminating the way. A few steps through the doorway and immediately on the left we came to a set of stone steps.

"That's the way out," he said. "Follow it to the end. You'll come to a ladder. Climb up it and you'll reach a hatchway. Pull back the bolt and make your way through and you'll be in the kitchen of a small farmhouse. Close the hatch after you and leave. When you get outside you'll be on the road to Saint Pierre."

"Aren't you coming to show us the way?"

"I'll be missed. I came into the lab to get something; if I don't return with it soon things are going to look suspicious. Go on – trust me. I'll see you at 11am tomorrow."

Trust me. Weren't people who said that the very ones you couldn't trust?

"OK, 11am, and remember, you'd better be convincing."

The passageway twisted and turned and every thirty or forty yards there were more stone steps. Eventually we reached the end and saw the ladder, which disappeared up through a vertical shaft. I tested its strength, making sure it held my weight, my hands feeling the dampness in the wood. Looking up into the blackness, there was no way to see how high the shaft went.

"You sure this is all right?" Tara asked.

"No, but we can't go back now, can we? This must be the way they get in and out of the convent without the nuns seeing them. We've got to try it."

I began to climb, placing each foot gently on the rungs, hoping they would hold me, gripping the sides of the ladder firmly. Halfway up, the end of the ladder became visible through the darkness.

"Tara, don't follow me up until I'm through the hatch – it might not take the weight of both of us."

At the top of the ladder was a wooden hatch. I pushed it with my left hand, but it wouldn't move, something was holding it shut. Groping around the sides, my hand found a bolt and slid it back. Now when I pushed against it the door moved, but was heavy. I bent over and climbed up another four rungs, placing my back against the door, and when I pushed with my legs it opened and I found myself emerging through a trap door in a kitchen floor. I climbed through and called down to Tara.

"It's OK. Come on up."

Three minutes later we both sat on the floor of the kitchen getting our breath back.

"Do you think we've done the right thing, leaving him like that?" Tara asked.

"I don't know, but he's not going to be able to get rid of the evidence by 11am tomorrow morning, that's for sure, and if he doesn't have something pretty spectacular to say then he's just been stalling for time and we'll go with the story we have. You have to ask yourself why he let us go – he doesn't know for sure we're going to turn up."

I looked around the kitchen; it was simple and dusty from neglect.

"We must have come along an old escape route from the time when the town was built. Someone must have built the cottage on top of it a long time after. Come on, let's find our way out to the road and get back to the car."

That night I had a bizarre dream of Little Red Riding Hood entering her granny's house. But *I* was Little Red Riding Hood, and sitting up in bed playing the part of granny was a creature with Michael Richard's face and a wolf's body, its claws sharp and metallic looking, the light from the bedside candle making them glint. The creature tilted its head back, gave a blood curdling howl, and I awoke with a start, perspiration on my forehead.

Chapter 13

At 10.57am I parked the car in the small car park in front of the restaurant. We got out and made our way to the entrance, scanning the scene for anything suspicious. I was still furious at being conned by Cleaver and a part of me relished the thought of an ambush; it would give me the chance to punch someone.

I opened the door and looked inside. On the right sat a couple of tourists, wearing shorts and T-shirts. Their faces were red and puffy from too much sun. On the left sat an old man with a whiskery face and a black beret. Thankfully there were no heavy looking guys with bulges under their armpits and I sighed with relief.

A woman with bright red hair and a stained white apron approached.

"*Bonjour,*" she said in a high-pitched musical voice.

"*Bonjour,*" I replied.

"*Deux personnes?*"

Michael Richards sat at the back of the restaurant. I pointed and said, "We're with him."

The windowless walls were panelled with stripped pine. An old mirror with half of its silvering missing hung to the left, and a picture of the Nice football team hung on the wall to the right. In the corner a rubber plant stood in a plastic, terracotta-coloured tub, its leaves covered with a film of dust.

Michael Richards stood up. He looked younger in his white T-shirt and blue jeans, more like a mature student than a mad scientist. He reached out his hand.

"Thanks for coming," he said.

Automatically my right hand moved to shake his, but then I paused for a moment, not wanting to appear too accommodating – he was the High Priest's accomplice, for Christ's sake – but he'd already seen my hand move towards his and it seemed churlish to stop halfway through, so I shook it. He smiled openly, gripping mine firmly, and then we all sat down in unison.

"Coffee?" he asked, and then ordered for us in what appeared to be perfect French.

The waitress disappeared and for a moment I studied him. He was cool, innocent looking, and credible – perfect credentials for a conman. Cleaver had his upper class mannerisms, the clothes and voice to lend him authority – but was a lying bastard. Richards was also a lying bastard, and probably more dangerous, although he was cut from different cloth.

"Sorry, I don't know your names," he said.

I looked at Tara, then back at him.

"This isn't a social meeting, Richards. You said you've got something to tell us." I looked at my watch. "My editor's sitting in his office waiting to see if I'm going to call and tell him to continue holding the story for a while longer. You don't have much time, so I suggest you start talking."

If Richards did have a bunch of hoodlums waiting to jump us, hopefully now he'd believe it wouldn't stop his operation from being exposed for the evil monstrosity it was. It seemed to do the trick. His cool expression changed and for an instant he looked horrified.

"How long have I got?"

"Thirty minutes."

He looked down at the table for a second and said, "This has nothing to do with weapons of mass destruction."

"Yeah, well you *would* say that wouldn't you. Are we supposed to just believe you, cancel the story and leave you to get on with it?"

He swallowed hard. "No."

"Good. 'Cos you've got to do better than that."

"Who told you we were involved in weapons of mass –"

"Hey, *I'm* asking the questions – you're giving the answers. All right, let's cut to the chase. Do you know who Virginie Lavelle is?"

"Who?"

"Virginie Lavelle."

He shook his head. "Did *she* say it was weapons of mass destruction?"

Useless. I tried another tack.

"Tell me how you met this High Priest character."

He nodded.

"I met him back in the States. Graham Farrow, a friend of mine I knew at school, introduced me to him. Graham's from a Christian family and he told me he'd met this guy who claimed to be the Son of God – *The Second Coming*, if you like. Naturally I thought Graham was a few dimes short of a dollar, but he insisted I meet the guy, so I did. He called himself the High Priest – I never knew his real name, no one did."

The waitress returned with the coffee and he stopped talking. While she served us I considered what he had said up until then and so far it seemed to tie in with what Tara's Uncle Jim had told us.

The waitress left and he continued.

"I'm not a religious man and I'm not so crazy as to believe he *is* the Son of God, but in a way I could understand my friend Graham believing he was. The guy had long hair like Jesus and weird piercing eyes, and he spoke with a voice that was... what you might call resonant. If you were sold on Christianity, like Graham was, you could believe it for sure. Graham's not stupid – none of the small band of followers are – he's the CEO of a software company and the others are all guys in business. The High Priest was pretty careful about who he had for his disciples – they had to have money and be willing to donate to the 'cause', as it were. They still do."

"What cause?"

"Preparation for Armageddon."

The matter of fact way he said it stunned me. "And it seems to me like you two want to speed up its coming."

"Hang on a minute. Let me finish."

I managed to hold on to my cool.

"You're jumping the gun. The High Priest had everyone convinced – he did tricks, performed miracles if you like."

"You mean card tricks or something?"

"No. There was no trickery. These *were* miracles, or appeared to be if you weren't a scientist like me. He would cut himself with a razor – genuine razor, genuine blood. Then he'd put a bandage over the cut and in the morning it would have healed – no stitches, just a small scar.

A day later the scar would disappear too. That's how he explained not having scars on his hands and feet after supposedly being nailed to the cross two thousand years ago."

"Yeah, but there must have been some kind of trick," Tara said.

"No trick. The guy was and is genuine, but I took some of the bloodstained bandages and did some analysis – genetics is my field. I used to work for a company that produced genetically altered crop seeds. When I ran some tests I discovered something… something incredible."

"What?"

"The guy's a genetic freak. He has an immune system that functions on overdrive. It was as if any virus introduced to his blood was destroyed by it, instantly. I'd heard he had never had a cold, so I experimented with the common cold virus and his immune system just blasted it away – it was freakish."

"So if what you say is true, and he *is* a genetic freak, how come?"

"I don't know. Darwin's theory of evolution says we evolved into what we are through natural selection – the survival of the fittest. The changes took place over thousands of years. I don't know if there were quantum leaps in our evolution – but maybe there were – like a chance in a billion of certain genetic conditions coming together to create a… a giant leap forward in our progress. It's hard to work out how it happened without meeting his parents, but he exists, so it happened. Of course *he* just says he's the Son of God."

"So if what you say is true, what are you doing over here in a convent in France?"

He shuffled around in his seat.

"Well – you see. Genetic freak he may be, but he's also insane."

"You know he's insane and yet you still stay with him?"

"Armageddon and all that – he believes it. He thinks the world is going to end soon and he's been sent here by God to prepare for it by creating a race of pure people to populate the world. Sort of like Noah building an ark for the animals before the floods came, except that, rather than save the animals, he's going to create new ones and allow the old ones to perish."

I shivered. "This guy needs locking up."

"I agree," Richards said.

"You agree and yet you traipse halfway around the world with him?"

"It wasn't my idea to come to France, it was his. He knew the CIA and the FBI were pretty hot on religious types, especially after Waco. So he wanted to get to another country where he could start to prepare in peace, as it were. We went to England first, but eventually decided on France – he liked the privacy laws here. He managed to convince the Mother Superior of the convent that he was the Son of God with the usual thing – razor and instant healing – it always works, especially with anyone who's devoutly religious. They're just waiting for the Son of God to turn up – he's the answer to their prayers."

"If you knew he was nuts and dangerous, why didn't you just turn him over to the police in the States?"

"I thought I could control the situation if I stayed close by. Like in *Sun Tsu* – The Art of War – keep your enemies close, and I had a constant source of DNA I could use to develop all sorts of cures for illnesses."

"So you thought you'd risk this lunatic doing Christ knows what, just for your own ego – so you could claim the glory and riches for coming up with some kind of new potion? Don't you think that was irresponsible?"

He nodded. "Maybe."

"All right, so what's going on with the nuns, the laboratories and all the rest of it?"

His forehead furrowed. "What do *you* think?"

"I think your High Priest is having himself a high old time on Saturday nights building himself a master race – that's what I think. I don't know which one of you is the sicker, him for doing it or you for letting him. At least he's got an excuse – he's nuts."

He looked up, anger written all over his face.

"I'm not proud of that," he said.

I heard a noise. Startled, I turned around, but it was just the two tourists getting up to leave. I turned to face Richards again and glared at him.

"Just how many fucking High Priests were you planning to breed before Armageddon?"

"Those babies are not High Priests. They're not clones. He doesn't know a thing about genetics, and anyway, none of them have inherited his immune system, I've checked."

"But he thinks they have, right?"

Richards nodded.

"Well, if he thinks all he has to do to create more like him is to fuck a bunch of nuns, I don't see why he needs *you*. So just what exactly does he think you're doing in that lab?"

He didn't speak. He looked up at the ceiling, sighed and slowly shook his head.

"Well? Come on, answer!" I shouted.

He paused for a moment and then said, "Making a gas to kill everyone on earth."

"You what?" I leapt to my feet, knocking my chair over in the process. "So it's true – *Weapons of Mass Destruction!*"

The waitress came running over.

"Monsieur? Monsieur?"

Richards raised his hand in a calming gesture.

"*Pardon, Madame, il n'y a pas de problème. Il a entendu des mauvaises nouvelles.*"

He smiled and, satisfied there wasn't going to be a fight, she left us. I picked up my chair and sat down.

"So you admit it. You are doing WMD." I turned to Tara. "Come on we may as well go. Everything he's told us we already know. Lets just go and print the damned story."

"No, please. For God's sake, calm down. You haven't heard everything yet!"

"I think we have."

"You haven't. Don't you want to know about the Secret Service?"

I sure as hell *did* want to know about the Secret Service and how Cleaver and the British Government were involved in all this.

"OK. Keep talking," I said.

"They planted an operative in the convent – a nun. I caught her sniffing around in the laboratory one day – just like I caught you. She told me who she was and that we'd been under surveillance by the Secret Service when we were in England and had been followed to France. She looked through some papers and was knowledgeable enough to see I was doing something with diseases and the production of gases. She put two and two together and told me she would let me continue with my work as long as I gave the gas to the British Government."

"Fuck! Then it's true, they know what you are doing and they approve! Just what the hell is this gas – is it anything to do with AIDS?"

"You know what happens to people with AIDS – their immune system breaks down. But death happens after a period of time. I told them I was developing a genetic mutation of the AIDS virus that was so virulent it would totally destroy a person's immune system in two weeks. They loved it. In theory you could put undercover operatives into a country and just add the virus to the water supply. The operatives could escape, sit back and wait for the whole population of the country to die off – killed by the common cold or any other virus lying around. Think about it – total death plus zero destruction. If you could then clean up the virus you could march into the country, clear away the bodies and just take it over."

"You twisted piece of..."

"*Not me! Your* government! They're the ones who want it!"

"And what about *your* High Priest?"

Richards put his head in his hands and rubbed his eyes.

"He wants it too. Once he's created a few more children in his own image."

Rage coursed through my veins. I clenched and unclenched my fists and a sick feeling infected my guts.

"But *you* are the one who is giving it to them! *You* are the sickest of all!"

"*No!*" He stood up. "Listen! I already told you the High Priest doesn't know a damned thing about genetics, didn't I? Those babies do not have his immune system! I'm pretty sure that if such a virus were created and released the High Priest would probably survive it, but those babies wouldn't. So you see there would be no master race, no ark to protect against the coming flood. Everyone would die except for the High Priest, and unless there really was a God to create an Eve, the whole human race would die out."

"OK, so it won't work for the High Priest, but it would still work for MI6."

"Yes, it would. They know that and that's why they haven't shut the convent down. They want the gas badly, but I'm not making it."

I screwed up my face in puzzlement. "You expect us to believe that? We've got an informer who says you're producing WMD."

"I know you have. You wouldn't know what you know without having an informer."

"So why should we believe you?"

"Because... because I'm not insane."

"And that's it?"

"There's not much else I can tell you. I came to France with the High Priest to study his genetics so I could do something good, not evil."

"Like what?"

"Something that no government wants anyone to produce."

"Like what? It's not a cure for AIDS is it?"

"No – not exactly. A cure for AIDS would be good for governments. It would take the burden off the hospitals, free up some cash."

"It would save a lot of lives too."

He hadn't even considered that.

"Yes, but I'm not sure that's something always uppermost in the minds of a lot of government officials."

I mellowed slightly. Those words could have been my own.

"So what is it that you claim to be producing that's good, and at the same time something that every government would want you *not* to produce?"

Five long seconds passed while I waited for him to answer.

"You ever listened to the politicians come election time?" he asked.

"Difficult not to."

"Heard them go on about the problems in the country; transport, health, education – the usual mantra?"

"Of course."

"Politicians point out problems – and blame the opposition for them of course, and then say: *Vote for me and I'll solve all these problems. Put your faith in me – hand me the power to do things and I'll solve all your problems for you.* Short of any alternative, the people vote them into office and the politicians spend the next few years concocting ways to avoid responsibility for *not* solving the problems."

Richards was definitely talking my language.

"Imagine how terrible it would be if there were no problems? With no problems to solve there'd be no reason to vote."

"I see what you're saying, but you can't be developing something to solve *all* problems."

He didn't answer and his silence intrigued me. If he thought he had developed a way of solving the whole world's problems he really was nuts, and I began to wonder if he was some warped Jim Jones type thinker who thought if we killed ourselves we'd be free of our troubles.

He looked me in the eye.

"Something concerns me. Our thirty minutes are up. Are you going to make that call to your paper?"

I'd forgotten about that. I didn't yet understand what he'd been talking about, but I was sufficiently curious to want to find out more.

"I... I guess so."

"There's a phone box outside. You got change?"

I looked at Tara. "Come with me."

She stood up and we went outside. The telephone box stood by the side of the road just in front of the car park. I approached it and picked up the receiver.

"Stand in front of me with your back to the restaurant."

I mimed putting a coin into the slot and positioned myself behind Tara so Richards wouldn't be able to see my mouth if he was watching us.

"What do you make of it?" she asked.

I pressed the receiver to my ear.

"I don't know. He hasn't told us anything we didn't know or couldn't have worked out."

"You think he's just playing for time – stringing us along?"

I thought about it. An hour ago I would have said yes and that the guy was a sick-minded psychopath engaged in something insane and dangerous with the High Priest. Even now a part of me wanted to hate him as much as I had then. But he had made an impression on me, and there were things that persuaded me he wasn't what I had first thought. He *had* let us go the night before; he'd even shown us the secret tunnel. He *had* turned up today, as he said he would, and as far as I knew he didn't have a team of henchmen ready to take us away. If he did they were taking a long time about it. There was something about his manner too, a kind of calmness that made me feel he was not the devil incarnate, not the kind of man who sixty years ago would have been working as a doctor in a Nazi concentration camp. He also had an obvious dislike of the political establishment, and through that we had an affinity, despite whatever else he had done.

"I don't know, Tara. I don't think so."

"You believe him?"

I hated to admit it, but everything about the guy, the way he spoke, his mannerisms, made him seem credible. I asked myself who else but an innocent would offer up such a simple defence as: *Because I'm not insane?*

"Let's just say I'm eager to hear the rest of his story. Come on, let's go back inside."

We entered the restaurant. Richards hadn't moved. On the table were fresh cups of coffee. Cleaver had ordered for us, but the manner of it had been different. This guy just seemed... well-mannered.

"You've told your editor not to print the story?"

"For now. I have to call him back in another hour and a half."

"I'm grateful."

"OK. You said you were working on something to cure all the world's problems."

I felt stupid and naïve uttering such silly words. Richards looked down at his coffee, his hands positioned on the table forming a protective ring around the cup, frown lines on his forehead. He didn't answer.

"Are you going to tell us? There *is* something more to tell, isn't there – or are we all just wasting our time?"

He looked up and shook his head, an earnest expression on his face.

"No, no, we're not all just wasting our time."

He glanced at me and then at Tara, as if he was weighing us up, which was ironic because we were supposed to be weighing him up.

Then he said, "I will explain it to you, but there is something I must ask. I know your editor has the story so far and there is nothing I can do about that, and you know I'm appealing to you to tell him not to run it. I just hope you can persuade him somehow. But whatever happens after this discussion I would ask you a favour: Please don't tell your editor what I'm about to tell you."

"Well, that sort of depends on what it is, doesn't it?"

He nodded. "Yes, I suppose it does."

He sipped his coffee and cleared his throat and it struck me that he had the look of a man who was about to tell his best friend that his wife was cheating on him, as if he knew he had to say something, but thought at the same time that it might be better if he didn't.

Finally he said, "OK. "What's the biggest fear people have?"

I thought for a second.

"I don't know, fear of failure, fear of looking stupid?"

"Bigger than that."

I couldn't think of anything more than that, but maybe they were just my own fears.

"I don't know, what?"

"What about fear of dying? Threatened with death, aren't we all terrified? How would you feel if a man pointed a gun at your head? How would you feel if you jumped from a plane, enjoying the thrill of the wind rushing past you and the sense of freedom, and then when you reached for your ripcord you realised you'd forgotten to put on your parachute?"

"Like everyone else I'd feel like I needed a change of underwear, how do you think I'd feel? Then again if I were stupid enough to jump out of an aeroplane without a parachute I'd think I deserved to die. You aren't making a device to remind people to put on their parachutes are you, so what is it?"

"Ever thought maybe some people are afraid of living?"

"No."

"Really? You ever look around at people going about their everyday lives, dead, joyless expressions on their faces? You seen many people over the age of six or seven get excited about life – just bubbling over with sheer joy and the endless possibilities of living?"

"Can't say I have."

"Ever wondered why?"

"Because they're too worried about the mortgage payments, the gas bill, whether their partner's cheating on them, or if their kids are going to turn out to be well-adjusted adults or doped-up delinquents."

"You worry about getting old?"

"Sometimes."

"Think you might have plastic surgery – a little nip and tuck here and there?"

"No, I don't think so."

"A lot of people do."

"Look, what's all this about?"

"They say there are only two things certain in life – death and taxes, right? What if we changed that? How would you feel about living forever?"

I imagined myself hobbling around with a Zimmer frame, stooping, my face lined and cracked like mud on a dried up riverbed.

"No thanks. Think I'll step off the merry-go-round when the time is right."

"Oh, really? You know I heard about an old man at his birthday party. A young kid came up and asked how old he was. The old man said, 'I'm eighty'. The kid said, 'I don't think I'd want to live to be eighty'. The old man said, 'You wait 'til you're seventy-nine'. If you don't want to live forever, when would you like to die?"

"Yeah, OK, I get your point."

"Don't think you do yet. How old are you?"

"Thirty-five."

"Still young enough to get it up when you want to – although maybe not as readily as you might have when you were twenty-one. Remember how you used to get a boner just looking at a brassiere advert?"

I couldn't stop myself smiling at that.

"Not quite the same now though, huh? Be nice if it stayed that way – maybe then you'd want to live forever?"

"Maybe you're right, but I was even more stupid when I was twenty-one than I am now."

"Maybe you can have both – ever expanding knowledge and a constant supply of testosterone. Is that sounding more attractive?"

"Tell me where the nearest pharmacy is, I'm on my way."

"Good. Now maybe you're getting the picture."

"So you're making some anti-aging pill – is that it?"

"If that's what you think then you *haven't* got the picture. Look, you said you don't see people over the age of seven walking about full of joy, right? And you said people were bogged down with bills to pay and kids etc. But is that it – is that the real reason?"

I looked down at the table and thought for a moment. I looked at Tara; she was as enthralled by this conversation as I was.

"I don't know, but if not then, what else?"

"Wouldn't you say that the look on their faces was one of hopelessness?"

That seemed to sum it up for me.

"I'd say so."

"But why?" he asked.

"Because that's just the way life is. We are born, then for most of us we get married, have kids and then…"

"Then we die."

"Yes."

"And that sounds pretty grim to me. Death is inevitable and getting old is too. Isn't there somewhere, deep down in our subconscious, the looming thought that if that's so then what's the point in bothering at all? Why bother to get fit and eat right – we're all dead in the end? Maybe it's better to live like a slob and get it over with sooner? What's that joke about the guy who doesn't exercise, smoke or drink? Did he live to be a hundred? No, but it sure as hell felt like he did."

"You're saying that if we don't age we won't have any problems?"

"I'm saying that if you stay forever young and healthy you have *time* to sort out whatever problems you have, and the motivation to do it. Death isn't coming around the corner to save you from your miserable life, so either you sort out your own problems or you'll live forever with them with no way out other than an accident or suicide – probably suicide."

"Why suicide rather than an accident?"

"Because the world is getting safer as technology improves – cars are safer, we'll have early warning systems built into them, and probably ourselves, to warn us of danger. If the most productive, inventive entrepreneurs in the world are also going to live forever, without getting old, think of the endless stream of ingenious products they're going to make that will improve our lives."

"OK, so you're saying if you remove death as a kind of limitation, everyone will have to lead more productive lives?"

"Yes! Or kill themselves if they don't want to participate. My guess is they'll get productive, but they'll have the choice."

"But not everyone's going to want to take the pill are they?"

"Not at first, but they will *eventually*, through the forces of competition."

"What do you mean?"

"If there are a lot of guys running around with sixty years' experience of life, plus the wealth accumulated over years of work, and they look like Brad Pitt, you aren't going to get a look in if you've got the money and experience, but the body of an old man – so you'll take the pill."

I nodded.

"Youth would be a given. Right now it's prized and everyone's doing what they can to retain it. Rich old guys want young looking women, even though they don't have anything in common. Reverse the ageing process and old people become the most sought after – people with youthful bodies plus experience and knowledge of life."

I got a taste of the enormity of what he was saying. "If it happened the world would be turned upside down."

"Not would be. *Will* be."

"You trying to tell me you're really going to make a pill that does this?"

"No."

"Then what the fuck are we talking about?"

"I'm saying I *have* made a pill that does this."

"You must be joking!"

"Did you see the animals in the cages?"

"Yes."

"The mice. Did they look young to you? They were looking pretty old a month ago."

It was incredible. I was listening to a man who was telling me he had produced the ultimate – a pill that could make everyone young and live forever, a pill that was going to change the way we lived, a pill that was going to turn the world as we knew it on its head. For a moment I wondered if I was living through some science-fiction fantasy.

"But we're not mice," I said.

"Genetically we're not that far off, actually, but if you don't believe me, just wait a while. I'm about to do the same thing with Harry. Harry's the chimpanzee."

My head was spinning. "I think I need another coffee."

He called the waitress. She cleared away the empty cups and took the order.

"But the High Priest, he doesn't know about this?" I asked.

"No, he just thinks I'm producing some killer gas."

"What about the babies?"

His face coloured slightly and he looked down at the top of the table.

"I knew he was going to do something like that eventually, but I was hoping to have finished my work before he got around to it. All I can tell you is that they're well looked after by their mothers, and they're all healthy."

"Ends justifying the means?"

"I don't really believe in all that, but in a way, yes. If no harm comes to them… well, if I have produced what I say I have, then they will have been born for a damned good reason. In fact I have to finish it – I owe it to them."

"I suppose that's another reason why we should keep our mouths shut?" He didn't answer. I looked at Tara. "Let's go outside and talk for a moment."

She got up and followed me outside.

"Danny, this is incredible. Do you believe him?"

I folded my arms and walked around looking at the ground. I kicked a pebble and then looked up at the sky. Did I believe him? Did I believe the most fantastic thing I'd ever heard?

"As crazy as it all sounds, yes, I do."

"What makes you so sure?"

"I didn't say I was sure, it's just the way he told us. He didn't just come out with it – he put it to us in such a way that we saw his vision – at least I did. Did you?" She nodded. "He couldn't have done that unless he'd been thinking about this and the massive implications of it for a long time. It didn't sound to me like something he'd just thought up over night."

"So he's been stringing Cleaver along all the time?"

"If what he says is right, then he would have had to have done that to buy time and to stop the British Intelligence Service from interfering."

"What about Deep Throat?"

"Deep Throat's getting his information through Cleaver; he only knows what Cleaver knows."

"Danny, we've been fooled and misled before."

"I know, but you've got to admit, if he's telling the truth... well... it's the most amazing thing... I mean how the fuck can we risk blowing the whistle on it?"

Tara didn't answer. I walked around thinking more about it, then threw my head back and laughed out loud.

"What's so funny?"

"Nothing. But can you *imagine* living forever, never getting old? The things you could do... the places you could see... You could have dinner on the moon one day, or on Venus!"

"Are you crazy?"

"Well, you could, couldn't you? We'd just have to wait until personal rockets were developed – and for someone to open a restaurant. Shit, maybe we could open one ourselves!"

Tara caught the idea and laughed with me. "So what do we do?"

"Order a rocket!"

We both cracked up at that.

Back inside the restaurant Richards looked up at us apprehensively, then he saw the remnants of my smile and his tension appeared to ease. I said, "We were just wondering whether we should open a restaurant on the moon or on Venus."

His face beamed. "You see, now you've got it!"

Tara and I sat down, and for a moment it felt as if we were all connected in some way, as if we'd shared an experience, a glimpse of a better world, and a warm, euphoric feeling spread through me. My head was light, and all my earlier thoughts of Richards – that he was dangerous, sick and crazy – had dissipated, lost in a sunshine vision of the world to come.

"You think you are playing God?" I asked.

"I'm a non-believer, but to those who believe, I would say if there is a God and he gave us freewill, then this is part of His design. How long have I got?" he asked.

"What do you mean?"

"I'm a realist. Your editor isn't going to sit on that story forever – wrong though it may be."

"I... I don't know. I'll keep him sitting on it for as long as I can. I'll tell him we haven't got it all yet, that I'm still working on it." I wasn't ready to end the charade of the waiting editor just yet. "When are you going to do whatever it is you do to the chimpanzee?"

"I'll be able to start in about a week."

"Can we see the results?"

He looked directly at me, holding my gaze, and then he nodded.

"You know everything now. No reason why not."

We drove back to Cannes, both agog at what we'd heard. The prospect of everlasting youth and a life full of endless possibilities invigorated me, and I tingled with excitement. Maybe Richards' theory was right and people's experience of life would transform with the realisation that getting old was a thing of the past.

"Hope we're not being fooled," Tara said.

"Yeah, me too. I like the sound of what he told us. I guess we'll know soon enough."

That night, walking alongside the port of Cannes, on our way to dinner, my thoughts turned to Deep Throat. He'd been wrong about WMD, and I wondered if there was some way I could let him know that everything was OK and that we didn't need him any more – without, of course, telling him what was really going on.

Tara said, "Why take the chance – shouldn't we just say nothing?"

"Because he's taking a risk in contacting us and if he keeps doing it he might get caught and that would jeopardise everything Richards is trying to do. Assuming Richards has been straight with us, I wouldn't want him stopped, would you?"

"So what do we do?"

"Let's get back to the cyber café."

When I logged on I saw I had mail from Deep Throat.

It said –

> *YOU HAVE BEEN SEEN MEETING WITH RICHARDS*
> *YOU ARE IN DANGER*
> *GET AWAY*
> *DESTRUCTION OF WMD OPERATION IMMINENT*
> *WARNING – YOU ARE A TARGET!*

Chapter 14

I jumped up off my seat, my chair flew back, toppling over, and I stood there, open-mouthed, comprehending but not believing what I had read, searching for a sign that I had misunderstood.

Seconds passed before I became aware of Tara's hand on my arm.

"Danny!" she whispered, bringing me back into the room.

I looked at her for a moment, then around the silent room at the puzzled faces staring in my direction, before righting my chair and sitting down, smiling at people apologetically. The message was still on the computer screen and I felt the rapid thump of my heart against my ribs.

The game had changed. We had been the hunters; now we were the hunted.

Quickly we left the cyber café.

Out on the street, the faces of the people walking by seemed to change before my eyes – smiles became leers and blank, indifferent expressions became sinister masks. A woman in her fifties approached wearing a yellow blouse and a short white skirt, her gold necklace glinting around her plump sunburnt neck. She tottered along the pavement on her high heels, her over-fed white miniature poodle waddling beside her, as if mimicking its mistress. I looked into the woman's eyes. She noticed my stare and tilted her head back, lifting her nose skywards, as if I was something her dog had deposited on the pavement.

"Danny, what are you doing?" Tara said.

I pulled myself out of it.

"Sorry – getting paranoid." I took Tara's hand and we hurried along the pavement, dodging pedestrians.

The hotel came into view. What was it now, a sanctuary or a trap?

"Tara, we have to leave," I said.

"You mean leave Cannes or France?"

"Probably both, but we'll start with the hotel."

"You think they know where we're staying?"

"If they don't they will soon — it won't take them long to check the hotels if they haven't already. They could be watching us right now. We're going to walk in there as if nothing has happened, get our things and get out. If they're watching us we've got to make sure they don't think we're about to run, so walk slowly."

I put my arm around her shoulders and we strolled into the hotel like two carefree lovers. Passing the concierge, I pretended to whisper in Tara's ear and then laughed. She followed my lead and laughed too.

"Bonjour," I said to the concierge.

"Bonjour, monsieur !" he replied.

The lift juddered as it began its ascent, and for a moment I felt safe, cocooned in the small metal cube. We reached our floor and hurried along the corridor to our rooms.

"Pack as fast as you can," I said.

Five minutes later, with a stuffed suitcase and two sports bags, we met up in the passageway and Tara turned right towards the lift.

"No, not that way. Follow me," I said, making my way along the corridor in the opposite direction. There had to be a service lift somewhere. Yes, there it was! I pushed the button and the whirring sound of the motor told me it was on its way.

"Where does this lead?" Tara asked.

I shrugged my shoulders.

Seconds later the doors parted and to my relief there was no one inside. We got in, pushed the lowest button on the panel and descended, eventually coming to an abrupt stop. The doors opened and my ears filled with a loud hissing noise. Opposite was the entrance to the kitchen. A plume of steam rose into the air, shielding us from whoever was in there. We exited the lift and hurried along a corridor leading to the rear of the hotel, the suitcase repeatedly banging against my knee. Reaching a covered delivery area and the street behind the hotel, I set off along the pavement.

"Where are you going? The car's this way," Tara said.

"Leave it. Come on!"

At the end of the road we waved at a passing silver Mercedes.

"Taxi!"

It didn't stop.

"Danny, why don't we get our car?"

"No, leave it. If we're being watched they'll be watching the car too."

Another taxi came and this time I flagged it down. The driver got out and walked around to open the boot and we threw our luggage inside. I looked up and down the street for a sign of anyone watching us, but saw nothing suspicious.

We got in.

"Hertz car rental, s'il vous plaît," I said.

"Comment?"

Shit. He must understand *Hertz*.

"Hertz car rental," I repeated.

He still looked puzzled so I mimed gripping a steering wheel.

"Hertz!"

"Ah, oui. 'Ertz!" he said.

We pulled away.

Thirty minutes later we loaded our luggage into the boot of a white Peugeot we had hired using Tara's credit card. The roads were empty. I felt a lot safer; sure we weren't being followed. I sat back in the passenger seat, but in my mind I kept seeing Deep Throat's last email – one line of it in particular –

DESTRUCTION OF WMD OPERATION IMMINENT.

The implications of it churned around in my head.

We came to a crossroads and Tara slowed the car down.

"Where to?"

It was ten seconds before I answered.

"Saint Pierre."

"What? Shouldn't we be halfway to Spain by now – or maybe Iceland?"

"That email said, 'Destruction of WMD Operation Imminent'. For some stupid reason I believe Richards, and I don't want to see his work destroyed – it's too valuable. And there's something else – the babies. I don't trust the Intelligence Service to give a shit about what happens to them, do you? We can't just leave it like this."

For a few seconds she thought about what I had said, drumming her fingers on the steering wheel.

"You're right. But Danny, we're a couple of amateurs – what the hell can we do?"

"We'll think about it on the way."

She pressed the accelerator and the car picked up speed.

Twenty minutes later we turned onto the track leading to the cottage that concealed the tunnel entrance. Tara pulled up outside the green front door.

"Danny, if we're going to warn everyone and get them out of there shouldn't we just smash our way through the front gates of the convent? I mean wouldn't it be better if we made a big entrance to get their attention?"

I paused for a moment, then said, "If *you* wanted to destroy what you thought was a laboratory for weapons of mass destruction, what would you do?"

"I don't know. Start a fire or blow the place up, I guess."

She realised what she had said and gasped, putting her hand over her mouth.

"Tara, if we go steaming in there, whoever has their finger on the button might push it before we get a chance to get everyone out. We've got to get in through the tunnel."

We jumped out of the car and ran to the door of the cottage.

"Shit – it's locked!" I said.

There had to be something heavy lying around we could use as a battering ram – a log or something. I looked around and saw thirty yards away the stump of a dead tree, lying on its side, the bark stripped off. I ran over to it.

"Help me."

Tara followed. We gripped it and immediately I felt its immoveable weight.

"We'd need a damned crane to lift this," Tara said.

I ran back over to the cottage and charged the door with my shoulder. It didn't budge. The second time it still didn't budge, and a sharp pain shot through my shoulder, as if my tendons had been torn out. I gripped it with my hand and screwed up my face in agony.

"Danny, are you OK?"

I walked around in a circle, rubbing my wound and eventually the pain subsided.

"Open the boot," I said.

Tara reached into the car, pulled the lever and the boot lid popped up.

"Help me move this luggage."

My shoulder was still sore, but together we lifted out the suitcase, took out the sports bags and pulled back the carpet. Out of the toolkit I took the instrument for removing hubcaps, ran to the cottage and inserted its tapered end into the gap between the door and the frame. After much prizing and yanking the frame began to give way and two minutes later it splintered, the door flying open.

"OK, let's move; we might not have much time."

Once in the cottage, we ran through to the kitchen and I kicked away the rug on the floor, grabbed the recessed handles of the trap door and heaved it open. Standing side by side, we looked down into total blackness.

"Fuck! The flashlight! Where is it?" I said.

"Oh, shit. It's in the car at the hotel."

The tunnel was as dark as outer space and smelled of dampness and decay.

"There must be a light switch at this end of the tunnel," Tara said.

I scanned the walls of the kitchen, looking for one.

"There, by the door," she said.

I tried the switch, but nothing came on. I saw another under a wall cabinet and clicked it on and off, but still nothing happened. The power must be cut off. Tara opened the wall cabinets, but they were all empty. The house looked like it hadn't been lived in for years. I opened some of the base cabinets, then turned around and saw Tara on her knees, stretching her hand down inside the shaft, groping along the sides.

"Got something!" she said.

I heard a click and ran over to her. Down at the bottom of the shaft was a faint amber glow.

"OK, I'll go first," I said.

Carefully I began descending the ladder, gripping the rungs, feeling again the dampness of the wood on my skin. I continued, transferring my weight slowly with each step, expecting one of the rungs to give way at any moment, and then with three feet to go I jumped and landed on the solid rock floor.

I called up to Tara, "OK. I made it. Be careful."

She began her descent and I held the bottom of the ladder, hoping she didn't come crashing down on top of me. She reached the bottom and we wiped the mildew off our hands and set off along the tunnel.

Half way along it a terrible thought struck me: What if they blew up the convent while we were still down there? Would the tunnel hold up or would we be entombed? I looked up at the incalculable weight of solid rock above us, held up by… I didn't know what, then shook the thought from my mind. We climbed the steps; I had forgotten how much higher the convent was than the cottage, and in the cool damp air sweat trickles ran from my hairline down my temples.

"Almost there," I said, stopping to bend over and catch my breath.

Two minutes later we stood at the ancient wooden door that separated the tunnel from the laboratories.

"Ready?" I asked.

She nodded.

I took a deep breath.

"Go!"

I grabbed the handle, turned it and pushed against the door.

"It's locked!"

I looked around for a huge medieval key dangling on a hook, but there was nothing.

"Michael!" I shouted, banging on the door.

"Danny, they'll hear you!"

"It doesn't matter now. Come on, help me!"

Together we beat on the door and kicked it with our feet, shouting, "Michael! Michael! Michael!"

"Keep going, we've got to make him hear!"

"Michael! Michael! Michael!"

Then I heard a muffled voice from the other side of the door shouting, "OK, OK, I'm coming!"

The lock rattled, the handle turned and the door opened.

"What the hell are you doing?" Michael asked.

I stepped through the doorway.

"Michael, you've got to get out of here! They're going to destroy the place. Get everything and get out!"

I tried to push past him, but he grabbed my shoulder.

"What are you talking about?"

"We don't have time to explain. We know they're going to destroy the place. The Secret Service – they saw us talking in the restaurant. We were followed!"

"Are you sure? Who told you?"

"Our informer. He told us they were going to destroy the place immediately and that we were targets. You must be a target too. We've got to get everybody out of here, the nuns, the babies – everyone."

"Danny, for Christ's sake, there must be some mistake!"

Tara said, "There's no fucking mistake – I saw it too – you've got to get out of here, *now*!"

The penny dropped and his expression changed.

"Grab what you can," I said. "I'm going up to get the nuns and the babies out of here."

I moved to pass him and he stopped me again.

"Wait! The High Priest – he needs to tell the nuns to get out of here, they'll listen to him. Come with me."

We ran along the corridor, past the laboratories towards the wooden door with the large, blood-red cross on it. Finally I was about to come face to face with the mad, genetically modified, Jesus-Christ-look-alike.

Michael banged on his door. It wasn't locked; it swung open. He turned to look at me, puzzlement on his face.

We stepped inside and made our way down the narrow corridor. Twenty feet ahead it opened out into a room. Michael went in first.

"Oh shit!" he said.

I followed him in and saw the High Priest lying on the floor, his legs twisted under his body, his arms lying limply either side of him and his face pointed to one side. A hole in his forehead seeped dark, gelatinous blood and his long hair was soaked in the red pool coming from the exit wound in the back of his head.

Michael knelt at his side and placed a hand over his heart, but there was no point in checking for signs of life. Not even the High Priest's genetic mutation could save him from a bullet in the brain.

I bent over his body and looked at his eyes. Curiously, one was now a dull grey colour, but the other was still a piercing blue. Something brightly coloured lay on the floor beside his pale face. I picked it up.

"Contact lenses. He wears contact lenses," I said.

"A magician's prop," Michael said quietly, staring down at the body of... what... a former friend, or just a never-ending source of genetic material?

I looked around the simple room. He had certainly lived like Jesus. There was nothing ostentatious about the hard-looking bed, the rickety old desk, the wardrobe made of pine or the washstand. A floral screen lay toppled over on the floor and in the wall behind where it had stood was a wall safe with a combination lock – the door still shut and unmarked. It appeared that whoever had killed him hadn't tried to get into it.

I put my hand on Michael's shoulder.

"Michael, now you know we aren't making a mistake – we've got to get everybody out."

He looked up at me and nodded, then snapped himself back into the present.

"OK, let's go and warn the nuns."

"No, we'll go upstairs. You get what you can salvage from the labs – have you been working in them today?"

"No, why?"

"Because whoever's done this is going to blow the place up, and judging by the way the blood has congealed on the carpet, they must have shot the High Priest a time ago. It's possible they've already wired up the labs with explosives."

"I won't need long."

We left him and ran down the corridor, turning right, sprinting up the spiral steps and through the doorway to the great hall. The chairs were still positioned in neat rows and the silver effigy of Christ on the cross still flickered in the candlelight.

"Where to?" I said.

"Follow me."

She yanked open the door that led to the gardens and we sprinted across the manicured lawn to the cloisters on the other side. A short, fat woman was walking along with her head held high, a large ornate crucifix swinging from the chain around her neck.

"It's the Mother Superior!" Tara said.

The Mother Superior turned to face us, and gasped in surprise. "Sister Amelia!"

It was a few seconds before I remembered Tara telling me the nuns didn't use their own names and that she had been known as Sister Amelia.

"Stop running at once! How did you get here and what is that man doing in this convent?"

"You've got to get out of here – now!" Tara shouted.

"What on earth are you talking about, child?"

"You are all in danger. You *must* get out!"

"Nonsense. The Lord is watching His flock. You must get back to the sanatorium and continue your treatment."

"Listen to her!" I shouted.

The nun stepped back in surprise and scowled at me, seemingly outraged that I should speak to her in such a manner.

"Young man, you have no business in this place!"

Tara stepped closer to the nun, who retreated, as if fearing an attack. Then Tara said, "You must listen to me. This place is no longer safe. You've got to get the nuns out of here! Tell them to take the babies and leave. *Now!*"

The nun looked at me and then back at Tara, her face registering shock, but curiously I sensed it was not the talk of danger that had spooked her; it was that Tara had spoken of the babies in front of me – a man from outside. Their secret was out.

She drew herself up defiantly, looked at Tara and said, "You are to be detained. I shall speak to the High Priest about you."

Tara lost control.

"You stupid old witch! The High Priest is dead! *Dead !* Do you understand?"

The Mother Superior looked at Tara pityingly, as if she was insane.

Tara turned to me.

"Come on, we don't have time to convince her, we've got to tell the others."

We left her, hurried along the cloisters, then up some steps and through the entrance to another building where we bumped into another nun.

"Sister Gwendolyn, thank God!" Tara said.

"Sister Amelia! What are you doing here?"

"You've got to help us! You speak French don't you?"

Tara quickly told Sister Gwendolyn that the convent was in danger and that all the nuns were to be gathered together in the main hall immediately. The nun looked puzzled and then Tara said, "Don't question it – just do it – by order of the High Priest!"

The lie worked. Sister Gwendolyn ran along the corridor into what appeared to be a dormitory and began shouting in French. Nuns hurried towards her. She said something else and three of the nuns ran off, presumably to gather the flock. They disappeared from view but I heard their distant cries, first in French and then in English, telling everyone that the High Priest had ordered them to assemble in the main hall.

"Come on, let's get over there fast," Tara said.

Retracing our steps, we came face to face once more with the Mother Superior, who began shouting at me.

"You are the devil! Get out of here. The High Priest will hear about this!"

"He's dead!" Tara said.

"Sister Amelia, you will burn in hell for that! The High Priest is the Son of God! He cannot die! You are a devil too!"

I looked around me. If any of the nuns heard the old woman ranting they would believe her rather than us – I had to shut her up. I grabbed her and put my hand over her mouth.

"We've got to take her with us or she'll screw up the whole thing," I said.

"How the hell are we going to keep her quiet?" Tara said.

I whispered into the Mother Superior's ear.

"Look, you stupid woman, we are not alone. The High Priest is being held, and if you don't shut up he will be shot!" I put my hand in my trouser pocket, made a loose fist and pulled it out, raising my arm as if holding something concealed. "If I push this button, he dies, do you understand?"

Looking terrified, the Mother Superior nodded and slowly I relaxed my grip on her mouth. "Now walk with us, quietly, if you want to see the High Priest again."

We approached the great hall as two nuns hurried inside, and we followed them in. There were many more inside sitting on the rows of chairs, and when they saw me a look of alarm spread over their faces. Some of them seemed to recognise Tara and whispered to each other.

Tara, the Mother Superior and I stood in front of the altar and waited while the rest of the nuns filed in, each of them seemingly confused by the legitimacy the Mother Superior's presence lent us.

At last Sister Gwendolyn entered the hall and approached us.

"I think that's just about everyone," she said.

I noticed her strong North of England accent.

"Thank you," Tara said.

Sister Gwendolyn nodded and turned to take a seat with the others.

"Hang on," I said. "I need you to translate for me."

She turned around and came back to stand beside me.

Looking out at almost forty nuns sitting expectantly, waiting for the arrival of the High Priest, I realised I was standing exactly where he had stood when conducting his 'fucking-services'. My sermon would be a lot different.

"Just repeat in French everything I say, OK?"

Sister Gwendolyn nodded.

"Listen to me. This place is not safe. You have to get out, now."

Some of the nuns understood me immediately and when Sister Gwendolyn repeated it in French I saw the expressions change on the remainder.

"Go now, quickly. Those of you who are mothers must get your babies. You must all leave at once."

Some mouths dropped open when I mentioned the babies.

"Get out now!"

They sat, like obedient dogs, waiting for the command to move from their master.

One of the nuns who spoke English stood up and said, "Where is the High Priest?"

How the hell could I get through to them?

"I am a messenger from the High Priest. He wants you to leave now, for your own safety. He'll join you later."

I looked at the Mother Superior and put my hand in my pocket, pretending to grip my imaginary button. She stayed silent.

"There are forces of evil here! Leave!" I shouted.

They still didn't move.

"I know about your babies, the High Priest has told me everything, but he commands you to leave, at least for a short time, until it is safe. You must save yourselves and your babies. Now move it!"

I leapt forward and grabbed one of the nuns, pulling her to her feet.

"Come on, get your things and get out! There's no time to waste!"

I yanked another one out of her chair.

"Leave!"

Tara stepped forward.

"He's speaking the truth! You have to leave. The High Priest commands it!"

I pushed some of the nuns out through the doorway and finally the message seemed to penetrate their confused minds. All the nuns were now on their feet, filing through the door, panic gripping them. With my arms outstretched by my sides I herded them into the gardens, like a farmer shooing chickens. The last one to go through the doorway was Sister Gwendolyn.

"You are speaking the truth, aren't you?" she said.

It was not the time to come clean about the High Priest.

"Sister Gwendolyn, this place is not safe, I promise you. Get out of here quickly and make sure the others leave too."

"We... we have nowhere to go. What shall we do?"

"Bring up your babies."

She seemed to sense that what I had said had an air of permanence about it.

"I don't know who you are or if you are a messenger from the High Priest, but you seem to know what is going on here. Tell me, has the High Priest left us? Has he gone to be with his father?"

She couldn't have said a truer word.

"The time wasn't right for him."

She nodded as if comprehending. "But he will be back, right?"

"I'm sure you won't be deserted."

She looked at the floor and I felt a rush of sympathy for her. They were all so... brainwashed, institutionalised — how would they survive out in the real world?

"Make sure when you leave here that the nuns keep quiet about the High Priest — you must not tell anyone who fathered the babies — the world will not understand, and they will be looked upon badly. Tell the nuns with children that they must say the convent took them in as destitute single mothers. Do you understand?"

She looked up at me.

"Yes, I'll tell them."

"Go on, hurry!"

She gathered up the skirts of her habit and ran after the other nuns, shouting to them in French. I turned to look at the Mother Superior, still standing in front of the altar.

"You must come with us too."

"No! You are the devil. You told me he is dead, but now you talk as if he is alive – I knew it! You are not his messenger, you have tricked the sisters!"

"I'm sorry, but I told *you* the truth. He *is* dead and you have to get out of here – it's not safe."

Tara and I moved towards the door that led to the gardens and I gestured for the Mother Superior to follow us.

"I'll not leave. I know he lives. The Lord protects his own!"

She ran over to the door that led down to the laboratories and pulled it open. And then my ears filled with a deafening thunder crack, the ground shook beneath my feet, and a fireball of angry flames gushed out from the spiral stairway. The Mother Superior flew into the air, landing amongst the first row of chairs, like a bundle of flaming rags, and the room filled with smoke and dust. Shock waves rumbled through my body and I felt sick, deep in my stomach. The blistering heat forced Tara and I to back away out into the garden. Clouds of black smoke billowed out of the entrance and then up into the sky, and I lost all sight of the Mother Superior.

"Jesus Christ, they've pushed the button!" Tara said.

I put my handkerchief over my mouth and stepped forwards to enter the building. Tara grabbed my arm.

"Danny, no! The whole place is burning; there's nothing you can do for her. We've got to get the others out. They might blow up the rest of the convent any minute!"

She was right. I prayed the blast had killed the Mother Superior outright – it would be better than burning to death. And I knew Michael was dead. No one could survive a blast like that.

Sister Gwendolyn ran up behind me, followed by two other nuns.

"Get the hell out of here!" I said.

"But what about..."

"Get out! You can't help anyone in there – just pray for them later!"

The three nuns turned and ran towards the cloisters, Tara and I following, screaming for everyone to get out. I looked over at the building adjacent to the great hall. Six nuns were exiting through a doorway, clutching babies close to their chests. To my right I saw a group of nuns hurrying out of the dormitory, some carrying small bags, others clinging on to their meagre possessions.

"Get out! Go into the town!"

I turned around to look at the hall and saw flames flickering in the roof, their orange glow visible through the gaps in the tiles. Sister Gwendolyn waved her arms, directing four nuns through the gateway that led out of the inner sanctum and into the main convent grounds. I ran over to her.

"Have we got everybody out?"

She looked around her as if searching for someone.

"I think so, but I can't find Sister Olivia."

Then I knew Sister Olivia was the agent working for Cleaver, the one who had shot the High Priest and planted the bombs.

"I think she's accounted for," I said.

We followed behind the last of the nuns, through the gateway and into the gardens of the main convent building.

"Keep going!" I shouted. "Get all the others out of here! Right out into the town!"

Some of the nuns who were not from the inner sanctum had come running through the gardens towards the blast and were being told what had happened. Sister Gwendolyn shouted to them in French and they ran back towards the main convent wall.

"There's no time to get anything – just get out!" I shouted.

Tara shouted to Sister Gwendolyn, "Tell them! Tell them to leave everything and get out into the street! The other buildings may have bombs in them!"

Sister Gwendolyn relayed the message and a hundred nuns hurried through the main convent and out into the town as fast as they could, some running, some helping the older nuns.

I heard a distant crash and I knew the roof of the main hall had collapsed. Tara and I looked at each other, and I knew in that moment we were both thinking the same thing: *Cleaver — that bastard, Cleaver!*

Five minutes later we followed the last of them through the gates and into the melee of nuns corralled in the street. Beyond them people from the town gathered to help, and in the distance I heard sirens.

Tara grabbed my arm.

"We've done all we can; we can't stay here."

I nodded. We were still targets, and there was no doubt now about the nature of the people who hunted us.

"Push your way along the street to the right," I said.

I took Tara's hand and we squeezed our way past the nuns and then through the gathering crowd of onlookers, finally breaking through to the other side of them.

"OK. Let's get back to the car."

Tara set off and I began to follow, but then turned for one last look at the pandemonium. Through a gap in the crowd I saw a familiar boyish haircut. I moved my head to get a better view.

Yes — it was Sylvie.

Chapter 15

We hurried along the narrow streets of Saint Pierre, sometimes breaking into a trot, cutting through the side streets to avoid the town square, turning a corner and stepping into a doorway when an ambulance and fire engine passed, the sound of their wailing sirens reminding me of the morning I was wrenched from my sleep to find Virginie Lavelle, dead, being carried out of the hotel room opposite mine. So much had happened since then it seemed like a memory from another life. Back then I had difficulty deciding what to do with my life – now every decision I made would determine whether I would stay alive.

Ten minutes later we arrived at the track that led to the cottage and I looked around for a sign that someone might be lying in wait for us. Every bush, every tree trunk, every shadow took on a sinister appearance. Slowly we made our way towards the car, listening for any sound, but all I heard was the distant wailing of sirens. I glanced to my left and saw plumes of smoke rising from the convent.

"OK. Let's run for it."

We sprinted the last hundred yards to the car, jumped in, Tara started the engine and we pulled away, the wheels spinning, the back of the car sliding from side to side, like a slalom skier.

"Where the hell do we go?" Tara asked.

"I don't know. Just drive. Head out into the country somewhere – anywhere."

The car rumbled on into the mountains. I sat in silence, oblivious to my surroundings, consumed by images of the Mother Superior being blown across the main hall, landing in flames. And then I saw the face of Michael Richards – the man I had mistakenly thought evil, but now knew was an innocent scientist with a vision – a vision he had shared with us of a beautiful new world, free of disease and death – a vision for which he had died. And I kept thinking that if I had seen Deep Throat's email thirty minutes earlier I could have saved him.

Tara turned to me and said, "We need some gas. I'll have to stop at the next town."

Her voice jolted me out of my thoughts and I realised it was dark outside.

"You know where we are?" I asked.

"No, but there was a sign back there saying some town or other was ten kilometres away. We'll be there soon."

Five minutes later we entered the main street of a small town. Tara pulled up at the petrol station, filled the car and paid the attendant. She got back into the car and I said, "We may as well find a place here to stay for the night. We don't know where we are, let's hope Cleaver's men don't either."

We found a small hotel, checked in, took our bags to a simple square room with a double bed and an en-suite with a shower, and then we both collapsed on the bed, still numb after the incident at the convent and weary from the journey. We fell asleep, shutting out the horrors of the day.

The next morning we sat in silence in the hotel restaurant, eating croissants and drinking black coffee. Behind me I heard footsteps. A tall thin man wearing a dark suit came into view. His face was angular and his swept-back blond hair was either wet from the shower or had been gelled.

He sat down at a table, positioning himself so he had a good view of us, then opened his newspaper and began to read. He turned a page and surreptitiously glanced in our direction, then looked away. Tara continued buttering her croissant. I heard the pages turn again, looked across at the man and he glanced at us once more, just for an instant, before turning back to his paper.

I gripped my knife firmly, my heartbeat quickened and I swallowed my mouthful of croissant, but it lodged in my throat. I choked loudly, dropping the knife and then gulped some coffee.

Tara looked up at me.

"Are you OK?"

I coughed again, swallowed some more coffee and then with a red face and watering eyes, nodded to Tara to indicate that everything was OK.

The man was still reading his paper and I wondered why he hadn't looked across when I had choked. Then I thought: A dark suit in a rural town? How come he has blond hair? French people didn't have blond hair.

I grabbed my knife again. Was it possible that they knew where we were already? Didn't they work in pairs – or was that just in the movies? I glanced behind me, checking there was no one there.

A voice behind me said, "Henri!"

The plump French woman who owned the hotel went over to the blond man who stood up and embraced her in the French fashion.

Seemed he was a local after all. I relaxed.

Tara seemed to notice the look of relief on my face.

"You OK?"

I nodded.

"Yes. Just my imagination going nuts. Let's get out of here."

The little Peugeot ate up kilometre after kilometre of winding roads. As long as we were in it I felt safe, but we couldn't drive around France forever. How long would we have to stay on the run before they forgot about us – or if they ever would? What we had found would embarrass the hell out of the British government – a government who regularly demonised any state engaged in the production of WMD. They had allowed a religious nutcase like the High Priest to indulge in his fantasies in order to get hold of one of the nastiest gases man had ever produced – a gas with no defensive use, no purpose other than to destroy the population of another country. Every pious politician who had ever spoken of evil rogue states whilst espousing the virtues of British fair play would be quaking in their boots if they thought we were going to publish our story. What government could survive the cruel tide of public opinion after such a revelation? It was clear to me that they would never rest until we were silenced.

I glanced across at Tara. She had been having the time of her life, so she said, but I was the person responsible for getting her into all this. I had been the one with a chip on my shoulder about governments.

We weren't Bonnie and Clyde, and a fugitive's life was not for us. Running forever was not an option; we had to deal with this head on. But how?

My brain worked overtime, trying to come up with some sort of plan, and then something came to me and I gripped the edge of my seat.

"Tara, we're going to Saint Malo."

"Excuse me, but where is Saint Malo?"

"Brittany." I rummaged around in the glove compartment and took out the complimentary map. "We need to pick up the A6 auto route north of Lyons."

"You going to tell me why we're going to this place?"

"So we can get to England undetected."

I took over the driving to give Tara a rest and we headed west to Orleans, then on to Le Mans, Rennes and finally we reached the old walled seaside town of Saint Malo, where we checked into the small Hotel de la Manche, dumped the luggage in our room and walked the streets, searching for a shop where we could buy a computer.

"Why don't we just find a cyber café?" Tara asked.

"I don't just want to send an email this time."

We found a small computer shop.

"This is going to be expensive," I said.

"Hey, I'm a trust fund baby. As long as you don't want to bid for IBM my credit card will stand it."

Twenty minutes later we left the shop carrying a large box and a carrier bag. In the hotel room I cleared the small writing desk in the corner of the room, opened the box and took out our new Toshiba laptop, I booted it up and plugged the modem into the telephone socket.

"I need you to open an account with AOL using your credit card."

Tara sat in front of the computer, clicked on the AOL icon and went through the account opening procedure.

"OK. Let me get onto hotmail now."

I checked for incoming mail, but there was none.

"I just hope to God Deep Throat is still monitoring this."

I typed the message –

*CONVENT DESTROYED. HIGH PRIEST DEAD.
SCIENTIST DEAD. WE ARE UNHURT, BUT NEED HELP.
THERE IS MUCH YOU DO NOT KNOW.
BRITISH SECRET SERVICE HAS BEEN FOOLED.
WE MUST MEET ASAP.*

I clicked on the icon and the message whizzed its way through cyberspace.

Tara looked at me.

"You think he'll meet us?"

"He'd better. We need to get to Cleaver through him, and I can't think of another way to do it that won't put our lives at risk. I'm banking on his curiosity getting the better of him; he'll want to know what we mean by the British Secret Service being fooled."

"Could be a long time before he picks up the message. So what do we do now?"

"Well, I'm supposed to be a reporter – so I'd better get reporting."

I began writing a full account of everything that had happened since waking up to find the pregnant Virginie Lavelle dead in the room opposite mine. I wrote how Tara had been kept against her will in the sanatorium, the meeting we had had with Cleaver, the lies he had told to mislead us, the real reason for the British Secret Service placing an operative in the convent and details of the deadly gas they were secretly trying to procure whilst operating in France – a friendly foreign country.

The next day we moved to another hotel and I continued my story, detailing the activities of the High Priest and concentrating on the culpability of the British Government in allowing his activities to go on to serve their own ends.

When it was finished, Tara read it.

"Shit. *That* is a damning report."

"I left out the help we got from your Uncle Jim, and of course, Deep Throat. Deep Throat won't show it to Cleaver if it's going to implicate him."

I connected my digital camera to the computer, downloaded the pictures we had taken in the laboratory and inserted them into the document.

"There. Pictures don't lie. All we have to do now is meet with Deep Throat."

I plugged in the modem and went straight into hotmail. There was no reply.

Tara frowned.

"What if he's stopped looking? Maybe he thinks we're on the run and aren't going to contact him. Maybe he thinks we're dead."

"He'll look again. He has to," I said.

If he didn't I had no idea how we were going to get to Cleaver. I stood up and put the computer in its case. "Come on, let's pack our clothes – we've got a boat to catch."

We caught the hydrofoil from Saint Malo to the island of Jersey. From there we took a flight to the Isle of Man, sixty miles off the north-west coast of England, the plane touching down with a bump on runway 06 at Ronaldsway. Under a grey, overcast sky we walked across the apron to the terminal building, bending at the waist to combat the wind that caught us as if we were sails on a yacht. We collected our luggage, changed some money into English pounds and took a taxi to Douglas, the capital of the island.

Tired and dry mouthed, we entered the reception of the seafront Sunshine Hotel, a misnomer if ever there was one.

I said to Tara, "What do you want to be, Mrs Smith or Mrs Jones?"

"Too obvious. How about Mr and Mrs Johnson?"

I signed the register as Mr Ian Johnson and paid three nights in advance, in cash, telling the receptionist I had lost my credit card and was waiting for a new one. She took the money and asked no more questions. When we got to our room we dumped our luggage on the stand, sat on the bed and, feeling thirsty, I picked up the phone, pressed the button for room service and ordered a pot of tea for two.

"You sure we're going to get to the UK from here without being discovered?" Tara said.

I nodded.

"You've been here before, right? A romantic weekend for two?"

"I was here a couple of years ago to cover the TT races. This little island has a world-famous motorcycle racing event every year. The place is deluged with bikers from all over the world and I was sent here once to cover it for the *Leyton-Middleton Advertiser* and no one asked me for any identity papers at the airport. In any case, I can't believe Cleaver would bother to watch the flights to the UK mainland from here."

"So we wait for Deep Throat to answer the email?"

I nodded again, and then Tara said, "Hang on a minute – Uncle Jim! He put us in contact with Cleaver before and he could do it again. Shall I call him?"

She dived onto the bed, grabbed the phone and looked at her watch. "He'll be at home still."

She dialled his number.

Seconds passed.

"Hi, Uncle Jim…Yes! I'm fine, how are you? I'm in Europe… No, I can't tell you that… Uncle Jim, I need a favour; I need to get hold of that English guy, Cleaver. Can you give me a number I can call? Yes, I know he's not exactly listed in the *Yellow Pages*, if he was I wouldn't need to call you…"

There was a knock on the door and I opened it. Room service. A woman carrying a tray of tea entered the room and I gestured for her to put it on the dressing table.

Tara was still talking to her uncle.

"But why not?" She looked at me and shook her head. "But it wasn't a problem before… No, I can't tell you why – does it matter?" She listened to her uncle for a minute. "But… but… no, I can't tell you that… I've got my reasons… No, I'm not in any danger – really." She looked at me and shrugged her shoulders.

The waitress heard what Tara was saying and looked at me quizzically.

I tried to distract her. "Um, the hotel's a little quiet isn't it?" I said.

"Oh, it's always quiet here, sir," she said. She looked disapprovingly at Tara. "Except during the TT races of course. We're always full then. Do you want me to pour it, sir?"

"Er… no, no that's all right, we can manage."

"Loads of biker types we get here during TT, all leather jackets and grease. Mind you it keeps us going. Have you been to the island during TT week, sir? Not a biker, are you?"

Tara said, "Uncle Jim, I have to have the number! It's important… But Uncle Jim!" She slowly took the receiver away from her ear and replaced it on the phone.

The waitress looked at Tara again.

I coughed and said, "That'll be all, thank you." Then I gave her a tip and she left the room.

I sat on the bed next to Tara. "What did he say?"

"No way. He says the High Priest is dangerous and he should never have allowed me to get involved. He wasn't too complimentary about you either for getting me mixed up in it."

A pang of guilt shot through me and Tara saw the look on my face.

"Danny! It was my decision, I'm a big girl now!"

I wasn't convinced. If anything happened to her I would never forgive myself – and neither would Uncle Jim.

I poured Tara a cup of tea.

"What, no biscuits? I'm hungry," she said.

We left the tea and went down to the restaurant to eat. After we had finished our meal Tara saw me gazing into space.

"Penny for them," she said.

"I was just thinking about Michael Richards."

Tara nodded. "Do you think he really had discovered a cure for ageing?"

I pondered on the question for a few moments.

"He sounded convincing to me. People die for noble causes, and I can't imagine a cause more noble than that. If he had discovered a cure he had the means to save us all. I guess someone else will discover it in the end, but how many people will die of illnesses or just plain old age in the meantime?"

"Do you think he was right about governments not wanting a discovery like that to be made – you know, upsetting the order of things?"

"They killed him because they were afraid he'd told us he was producing a deadly gas; maybe they're crazy enough to have killed him anyway if they knew what he was really doing."

"Are they going to kill us?"

"No," I said.

But I knew they would try.

Chapter 16

Two days later at 6.10pm I received the email I had been waiting for. "Tara – I've got it!" I heard the shower being turned off and a minute later she emerged wrapped in a bath towel. She looked over my shoulder and read –

MEETING TOO DANGEROUS. EXPLAIN 'FOOLED'.
DEEP THROAT.

I typed my reply –

MEETING IMPERATIVE!
I SAY AGAIN, IMPERATIVE!
WE HAVE SOMETHING FOR YOU.
YOU MUST GIVE IT TO CLEAVER. URGENT.
TELL US WHERE AND WHEN.
WILL MEET YOU AND EXPLAIN 'FOOLED'.

I clicked the icon and sent the message.
"He *has* to meet us now. He'll be wondering what we have."
Minutes passed.
"Come on, God damn you! You owe us a meeting for Christ's sake!" I shouted.
"You don't think he sent the email and went home do you?" Tara asked.
"No, the bastard's still there, I'm sure. He asked us to explain what we meant by 'fooled'. His curiosity's aroused – he'll be waiting to see if we reply to that. Come on answer! Yes – here it is!"
It said –

MEET TOMORROW 4.30PM KINGSLEY ARMS HOTEL, WATFORD.
BE CAREFUL – DANGER! CONFIRM?
DEEP THROAT.

I replied –

MEETING CONFIRMED.
WILL MEET YOU IN THE CAR PARK.
WHAT IS YOUR CAR REGISTRATION NUMBER ?

Two minutes later Deep Throat replied giving us the number.

"Now we'll see how weak the security is between the Isle of Man and the UK."

I made copies on two separate disks of the document I had written. I put one in an envelope addressed to: Mr Johnson, Room 313, Sunshine Hotel, Douglas, Isle of Man, marking it: *Please retain until Mr Johnson's return.* The other copy I would give to Deep Throat at our meeting.

Next morning I put the envelope in a post box just up the road from the hotel, and then we checked out.

"Did you enjoy your stay, Mr Johnson?" the receptionist asked.

"Very nice, thank you."

"I see you've paid in advance for the room, so there's just £34.80 to pay for additional items."

Tara handed her the cash. The receptionist smiled and gave me the bill. We turned to go.

"Oh, Mr Johnson, please take one of these – it's our special weekend offer. You get a free dinner if you come back for a weekend break."

To please her I took the leaflet and stuffed it into my inside jacket pocket.

"Thank you that's very kind." I glanced at my watch. "We have to go now. Can I get a taxi to the airport?"

"Of course."

She called a taxi.

We arrived at Ronaldsway Airport at 7.15am.

"Have you got enough cash on you?" I asked Tara.

She nodded. We approached the ticket desk.

"Two tickets to Manchester please."

"Certainly. Return or one way?"

"Return."

I gave our names as Mr and Mrs Johnson. The girl typed away on the computer and seconds later the ticket printing machine sprang into life. Tara took out some banknotes, paid the woman and then we checked in, keeping the computer as hand luggage.

"Jesus, that was easy," Tara said.

Forty minutes later we were drinking coffee at twenty-one thousand feet.

We landed at Manchester Airport, collected our bags and took a taxi to the station where we bought two first class tickets to London. From there we hired a car, but as we pulled away Tara saw the look of unease on my face.

"What's up?"

"This might be a mistake."

"Why?"

"We're no longer Mr and Mrs Johnson. That credit card transaction is traceable."

"You think they can trace it that easily?"

"More easily here than in France. I just don't know what they can do, but we can't take any chances."

"We can't take it back, the transaction's already gone through."

"Let's just get this over with as fast as we can and then get the hell out of here."

At 3.57pm we pulled into the car park of the Kingsley Arms Hotel on the road out of Watford. The building looked as if it had been constructed in the 1960s – typical of the kind of low-cost hotels used by travelling salesmen and businessmen on a tight budget – functional and characterless.

"Park it there – we'll be able to see all the cars coming in," I said.

Tara reversed into the space, turned off the engine and we waited. Vehicles entered and exited the car park, mainly Fords and Vauxhalls. Executives carrying briefcases and suitcases made their way to the hotel entrance, but as yet there was no sign of Deep Throat.

I glanced at my watch.

"He'd better turn up after all this. If he doesn't we're fucked for getting hold of Cleaver."

I drummed my fingers on my knee and felt the moisture forming on my palms. Another car came in, an old black mini. I stared at the number plate. It wasn't it. Suddenly a thought struck me: What if Deep Throat had decided to turn us over to Cleaver? Nervously I looked around.

"What is it?" Tara asked.

"Nothing, I was just checking to see if he's already got here." No, he couldn't turn us in – he was definitely on our side. If he turned us in he would know that we would tell Cleaver about the emails and the help Deep Throat had given us – unless of course the whole thing had been a set up from the start. I quickly went through how Deep Throat had contacted us and what he had said. No, it couldn't be a set up – that was crazy – what would have been the point?

"More cars coming," Tara said.

I looked up. A blue Ford came in; not the right number plate, and then a silver Ford Puma. I checked the number: W361 AGR.

"That's it!"

The Puma passed in front of us and slowly made its way to a space nearer the hotel entrance. I paid no attention to the two other cars entering the car park – we had found the one we were looking for. It reversed into the space and we waited a few seconds.

"OK, let's go," I said.

We got out of the car and walked towards the hotel.

"Danny, watch out!" Tara said.

I turned around and just managed to jump out of the way of a black Transit van I had inadvertently walked in front of. The driver braked hard, I raised my hand acknowledging my mistake, and he reversed backwards into a space near the car park entrance.

"Sorry, Tara. That would be a stupid way to die."

She looked at me in a way that said, *You're telling me*.

When we were ten yards away from the Puma, the door opened and the driver got out. She wore a navy blue business suit over a white blouse, her hair immaculately coiffured in blonde waves, a thin row of pearls encircling her neck. Tara and I looked at each other. Was this Deep Throat? For some reason I had never imagined Deep Throat to be a woman. She positioned her black handbag on her arm and began to walk to the hotel entrance. We followed, and as I passed the Ford Puma I looked again at the number plate – W361 AGR – definitely the one.

We caught up with her just in front of the revolving door.

"Er... excuse me. Have we met before?" I said. She turned around and I saw a trace of fear in her eyes. She looked directly at me and then at Tara, but said nothing. "I'm sorry, but we've just returned from a break in the South of France and we're supposed to be meeting someone here. I thought I recognised your car, but I might be mistaken."

Her expression changed.

"You're not mistaken. Let's go inside."

We followed her into the hotel and I noticed her court shoes – expensive looking.

The Kingsley Arms was just as I had thought; green carpet, a curved reception desk, the front covered in studded red leatherette, and recessed lighting – very tacky. The place looked as if all expense had been spared and the cleaners hadn't turned up for a couple of days. It was definitely too downmarket for Deep Throat, but she seemed to know her way around. We passed through reception into a restaurant area, and then she paused at a table in the corner, gesturing for us to take seats on the far side of it, with our backs to the window. She sat down opposite Tara, and placed her handbag on the empty seat beside her.

Damn it! I'd left the disk in the car. I would have to give it to her on our way out.

A waitress came. Tara and I ordered coffee, Deep Throat ordered tea.

"You thought I would be a man didn't you? I seem to have spent my life disappointing people because I'm female. Apparently my father went into a sulk when I was born – he wanted a son to play fly-half for the England rugby team."

Her accent was pure public school and she held her head aloft when speaking, her face impassive apart from the minimal movement of her lips. Her youthful eyes shone bright blue, contrasting with her pale, lined skin.

"Deep Throat doesn't seem like an appropriate name for you, what do we call you?" I asked.

She thought for a moment. "You may call me Elizabeth. It's not my real name of course, but I've always liked it." She adjusted the bracelet on her wrist. "So, Mr Avery, you have something you wanted to tell me?"

She was incredible. We were trying to keep ourselves alive, her colleagues were trying to finish us off, and she said quite calmly: *So, Mr Avery, you have something you wanted to tell me?* – as if I was an errant son who had come to confess a wrongdoing.

Anger rose within me. "You just sit there and –"

Tara put her hand on my arm, drawing my attention to the approaching waitress, who served the coffee and tea, along with an assorted plate of dry-looking biscuits. When she had moved away I began again.

"How the hell can you sit there so calmly? You know what Cleaver is trying to do to us."

"Yes, Mr Avery, I know, and I agreed to come here at your request, and at considerable risk to myself, so please moderate your tone."

I considered what she said. She was right of course, she would be in danger coming here, and she had already put herself at risk by sending us all those emails. I calmed down.

"You have to appreciate, it's not easy staying cool with half the Secret Service out to kill you."

"I quite understand, but the longer we stay here, the longer we will all be in danger."

Tara said, "Just how much danger are we in?"

She paused for a moment and then said, "I would describe your situation as… *grave.*"

The matter-of-fact way in which she said it was chilling.

I said, "I take it you knew all along what was going on down in that convent?"

"I was party to the information for the most part, yes."

"Doesn't it bother you?"

"Mr Avery, that is a stupid question isn't it? Am I not here?"

"Why the hell did you send us all those cryptic emails – why not just come out with it in the first place?"

"It wasn't too hard for you was it? After all you are a reporter are you not? You must have done the odd crossword."

Done the odd crossword!

"What if we hadn't worked it out, what then?"

"I have signed the Official Secrets Act, Mr Avery, I do not speak about that which I should not."

"The Official Secrets Act? You're working for a bunch of murdering psychopaths who've bombed a convent, killing one religious nutcase who they encouraged to continue with his lunatic, perverted activities, an innocent scientist and the Mother Superior! All this in an attempt to cover up their attempts to procure probably one of the most deadly gases known to man, and you're worried about the *Official Secrets Act*!"

"I come from an age where duty still counts for something," she snapped. She looked down at her tea for a moment and when she looked up again I saw remorse on her face. "I'm sorry about the Mother Superior, I didn't know." She looked down again, seemingly disturbed, then raised her teacup to her lips and sipped, before delicately replacing the cup in its saucer and clearing her throat.

"When CABWINT was set up I –"

"CABWINT?" I said.

"Chemical and Biological Weapons Intelligence – that's who we work for."

"Never heard of them."

"You wouldn't have. We're new for one thing, and we don't advertise our existence. Of course I'm not an agent, just an administrator."

"You don't seem like the murdering type to me, so how can you work for such people?"

She sighed. "It wasn't always like this. Years ago things were different. We had an enemy – Russia. Things were black and white in those days. I thought I was doing something for my country, but nowadays it's all shades of grey. An ally from days gone by suddenly becomes your enemy. Now we're fighting against terrorists rather than countries and... well it's just all so messy."

"But if you have such a strong sense of duty, what made you decide to contact us? It doesn't make sense."

She sighed again. "It wasn't the gas. Oh, I know it's a terrible weapon and the world would be a better place without it, but it wasn't that. You see, as Alistair always –"

"Alistair?"

"Alistair Cleaver. As he always said, the gas will be produced one day and it's better that we have it rather than some rogue terrorist state. Toby Wilcox said the same thing."

"Who's he?"

"He's with the MOD. CABWINT works with the MOD and Toby's the man who liaises with us. It wasn't the gas that changed my mind – it was the children. You see… I never had any of my own, although I did fall pregnant once. *Fall pregnant* – that's how we used to refer to it in those days – like some terrible illness. I wasn't married of course and the father of the child insisted on me having an abortion. Being a single mother wasn't accepted then. It would have been a scandal and it would have wrecked my career and his."

Tara pushed her cup to one side. "Couldn't you have married him?" she asked.

"He said… he said he didn't love me. So it wasn't an option." She looked down at the table again. "After the abortion I was told I could never have children."

Tara said, "What about the father – what happened to him?"

"He did well in his career and I carried on loving him. Anyway, when I heard about the High Priest and the children of the nuns… Well I just couldn't stand by and do nothing – it was all so… so wrong. Something inside me changed and I realised that allowing innocent children to be put in danger was not acceptable for any reason, and I had to stop it. *You* stopped it for me. I'm grateful for that."

"Sorry things didn't work out better for you," Tara said.

"I'm going to retire. I have a fondness for cats and I intend to retire to Devon and buy a cattery. Anyway, after I realised he was prepared to allow innocent babies to be harmed I stopped loving him. You see the father of my unborn child was Alistair Cleaver."

My mouth fell open. She took a deep swallow, as if trying to suppress her bitterness.

"Anyway, the past is the past, Mr Avery. Do you have something to tell me?"

I shifted in my seat and said, "Just how ruthless is Cleaver?"

"He's ruthless, Mr Avery. Vain and ruthless – very."

"I have something in the car for him. I want you to make sure he gets it."

"What is it?"

"It's a disk with all the evidence we have on him and CABWINT. Pictures too – embarrassing for Cleaver and the government. Tell him I've sent a copy to solicitors in five different countries with instructions for it to be sent to the press if anything happens to either of us."

"What do you expect me to do – just go and hand it to him? Don't you think he'll wonder how I got it?"

"So don't hand it to him. Just slip it in his mail."

She considered what I'd said, then nodded. "You said Alistair had been fooled. What did you mean?"

"I'll tell you when you've delivered the disk to him."

"Was he really duped, or is this just a ruse to get me to do what you want?"

"Your operative in the convent was fooled by the scientist – he never was working for you."

She looked puzzled. "Well, if he was working for someone else… then *they* must have the gas." She looked agitated. "Mr Avery, this is no time for games. As much as you might hate the idea of the British Government getting hold of it you can't allow another government to get it – that would risk national security. You must tell me –"

"*When* Cleaver has the disk and has called off his dogs – I'll tell you then, and not before. Will you make sure he gets it – it's our only means of security."

She nodded. "Yes, yes of course, but afterwards you must tell us what you know. It really is…" Her mouth fell open, as if something had shocked her. She was looking over my shoulder out into the car park. "Oh no. My God, I… I was sure I'd taken enough precautions. I've been followed. That man… he's one of Alistair's agents."

I turned around and saw a burly man with dark swept-back hair, wearing a navy blue raincoat.

"Are you sure?"

"Yes – of course I'm sure! He's Ronald Simmons, I know him!"

"He knows your car?"

She nodded, wringing her hands in front of her chest. Simmons walked towards the reception entrance.

"Come on, there must be a back way out of here," I said. We stood up. "The kitchens! Hurry!"

I ran over to the doorway leading to the kitchens, Elizabeth and Tara following. We entered it, Elizabeth's heels clicking on the ceramic tiled floor, and three young men in chef's hats looked up.

"Hey, what's all this?" one of them said.

I pulled out my wallet, opened it up and flashed my credit cards at them.

"Health and safety inspection. You just carry on working – we'll be watching your procedures."

The chefs looked worried. One of them said, "We had one of those three weeks ago."

I did my best to look officious. "Not by us you didn't. We'll tell you when we're satisfied, all right?" They looked down and carried on preparing the food. "Right. Where's the rear entrance to the premises?"

"Over there," said one of the chefs, pointing.

"Let's check out there for anything hazardous. Come with me, ladies."

I led them through the back of the kitchen along a corridor and out to the rear of the hotel.

"Would Simmons be alone?" I asked.

"I... I don't know. He may have someone with him."

"Cleaver?"

"I don't know."

Shit. We couldn't risk going around to the front of the hotel, not if Cleaver was there. "We'll get away over the fields."

"That's a good idea. Go on, I'll be all right. I can go around the side of the building to get back to my car."

"But what if Cleaver *is* there and he sees you?"

"I'll make something up – tell him I was meeting an old friend or something. I can handle him, I'm sure."

"OK. But you'll have to get the disk from our car – it's in the glove box."

"Yes, of course. Give me the keys."

Tara handed them to her. "It's a red Ford Mondeo – near the front of the car park."

"I'll get it to Cleaver – I promise."

Somehow I knew she would. "Go on! Get moving. I'll email you." She trotted around the side of the hotel as fast as she could in her heels. The hotel had no garden at the rear, just a dismal strip of grass. Beyond that a four-foot high hedge formed a border between the hotel grounds and the fields behind. Blighted and sparse, the hedge had numerous gaps in it. We squeezed through one of them and were about to set off across the field when I stopped dead in my tracks.

"Hang on a minute. Let's make sure she gets it and gets away all right," I said.

Crouching low, we made our way alongside the hedge towards the front of the hotel, and then I saw her, walking purposefully towards a red Ford Mondeo, but it wasn't ours.

"No! She's got the wrong one!"

She pointed the key fob at the window and pushed the button to unlock the door, but the indicator lights flashed on our car, ten yards away. Thankfully she must have heard the beeping sound of the alarm being deactivated and the door locks clicking open because she turned around and hurried over to it. She pulled the door open, bent over and reached inside to open the glove box but it was too far away for her – she would have to get inside. She stood up and put one leg in the foot well, ducked her head below the roof and lowered herself to sit down. Her weight made contact with the seat, and then…

It was as if God had hurled a thunderbolt at the car and scored a direct hit. There was a flash of intense white and amber light and a smoke cloud, expanding instantaneously, along with an awesome percussive crack that punished my ears. The Mondeo lifted six feet up into the air, then landed with a crunch, half on top of the MG sports car that had been parked next to it, both the cars now reduced to a pile of flaming scrap under a descending shower of shrapnel.

"Fuck… That was meant for us!"

A man ran out from the hotel towards the black Ford transit van that had almost knocked me down.

"Look," I said. "It's that guy – Ronald Simmons!"

He was moving fast for a man of his bulk. The door of the van opened and the driver set off before Simmons was fully inside, but still he managed to clamber aboard and pull the door shut. The van sped around the car park and I could see it was going to pass in front of us on its way out. Someone had parked a car outside the white-lined parking zones, partially blocking the exit route, and as the van slowed down to squeeze through the gap I got a look through the side window. Simmons was in the seat by the nearside window; the driver was the same guy who had been driving it when it nearly ran me over, but there was a third man – sitting in the middle seat – tall and slim, and I recognised him instantly.

"It's Cleaver!"

The van pulled off the car park, the driver keeping it in first gear too long, causing the engine to scream. I looked again at the bonfire in the car park. Elizabeth was dead, that was certain.

"Come on, we've got to get the fuck out of here!"

We ran, arms and knees pumping, lungs burning, across the first field behind the hotel, and then a second one, causing two grazing ponies to take fright and gallop away from us. Gasping for breath we came to a stile, climbed it and then I slumped to the ground, my legs aching and my muscles in revolt at the demands I had placed upon them. Tara sat down beside me and I sucked in air as deep and as fast as I could, sweat streaming down my face. Running any further wearing my jacket would be impossible, so I discarded it and stuffed it in the hedge.

Tara said, "Are we safe?"

"I don't know. They could have people all over the place. They're not going to stop looking for us now. Come on, we've got to keep going."

We jogged along the side of the next two fields using the hedges as cover, the fear of getting caught or shot by Cleaver's men overriding the urgent desire to stop and ease the pain in my chest and legs. After heading for a time in a north-easterly direction, we pushed through a gap in the hedge, checking there was no one in sight, and eventually found ourselves at the end of a lane. In front of us was a sign saying: *Elstree Aerodrome*.

"Walk now. We've got to get our breath back," I said.

Tara wiped the sweat off my face. "You're not thinking of stealing a plane are you?"

"I can't fly, I'd kill us quicker than Cleaver would. Can you?"

She shook her head. "No, but Uncle Jim can. He's taken me up in his plane before."

Great. Where was Uncle Jim when you needed him?

"Is there any way of telling who's going up?"

She thought for a moment, and then looked around her.

"Come with me."

We walked over to a building with a large letter C on it. Tara opened the door, stepped forwards to enter the building and bumped into a middle-aged man with a beer gut that stretched his thin navy blue pullover to its limits. In his hand he held a pair of headphones.

"You all right, love?" he asked.

"Sure, I'm sorry – careless," Tara said.

"No problem."

He smiled, nodded at me, and then walked past us. We entered the small office. On the walls were aeronautical maps, weather reports, adverts for small aircraft for sale and two clocks – one marked 'UTC'. Tara found a large clipboard with a multicolumned sheet on it.

"Here it is," Tara said. I stood behind her, looking over her shoulder. "Look at this," she said, pointing to an entry. "This is the booking-out sheet. They write on here where they're going. This one – G-YBYY – says it's going to Liverpool. Look at the estimated time of departure. That's in ten minutes. Come on, we've got to find it."

We left the office and walked up and down the lines of planes – there were dozens of them, mostly single-engined, but we couldn't see one with the registration G-YBYY.

"It must be here somewhere," Tara said. "Over there, look. It's that guy I bumped into who was coming out of the office – let's ask him if he knows where it is."

The man was walking around his plane, doing his pre-flight inspections. He lifted the engine cowling and pulled out the dipstick to check the oil.

"Look at the registration," Tara said. "It's him! Just leave the talking to me."

She undid her shirt buttons, showing off her cleavage, her breasts still moist with sweat after running across the fields, then flicked out her hair and approached him. I stood five yards away.

The man looked up.

"Oh, it's you," he said. "You all right?"

She clasped her hands in front of her like an excited schoolgirl.

"Hi," she said, in a voice honeyed with sex. "You're going to Liverpool aren't you?"

"Aye, I am. How did you know?"

"Oh, I saw in the office – it said where you were going."

"You've been checking up on me, haven't you!" He flashed his piano-key teeth.

"Well, yes. I am a naughty girl, aren't I?"

"Are you? Oh, it's my lucky day then!"

The man grinned so wide the corners of his mouth seemed to extend beyond the width of his ears.

Tara grinned back. "I was wondering... You see, I'm hitch-hiking – but by plane." She reached inside her shirt and scratched her breast, the man's gaze following her hand. He swallowed hard. "I wanted to go up north, you see. You wouldn't like to give me a lift would you? I'd be *soooo* grateful."

Somehow he managed to wrench his gaze from her breasts. "Um... hitch-hiking in a plane, eh? That's a new one."

"Oh, we do it all the time in the States. My uncle has a plane. A Piper Saratoga – do you know that plane?"

"Your uncle, eh? Nice plane, love – very nice. You want to go to Liverpool? Just you, or your boyfriend too?"

"Oh, he's not my boyfriend – he's my cousin. He's just showing me around England, introducing me to people – you know."

The man's face brightened. "Your cousin, you say. Well, yes, I could certainly do with the company. You got any bags?"

"No, we're staying with my aunt up in Liverpool. We just came to London for the day by train early this morning – but flying is much better isn't it? A real sexy way to get around, I think."

The man coughed. "Um, yes. Well, you'd better get in then. I just need to attend to a few things and we'll be on our way."

"Thank you so much. You're a real English gentleman!" She bent forward and kissed him on the cheek. His face went red and he swallowed hard again before making his way over to the gent's toilets.

Ten minutes later he returned to his little four-seater aircraft, and I saw the look of disappointment on his face when he realised I was in the co-pilot's seat and Tara was sitting in the back. He climbed in and put on his headphones.

"Um, right. Well, we'll be off then." He flicked on the radio. "Golf, Yankee, Bravo, Yankee, Yankee," he said.

The reply came back, "Golf, Yankee, Yankee."

"Bill, make that three POB to Liverpool."

"Wilco, Harry. Have a good flight."

Five minutes later the little plane gathered speed on the runway, juddering and bumping over the potholes in the asphalt, until Harry pulled back on the column and we rose gently into the air. We flew in a straight line, gaining height until the altimeter said five hundred feet, then we turned left, continued our climb, and turned left again, rising out of the circuit. I looked down below at two single-engined planes and a dark green helicopter, which were now positioning themselves to land at the small airstrip.

Thirty minutes later, cruising at two thousand five hundred feet, travelling in a north-westerly direction, I glanced across at Harry. The look on his face seemed to say: *Who's taking who for a ride here?* I pictured Cleaver driving around in circles trying to catch us, and a wry smile played around my lips, but then I remembered Elizabeth's car turning into a ball of flaming scrap and I imagined the horror and the agony of being burned alive. It had so nearly been us. I shook my head, trying to get rid of the thought, forcing my mind to think of other things.

Two hours later, the rear wheels of the plane touched down on the runway at Liverpool Airport with hardly a bump. Harry could really fly. He parked the plane, turned off the engine and switched off the electrical systems.

"That was great," I said.

"Aye, it is that," Harry said.

We climbed out and Tara, still in her sex-kitten role, kissed Harry on the cheek. "Oooo, you're so clever!" she gushed.

He blushed and looked down, his gaze lingering on Tara's breasts again before it reached the floor. Then he led us through a door marked with a big letter C, up a stairway and on to a glass screen where he flashed his pilot's licence at a man sitting behind a desk.

"Think I know you by now, Harry," the man said. "Who've you got with you?"

"Just a couple of friends. I've brought them up from down the smoke."

The man gave us a quick glance and then pressed a button to release the door, allowing us into the airport terminal building.

"Right, well, I'll be leaving you here then," Harry said. "Got to go and put the plane away for the night."

We said our goodbyes and then made our way into the main terminal building. Ahead of us I saw a coffee shop.

"Let's get something to drink."

We sat down, each with a cup of coffee and a sandwich from the self-service counter. Somehow feeling hungry didn't seem right – almost disrespectful – so soon after seeing Elizabeth murdered. Behind Tara, through a large window, I saw a plane take off, probably full of holidaymakers on their way to a break in the sun. I finished the first half of my sandwich and sipped my coffee.

"Maybe this is a stupid question," Tara said, "but do you think we're safe here?"

Were we safe? Were we ever going to be safe again? I had no idea what sort of technology government agencies had at their disposal, but I couldn't see how they could have tracked us in Harry's little plane.

"Yeah, I reckon we're safe – for now anyway."

But I knew Cleaver would never give up – there was too much at stake for him and the government. Our only chance was to make it more risky to follow us than to leave us alone.

"We've got to get that spare disk I posted in the Isle of Man." Another plane took off behind Tara's head.

"How do we get it to Cleaver?" she asked.

I hadn't worked that out. "Let's just get it first."

Tara put down her coffee.

"So what do we do – take a cab to Manchester and catch a plane back to the Isle of Man?"

"We don't need to. They fly from here too."

Something moved outside, drawing my attention. It passed behind Tara's head, and then began to descend. I knew I'd seen it before, I was sure of it.

"Oh, fuck!"

"What?" Tara said.

I leapt up from my seat and ran to the window. Tara got up and followed me.

"What is it?" she said.

I stared at the dark green helicopter. It was the one I had seen landing at Elstree, just after we had taken off in Harry's plane – it had to be. It was hovering six feet from the ground. A feeling of foreboding washed over me. How many dark green helicopters were there? It wasn't the right colour for a private one – it looked almost military. It touched down and seconds later the rotors began to slow. A side door slid back and two men got out. I recognised them instantly – Ronald Simmons and the man who had been driving the Transit van. Then a third man emerged, and I found myself staring at the unmistakable figure of Alistair Cleaver.

Chapter 17

"Let's get out of here!" Tara said. We turned and ran through the cafeteria. A short woman with peroxide blonde hair carrying a tray jumped out of our way, toppling over her cup of coffee.

"Oi! Watch it, you fucking idiots!" she shouted.

We scurried down the stairs to the ground floor of the terminal – our legs a blur. The exit was right in front of us and we ran towards the two sliding glass doors, but ten feet away from them I grabbed Tara's arm, pulling her to a halt.

"Fuck it – look!"

A silver Mercedes with tinted windows came to a stop outside the door and two mean-looking men got out, both wearing sunglasses. They stood still, looking straight at the terminal door. We were trapped.

I looked around me.

"In here!"

I grabbed Tara's arm and pulled her into the gents' toilets. An old man stood at a urinal looking down, too engrossed in what he was doing to notice us, and I prayed that all the cubicles were not full of nervous flyers. In front of the first one stood a small traffic cone with a sign on it saying: *Out of Order*. The following two were engaged, but the next had a green strip showing on the lock. I shoved Tara inside, then dragged the sign from the first cubicle, positioning it in front of ours, before joining Tara inside and locking the door.

Tara looked at me, her face panic stricken. She made as if to say something, but I put my index finger to my lips, telling her to keep quiet. I stood on the lavatory seat and gestured for her to do the same. We pushed against the cubicle walls to keep our balance while the old man outside coughed and spat, and soon his feet made a shuffling sound as he made his way out of the toilets.

Tara whispered, "You sure those goons outside were Cleaver's men?"

"I don't know who the fuck they are, but they didn't exactly look like social workers. If he knows we're here he'll have got some back-up organised."

More footsteps outside.

We stood perfectly still, each of us carrying our weight on one leg – the toilet seat not big enough for us both to stand on it properly. For ten minutes we heard the sound of men pissing into urinals, coughing, farting, water running in washbasins and roller towels being pulled. The muscles in my thigh ached and I gritted my teeth, fighting against the dull pain, racking my brains to come up with a way to get out of the airport.

Had those guys with the sunglasses really been Cleaver's men? When I thought about it I realised they had been dressed to attract attention, and that couldn't be good for people in the Secret Service. Whoever they were I was sure that by now Cleaver, Simmons and the other guy would be searching all over the building for us.

The toilets went quiet for a few minutes and we got down off the lavatory to rest our aching legs. Then a door slammed shut and the partition walls rattled – someone had entered the cubicle next to ours. We jumped back up onto the seat. Two minutes later whoever was next door groaned and farted like a tuneless trumpet, and there was a plopping sound followed by a huge sigh of relief.

How long would we have to stay in here? When would Cleaver decide he had arrived too late and stop looking for us?

The man in the cubicle next door started whistling. Tara and I looked at each other and despite being in danger, the ridiculousness of the situation got to us and we fought hard to suppress our laughter.

A minute later we heard the man scrunching up lavatory paper and then the sound of the toilet being flushed. He belched, left the cubicle and walked out into the main terminal building.

"He didn't even wash his hands!" Tara whispered.

We got down off the seat once more and the humour of the moment faded. I still couldn't think how we were going to get out of there. Cleaver may have given up by now, but I wasn't prepared to gamble my life on it.

A minute later we heard more footsteps and jumped back up on the seat.

A voice said, "Where the fuck could they have got to?"

We froze, hardly daring to breathe.

A second voice said, "We can't have lost them. They'll turn up."

My heart thumped inside my chest and I swallowed hard.

"I'll bloody kill 'em," said the first voice.

"They won't be far. If I know Marjorie she'll be in the bloody dress shop getting another bleeding outfit. You should see her wardrobe, stuffed it is. More outfits than a fancy dress shop. Give 'em a bloody credit card and they go nuts."

"We miss this flight and I'll be going more than fucking nuts. Anyway what does she want to buy a dress here for – there's plenty of frigging dress shops in Malaga?"

The men left the toilets.

"Jesus, I thought that was them," Tara said.

"So did I, but they've given me an idea. I need you to go out to the shops. I saw a chemist's out there. I want you to buy a packet of disposable razors, a pair of scissors and two pairs of sunglasses."

"What?"

I outlined my plan to her and she looked horrified, but we didn't have a choice.

"It's either that or we could end up like Deep Throat," I said. Eventually she nodded in agreement, and I took off my shirt and trousers. "Take your clothes off and put these on."

She gave me a strange look.

"Just do it."

Two minutes later Tara was wearing my shirt and trousers, looking like a kid who had dressed up in her father's clothes. I rolled the legs of the trousers up so they showed her bare calves and I rolled up the shirtsleeves past her wrists.

"Hang on a minute, bend forward."

I scruffed up her hair until it was knotted, like it hadn't been combed for weeks, and then pulled it forwards so it hung over her eyes.

"Now you've got to walk like a pissed-off teenager."

"What?"

"You know, slouch, look down at the floor, drag your heels, put your hands in your pockets. Look like your mum just grounded you for a week."

"Jesus Christ, this better work."

I listened out for any sound coming from outside the cubicle, and then opened the door.

"OK. You know what to do. Keep looking down at the floor, and for Christ's sake don't be long."

I watched her walk towards the exit of the toilets. From behind she looked exactly like some angst-ridden youth. I closed the cubicle door and sat on the lavatory, leaning forwards, my head in my hands, praying Cleaver didn't spot her. Minutes went by. *Come on, Tara!* My foot tapped involuntarily. The cubicles either side of me filled up and I listened to more farting and grunting, and then someone knocked on my door. She was back. I unlocked the door and opened it an inch.

A man's voice said, "You all right in there, sir?"

He was wrinkle-faced with a flat cap pulled down low over his eyes, wearing a luminous yellow jacket that bore the word 'Maintenance', and I realised it was the attendant.

"Yes, of course. Bit of tummy trouble, but I'll be fine."

"Don't mind me, sir, you take your time. Only some joker's moved the Out of Order sign."

"Oh, I see."

"Trouble is someone's used the one down at the end that doesn't flush. Who says this is a crap job, eh, sir?"

He chuckled at his own humour and I wondered how many times he'd told the same joke. I shut the door.

For God's sake, Tara, don't come back now!

The maintenance man whistled an unrecognisable tune and I heard the sloshing sound of a mop being dipped in a bucket and then a shushing sound as it was pushed backwards and forwards over the tiled floor. The maintenance man's footsteps moved further away, and then I heard the sound of a cubicle door being pushed open and him saying, "God! Jesus!", and I imagined him holding his nose, fighting to keep down his lunch.

A minute later his fading footsteps indicated he had left the toilets, presumably to get something strong and powerful to deal with the stench of cubicle one.

Thirty seconds later someone knocked on my cubicle and I heard Tara call my name in an urgent whisper. I opened the door and pulled her inside.

"There's a maintenance man out there," I said.

"I know. I walked in earlier and saw him. I've been outside for the last five minutes waiting for him to leave."

"Did you get it?"

She handed me the bag and I looked inside.

"OK. You'd better get to it."

"You sure you want this?"

"Just do it."

I knelt on the floor with my head over the lavatory pan and she got to work with the scissors.

"Get as close as you can, but leave the middle."

My hair dropped into the pan and I began to feel cool air on my scalp. Five minutes later she finished with the scissors and began with the razor, the blade jamming up with hair and tugging.

"Ouch! Fuck this."

I took off the top of the cistern, cupped my hand and splashed water over my head.

"Rub it in."

With the remains of my hair wet, she continued to shave my head, but it wasn't much better – like shaving in cold water – except my head felt ten times more sensitive than my face, and I grimaced in pain. By the time she finished she had got through three razors and my scalp was cold, wet and sore.

"I've nicked you a couple of times," she said.

"I'll get over it. Now it's your turn."

Her gaze wandered over my new hairstyle and she put her hand to her mouth to suppress a laugh. I put my finger to my lips to tell her to keep quiet – someone was pissing hard into one of the urinals. But then my face started to crack up and I clamped my hand over my mouth to hold in my hysterical laughter. Tears ran over my hand and my body convulsed and then I reminded myself that Cleaver was waiting outside to turn us into toast, and I pulled myself out of it.

"Jesus, do I have to have a goddam Mohican?" she whispered.

"I'll just cut it short – no Mohican, OK?"

She knelt down and I went to work on her hair, cutting it down to an inch in length, revealing her slender neck. I finished the job, brushed off her shoulders and told her to stand up.

She looked at me with an expression that said: *Well?*

Crazy as it seemed, I thought it suited her. "Hang on a minute. It's not finished yet."

I opened the cubicle and peered out, making sure there was no one there, and then quickly moved over to the wall-mounted liquid soap dispenser and filled my cupped hand with the creamy pink solution before nipping back into the cubicle and closing the door behind me.

"Bend forward."

I rubbed the solution into her hair and teased it into spikes.

"That's it – we're punks. Just need you to go and buy me some clothes and then we're finished."

Tara put on the sunglasses. She was unrecognisable. She went out into the shopping mall and came back five minutes later with a black T-shirt and a pair of jeans, two or three sizes too big for me.

"Give me the scissors."

I stuck the pointed end through the material of T-shirt and tore diagonal rips in it, then did the same to the trousers. Suitably ripped, I put on my new clothes along with my sunglasses, and rolled up my trousers so they looked like Tara's.

"OK, let's go."

It was time to see if our disguises would fool Cleaver.

I opened the door and caught a glimpse of my new look in the mirror – it was pure Sex Pistols. A man walked in and saw us exiting the cubicle. He sneered at us.

"Dirty perverts!"

We brushed past him and once in the main terminal building made our way to the exit, shuffling along, shoulders hunched, looking down at the floor, and this time there was no Mercedes or mean-looking guys in sunglasses standing outside. The sliding glass doors opened and I glanced over the rims of my sunglasses, scanning the car park for any sign of Cleaver, but saw nothing unusual. To my left was a taxi rank and I led Tara towards it.

The driver looked at me with suspicion and disapproval written all over his face, but I opened the door and we got in.

"The docks. As fast as you can," I said.

"All right, mate. What's the hurry?"

"We're late, of course, what do you think?"

"Only asking, keep your hair on." He chuckled to himself. "You got any money, mate?"

"Of course we have."

Tara pulled out some banknotes from her trouser pocket and held it up.

"Robbed a bank have you?"

He shifted the cab into gear and pulled away with Tara and I still looking out for a tall thin man wearing a pinstriped suit.

"Is there a boat to the Isle of Man tonight?" I asked.

"Nah. Not 'til tomorrow morning, mate."

Shit. We'd have to hide out somewhere until then. But in a city the size of Liverpool that wouldn't be too difficult, would it?

Chapter 18

I awoke to find myself looking up at a mass of green foliage and it took a several seconds for me to remember where I was. Tara lay next me and she rubbed her eyes.

"What time is it?" she asked.

I looked at my watch. It was 8.15am.

"It's breakfast time."

My stomach felt painfully empty.

The previous night the cab driver had dropped us off at the docks and we had wandered along a main road until we had stumbled across a patch of ground that had been cultivated – presumably as an antidote to the drabness of the city. Unwilling to risk booking into a hotel while Cleaver and his men where searching for us, we had crashed out amongst the bushes and had drifted off to sleep at around 3.30 am. Now the rush hour was in full swing, the sound of traffic acting as our alarm clock. Emerging from our bush, I stretched and ran a hand over my face, scratching at my whiskers. My skin felt sticky and in need of a wash.

Making our way back towards Albert Docks, we came across a burger restaurant. "Two cheeseburgers and two coffees please."

"Do you want fries with that, sir?"

I shook my head, thinking I'd heard that line somewhere before. Tara made her way over to a table in the corner and slumped down onto a chair, still tired after a broken night's sleep. A minute later, carrying a tray with our breakfast, I joined her and we bit into our burgers, the soft bread and the cheesy-meat filling mixing into a paste in my mouth.

"I'm going to the bathroom to wash," Tara said.

Sipping my coffee, I wondered where Cleaver was and if he had still been at the airport when we had crept out of the toilets. We may have fooled him – after all we had only met him once; it would be difficult for him to see through our disguise.

I finished my coffee and then Tara returned.

"I feel a lot better for that," she said.

"My turn."

I went into the gents' and approached the washbasin, looking at myself in the mirror, getting used to the shape of my head and ears, which now they hadn't got any hair around them seemed to stick out more. I put on my sunglasses to see the full effect. Yes, Cleaver could well have been in the car park; there was no way he would have recognised us.

"Johnny Rotten eat your heart out."

After splashing water on my face, I dried myself off, went back into the restaurant and sat down opposite Tara.

"You getting to like your new look?" she asked.

"Oh, yeah. Like it's really me."

She laughed and said: Sleeping under a bush in Liverpool, the home of the Beatles, with a real punk rocker – my Mom would be proud of me."

We each drank another coffee and then it was time to leave for the docks.

Fifty yards from the boat I slowed down.

"What's up?" Tara said. "You think Cleaver might be here?"

"If I was him I'd think about it, wouldn't you?"

We stopped, both of us looking around for anything suspicious.

"Danny, if we don't take the boat where are we going to go? We've got to get that disk."

She was right. To get to the Isle of Man we had to take either the boat or the plane and Cleaver was probably staking out the airport right now, unaware that we had seen him yesterday, thinking we would try to fly out of the country. He was resourceful and I guessed he must have checked out all the planes leaving Elstree yesterday, and someone, probably the guy in the control tower, had told him Harry had taken two last minute passengers to Liverpool. Of course he couldn't know that we had come into the country from the Isle of Man – we'd bought our tickets with cash and travelled under the name of Johnson – so there was no way except by a wild guess that he could imagine we would be trying to get back to the island. I was being too cautious – it would be OK.

"Let's get on that boat."

We bought our tickets and joined the other foot passengers, making our way onto the ferry, the sea breeze catching our faces. Looking up at the rust streaks that stained the once brilliant white paintwork, and the huge rivets in the solid steel sides of the boat, I wondered for a moment how such a heavy vessel filled with cars could actually float.

Inside the main saloon holidaymakers and day-trippers, laden with shopping bags, tried in vain to control their excited children who ran around shrieking. The large open space with its rows of seats was too exposed and my survival instinct told me that if Cleaver or one of his men were on board they would spot us immediately – even with our new appearance. In any case, we were an oddity; punk rockers died out years ago and we were being stared at by a sea of incredulous faces who seemed to think we were a couple of deadbeats.

I looked around and saw a woman wearing a uniform sitting behind a small desk. Above her head a sign said: *Cabins.*

I tugged Tara's arm and we approached the desk.

"Could we have a cabin please?"

The woman looked up at my Mohican hairstyle and her welcoming smile faded. I wondered why anyone would want to be a punk rocker and suffer such reactions – but then of course, that was the point.

"Have you booked?" she asked.

"No, I didn't realise you had to."

She sneered at me as if I was an idiot, then looked at a clipboard with the names of the passengers who had reserved cabins.

"Sorry we only have the luxury cabins available now."

She gave me a gleeful, fuck-you smile.

"Luxury is fine," I said.

She looked defeated, and reluctantly reached for a key.

Tara paid the lady in cash.

"Here's your change. Upstairs, along the corridor and it's on your left."

Before I could say thank you she was already looking down at her clipboard again, as if we didn't exist.

We climbed the stairs and found the cabin.

"Hardly my idea of luxury," Tara said.

It had two narrow bunks, one on each side, and in between the bunks, on top of a cheap-looking teak bedside cabinet, sat a tray with two plain white cups, a small kettle, some packets of instant coffee, teabags, sugar and UHT milk. A shabby limp curtain in a pink floral design hung to the left of a rust-stained porthole. At the foot of the bed on the left-hand side was a door. I opened it.

"We've got a shower," I said. "Useful."

"And a TV," Tara added.

She picked up the remote, pushed the on/off button and a few seconds later Sky News came on and the newsreader announced:

Police have still not identified the body in the burned-out car at the Kingsley Arms Hotel in Watford. Initial reports suggest the car was carrying a terrorist bomb that went off by accident. An incident line has been set up and police want to hear from anyone who was in the vicinity yesterday afternoon who may have seen the car arriving at the hotel.

"Jesus Christ! That's Elizabeth's car!" Tara shouted.

We gazed at the burned out wreck and I was reminded that we were the ones who were supposed to have been blown up in it. The sight of the charred and twisted metal sent a shiver through me.

The newsreader moved on to another topic and for a few moments Tara and I stared at the screen, in silence, until Tara eventually said, "Danny, do you think if we get that disk to Cleaver he'll stop? I mean is he ever going to leave us alone?"

I really didn't know – the man was a fanatic. Blowing up convents, putting a bomb in our car – he was scared of what we knew getting out, that was certain. If I showed him what evidence we had and he wasn't impressed, what then? Would he kill us anyway?

"Let's just hope it does the trick."

"Have you thought about how we get it to him yet?"

"Something'll come to me."

We docked three and a half hours later, the throbbing engines fell silent and someone knocked on our door.

"Isle of Man!"

We waited in the cabin as long as we could, allowing the other passengers to disembark before us. With my punk clothes and haircut

I was feeling like a freak and I didn't want to stand around getting gawped at. Ten minutes later the steward knocked on the door again.

"OK. Let's go and see if that disk is waiting for us," I said, thinking that if it had got lost in the post we were going to have to spend the rest of our lives on the run.

At the Sunshine Hotel, the receptionist looked up, suspicion on her face.

"Can I help you?" she asked.

"We'd like to check in," I said.

"Do you have a reservation?"

"No." I removed my sunglasses. "It's me, Mr Johnson. We were here until yesterday morning, remember?"

She stared at me, her mouth falling open, and then said, "Oh! Um… yes, I didn't recognise you."

I smiled at her in a reassuring way.

"Well, that's probably a good thing. We've been to a fancy dress party – a punk rocker do – you know, like vicars and tarts, only not vicars and tarts – punks."

She laughed nervously.

"Oh, I see. Yes. Very good."

"Well it would have been a shame not to have entered into the spirit of things, wouldn't it?"

"Yes, indeed. Um… yes we do have a room."

I filled out the registration card.

"Did you find your credit card, Mr Johnson?"

"Er… no. Still waiting for the new one to come. We'll pay cash again. Do you want us to pay now?"

"No, that'll be OK. You can pay when you leave."

She handed me the key to room 403.

"I was expecting something in the post. Could you check to see if anything's arrived?"

She went into the small office behind the reception desk and returned a minute later.

"No, I don't think so – there's nothing here."

Damn – it had to be here. The postal service can't be that slow – the goddam island's only thirty miles from one end to the other.

"Are you sure?"

"Yes, I'm quite sure. Was it important? I hope it wasn't your credit card."

It's our fucking lives.

"No, it's not my credit card, but it *is* important. If something turns up you'll let us know?"

"Of course, Mr Johnson."

We turned to make our way to the room.

"Enjoy your stay," she said.

Without that disk it would be a short one. Next stop Borneo, or Thailand.

We had only walked five paces before she called after us.

"Mr Johnson, just a moment, sir!"

A weedy looking young man about twenty-five years old, wearing a black waistcoat over a white shirt approached the front desk.

The receptionist said, "Terry, have you seen anything in the post for Mr Johnson?"

"Yes, something did arrive; I put it in the safe."

I closed my eyes in prayerful thanks.

"Ah, you're in luck, Mr Johnson."

Two minutes later the envelope bearing my own handwriting was safely in my grasp, my fingers feeling the outline of the disk inside it. I thanked the receptionist, and then we stepped into the lift and pressed the button for the fourth floor. As it began its ascent I leaned back against the fire extinguisher that was attached to the inside wall, and then sighed in relief.

"You know, we're going to have to get another computer to make some copies of this. Do you want to get one now or shall we leave it?" I said.

The lift stopped at the fourth floor and the door opened.

"We can get one now if you like." Tara said.

I pushed the button for the ground floor, the doors closed and we began to descend, but then the lift immediately slowed down. Someone on the third floor must have called it.

It stopped, the doors opened and suddenly I found myself staring into the face of my worst nightmare…

Chapter 19

Before me was the unmistakable, impassive, and imperious face of the man who had brought darkness into my life – Alistair Cleaver; dressed in his pinstriped suit and white shirt. On his left stood Ronald Simmons – a thickset man with the intimidating presence of a nightclub doorman. Another mean-looking bastard stood on Cleaver's right – and just behind the three of them was… Uncle Jim!

My mind reeled. Uncle Jim of the CIA – Tara's loving uncle, working with Cleaver? Had we been set up all along? Of course! The CIA and the British Secret Service would be sharing information, swapping weapons technology. Uncle Jim had led us into Cleaver's clutches – we had been fucked from the start!

Along with his two henchmen, Cleaver looked at us, still poker-faced, no angry expressions, no attempt to grab us. He took a step forward, then one back, as if he was wondering whether there was enough room for us all in the lift. For a moment I felt as if I were in a strange dream, invisible to everyone, everything happening in slow motion. Then it dawned on me: he didn't recognise us. He wasn't looking at his quarry – the two people with the knowledge and power to destroy him and embarrass the government – he was looking at two scruffy punk rockers who were taking up too much space in the lift, inconveniencing him.

A second later he seemed to decide we were too insignificant to impede someone as important as Alistair Cleaver, and he stepped forward again. Tara gasped. She grabbed my arm and edged to the back of the lift, and then Cleaver caught sight of the terror on her face. His eyes narrowed and he concentrated his gaze first on Tara and then on me, and I watched him begin to salivate, like a dog awakening to find a juicy rat in its kennel. We were trapped. Flight was impossible. Now we must fight – or we were finished.

Cleaver's right hand slipped inside his jacket, and his movement seemed to flick a switch deep inside me. I grabbed the fire extinguisher off the wall, raised it above my head, and just as Cleaver's hand turned to level his pistol at me, its silencer confirming (as if any confirmation was needed) that he had come to assassinate us, I brought the extinguisher down on his wrist, knocking the gun from his hand, and then charged at him, my shoulder hitting his chest, sending him backwards.

Ronald Simmons made a move for his gun and I kicked him hard in the groin. He cried out and staggered back. I bent down to pick up Cleaver's gun, and as I came up with it in my hand, the other heavy was straightening his arm, almost ready to fire. In that fraction of a second I knew he was going to pull his trigger before I could pull mine. It was all over.

Suddenly the man's arm was knocked away and I saw Uncle Jim punch him in the side of his head. The man fell and Uncle Jim grabbed and twisted his wrist, forcing him to release the gun. Confused, I held my pistol pointing at Cleaver and Simmons. Then Uncle Jim said, "Easy, Danny. You used one of these before?"

"Sure I have," I lied.

Was Uncle Jim with us or against us?

"Back against the wall," Uncle Jim said to the three men.

He gestured with the pistol and they did as they were told. Still looking at the men, Uncle Jim said, "Tara, get out of here."

She stepped out of the lift and I saw her trembling. With his left hand, he took out his room key and threw it to her.

"This room here," he said, nodding to the door opposite the lift. "Open it."

She fumbled around for a few seconds, then got it open.

"Now step away from the door."

She moved away.

"Inside," Uncle Jim said. "Either one of you make a wrong move and I put a hole in your boss. Be a shame to make a mess of his nice suit wouldn't it?"

The two entered the bedroom.

To Cleaver he said, "You. Fold your arms in front of you."

Uncle Jim stood behind him, his left hand on Cleaver's shoulder and the gun barrel pushed into the nape of his neck. Slowly they made their way into the bedroom and Uncle Jim said to Tara and myself, "Follow me inside and shut the door."

Inside the room Uncle Jim spoke to the two heavies.

"You two assholes – on the floor – face down. Put your hands behind your backs. Move slowly."

They did as they were told and he turned to Cleaver.

"You sit in the chair. Put your hands on your head."

Cleaver sat and interlocked his fingers, resting them on top of his oily hair.

"How old are you?" Uncle Jim said.

Cleaver looked puzzled.

"Hey, I asked you a fucking question."

"Fifty-seven," he said.

"You want to make fifty-eight you keep your hands on that stupid head of yours."

Uncle Jim looked at me.

"Were you ever a boy scout?" He saw the puzzled look on my face. "Can you tie a knot?"

I nodded.

"Good. Put that gun down, unplug those two bedside lamps and use the cable to truss up these two turkeys ready for Thanksgiving – and don't be kind. I want to see the flex cut deep into the flesh, know what I mean?"

I put the gun on the bed and followed his instructions.

Uncle Jim looked at Tara.

"What in God's name have you done to your hair? No, don't tell me, we'll get to it later."

"How did you find us?" she asked

"Right now I'm asking the questions."

When I had the two men tied up Uncle Jim inspected the knots.

"Not bad." He looked at me directly and said, "That is some haircut, son." He held my gaze for a few seconds before slowly shaking his head from side to side. "Roll these two shit-heads over and search them."

I turned them over, searched inside their jackets and pulled out Simmons' pistol.

"Bring that here," Uncle Jim said.

I put it down beside him.

"Now check their ankles."

I hesitated for an instant.

"Do it, Danny."

I did as I was told and found a small pistol in an ankle holster strapped to Simmons' leg. I put it with the others.

"Quite a little arsenal we have here. Now I hope you guys don't embarrass too easily." He looked at Tara. "I hope you don't either." Then he turned to me. "Danny, I want you to take down their pants."

"What?"

"Don't go all shy on me. I know you're not that way inclined. Just do it."

It was an instant before I remembered that pants equals trousers to an American, and, although the request still seemed bizarre, I undid the trousers of the two heavies, pulling them down to their ankles.

Uncle Jim looked at Cleaver. "Stand up, Mr boss-man, and remember what I said about making your next birthday."

Cleaver stood up and I undid his trousers, letting them drop to the floor, revealing his purple boxer shorts.

"Pretty fancy," Uncle Jim said. "You can sit back down now, and you two assholes can roll over on your stomachs again."

Uncle Jim told Tara to sit on the bed and then he turned to me.

"You sit next to her."

I sat.

"Good. Now we're all comfy we're going to have a little talk."

He looked at Tara. "So, what the hell have you got yourself into?"

I began to speak.

"It's all on –"

"Shut up, Danny, I'm not talking to you, yet."

"Uncle Jim, listen to him. *Please,*" Tara said.

He looked at me and I sensed I had permission to talk.

"It's all here on this disk." I held up the envelope.

"What is?"

Tara said, "Everything. Just look at it Uncle Jim."

I said, "He can't – we don't have a computer."

"You're in luck," Uncle Jim said. "I have one. It's in the cupboard – you can get it out. I'm intrigued."

I booted up the computer, put in the disk, opened up the file and showed it to Uncle Jim.

"Looks like a load of words to me. You wrote it – you read it. Gentlemen, Danny here's gonna read us a story."

I began reading. When I reached the part about Tara being kept in the sanatorium against her will. Uncle Jim said, "Shit!" He looked at Tara, his face showing a mixture of anger and concern.

"Keep going, Danny," he said.

I read the part about me finding her in the gardens and rescuing her, and he interrupted again.

"Is this true?" he asked Tara.

She nodded. He looked at me, and his face seemed to soften.

"Go on, son."

When I had finished my story, I picked up the computer and carried it over to Uncle Jim, showing him the pictures we had taken inside the laboratory. Then I showed them to Cleaver.

Uncle Jim was red faced; he looked like an angry bulldog.

"We've never met, Cleaver, but we've spoken. Guess you know who I am."

Cleaver nodded.

"And you knew all along this was my niece you were trying to put away – I told you who she was when I asked you to tell her and Danny here what you knew about the High Priest."

"No offence," Cleaver said. "It's just business. You know the game, old boy."

Uncle Jim leapt at Cleaver and punched him hard in the solar plexus. Cleaver heaved and doubled up, wrapping his arms around his stomach, gasping for air.

Five seconds later Uncle Jim said, "What did I tell you about keeping your hands on your head?"

He pointed the gun at Cleaver who, still grimacing, put his hands back up there. A trickle of sweat ran down his forehead.

"You Brits have been naughty boys," Uncle Jim said. "Danny here writes a good story." He turned to me. "What are you planning to do with it?"

"We were trying to get a copy of this to Cleaver via his secretary. Unfortunately Cleaver tried to blow us up, but he blew her up instead, along with the disk."

"Careless," Uncle Jim said. "Good secretaries are hard to come by."

I looked at Cleaver. His passive smugness had disappeared and he had a weird look about him. It was a mixture of rage and confusion – the sort of look I had seen on the faces of street people – the ones who scream at the traffic, but don't know why.

"She was going to let him know that I have five copies of it with lawyers in different countries. Each of them has instructions to send it to *The Times*, *The Washington Post* and *Le Figaro* at the end of the month."

Tara remained impassive as she listened to my lie.

"The instruction can only be changed by a call from me and a code word. Tara has to call too with her own code word. The only instruction we plan to give them is to delay the order by one month, so if anything happens to either one of us the story will get out."

"We'd simply deny it," Cleaver said.

Uncle Jim looked at Cleaver.

"You're lying, Cleaver. If all it took was a denial you wouldn't be chasing around trying to kill these two. I think Danny here's done a pretty good job. It seems like you ought to be glad you didn't kill him or my niece – if you'd killed her I sure as hell would have killed you." Uncle Jim scratched his chin, pondering for a moment. "There's something I've got to do. Danny, hold this. You ever shot anyone before?"

"Er, No."

"Today could be your day. If that fucker moves, you have my permission to shoot him. This is a once in a lifetime offer, Danny – after this you don't get to kill anyone else. If he moves, take it. I'll be back soon and if you've shot him I'll tell everyone it was me, so you don't have to worry, OK?"

I nodded. Uncle Jim left the room, taking the disk with him, and I felt the lethal lump of metal in my hand, and the horror and thrill of having power over life and death under my sticky fingers. Suddenly I felt two-feet taller, and I understood why the streets were full of kids who would rather carry pistols than footballs.

I kept the barrel pointing at Cleaver and said, "How did you find us?"

"It was easy."

He smiled at me in a smug way, showing his distain for me, and I was irritated, because with the gun in my hand I felt I was due a little more respect.

"So, enlighten me."

"You left your jacket in the hedge. Careless. Inside the pocket we found a grubby little leaflet from this hotel, offering a free meal – I was sure you'd come back to claim it. The man in the control tower at Elstree was very helpful. He told us a pilot had picked up a couple of last minute passengers before taking off for Liverpool – so it wasn't hard to work out that you were on your way back here."

"But you didn't come straight here, did you?"

"No, Liverpool first, but the control tower said you'd landed ten minutes before us and left the airport."

I realised we had gone punk and spent a night sleeping rough in Liverpool for no reason. They had probably taken off while we were still hiding in the damned toilets.

The urge to rattle the smug son-of-a-bitch became overwhelming.

"Clever, Cleaver. So clever he blows up his own secretary."

His expression changed and I knew I was pushing the right button.

"What a stupid thing to do. You're such an asshole aren't you? Poor woman blown to bits by her murdering boss… You know you really shouldn't play with fire, Cleaver. You'll get burnt yourself one day."

His chest began to heave up and down, as if he was going into some kind of spasm.

"She seemed like such a nice woman, although what she was doing working for an idiot like you is beyond me. She told us a lot about you. Oh, yes. We had a very interesting discussion before you killed her. Was she just an expendable piece of rubbish to you, like the nuns in the convent?"

His face reddened and his cheek twitched involuntarily.

"Shut up!" he said, taking his hands off his head.

"Hands back up there, Cleaver. *Now!*"

I stretched out my arm and looked down the barrel of the gun, aiming right between his eyes. He folded his arms in front of his chest and then he said defiantly, "My arms are tired, Danny. I think I'll just keep them here."

For a moment I was confused. He was supposed to be compliant – I had the gun.

"So now what are you going to do, Danny. Shoot me?" He chuckled.

Now it was my cheeks that flushed. I stepped closer to him.

"Put them back on your head, Cleaver!"

"No."

I wanted him to feel afraid, to be in fear of his life, and the bastard looked anything but that. *I* held the gun, *I* had the means to end *his* life, and yet he stood there mocking me. I felt the power draining away from me.

"Put them up on your fucking head, you asshole!"

He smiled and shook his head and I desperately wanted to push the barrel of the gun up his nose. I stepped forward.

Suddenly he leapt up and with both hands made a grab for the gun, but my adrenalin-fuelled body reacted quickly and I jumped back, out of reach. He froze – the look on his face telling me he knew he had made a mistake – knew he had crossed the line. I still had the gun, he had given me the opportunity to take up Uncle Jim's offer, and I could kill the son-of-a-bitch, right now. And why not? It would be self-defence – he had tried to kill me, hadn't he?

In terror he looked down at the end of the gun barrel, and I realised he was waiting for the muffled sound of a silenced bullet. He stood bent forward, both arms still outstretched, and my heart pounded like a jackhammer, the mad desire to kill arising within me like some dark primeval instinct. My clammy hand gripped the gun, my slippery finger teasing the trigger. In my head I saw flashing images of the High Priest, Michael Richards, and the Mother Superior flying through the air. I saw the row of cots with the babies fathered by the High Priest, Elizabeth getting into the car at Watford, then the haunting face of Virginie Lavelle, and I knew this man before me, this evil bastard, deserved to die. I *could* do it now – with one wiggle of my finger I could rid the world of him. I increased the pressure on the trigger. Just a fraction of an ounce more and it would be over. The barrel began to shake, and I saw my father, full of despair and hate, lying dead, his heart given out after he had fought the politicians who had cheated him – the people who cheated us all – people like Cleaver. Now I could strike back! My lips pressed into a line, my eyebrows knitted together, the muscles in my forearm taut, like cords of steel.

Take it! Take your chance! Finish the bastard!

And then it was as if a great firework exploded in my head, and a spark of reason shot up out of the flames of my anger, before descending and smothering them like a wet blanket, and I felt the tide of my rage subsiding. My ears filled with a rushing sound and my consciousness seemed to be in a space above my head, looking down at what I was doing. I was not like Cleaver – not one of them – but for a few seconds I had wanted to be, craved to be. I had wanted to be a savage – to take a man's life. My consciousness seemed to return to my body and I was once again seeing things through my own physical eyes. No, I wouldn't pull the trigger – I wouldn't kill a man if I could avoid it – and I knew Cleaver believed that about me.

He hadn't moved – his eyes were still fixed on the gun, and I stepped forwards, lifted it and brought it down hard on the top of his head, the butt of the pistol making a dull thumping sound as it struck. Maybe I hadn't been completely civilised. He slumped back down in the chair, groaning in agony and rocking backwards and forwards, clutching his wounded skull.

"Ah, you've got your hands back on your head," I said. "That's a good boy."

The power was back with me now, and I felt like Clint Eastwood in *Dirty Harry*. I pointed the gun at the window and squeezed the trigger, the silencer muffling the sound of the explosion. The bullet made a neat hole in the glass.

"You know, Cleaver, the balance of this gun isn't right. You really should get it checked."

I sounded like an expert and Cleaver stopped rocking for an instant and looked up at me, stunned.

"I've never shot such a useless pile of shit. The gun I mean, not you." Which was true of course – I hadn't fired any gun before.

A noise came from behind me, I looked around and saw Tara with her foot on Simmons' neck.

"He tried to get up," she said.

I looked at the man beside him who shook his head, as if to tell me he would behave, and then I faced Cleaver again.

"You disgust me, Cleaver. What a worthless piece of crap you are. What the fuck do you think you have been doing with your life? You play these stupid, school-boy spy games – only you're fucking around with real weapons – and you kid yourself you're doing it for the good of the country? Do you think we want you to be out there getting hold of gases to kill the rest of the world? I didn't see that in the manifesto last election time."

"You're naïve, Avery. The world isn't made of icing sugar. If there weren't people like me you stupid saps couldn't sleep at night."

"You're wrong, Cleaver. It's because of people like you that I can't sleep at night. The gas you were trying to get hold of had no defensive capability. Use it and you'd wipe out millions at a stroke."

"It would have been a deterrent."

"Bullshit! For it to be a deterrent other countries would have to know you had it. When exactly were you going to let the world know, Cleaver? Going to put it out on Sky News and CNN were you? I don't think so. You'd have stockpiled it, just waiting for some conflict to take place, and then some mad bastard who'd been deprived of a chemistry set when he was a kid would push the button. Then what – Armageddon?"

"We would have been invincible!" Cleaver barked.

I saw the insanity of the man. In his sick, nihilistic mind he would have become a national hero. *He* would have been the one responsible for giving Britain its 'invincibility' – its ability to out-kill any other nation.

"Was it Britain you were trying to make invincible, or was it yourself? Somewhere inside your stupid head there's a great void, Cleaver, some feeling of inadequacy. Were you unloved as a child? Did they pick on you in the playground?"

He swallowed hard and looked down at the floor.

"Maybe you were the one they never picked for the football team? I bet that was you, Cleaver. I bet you spent your time alone in the dormitory, pulling the legs off spiders, hoping some day someone would love you. Well, no one does, Cleaver. The only people who did were your mother and your secretary – but you killed her."

He began to shake violently and then uttered a sound halfway between a sob and a squeak. He covered his face with his hands, heaved, and then threw up, coughing and gagging, sick dribbling through his fingers and onto his trousers. The smell of bile filled the air, and I felt disgusted and at the same time sorry for the pathetic man in front of me, gibbering and sobbing while the contents of his stomach soaked into his clothes.

Puzzled by the strength of his reaction, I stepped back, away from the smell.

"Tara, I think you'd better get him a towel."

She got him one and he mopped himself up, still snivelling, and then he dropped the white towel, stained with streaks of coffee coloured puke, on the floor beside his chair.

The door opened. It was Uncle Jim.

"Jesus, what a mess. What have you done to him?"

I wondered that myself.

"I'm disappointed in you, Danny. I was expecting you to have shot the creep."

He tossed a computer disk onto Cleaver's lap.

"That's a copy for you."

Uncle Jim looked at me holding the gun.

"You want me to take that, son?"

I looked down at it. A part of me didn't want to give it up; the feeling of power was addictive, but with some reluctance I eventually handed it over to Uncle Jim and then said, "What do we do now?"

"We wait," he said.

For some reason I didn't feel the slightest inclination to ask what we were waiting for. I just stared at Cleaver, smelling of sick, defeated, pathetic, and somehow I knew the nightmare was over.

Twenty minutes later someone knocked on the door.

"Get that would you, Danny?" Uncle Jim said.

I opened the door just enough to see who was there. It was the receptionist holding a large white envelope.

"Oh, Mr Johnson," she said. "I have a fax, but it's for –"

"It's all right, I'll take it. Thanks."

I closed the door.

"Open it up," Uncle Jim said.

Inside were four sheets of paper. I studied the first two and my mouth gaped like a goldfish. I read them a second time, unable to believe my eyes. Tara and I had been made members of the USA Diplomatic Corps, and the signature next to the seal at the bottom of the fax was that of none other than the President of the United States himself. The other two sheets were copies of the first two. I stared open-mouthed at Uncle Jim. How had he managed to get the president to sign something like that – and so quickly? Did he work for the CIA or did he run it?

Uncle Jim took a copy of each fax and held them out to Cleaver.

"Read," he said. "I hope your hands are clean."

Cleaver held the faxes in his unsteady hands and read.

Uncle Jim said, "Diplomatic immunity. These two are off limits. Rules of the game, old boy. You get the picture, Cleaver? Leave these two alone and if you do, then all this shit you've been trying to pull just might stay hidden, right?"

Cleaver nodded.

"Good. Those copies are for you, Cleaver, just in case you forget. The other two stay with Tara and Danny here."

Uncle Jim looked at me.

"OK. Danny, Tara, take off their ties and remove their belts from their pants."

Twenty minutes later, using ties and belts, Cleaver's legs were tied to the front legs of his chair and his hands were strapped together behind it and tied to its back legs. He was going nowhere. Simmons and the other heavy's legs were tied together and their arms linked behind the radiator pipe. Tara went down to reception to borrow some sticky tape. When she returned we gagged all three of them.

Uncle Jim packed his small suitcase, placing the guns inside along with his computer and the few possessions he had with him. We left in his hired car and drove to the airport by the coast road. When we found a track leading to the top of a cliff we reversed the car to the edge and hurled the guns into the sea.

At the airport Uncle Jim bought three tickets to Paris and when we were safely cruising at thirty-three thousand feet, Tara said, "So how the hell did you find us?"

"Easy. When you called me, I heard someone talking in the background. They mentioned the TT races."

I remembered trying to distract the waitress who had brought some tea to our room. She had been trying to listen to Tara's conversation with her uncle.

"I'm a biker for Christ's sake. Every biker knows where the TT races are held, so I just used a few contacts to get into the phone records of the major hotels on the island and find someone who had called my number. Easier to work that way around than to try to trace the number from the States."

"Pretty cool," Tara said. "But how the hell did you get us made into diplomats?"

Uncle Jim coughed and looked a little uneasy.

"Favours, that's all. Some people paying some debts."

I got the feeling he wasn't being entirely honest with us, but however he had done it I was grateful. With our immunity and the threat of my story getting out, we would be pretty much untouchable in any country.

We landed in Paris and thirty minutes later sat in an airport restaurant sipping coffee.

Uncle Jim said to me, "You know I'm grateful for what you did for Tara – getting her out of that sanatorium. Seems I may have misjudged you when we first met. That was quite a story you read out back there. Pity you can't make it into a film – it could be worth a lot of money."

"I don't need any thanks for rescuing Tara; having her with me is reward enough."

"Hey, I'm impressed. Better hold on to this one, Tara."

I said, "You know, when the lift doors opened and I saw you standing there, I thought for a minute you were with them."

"You did? I just went for the lift and found three other guys waiting for it. Took me a while to recognise you though, with that haircut. Tara I would have recognised, but I couldn't see her behind that Cleaver guy. Tall son-of-a-bitch isn't he? You know Danny, you've got to do something about that Mohican, it really isn't cool."

He was right. A few minutes later I found myself once again in the toilets of an international airport, cutting my hair. With the Mohican gone and my head totally shaved I wouldn't draw quite as much attention. I ran my hand over my smooth head and looked at myself in the mirror. It wasn't bad. Not bad at all. I stood there admiring myself and thought about what Uncle Jim had said about being paid for my story, wondering if maybe there was a way we could get some money for it without giving up our bargaining chip.

I returned to Tara and Uncle Jim, who said, "Jesus H Christ, Yul Brynner lives!"

Tara kissed my head and then Uncle Jim said, "You two are coming back to the States I take it?"

Tara and I looked at each other. A smile played on her lips and I sensed she was reading my mind.

"You know, now that we've sorted out all this business with Cleaver, I think it would be a good idea if Tara and I went back to where it all began. Besides there are a few questions still unanswered and it would be a shame not to tie up all the loose ends."

"Looks like you got yourself a real reporter for a boyfriend. Can't let it go, huh?" He leaned closer towards me. "You sure you aren't getting into something dangerous, Danny?"

"Promise. I think we've had enough of that kind of excitement."

We said goodbye and then spent an hour buying new clothes. Punk was never going to be our style.

Chapter 20

The scenery along the road from Nice airport seemed different now, my view of it changed by the passing of events rather than time. Everything looked newer and fresher.

We entered Saint Pierre through the stone archway and I parked the car where I had left Sylvie's van after returning from the sanatorium with Tara. Back then I had been convinced Tara was insane and dangerous. I took her hand and we walked through the town, passing the Pizza Roma where I had taken Tara the first night we had met, and I remembered her punching me in the solar plexus. To touch her then was to take your life in your hands, now her hand seemed to fit perfectly in mine.

We arrived at the walls of the convent, the tall wooden gates held together by a loose chain and padlock. I pulled them and they parted enough for us to look inside. The place was deserted – no sign of life. The lawns were overgrown and the once immaculately kept flowerbeds looked ragged and in need of attention. In the distance I saw the remains of one of the ruined buildings, destroyed by fire, a few charred beams were all that remained of the roof. In my mind I saw again the image of the Mother Superior, smouldering, lying dead in the great hall, and then the innocent, open face of Michael Richards, whose dream of ending the ageing process and the diseases associated with it had been cruelly terminated by Cleaver's operative. Good destroyed by evil. How different real life was from the movies, where good always triumphs in the end.

Tara and I hadn't spoken for at least ten minutes and I knew she was reliving her own memories of the place, more detailed and intimate than mine. She had spent a year in the convent and had known most of the people in it. I took her hand and we wandered back towards the town square, past a restaurant with people sitting outside, some eating, some drinking coffee and reading newspapers. I moved my arm up around her shoulders.

"What are you thinking?" Tara said.

"Right now I'm thanking my lucky stars that I chose to come here after Eddy Sinclair gave me the sack. Every cloud has a silver lining and all that."

We grinned at each other like two people who had just won the lottery and suddenly I felt a rush of love for her, and it was an innocent, fresh and raw love, the sort I hadn't experienced since I was a schoolboy in short trousers. Not since I had played kiss chase with... Ellen Brady! That was it! At last I had stumbled upon why I had been so drawn to Virginie Lavelle – she was the image of Ellen Brady, my first love!

"What's the matter?" Tara asked.

I shared my realisation and then said, "Ellen Brady... Whatever happened to *her*?"

"Oh. You want I should bore you silly with my first love too?"

I was surprised, but not altogether displeased by Tara's little lapse into jealousy.

We reached the square where at seven years of age I had watched the men playing petanque, the square where Sylvie's grandmother's shop was situated – and there she was! Sylvie was tipping some carrots from a sack into a half-empty green basket outside the shop front. She turned and saw me, but there was no sign of recognition on her face, just puzzlement.

"Sylvie!" I shouted.

We walked towards her.

"Oh, it's you. What happened to your hair? You're not..."

Then I realised what was going through her mind.

"No! Not at all, I'm perfectly healthy. Just a fashion statement, that's all – albeit a bad one."

She looked reassured.

"You remember Tara."

They shook hands.

"So what brings you to Saint Pierre?"

"Oh, we just thought we'd finish our holiday. Got called away a little earlier than we wanted to last time. I heard about the fire."

Sylvie nodded slowly.

"It was tragic. I don't know if the nuns will ever move back in. They said it was an underground explosion – probably natural gas building up for hundreds if not thousands of years, but I don't think they'll ever get to the bottom of it. They say part of the hillside has collapsed in on itself over at the far side of the convent."

"That's terrible," I said.

I swallowed hard and thought about Michael Richards, crushed and entombed forever under so many tons of rock, and a sick feeling swept through my stomach.

Sylvie continued, "One of the nuns was killed – the Mother Superior, but I think they were lucky that more people didn't die. There were babies in there, you know?"

"No, really?" Tara and I shook our heads.

"Apparently they had taken in several women with babies. The mothers had become nuns and they were bringing up the babies under the protection of the convent."

"Well, I suppose that's very charitable of the nuns – very forgiving you might say."

Sylvie nodded her head, but she still looked puzzled by something. "They were dazed and confused when we found them after the fire, I suppose that's natural."

"What happened to them?"

"They went to the hospital for a medical check. After that, I don't know."

I changed the subject.

"How's your grandmother?"

Sylvie looked at me suspiciously and I held my hands up in a surrender gesture.

"Hey, it was just a question."

Seemingly reassured about my motives for asking, she said, "Very well thanks. What's that English expression… sharp as a tack? Are you two staying at the hotel?" She nodded in the direction of the hotel opposite and I remembered the manager with his hideous eye.

"No, we're staying in Nice. The manager wasn't too friendly towards me for some reason, in fact when I was staying here the whole town made me feel as welcome as a cockroach in a fridge."

Sylvie chuckled and said, "It wasn't anything personal; it's just that we don't trust reporters. We had some trouble from one once. A tourist let his three-year-old son walk on the ramparts and he fell off and was killed. There was a reporter from a national newspaper who did a piece on us, saying that health and safety laws were being broken and that we should put up fencing on top of the walls. Some local politicians jumped on the bandwagon saying we should put the wire fencing just about everywhere – and we resisted. Some of us marched in the streets. We didn't want the beauty of our town destroyed just because some irresponsible tourist had allowed his son to get killed. I mean no one in their right mind would allow their son to do what he did. The reporter said we were 'socially irresponsible' and 'backward thinking retards', so when you registered at the hotel and put 'reporter' as your profession, Claude was over to the Café de la Place like a shot to tell us. Sorry we misjudged you."

So that's what it had all been about.

"Thanks for telling me. I thought I was using the wrong soap." Sylvie laughed. "But this Claude character got upset when I tried to find out the name of Virginie Lavelle. Why?"

"Ah, there would be a simple explanation for that. He told me he didn't know her name. When she turned up she wanted to go straight to her room and register later. I think she wasn't feeling too well, and she paid cash – in advance. Claude put the money in his pocket, not through the books, so under the circumstances he wouldn't have been happy about a reporter asking questions. And anyway, he really didn't know who she was."

That explained why I couldn't find her name in the register. There had been no town-wide conspiracy after all. Suddenly I felt foolish for thinking anything so far-fetched.

We carried on talking for another five minutes and then Sylvie said, "Are you going back to Nice now?"

I thought about it for a moment.

"You know, I think I'd like another look at Virginie Lavelle's monument."

I wanted to say a final farewell to her, so Tara and I walked along the edge of the square, then turned left. I looked at my watch. It was 6.05pm and the sun was getting lower in the sky, casting a softer light and longer shadows.

After we entered the cemetery we walked towards the place where Virginie Lavelle lay buried.

Tara nudged me.

"There's someone there," she said.

I looked over at the monument and saw the tall lean figure of a man with his back to us. He wore a dark blue blazer and light tan coloured slacks. His dark hair was brushed back and when we drew nearer I could see it had been blow-dried, although not carefully enough to conceal the balding patch at the back of his head. Tara stopped and suddenly grabbed my elbow. She looked afraid for some reason.

The man heard us and turned around. His narrow face was tanned and clean-shaven, and he had a prominent nose.

He looked directly at me.

"Excuse me," I said. "We didn't want to disturb you. We just came to pay our respects."

"You knew her?" the man said.

Did I know her or didn't I? I remembered the strange connection I had felt when I had met her, but no, of course I didn't know her – not in the way he meant.

"We met once." I noticed the man's sorrowful eyes. "I never really got to know her, but I would have liked to. She seemed to me to be a remarkable woman."

I became aware that for some reason Tara was keeping her gaze pointed down at the ground, and then I felt her hand shaking.

I asked, "May I ask how you knew her?"

"She was the mother of my child," the man said.

The mother of his child? Did Virginie Lavelle have another child, or did he mean the child she was carrying when she died? Was this the man I had cursed for not being with her when she and her baby had died in the hotel room opposite mine?

Tara looked up, and when the man saw her face his expression changed,.

"You!" he said.

Tara drew herself up defiantly.

"Yes, me."

Her eyes burned with pure hatred. I tried to work out what was going on, my gaze moving from one to the other.

"You've changed your hair," he said.

Was he an ex-lover of Tara's?

He continued, "I didn't expect to see you again. Once you left I thought you'd stay well away, thought you would have gone back to America."

"Oh, so you knew I was *capable* of doing that?" Tara said. "What I ought to have done was to go straight to the police."

I stiffened.

"Tara, who is this guy?" I said.

"This is the bastard who abducted me. The man who asked me what my problem was and when I told him refused to believe me and pumped me full of drugs to keep me quiet. This is the man who robbed me of my freedom – the man you saved me from – Dr Dupont."

The penny dropped. Dupont looked at me nervously, as if he was trying to work out what I was going to do.

Tara said, "Did you think I was mad?"

Her voice trembled as if she was trying to control her anger. Dupont didn't answer. Her voice became louder.

"Well, did you? Answer me!"

Dupont looked down at the ground and then in a gentle voice said, "Not mad, but perhaps a little… disturbed."

"Not mad? Yet you pumped me full of drugs like a junkie, day after day! Why did you do it – why?"

"You were paranoid. The things you said happened to you in the convent were…"

"Were true, God damn you! You think I was making all that shit up? What kind of a crazy fucking mind do you think I have?"

"But the things you said were… bizarre to say the least. Of course it was possible that the drugs I gave you encouraged you to imagine things in a more… colourful way, but you…"

I had to cut in. "Dr Dupont. Believe it. Everything she told you happened to her was true – I can verify it. Virginie Lavelle would have verified it too, if you'd asked her."

A look of pain etched across his face.

"Do I look mad to you?" asked Tara aggressively.

"No," Dupont said.

"Amazing isn't it. I'm in your sanatorium, drugged up to the gills and you think I'm crazy. Here I am, out of your sanatorium, drug-free, and you say I don't look crazy. Just how did you make such an incredible diagnosis?"

Dupont didn't reply.

"I think the police need to hear about you and your house of horrors. I don't think they take too kindly to abductors and kidnappers."

Dupont looked uneasy.

"Look, I... um, I may have made a mistake, but if I did it was an innocent one. I might have listened to the Mother Superior too much without carrying out enough tests to make up my own mind, but I beg you, please, not to go to the police or cause trouble. We have many people in the sanatorium who certainly should be there and need our help. And we also have some other people, some... special people, who need looking after right now – people who have nowhere else to go."

"What do you mean, 'special people'?" I asked.

"Do you know about the explosion in the convent?"

"Yes, we heard about it."

"There had been some nuns in there with children – single mothers who had found God and wanted to devote their lives to worship – women who had repented for their sins, for having a child out of wedlock. We have taken them in at the sanatorium."

Tara and I looked at each other and then she said, "That's very charitable of you. Don't tell me you've found God too?"

Dupont said nothing, but he looked guilty.

"Does this have anything to do with Virginie Lavelle?" I asked.

Dupont was still silent.

"Look, I need to know about Virginie Lavelle."

He stayed silent. I turned to Tara.

"This guy isn't going to help us. I'd have thought he owed us something after what he did to you. Come on let's go to the police, I don't trust him and I don't think we can let him get away with what he did to you."

"No, wait. Don't do that." Dupont said.

Tara and I stood still, waiting for him to continue.

Eventually he said, "Why do you want to know about Virginie?"

"I've got my reasons. What did you mean by, 'She was the mother of my child'?"

"She was pregnant when she died. I was the father."

"OK. I'm going to be blunt. The police said she was a prostitute. Were they right or wrong?"

"She was a prostitute when I first met her, but she stopped all that and in a reaction to what she had been she turned religious. Then she entered the convent and changed her name to Sister Edith."

I felt Tara gripping my elbow again.

Dupont continued, "I tried to stop her, I wanted her to stay with me, but she didn't want me. I think I was just a crutch she leaned on when she was trying to stop being a prostitute. Her being in the hotel when she died... I can't help wondering if she had somehow changed her mind and was on her way back to me."

"Did you know she was pregnant when she went to the convent?"

"No. If I had I would have tried even harder to stop her going in there."

"How do you know you were the father of the child?"

"Because we were together for a year and I know she only slept with me during that time, and besides..."

"What?"

"I did a DNA test on the baby – my son." His face crumpled in pain, and then in a shaky voice he continued, "Do you know how it feels to be called in to do an autopsy and when you get there you find out you have to cut up the woman you love and your unborn son?"

We stood in silence for a few seconds and my heart went out to him. I had understood grief, ever since the deaths of my parents.

"How did *you* know her?" Dupont asked.

"I only met her briefly, but in a strange way she had an effect on our lives – we owe her a lot." I took Tara's hand in mine. "Sorry about your son." I turned to Tara. "Come on, let's go."

We left Dupont to grieve.

When we reached the car we got in and Tara said, "I think I know why Virginie Lavelle was in the hotel the night you arrived in Saint Pierre."

"You do?"

"One of the nuns told me about Sister Edith. She was taken into the inner sanctum very quickly and was chosen by the High Priest – I think he liked them cute as well as religious. I heard he did his thing with her and it looked like she had got pregnant by him, but the baby grew quickly – too quickly – and it was obvious she'd already been pregnant when she arrived at the convent. They threw her out. Said she was impure."

"Why didn't you say anything to Dupont, just now?" I asked.

"It might be kinder to let him think she was on her way back to him."

She was right and she'd answered the last question I had about Virginie Lavelle. I was glad we had come back to Saint Pierre and had tied everything up, but with all my questions answered it seemed there was no longer any reason to be there.

"You know what? I think I've finished with France."

Tara squeezed my thigh and said, "We've been around so much death and fear of death… it's made me appreciate life and what I have. Danny, I think I need to see my mom again. Fancy a trip to the States?"

Chapter 21

We turned into the driveway and the armed guard opened the gates and saluted when we passed by. Tara's mother, Isobel, came out to greet us, and I noticed her respond differently to Tara's hug this time – she hugged back. Isobel quickly got over our new haircuts; no doubt she had appalled her parents many times when she was young.

We took tea in the same room as before and later we sat down to dinner.

"Danny, I do hope you like fish," Isobel said.

She was charming and polite. How different to the frosty reception I had received last time. Was she beginning to accept me, or had she been tipped off by Uncle Jim that I was not the gold digger she had first thought I was?

"Fish is fine by me," I said.

We dined on succulent poached salmon in hollandaise sauce, green vegetables and new potatoes. I finished my last mouthful of fish, the flakes melting over my tongue, releasing their distinctive flavour, and then I sipped my Chablis.

Isobel casually said, "Uncle Jim told me he ran into you both in Europe."

Tara was about to put a piece of fish into her mouth, but she stopped, holding her fork six inches in front of her face.

"Did he tell you what we were doing?"

"He said you were… in difficulties – whatever that means. He said he couldn't tell me more because he would have to let me know what he had been involved in and it was classified. Are you going to tell me?"

Tara looked at me, then at Isobel.

"That would be difficult, Mother. Just like Uncle Jim said, it's classified."

Isobel didn't look convinced.

"Well, how on earth did you get mixed up in whatever he was involved in?"

I jumped in.

"Pure coincidence. I was working on a story and Tara was with me, and… things just sort of crossed with something Uncle Jim was working on."

She looked at me with piercing eyes, and for a moment I had an impression of how beautiful she must have been when she was Tara's age.

"Young man, I hope you are not telling me an untruth. That would be most regrettable, especially as my brother has sung your praises, although for what he wouldn't say."

I held her gaze and after a few seconds she continued, "Anyway it wouldn't be right for you to be so discourteous, now that you are both members of the Diplomatic Corps."

Tara said, "He told you about that?"

"Do you want some dessert?"

"Mother, forget dessert. I'm surprised he told you that."

"You were in a lot of trouble, weren't you?"

Tara didn't answer.

"I'll take your silence as confirmation. Tara, I may not have been the best of mothers over the years, but I *am* your mother and I *do* care. You are all I have and I do love you. Whatever you've got involved in I want you to stop it – now."

She seemed to have lost her laissez-faire outlook all of a sudden.

"Mother, you don't have to worry. It's all over."

"I hope so."

Isobel said to me, "I thought it was all your doing, Danny, but Uncle Jim tells me otherwise and I am inclined to believe my brother."

She turned to Tara again.

"You *were* near death weren't you?"

"Did Uncle Jim say that?"

"No, he told me very little and it appears his CIA training has enabled him to resist any inquisition from me."

Tara grinned. "He can be a little secretive, can't he? Just what exactly does he do in the CIA – he's never said? He's not the director of it, is he? I mean how did he manage to get us enrolled so quickly as diplomats? We got faxes from the *President*, for Christ's sake."

"Uncle Jim is resourceful, but Tara, just tell me, you *were* in great danger weren't you?"

Tara held her mother's gaze for a few moments, as if she was wondering how much she should reveal, and then she nodded slowly. Isobel closed her eyes and swallowed hard.

"If I had lost you, I…"

Tara seemed surprised, as if she had never heard her mother say anything like this before.

"Life is so fragile, Tara, I realise that. It's something you'll see for yourself as you get older."

"Mother, there's nothing wrong is there? You're not…"

"No, I'm in good health, as far as I know, but life can be snatched away from us at any time."

We sat in silence and I sensed something momentous was happening between Tara and her mother, although I couldn't tell what.

"Mother, are you trying to say something to me?"

Isobel didn't reply.

"Mother, what is it?"

For a few seconds Isobel didn't answer, but then said, "Eventually the record has to be put straight."

"What?" Tara said.

Isobel looked at me and I sensed she wanted me to leave.

"Um… look, I'm sure you want to talk alone," I said. "I'll just take a walk in the garden."

"No," said Tara. "Danny and I are partners. You can say anything in front of him – no secrets." She held my hand.

Isobel seemed to sense the strength of our relationship and that it was OK to say anything she wanted to in front of me.

"You don't have to tell me what happened – I don't want to hear how my daughter nearly died, but then I always was good at sticking my head in the sand. We must have an ostrich somewhere in our family lineage. When I contemplated losing you… well the thought was devastating, and I realised that I *will* lose you one day, because I am getting older, and some day I will die. I don't want to leave this planet without setting the record straight; it wouldn't be fair to you.

No, I'm not ill, I'm healthy, but there are accidents every day aren't there? I guess if anything did happen to me Uncle Jim would set things straight – but I'd feel bad not having looked you in the eye and told you myself."

Tara looked apprehensive.

"When I was young, Tara, things were different. No AIDS, no worries about getting pregnant, we were all on the Pill."

"For God's sake, Mom. It's a bit late for the birds and the bees talk."

"I'm just trying to tell you things were different in my... Oh, what does it matter? I don't have to justify myself. Look, I slept around a lot, OK?"

"Yes, you told me."

"I didn't tell you that when I was at college I met someone I fell in love with, and I stayed faithful to him for a year."

"Jesus, a whole year!" Tara said, her voice laced with sarcasm.

"Believe me that was a long time for me back then – and very uncool."

"So what are you trying to tell me, that you were a bad hippy? Is that it?"

Isobel closed her eyes and shook her head in exasperation.

"What I'm telling you is that during that time I got ill and took some medication, which stopped the Pill from working."

Tara shut up.

"I was hanging around with a bunch of political activist types at the time, and we were planning world peace and protesting against war. Democrats of course – I could never sleep with a Republican. The man I fell in love with, he – well it doesn't matter what he was like, except that he was ambitious and not the family type. He went off with some blonde bimbo called Clara Maguire and we were finished. I had you and he never came to see you, not once. I have to say I didn't mind; it was better that way. The last thing I wanted was some guy popping around every month just to ease his guilt, and it would have got you all mixed up, so we never saw each other after you were born."

"You knew all along who he was?"

"It was for the best... best for you. At least I thought it was then. Now it's best for him."

Tara snapped, "Best for *you*, you mean."

"No. It was never the best for me. It was a long time ago and he's married now. I knew it would damage him if it got out that he had a daughter, and I didn't want to hurt him – although *you* may want to. I'm telling you this because as much as I don't want him or you hurt, more than that, I want you to know who your father is."

Tara balled her fists.

"All my life you've lied to me!"

"Tara, it wasn't that simple."

"Bullshit, Mother! I've lived my life thinking you'd got fucked in some gangbang and hadn't a clue who my father was. I have lived my life as if he were dead and I had no chance of finding him. Why? Why did you lie to me all my life?"

"Because I love you and because I loved him. Tara, it's not so simple. There were times when I wanted to tell you, so many times, but it got worse as time went by. In the end I couldn't tell you, because of the damage it would do to him, because of the damage it *could* do to you and… and because… because your father is The President."

Chapter 22

The Turks and Caicos are wonderful islands. We swim and fish and make love and explore the coves and secluded beaches on our forty-five foot boat, named *Immortality*, in memory of Michael Richards. I have taken to snorkelling and adore the myriad of colours and the tranquillity of the world below the waters of the Caribbean. At night we eat at Jake's Tavern, run by Rufus 'Crayfish' Foley, a wizened-faced blues guitarist and purveyor of the finest seafood on the island. Tara does a guest spot twice a week and after her shows we sometimes mix with the holidaymakers. Every now and then we meet people we like and we invite them back to our home for dinner, or take them out on our boat to fish and share the beaches we know. Heaven on earth.

Leyton-Middleton has faded far away into some distant fuzzy corner of my mind. Cleaver has been blotted out of my mind for the most part – I don't want to live in the past. I have come to realise the path I had followed for so long (trying to become a Bernstein or Woodward) was not the path for me. Izzie had been right – I had been trying to avenge the death of my father and my need to strike back at the political establishment had consumed me. And for what? My father would never come back, and the elusive, slippery foe I had tried to fight would never die. It would only metamorphose and come back at me, like some alien creature in a sci-fi movie.

I have found an inner peace by accepting what I can't change, and by removing myself as best as I can from the tentacles of the political monster. Anyway, I achieved my goal. I found the big political scandal I had always sought and I struck against the forces I detest. Although the story we uncovered was never published we profited by it – greatly.

How?

Well, whatever remnants of the reporting instinct I had left within me did not die easily, and I was irked by the prospect of not being able to publish the biggest story I would ever find. After all, we had risked our lives to get it and had only narrowly escaped being murdered by Cleaver and his men. I wanted retribution for what had happened to me, and for what had happened to Tara, Michael Richards and the nuns in the convent. So I sent a copy of my disk to the British Prime Minister at 10 Downing Street. In the accompanying note I said that it was a great sacrifice for Tara and I to agree not to publish it. I gave an impression of what I thought would be the likely cash figure we would get for the rights after a frenzied worldwide bidding war.

Soon afterwards I received a reply from a prime ministerial aid telling us to get lost and of course denying there was any truth in the 'work of fiction' we had submitted to them.

Curiously, three days later someone knocked on our door. Tara was upstairs and I was eating some fruit in the kitchen. I wiped my hands, went through the house to the front door and opened it. A square-jawed man with slicked-back dark hair, perfectly parted at one side, asked:

"Are you Mr Avery by any chance?"

The man's eyes were almost black and his face pitted with pockmarks. He stood up straight, his chest thrown out.

"Who wants to know?" I asked.

He seemed to take my answer as confirmation. "Name's Wilcox, Toby Wilcox."

He thrust out his hand and shook mine firmly and enthusiastically. That name – Toby Wilcox… I trawled my memory for it, and then something flickered in the recesses of my mind. Elizabeth, or Deep Throat as we had known her, had mentioned that name to us. He was someone who had worked with Cleaver. Toby Wilcox was the man from the Ministry of Defence!

Alarmed, I took a step backwards, then looked down at the pockets of his trousers, but there were no bulges indicating he might have a gun in them, and his khaki coloured shirt was too tight to conceal a weapon. He carried a leather document pouch, but it was very thin.

"May I come in," he said, with military crispness.

I looked over his shoulder to check he was alone and then, with what was probably breathtaking stupidity on my part, I stepped to one side and beckoned him in.

I sat him down on the simple pine-framed sofa next to the French windows that looked out on to our small patch of land at the rear, and offered him a drink.

After I returned from the kitchen with two ice-cold cans of Coke, Tara came down the stairs. She had been taking a shower and was towelling her hair dry. Luckily she had put a robe on; she usually walked around the house naked, showing off her amber-coloured all over tan.

"Oh, hi," she said, surprised to see someone in the house other than me.

"This is Toby Wilcox," I said, waiting for the any signs of recognition to show on her face. After a few moments I helped her out. "He... er, he works with Cleaver."

Tara looked stunned. In an instant Wilcox was on his feet with his hand outstretched. "Used to," he corrected me, then said, "Look, could we all sit down?"

For a moment I was unable to move, rooted to the spot in my confusion, until eventually Wilcox retook his seat on the pine sofa, and, following his lead, Tara and I each took a chair. He sipped his Coke, looking like a man unused to drinking from a can, and then said, "Mr Avery, this is a delicate matter. Officially this meeting is not taking place and if you ever refer to it, its existence will be denied – do you get my drift?"

I said, "Why don't you fill me in on what it's about, then I can decide whether it exists or not."

"Quite." He cleared his throat. "What you sent to Number Ten has created quite a stir. I have been sent here to... come to an agreement with you, as it were. Of course the government denies everything you put in your story."

"Denies everything, but still wants to come to an agreement," I said.

He cleared his throat again. "Shall we just say that someone read the story and decided they would like to buy the rights to it – exclusively of course, and for all time."

It was an interesting way of putting things. "Don't tell me you've left the MOD and gone into publishing?"

"Er... no, not exactly. However, as I said, somebody does want to buy your story. Someone who... is prepared to reward you for all the time you put into it, and for a considerable sum, I might add."

"How much?"

"You indicated that the rights to your book could fetch up to five million pounds sterling. The purchaser does not disagree with your estimate."

Five million pounds! Tara and I looked at each other, the corners of our mouths lifting, our eyes twinkling – we always did things in harmony these days.

"The money wouldn't be paid directly to you of course. The purchaser wishes to remain anonymous, but he has deposited the sum in a numbered Swiss bank account and I have been instructed to provide you with the details of the account and how to access it, should we reach an agreement."

I sat back in my chair. "Well, at least you're not trying to kill us this time."

"Seems that would be counterproductive, wouldn't it?"

He obviously knew about the disks I had deposited with lawyers in different countries since our encounter with Cleaver in the Isle of Man. He opened a leather pouch and pulled out four copies of a contract.

"If you would read through this and sign it, then I can provide you with details of the account and you can… go on a spending spree."

The contract was short and to the point. It was effectively a gagging order and gave all rights to the story to a company called Lavender Publishing.

"If you'll excuse me, I think we need to talk about this," I said.

"Of course."

I stood up and beckoned Tara to follow me into the kitchen.

"Five million fucking quid!" I said in an excited whisper. "The bastards are shitting themselves!"

Tara held my hands and we jumped up and down like children on Christmas morning, struggling to stop ourselves from screaming. Eventually we calmed down.

"Do you think we should take it?" she said.

"Of course we should take it. Why? Do you think we should ask for more?" She didn't answer and I knew what she was thinking – that the money would be tainted somehow. "We earned it, Tara. Anyway, I have an idea – something we could do with it."

We went back into the room and sat down again.

"We're considering it," I said. "Seems like you want to bring this matter to an end – we'd like to do that too. Closure is what we are seeking, to use an American expression, but there are a few questions I'd like answered first. You said you used to work with Cleaver. I know you are MOD and he was with CABWINT. How come you don't work together any more?"

"That, I am not at liberty to say."

"Bullshit, Mr Wilcox. This meeting isn't taking place remember? You can say whatever you like. So why don't you indulge us for a moment. As I said, we'd just like to achieve closure, if you understand me."

He coughed again. "All right, I suppose you have a point. If it helps to bring this matter to an end then I can tell you that Cleaver is not currently with CABWINT. He's on… extended leave."

"How come?"

"He uh, he went a little off the rails, shall we say. This whole episode was a fiasco, people getting killed, you getting hold of your story – most embarrassing. I shall deny any of this if it gets out, you understand?"

Cleaver gone off the rails? I found the idea quite surprising. He came across as someone who was always so sure of himself.

"He killed his secretary, he should be tried for that, or has she been classified as just another operational casualty?"

"We think that contributed to his going off the rails."

"Filled with remorse over that was he?"

"Yes."

"What? That cold hearted son of a bitch? I don't get it. He didn't seem to be that disturbed when we had our run in at the hotel on the Isle of Man." And then I remembered the way he had looked when he had been tied to the chair with vomit stains on his shirt and trousers. Toby Miles said nothing. "Come on, there's more to this, isn't there?"

"I think I've said enough."

"Bullshit. If you want me to sign that contract you're going to have to help me to *get closure* on this. And that means telling me everything I want to know. We were nearly killed by that murdering bastard. I want to know what's been going on since we last saw him. So fill me in. This meeting isn't taking place, remember?"

He thought for a moment before answering. "If it gets you to sign the contract ... What the hell – I'm retiring in a week. He's been seeing one of our army medics, a psychiatrist who councils soldiers returning from war zones. Some things have come to light that are, irregular, shall we say?"

I was intrigued. "Go on."

"The lady you referred to as his secretary was called Mary Finch. Unbeknown to us, Cleaver was having an affair with her before he got her a job with the service. We knew about the affair later of course, but to be frank about it, we turned a blind eye. Everyone needs loyal staff and I suppose if you have a secretary who is in love with you, you can count on her loyalty. Problems can occur when and if the affair ends of course – and we know it did end, although Mary never caused us any problems. It seems Cleaver met her at a party given by his father – it was his father's sixtieth birthday party. They hit it off immediately – shared an instant bond, a kind of affinity. Unfortunately that became a problem. You see, after Cleaver was born his father sired another child, only not with Cleaver's mother, with a woman who ran a dress shop in Chelsea. For a long time neither Cleaver or his mother knew about this, although Cleaver did eventually find out – albeit too late."

"What do you mean, 'too late'?"

"It turns out that Mary Finch was the daughter of the woman who ran the dress shop in Chelsea."

"Jesus Christ. You mean he was having an affair with his sister, and then he killed her – his own sister?"

Wilcox nodded. "He didn't know who she was when he met her. His father introduced them wanting his two offspring to get to know each other, but didn't reveal to Cleaver who Mary was until it was too late and they were already in love. The father only revealed the truth about Mary when he was dying – it was a sort of deathbed confession. But Cleaver didn't tell Mary he was her bother."

"And so he carried on the affair, right?"

"For a while, yes. I suppose it was difficult for him to stop it, but it ended eventually."

"That would have been when she got pregnant."

"Pregnant?"

"You didn't know?"

"No."

"Typical Cleaver. He hasn't told your psychiatrist everything. We met her before she was killed and she told us about her affair with Cleaver. She got pregnant and he told her to get an abortion, which she did, though she regretted it and as a result fell out of love with him. Jesus, it's not surprising Cleaver wanted her to abort."

Now I knew why he had reacted so strongly in the Sunshine Hotel when I had brought up her death.

"I take it he's finished at CABWINT now?"

"Well, I wouldn't go so far as to say that."

"After all this you would keep him on?"

"It's not easy to find people who can operate in the way Cleaver can. You may not like it, but we need people who have a sense of duty, which is… unencumbered by the restraints of conscience."

"Delicately put. A ruthless son-of-a-bitch, you mean."

"Quite."

Cleaver would be back, I was sure of it. There was another thing I wanted to know, something that had been playing on my mind, something I hadn't been able to work out.

"How did Cleaver know we were going to meet Elizabeth – I mean Mary, at the hotel in Watford?"

"That was simple," said Wilcox. "It was the first email she sent you. When your house was broken into, Cleaver had a device put on your computer that sent him a copy of all your emails, and he saw it. It was from a hotmail account, the name had a series of numbers in it. If you reversed them you got the date of a birthday – Mary Finch's – not very original really. Cleaver was on to her and had her watched from the first time she contacted you."

"You mean he saw all the emails she sent us?"

"No, but he knew she had contacted you once. I think he was in two minds to know what to do about it. She was the woman he loved, and his sister. I think he thought he could contain the situation somehow if he just had her followed. The day she met you, she took time off work, something she never did, and he guessed what she was doing."

For Tara and I that was closure. We knew everything now. But there was something in the contract I wanted changed.

"If anything happens to either one of us, then the rights to the story revert back to us – or our estates. You understand what I'm saying, don't you?" I wanted to make sure the purchasers of our story still had an interest in keeping us alive.

Wilcox raised his eyebrows and I saw the trace of a smile on his lips, as if he was impressed with my thoroughness.

"I think we can agree to that, Mr Avery."

We wrote in the additional clause, signed and dated it, and then signed the bottom of the contract. Two days later we got access to the cash, and it was one in the eye for Eddy Sinclair, who said I would never make a penny as a writer. Tara had been right about the money – it did give us an uneasy feeling, so we took a final trip to France – back to the sanatorium where Dr Dupont was giving help and support to the six nuns and their children. Once we had established the names of the children, and with the help of a lawyer in Nice, we set up individual trust funds for the children, which allowed interest to be paid to their mothers to help them bring up the babies. The capital sum would go to the children when they reached the age of twenty-one. We put half a million pounds in each trust. That left us with two million pounds, which we kept. Our altruism had limits and we were entitled to something.

After buying the house we had been renting on the island, we set up a recording studio. Tara wrote and performed her songs, and I became her manager, marketing her music directly from a website, building up quite a following. Sometimes we rented studio time to local musicians, and I developed a taste for reggae.

And then one day we had a couple of visitors.

I answered the door and found myself looking at two young men in their early twenties. For a moment I thought I'd gone cross-eyed – they were identical twins, each a carbon copy of the other; blond hair, blue eyes, smooth elastic skin, vibrant with youth. Both wore shorts, T-shirts and trainers.

"Excuse us. We're fans of Tara's and we're passing through on vacation. Any chance we could meet her?" said one of the twins.

These weren't the first fans to call on us; we were easy to find – our website said we lived on the Turks and Caicos Islands.

"Hi," I said, a big cheesy grin on my face. When you're trying to break through you can't afford to alienate any fans. "She's in. I'm sure she'd be more than pleased to say hello. Why don't you go around the back and sit on the bench under the tree? She'll come out and see you in a minute."

The two fans smiled politely. "You must be Danny Avery, her manager."

It was the first time any fans had known who I was; there was no picture of me on the website, although my name was mentioned.

"Yes, I am."

The twin on the left said, "It's a pleasure to meet you, sir." He stretched out a hand and I shook it. "I'm Mickey and this is Albert."

I shook Albert's hand too and then said, "Well, guys. Go around the back; we'll be out soon."

I closed the door and hunted around in the small storeroom where we kept the T-shirts that we sold on the website with Tara's picture on the front. It would be good PR to send the fans away with something after they had taken the time to seek us out. Tara was in the kitchen, preparing vegetables and fish. I told her some fans had arrived to see her.

"Oh shit, it's almost lunch–time," She said.

"They won't be here long. Come on, babe, got to be nice; we need the fans right now."

She wiped her hands and we both went out to the back.

"Tara, this is Mickey and Albert, right. Or have I got it the wrong way around?"

The twins grinned, each showing off their fresh white teeth. "You got it right," said Albert.

"Mickey's in the white shirt and Albert's in the blue," I said, helping Tara out.

"Hi guys," she said. She shook their hands. She was good at this. "It's real nice of you to drop by and say hello."

Mickey said, "I can't tell you how thrilled we are to meet you. We love your music."

"Well, that's really kind of you. Sit down, please. Would you like a Coke?"

I went into the kitchen to get a couple of cans from the fridge and when I returned Mickey and Albert were talking to Tara about her music, telling her which tracks they liked best on the CD and why. I handed them their Cokes and they opened them, each taking a long suck. They were nice kids. Sometimes you meet people and something just clicks. You get a sense of who they are and what they stand for and it's almost as if you've known them forever. With Mickey and Albert it was like that, even though there was a big age difference between us and I wondered if we should rethink our marketing strategy – I had assumed people of the twin's age were only into rap or new metal music.

Then Mickey said, "Did you enjoy your time in France?"

Tara paused for a moment then said, "Um… yeah, sure. France is a beautiful country."

Strange. There was nothing on the website about ever being in France.

Mickey said, "I don't detect any religious influences in your music."

"Um… no. Religion's not my thing."

The mood changed and I felt my stomach tighten.

"But you spent time as a nun. It seems strange that you don't express any religious beliefs in your songs."

Tara looked at me and I wondered who the hell I had invited into our home.

Mickey said, "How about you, Mr Avery – did you like Saint Pierre? Such a nice looking place I think – perched up there on that hill. Great views of the mountains and the sea." There was something sinister about these two. "*Echoes from the Past* is one of my favourite numbers. I like Tara's vocal on that one, and of course – *We Must Dance*. Interesting title that. The initials are WMD."

I stood up.

"OK. The meeting's over. Time to leave." I jerked my thumb towards the entrance. "Move it."

They sat still. Albert seemed to be suppressing a smile and Mickey looked strangely impassive.

"Danny, I'm sorry about that, but I had to do it. Don't you recognise me?"

What the fuck was this little shit talking about? I didn't know him – of course I didn't know him. He was a different generation to me and I couldn't think of anyone I knew who had twins.

"Just get out of here. Your time's up." I jerked my thumb again. "Out."

"Danny, relax," he said. "We mean you no harm."

They'd better not. After going through all that shit with Cleaver, I had grown harder and more aggressive.

Mickey continued, "We've met before." I tried to remember seeing him, but nothing came to mind. "Remember Saint Pierre? There was a restaurant just outside the town. We once had a very interesting discussion there, and of course before that we saw each other in the convent – or rather underneath it. In a laboratory."

No one knew about any of that. Not even the lawyers who had copies of my disk. The only people who knew about it were myself, Tara and the one other person who had been there… Michael Richards.

Mickey – he said his name is Mickey.

"Danny, you must know me now. The last time we spoke we had just found the High Priest lying dead in his room."

I looked at him as if he were a ghost, and struggled to get my breath. The young man in front of me with his twin brother was not much more than twenty-five years old, or at least he *looked* that age. He began to grin as he watched me trying to come to terms with what I had heard. Suddenly I felt like the apostles must have felt meeting Jesus Christ after He had risen from the dead.

"Are you… Michael Richards?"

He nodded. "You know I am."

"How did you…?"

"It works."

"Yes. I see it works. You look younger… But you were killed in the explosion."

He chuckled.

"I got out down the tunnel. It's all right, I haven't discovered how to bring people back from the dead, but then maybe in the future that won't be so necessary."

Our meeting with him in the restaurant outside Saint Pierre came back to me and I remembered everything he had said – how the order of things would be turned on its head. Old people would be regarded as highly prized human beings – just as youthful in body as the young, but along with youth they would also have the benefit of their whole life's experience. I gazed at him in awe. The massive leap forward for mankind that he had spoken of was here – now! Anti-ageing creams would be a thing of the past. Old people's homes would be read about in history books. Now people could dream their dreams, knowing they had forever to achieve them, and lovers need not grow old together – they could just *grow* together – forever young.

"Michael, I… you did it. You actually did it!"

He nodded. I stepped towards him and shook his hand, then he grabbed me and hugged me and I felt the litheness of his body – he really was young again. I stood back and gazed at him, then at Albert.

"I've got to ask; how old is your brother?"

"Danny, this is my father. He's sixty-six years old."

Shit, I was dreaming.

They stayed to lunch. Tara cooked some more vegetables and fish and I opened a bottle of wine. Michael told me how he had escaped before the explosion with enough of his records on computer disk, some genetic material from the High Priest and a load of cash from the High Priest's wall safe – all he needed to finish his work. He had gone to stay with his father and after trying it out the treatment on himself he had given it to Albert.

"We saw your website and we really are fans of yours, Tara," Michael said.

"Thanks."

"But we didn't track you down just to get a T-shirt. I wanted to thank you both."

"For what?" I said. "We didn't do anything."

"Exactly. You didn't and that's why I'm grateful. I have to admit I was expecting to read the story in a newspaper somewhere. I didn't think you'd be able to resist the urge to sell it. I misjudged you – sorry."

There was no need to tell him any different.

"When does the world get young, Michael? This must be the most radical thing to happen to the human race since… since forever."

"Not yet, it's too soon. We're the human guinea pigs. We don't know if there are any side effects yet. It'll be ten years before this becomes available – we have to wait." He looked sad. "Of course people will die in the meantime, people who needn't, but it's coming, Danny. Eternal life is coming and I hope the world will be ready for it."

They stayed with us until dusk, then Michael looked at his watch.

"We're late," he said. "Got a plane to catch."

Tara and I waved them off and they ran down the road, looking like two energetic students.

After dinner that night Tara and I made love. We made love every day, sometimes three times a day, and the excitement I felt when our bodies touched never diminished. I was living in an almost permanent state of sexual arousal, and it would be like that forever, because one day we would have some of Michael's pills.

We lay still, gently caressing each other, the air moist with our perspiration, and at that moment I wished other people could share the same joy of lying in their lover's arms, dreaming of an unlimited future. And I thought how ironic it was that the nuns had been duped into believing the High Priest was The Second Coming, the saviour of our race, because with the help of Michael Richard's, he had been.

Danny finished reading, gathered the pages together and put them back in the large manila envelope. It had been good to add the last few chapters to the story. Of course there was no need to add them to the copies he had lodged with the solicitors in five different countries, but this was Danny's personal copy, and as time went by he would add more chapters and it would become *their* story – Danny's and Tara's.

He stuffed the envelope back in its hiding place in the rafters of the roof and then sat on the bed wondering what Michael and Albert were doing. Would he ever see them again? He smiled to himself as he always did when he remembered how they looked when they had turned up on the island – fit, young, healthy and twenty-five years old.

Was it possible to turn the *whole* world young, or was that just a crazy dream? Ten years they had said – ten years before they could release the cure for aging.

But they were wrong about that.

Part II

Chapter 1

Alistair Cleaver approached the 1930s semi-detached house at 31 Mayberry Gardens with the feeling of trepidation he always felt when he met Joss Whelan. He rang the bell and the door was opened by a frail woman dressed in a yellow cardigan. She had a bewildered expression on her face and a trace of spittle on her lips. She was Joss's wife, Alice. Without saying a word she led him through to the back of the house and shooed him out into the garden. He smiled and nodded at her, letting her know he understood, and then stepped out onto the patio. She closed the French windows behind him, and then he saw Joss halfway down the garden. Cleaver stepped onto the smooth, green lawn and made his way towards the thickset, grey haired man.

"Good morning, Joss."

Joss was looking intently at a weed sprouting in the soil. He bent down and pulled it out, shaking his head. "You know, you let one of these grow and pretty soon the place is overrun with them."

"It all looks good to me," Alistair said.

Joss took the secateurs from his pocket and snipped off a miniscule clipping from a rose plant, making it perfect. "See that rhododendron over there? Took me five years to get it looking like that."

"You've done a marvellous job with it."

Joss glanced at him. "You know... there are some things we can't take credit for. You believe in God, Alistair?" Before he could answer Joss continued, "We're all gardeners on this earth. The Almighty has his design for us; *He* makes all these plants grow. We just tend His garden, as it were, pick out the weeds, sometimes add a little fertiliser, keep things in check, stop the place running wild."

Joss led Alistair back up the garden to the patio in front of the French windows. They sat down at the round, wooden table and a minute later Alice arrived, shuffling along, carrying a tea tray, some of the milk spilling from the jug onto the cake. She put the tray down on the table.

Joss looked up at her with what appeared to be an expression of genuine affection. He patted her on the arm. "It's OK dear, I'll pour it. Run along now."

He handed Cleaver a cup of tea and then cut them both some fruitcake. Holding a slice up to his mouth, he looked down at it wistfully. "She used to make wonderful cakes, but I had to stop her. She got confused and put salt in instead of sugar. Still, can't be helped."

"No, quite," Cleaver said, waiting for Joss to come to the reason why he had summoned him.

Joss put down his plate and finished chewing. He looked directly at Cleaver, who saw the familiar coldness return to Joss's eyes. "Something's come up. Has to do with that business in France three years ago – the gas."

Cleaver had that sinking feeling in his stomach again – the one he always had when *The French Incident*, as it had become known, was mentioned. Looking sheepish, he said, "Joss, I, er…"

"Don't worry about it, Alistair – it's history. Wasn't your fault anyway. There's something you don't know. Something you didn't *need* to know – until now, that is. You see, Olivia, or Sister Olivia as we called her then, took some items from the labs down there before she blew the place up. When we debriefed her she told us a few things that were…curious to say the least. We got the boys in our labs to look at what she'd taken and… well, we were more than a little surprised by what we found. Our boys were scratching their heads for a while, I can tell you. It all looked… like something… strange, unbelievable and… quite frankly, bloody disturbing."

Alistair sat up straight in his chair. "What was it?"

"What I'm going to tell you is not to be spoken about in CABWINT or anywhere else, do you understand?"

"Yes, of course."

"Good. Alistair… there never was any gas. We were being duped by that scientist chap, Michael Richards."

"But there must have been. All that–"

"It was a smokescreen – all of it. Our scientist friend was making something else – even more disturbing."

"More disturbing than a gas that could wipe out a country in two weeks?"

"Yes. You see… it appears he was working on some ridiculous cure for aging."

Cleaver sat back in his chair looking puzzled. "Joss, I don't understand. You mean he was making a health potion?"

Joss cleared his throat. "No, you *don't* understand do you. It was more than a health potion, Alistair. And he wasn't in the process of developing it. We think he had actually succeeded, albeit in perhaps a limited way. You see, Sister Olivia told us that some mice he had in a cage down there suddenly became young."

A faint smile played on Cleaver's lips. "I see. So there never was a gas. Well…"

"I take it that smug, relieved look on your face is born of the mistaken idea that this somehow exonerates you for failing to procure what was never there in the first place. I should remind you that you still allowed yourself to be fooled by a delusional scientist and his half-mad religious cohort. So I wouldn't feel too smug if I were you. Your arse is not off the hook, so to speak." The smile on Cleaver's face disappeared. "Now… perhaps we can concentrate on the issue at hand."

"Er, right. Sorry. So he turned some mice young. Quite remarkable really."

"Remarkable?" Joss's forehead furrowed. "He would have been experimenting on humans next. Joseph Mengele comes to mind – the Nazis building a master race. It would have been evil!"

Cleaver sensed Joss descending into one of his dark moods. "Yes, I see."

Joss clenched his fist. "Think what would have happened if it had got out. There would have been chaos – a breakdown of order! People would have got above themselves, developed harmful expectations – very dangerous. There'd have been a population explosion; the world would have starved to death in no time at all. A world without order? My God, it's unthinkable! Life has its *own* order, and death is a part of it. We need death, Alistair; it brings certainty… and renewal. We live and we die. We are put back into the earth, and so we replenish life itself."

"Like compost."

Joss glared at him. "The Almighty, in his wisdom, maintains order with all of us through death – that's why it's there. You take that away and… well it doesn't bear thinking about. We'd… we'd run amuck and destroy ourselves for heaven's sake! Life, the world – it's like a finely balanced watch, all the wheels whirring around, connected to each other. You mess up one cog, you mess them all up. Balance and order – without it we have nothing."

Cleaver paused for a moment, making sure Joss had finished. "Yes, I see that, of course. But why are we talking about all this? I mean the lab was destroyed, we blew away half the hillside."

"Yes…" Joss sipped his tea. "But, as I said, something's come up. As you know, my role is… undefined. Some idiot in The Ministry for Defence called me a 'floater', of all things. Makes me sound like an unflushed turd. However, not being chained to a singular role gives me an overview of all departments, which is how it came to my attention that we'd heard something from our people in Zagreb. You see the Croatians have a recent history that makes them particularly vigilant when it comes to possible terrorist activity. They got wind of a couple of young men, Americans as it happens, who were running a laboratory from an apartment. They suspected it was a bomb factory. Our chaps heard about it and broke in to take a look around. There were some animals in cages, lots of equipment for doing experiments, and a laptop computer, which they stole to make it look like the place had been broken into by kids. Trouble was there was nothing on the computer – just a bit of software linking it to a computer server in Russia, which they've been unable to access."

"So they don't know what was going on?"

"No. But here's the thing that caught my attention. The locals said the two Americans seemed to be particularly fond of taking in stray dogs. They took in any old mutt, apparently. The thing is, the dogs went in looking haggard and whiskery and came out looking fresh, fit and playful as puppies."

"My God. Didn't they question them?"

"They left it too late. After the break in they both disappeared, which was suspicious in itself. A break in is a break in. They happen. You don't pack up and go just because you have one. Unless, of course, you are doing something you really shouldn't be doing."

"I see."

"The point is, Alistair, do we know for sure that Michael Richards is lying beneath the rubble of that hillside in France? Could he have got out?"

"What does Olivia say?"

"Nothing. She set the charges, took what she could and cleared out of there. She can't say what happened to him." Joss took another sip of tea and then said, "What about that reporter chappie?"

"He's in the Turks and Caicos Islands as far as I know. We watched him for a while, but... There was no point in continuing – he wasn't doing anything other than messing about with his girlfriend and writing some online newspaper. Blogs, I think they call them. He has his rant about this, that or the other, but he's living quietly, as far as I know."

"If something is going on, could he be part of it?"

"I suppose he could... But then... no... I don't think so. You see he wrote that damned account of everything that happened and gave it to five lawyers in different countries with instructions for it to go to the newspapers if anything happened to him. There was nothing about an anti-aging pill in what he wrote – I had a copy of it. Surely he would have said something about it if he had known? Anyway, he's a reporter – he'd have loved to get a story about age reversal. He'd have written about it. When I caught up with him in the Isle of Man all he went on about was weapons of mass destruction. No, I'm sure he's been duped too."

"Well, let's hope so."

"What do you want me to do?"

Joss picked up a manila envelope from the table and gave it to Cleaver who opened it and pulled out a photograph of two sandy-haired young men. They looked like twins, about twenty-five years old.

"These are the two Americans. See what you can find out, would you?"

Chapter 2

It was midnight. They walked back from Jake's Tavern, where Tara had been playing her usual mid-week session, talking about the two new songs she had sung for the first time. Rufus 'Crayfish' Foley, who owned the bar, loved one of them, but not the other. He had said it needed work on the middle eight bars.

Danny said, "I think he's right, you know?"

"Why?"

"I just think we need to change the chord structure. There's something missing – it just doesn't... lift you to another place, that's all."

"Maybe I wanted to keep you right where you were."

"Come on Tara, you know what I mean."

She slipped her hand in his. "Yeah, I guess so. I've been working on this album for so long I just want it to be finished. I'll play around with it in the morning." She pulled him closer and kissed his cheek. "I'm beat. Can't wait to get into bed."

They arrived outside the house, Danny reached inside his pocket for his keys and then he heard a twig snapping. He looked up and caught sight of a figure disappearing down the side of the house. He grabbed Tara's arm.

"What is it?" she said.

"Someone's there, I saw them."

"Where?'

"Behind the house. I saw them going around the corner."

"You sure you're not imagining things?"

"For God's sake Tara, believe me."

Danny bent down and picked up a fallen branch. It felt good in his hand, heavy enough to do some damage, but not so heavy that he couldn't swing it with ease.

"You think it's burglars?" Tara said.

"What else at this time of night?"

"What if there's more than one?"

"I only saw one."

Danny walked silently towards the house, taking slow deliberate steps, Tara following. She tugged his shirt.

"Maybe we shouldn't do this."

"Bullshit. We've got all sorts of recording equipment in there. You think I'm going to sit back and let them take it, hoping the police get here before they leave? No chance. Come on."

They approached the front corner of the house. Danny held the branch up high, ready to strike, waggling it slightly, like a golfer preparing to tee off. He shuffled his weight from one foot to the other, preparing himself mentally. Then he turned the corner and let out a gasp. There were *two* of them, and they were coming back around to the front of the house. The first one almost bumped into Danny who drew the branch back and swung it at the man, but he was too quick and jumped out of range.

"Danny! For Christ's sake don't kill him!" the second man shouted.

Confused, Danny froze. How did they know his name?

The two men drew nearer and Danny backed away holding the log like a baseball player about to hit a home run. Moonlight lit up the first man's face. For a second nothing registered, but then Danny's eyes widened in surprise.

"You! What the hell… ?"

"Danny, who are these… ?" Tara said. "Oh my God! We didn't expect to see you two…"

Danny said, "Where have you been? Or more to the point, what're you doing here?"

Michael and Albert looked serious and suddenly Danny realised this wasn't a social visit.

They sat in the living room and Danny opened a bottle of wine. Tara made a toast:

"To reunions!"

They each took a sip and then Danny said, "Well, you don't look any older than you did three years ago. Is this how it'll always be – you're never going to look any different?"

"I guess so. The cure takes you back to the point when you are fully developed physically and keeps you there. There's not going to be any... degradation, for want of a better word."

Tara said to Albert, "How are you feeling now you're forty-odd years younger? Is it like when you were twenty-five?"

"Better. At least I think it's better. When I was twenty-five I never knew any different, so maybe I didn't appreciate being strong and fit. And I was pretty stupid at that age. Now I know what it's like to get old and weak, stooping around the house, breathing hard when you get to the top of the stairs – all that stuff. So I guess I'm just appreciating it more."

"Any drawbacks?"

"Nope. Except one, maybe. It's the ladies. I get young girls looking at me, which is nice, of course, but we just don't have anything in common. The older ones think I'm just a cute kid and so they aren't interested in me. What I really need is a woman who's a gym-freak, about twenty-one years old, who appreciates Duke Ellington and Ella Fitzgerald. Now where the hell am I going to find a woman like that?"

Danny asked Michael if there had been any side effects.

"I've monitored our bodily functions for three years now and there's been nothing. Everything works like... a shiny, new, well-oiled machine."

Danny shook his head in amazement. "So where have you been?"

"Croatia."

"Croatia? Why there?"

"Somewhere away from Cleaver. At least that was the idea."

"The idea?"

Michael told Danny and Tara about the laboratory they set up in the apartment and the break-in.

Danny said, "How do you know it wasn't a bunch of kids?"

"Because we rigged up a camera in the air-conditioning vent, and when the movement sensor triggered it to work it recorded their every move. They weren't kids. Three professional guys, dressed in black, ski-masks, all the kit. They searched the place thoroughly and carefully, not making a mess. You wouldn't think anyone had been there they were so neat. But they took a laptop computer."

"Your computer? But that's going to tell them everything."

"No it won't. You see... we took precautions. All we used the computer for was to access a remote server. All my data is stored on a computer in Russia. There was nothing on the laptop, nothing at all."

"You have no idea who they were?"

"Their names – no. But the video recorded their voices. They had English accents. Now, you've got to ask yourself, why would English guys, wearing black, break into an apartment in Croatia?"

Tara asked, "But if it was Cleaver, how the hell did he find you?"

"I don't know."

Albert said, "It was the dogs."

"The dogs?"

Michael said, "I may have made a mistake. There were some stray dogs – poor flea-bitten old things, arthritic, hobbling around. I took them in and made them young again, and then they became boisterous, too much of a handful to keep in the apartment, so I let them go. Trouble was they were known to the locals, who sometimes threw them scraps. I guess when they suddenly saw them young somebody got a little spooked. I got some funny looks for a while, like I was the town witch or something. Guess we're lucky we weren't burned at the stake."

"Jesus, if it really was Cleaver... So what did you do?"

"We got the hell out of there as fast as we could."

Albert said, "We left everything. Couldn't risk hanging around a minute more than we had to. Those guys in black... they were like something out of a spy movie. I don't think they'd think twice about coming back and.... you know what. And what if they had? What if they had come bursting through the door with machine guns and blasted away? All this that Michael has worked for... it would be lost. And that would mean they wouldn't just have killed us, they would have condemned the whole world to death... for what? For nothing."

"You don't think they could have followed you here?"

"No. We were careful. We didn't just jump on a plane and fly here. We went through five countries in all. I don't see how they could have followed us through that. But I'm sure they'll be looking. Probably they'll be watching Albert's house in Ohio thinking we'll turn up back there."

Danny said, "You know, Albert's right. If anything happened to you two..."

"I know. That's why we've come to a decision. We're not going to wait any longer. We've got to make this available to people now."

"But I thought you said it would take ten years before you were ready for that?"

"Albert and I have been the guinea pigs. We don't have any ill effects, just more energy than we have ever had, freedom from colds, illnesses – great health. In an ideal world I'd wait longer, but the world is not ideal, is it? What if we don't make it and Cleaver catches up with us? It's not as if I'm ever going to be able to do proper clinical trials on this. I'm not going to get a licence to sell it from the FDA now am I? Where we are now is where we'll be in ten years time."

"The difference is we're alive now, we may not be then," Albert said.

Danny listened to their words and he knew they were right. There was nothing to be gained by waiting any longer. And then the significance of the moment became apparent and he began to feel shaky inside. As crazy and melodramatic as it sounded, he knew this could be a turning point in the history of mankind.

He swallowed hard.

Michael said, "Look, we realise this is not your fight. You stumbled across what I was doing in that lab in France. You weren't looking for this – I was. We have no right to ask you to get involved – so I won't."

"I appreciate that." Danny said.

"But if you *want* to get involved... well, we're not going to say no."

Danny looked at Tara and said, "I think we need to sleep on it."

They lay side by side looking up at the ceiling, holding hands, too charged to think about going to sleep.

"You know what this means – I mean, you *really* know what this means?" Tara said.

"You mean can I imagine what the world would be like if six billion people were all twenty-five years old? No, I can't imagine that. I try to, but it's just... impossible. Everything would be turned upside down..."

"I meant what it would mean for *us*."

"Yeah. We'd be together until the end of time."

"No! You're quoting song lyrics at me here! I'm talking about what it will mean to us in terms of... being on the run from Cleaver and his crew again, only this time it would be worse. There's nothing, absolutely nothing they wouldn't do to stop this. We could be killed. Uncle Jim isn't going to save us – not this time. We could just carry on as we are. My CD's are selling well; you're doing your Internet newspaper. We're happy aren't we? I mean... life's good for us right now."

"Yeah, I know."

"Michael's right. I mean we didn't go looking for this."

Danny sighed. "No. We didn't go looking for it." He turned over onto his side. "But whichever way you look at it, it's still our fight."

"Why do you say that?"

"Because we *know* about it, that's why. We know that everyone in the world will die needlessly if Michael doesn't succeed. And if he fails and we didn't do anything to help... how are we going to live with that? Could *you* live with that?"

Tara caressed the side of his ribcage. "No... No, I guess I couldn't."

In the morning Tara made fresh orange juice in the kitchen. Danny came downstairs, his hair wet from the shower.

"Where are they?" he asked.

"I don't know. Out, I guess." Danny looked worried. "Come on Danny, Cleaver hasn't come here and stolen them from their beds. If you're going to get jumpy like this when they're out of sight you better handcuff yourself to them." She looked out of the window. "Look. Here they come now."

Danny looked outside and saw Michael and Albert sprinting, racing each other, neck and neck, their finely muscled torsos glistening with sweat.

Danny shook his head in amazement. "My God. That guy's seventy years old."

Ten minutes later they sat on the porch at the front of the house, sipping orange juice.

Tara said, "Do you run every morning?"

Albert said, "Have to. If we don't we get twitchy. It's like we've got so much energy we have to find something to do with it."

Danny vaguely recollected feeling that way when he had been a teenager playing football back in England. He tried to remember when things had begun to change but couldn't pinpoint an exact moment in time; he just knew that a vital spark had faded within him over the years.

"We talked last night," Danny said. Michael nodded. "And... we're in."

Michael grinned for a moment and then looked solemn. "Thank you."

"Do you know what you want to do... how to go about this?"

Michael shook his head. "You know... I really don't have a clue. I'm sitting on the greatest discovery mankind has ever made, and I can't tell anyone about it for fear of getting shot. I think I know how Gallileo felt when he tried to tell the world the earth was round. You shake things up and... well, people get scared."

Tara said, "What do you need to make it – I mean on a big scale?"

"I need a pharmaceutical manufacturer. But no one's going to start manufacturing something that will eventually put them out of business. No aging equals less illness, equals less drug sales.

Tara said, "It's crazy. Are we the only people that know about this?" Michael nodded. "If we tell anyone about it we could end up dead. I don't see what we can do?"

"Move and you're dead. Don't move and everybody dies. It's impossible," Albert said.

They sat in silence for a moment, looking at the ground. Then Danny said, "The eradication of death... It's something – maybe the only thing – worth dying for."

Michael grinned. "Quite a paradox, isn't it?"

Tara said, "But how can we do it? We're just four ordinary people – well, two of us are ordinary. On our own we're... powerless."

Danny sat back, gently tapping his lower lip with his fingertips, and then a memory and an image of a man's face came into his mind. Slowly he lifted his gaze and said, "All right. If we're *really* going to do this, maybe there is someone who can help."

"You know somebody?"

"Maybe. But we need to take a trip to England."

After listening to Danny's idea, Tara called her mother in Florida.

"High mom, it's me!"

"Oh. So, you decided to call. What is it – are you in trouble?" Her voice was unusually flat and lifeless.

"Are you all right, mother?"

"Typical. Avoid a question with a question."

"No, I'm not doing that. You just sound off colour, that's all."

"So now I have to be a mother to you and always upbeat and cheerful with it, is that it? Am I not bright and cheerful enough for you?"

This wasn't going as Tara had hoped it might.

"Lets start again. I want to ask you a favour."

"What?"

"I want to take some friends on a plane trip – to Europe. Someone we know has never been there and Danny and I said we would take him, and… well I just thought, as an extra special treat, we could go in the private jet, that was all. I mean you don't use it much and, it would be great if we could-"

"Yes."

"Yes? You don't mind? But I thought-"

"I said yes, didn't I?"

"I just thought it would-"

"You thought I'd put up more of a fight. Tara, there comes a time in life when you get tired of fighting."

"Er, right. It's just not like you to-"

"You want me to change my mind?"

"No!"

"Then stop bugging me about it. Call the pilot and tell him what you want to do."

"Thank you mother, that's very kind of-"

"And it would be nice if we met again sometime soon. If that wouldn't put you out. I'm sure you have such a busy schedule…"

"Cut the sarcasm, mother. It's not your style."

Tara called Graham, the pilot, told him where she wanted to go and they agreed a time for him to pick them up from the airport on Turcs and Caicos.

"Just one thing, Graham. I want you to bring a few extra of those neat little captain's shirts you wear. You know, the white shirts with the cute gold epaulets. And as far as anyone is concerned you're on a positioning flight, just you and the co-pilot, no passengers, okay?"

Forty-eight hours later they landed at Biggin Hill airport, just south of London. Graham and the co-pilot checked in with airport control and notified customs of their arrival. Security was lax to the point of being almost non-existent, as it was at all small airfields. Graham moved back and forth easily from the airport offices to the jet, each time taking with him one of his four passengers wearing their crew shirts. An hour after landing all four passengers were safely outside the airport building, undetected, climbing into a taxi.

Cleaver turned to his computer terminal and saw he had mail on the secure server. He opened it up and downloaded the attachment. A scanned image appeared of a young man with a broad smile and sandy hair. It was a picture of Michael Richards taken from his College Yearbook. Cleaver sat back and stared at it for a few moments, squinting to get a better look at the blurry detail. He took out the photograph of the twins in Croatia from the manila envelope Joss had given him and held it beside the screen, comparing the eyes, the line of the nose and the size of the mouth. My God... it was definitely the same person! Or at least, one of them was. Cleaver read the note attached to the email, which confirmed Michael Richards was an only child.

The gravity of the situation dawned on him. Richards had somehow got out of the convent before it had blown up, and now... (Cleaver could hardly bring himself to allow the thought to enter his mind)... he had used his invention, or whatever it was, to ... turn himself young. But how come there were two young men in Croatia? Had Richards cloned himself? No, that was impossible. If he had cloned himself he would have ended up with a genetically identical *baby*, not a twenty-five-year-old twin. It didn't make sense. He would work it out later.

Cleaver needed to see Joss.

The four of them stood in a huddle under a tree, lying in wait, grim, determined expressions on their faces.

Danny said, "Get ready. He'll be here any minute."

Tara nodded and then Albert said, "Just how rich is this guy?"

"We're talking billionaire here," Danny said. "Exactly how rich, I don't know. Once you're up there what difference does it make?" He was feeling jumpy and charged. "We're only going to get one crack at this."

Tara said, "If it goes wrong we better get back to the plane and get out of the country – fast."

Michael said, "But we're not going to mess up, right?"

Danny looked over the wall and saw a silver Bentley approaching. "Okay, this is it – he's here."

Chapter 3

David Lane sat in the back of the Bentley shuffling some papers, unable to concentrate, his mind drawing him back to the conversation he had had at home that morning. He'd awoken to find himself in bed alone, just the impression on the sheets where Helen had been lying. She was up early again, but these days that was nothing new. He got out of bed, put on his robe and made his way into the living room. There she was, sitting at the table, leaning forwards, concentrating on some paperwork, her silk dressing gown open, revealing the side of her breast and her long slender legs. She ran her hand through her short blonde hair and adjusted her dark-framed reading spectacles, unaware that he had entered the room.

"You look busy," he said.

She looked up. "Oh, hi. Yeah. Course I'm busy; there's a lot to do. You know profits are up by 15% already this year?"

"My oh my. Who'd have thought it, Helen Andrews the business woman."

"You've got yourself to blame for that. Don't you remember that discussion we had when I was just a doctor? You told me that I would cure more people by building a hospital and putting other doctors to work than I ever would on my own. You were right."

He remembered the conversation, though he was sure she had changed the context. "I didn't expect my words to have such an effect on you."

She looked back down at the spreadsheet and said absently, "Well, I'm glad they did." She turned the sheet over and said, "You know if we put a little more pressure on our suppliers I reckon we could reduce our costs by another ten percent, and if we hold off on paying them so promptly we could use the additional cash flow to help fund the new hospital. What do you think?"

"I think you need to look at the long term. Don't piss off your suppliers too much; we need them as much as they need us. Possibly more."

"Wow! David Lane, billionaire industrialist, gets soft in his old age! Well I never – who'd have thought that?"

Then he had said, "Are you forgetting why we set out to build these hospitals?"

And she had replied, "Have you forgotten the joy of making money, David? It's easy for you to forget, you've got so much of it."

Now he sat in his car, the conversation replaying over and over again in his head, and it disturbed him. Helen didn't get it. She couldn't see that for him it had never been about making money – it had been about making a difference. The money was just a by-product. The trouble was he knew if your reason for getting up in the morning was just to make money, you probably wouldn't. You'd be too inclined to take shortcuts and then everything you tried to build would collapse around your ears like a cheap block of flats in an earthquake. He would talk to her later when they got back from work. Right now he had other things to think about, like the site meeting later that morning at the new hospital. Things were running a couple of weeks behind schedule.

In the front of the car, the chauffeur, Alex, a giant of a man and one-time amateur bodybuilder, turned the wheel and the Bentley smoothed its way around the corner and into the hospital car park.

"Will you need the car again this morning?" Alex asked.

"No. I'll be here all day. I'll call you when I've finished."

The car stopped in David's reserved space beside the hospital entrance. David got out, shut the door, and as he took a step towards the entrance he caught sight of something moving in his peripheral vision. He turned to look and saw four people running towards him, weaving their way between the parked cars. Alex saw them too and he sprinted around the car to get between them and David, taking up a get-set position, fists raised, ready to fight.

Danny stopped two yards away from the big chauffeur who said, "Another inch and you cross the line. You understand me?"

Danny said, "Mr Lane, we've got to talk to you."

David shook his head and said, "Not interested… whatever it is."

"You will be – I promise."

"Great. Call my secretary and make an appointment." He turned and began to walk towards the hospital entrance.

"We tried that already. Please you have to talk to us!"

Michael tried to make his way past the chauffeur, which was a mistake because the big man jabbed him in the face, grabbed him, lifted him off the floor and threw him to the ground, cracking his head on the tarmac.

Danny and Albert picked him up. His eye was beginning to swell and blood trickled from the gash on his head. Danny shouted, "You know me! For Christ's sake, we've met before. I interviewed you!" David looked him in the eye for a second, and then a flicker of recognition seemed to flash across his face. "I swear to you this is serious, you've got to see us!"

David said, "What's it about?"

"Not here. In private."

David led them into the starkly furnished boardroom – just a long table with seating for twelve people, a cabinet on one side of the room with a coffee machine resting on it, a desk with a computer terminal on the other side.

"You better all take a seat," he said. One of the two sandy-haired guys was holding a handkerchief against his wound, stemming the flow of blood. "I'll get a nurse to look at your head."

"No, it's okay, really. I don't need one," he said.

"That gash looked nasty to me."

"I'll be fine."

"Well, if you're sure…"

"I'm sure."

David said to the tall dark-haired one, "So, remind me of your name."

"Danny Avery."

"Oh, yes, that's it."

"This is Tara, Albert, and the one your man hit is Michael."

"Alex was just doing his job." He looked over at the man-mountain and nodded his approval. Alex gave him a self-satisfied smile.

David said, "You seemed eager to see me, so I hope this is good. You don't have much time, I've got things to do this morning, so you better get on with it."

Danny nodded towards Alex. "Not with him in the room. No offence…"

Alex glanced at David, waiting for instructions.

"It's okay, Alex. I know who this guy is. There'll be no trouble."

Reluctantly Alex left the room.

David crossed his arms, looked at Danny and said, "I'm all ears, so talk. No, wait. Let's clear something up first. That article you wrote about me – you said I was a rich man playing with a football club. Something about jeopardising the hopes of the working class fan. Yes, that was it, wasn't it? You weren't too impressed after our interview."

Danny said, "I, er… I made a mistake."

"Damned right you did. You should have checked the accounts of the club before you came out with that nonsense. They *asked* me to buy it. Playing with it? I was *saving* it. And it's still going strong and a lot of fans, working class or otherwise, are pleased I stepped in. It would have been nice to have had the support of the local press."

"Like I said, I made a mistake."

"I take it this isn't about football?"

"No."

"So… ?"

Danny swallowed hard and took a deep breath. How on earth did you begin to tell someone you had the secret to eternal life? There was no way of knowing how David Lane would react. He could come to the conclusion that they were all lunatics and try to get them locked up. Worse still, he could get a sense of the power of the discovery and how it would turn the world on its head and then side with Cleaver and his cohorts. As someone who had made billions from healthcare and pharmaceuticals he had the power to help them, but he could destroy them too.

"It all started when I took a trip to France…"

Chapter 4

It had been a surreal hour. Danny had told David an abridged version of the story he had lodged with five solicitors in different countries – the story that had protected Tara and he from the British Secret Service. For the most part the billionaire listened with an impassive look on his face, but once or twice he exhibited an expression of disbelief, the trace of a smile on his lips. Danny kept going until five empty coffee cups stood on the table and he got to the part where Mickey and Albert turned up for the first time in The Turcs and Caicos Islands looking like twenty-five year old twins.

David grinned. "So you are telling me these two friends of yours are, how old? One nearly forty and the other close to seventy?"

Danny nodded.

"You've wasted my morning. You told me there was something important I'd want to hear, and this is it? This is what you wanted to tell me? Are you mad? I don't have time for this." He stood up. "This meeting's over."

"Wait!" Tara said. "Please! Listen to him. He's telling you the truth."

"You really thought I'd believe all this? High Priests, Secret Service, nuns, eternal life potions or pills or whatever it is you say you've developed – just what did you expect to gain from this? Strikes me Danny should forget being a reporter and start writing fiction. But you better make your plots more believable or you'll never get them published. I'll have someone show you out." David took a step towards the door.

Danny said, "Don't leave. For God's sake don't – not yet!"

David turned around, "Why? You got more to add to this… story?"

"What you just said, 'just what did you expect to gain from this' – it's a good question isn't it? Just what could we gain from telling you something like this if it isn't true? We've been trying to get to see you for three days. Your secretary fended us off with one excuse after another. Your gorilla assaulted Michael and still we're here, telling you what actually happened – what Michael achieved three years ago. Now, *really* ask yourself, what we have to gain from telling you all this if it isn't the truth. Nothing, right? Absolutely nothing. Now ask yourself what we have to *lose* by telling you all this if what we say *is* true and the British Secret Service are trying to kill us."

David paced the room, pinching his chin with his thumb and forefinger. After a couple of lengths he said, " I take your point, but you are asking me to believe that these two people are… I don't know what, exactly… genetically modified freaks who'll never grow old. You are telling me you have the cure for death! It's not possible – it just isn't."

"So why the hell *have* I told you all this? What *are* we doing here?"

Michael took his handkerchief away from his head, put it in his pocket and said, "He's has told you the truth – everything. We are what he says we are."

Danny pointed at Michael's head, "Look! Look at his head! You saw what happened when he got thrown to the floor. You saw the bruise on his face, the gash on his forehead. You even asked him if he wanted a nurse. Look at it now!"

David walked over to Michael, looking intently at his face. He bent down and peered at the scar tissue that had already formed where there had once been an ugly gash, oozing blood.

Danny said, "How do you explain that? Scar tissue formed in what… an hour? Anyone else would have needed stitches in a wound like that. Where's the blood? Where's the bruising on his face? Gone. There's nothing. By tomorrow morning there won't be a mark on him. You won't know he's been injured. You run hospitals – ever seen someone heal like that?"

David shook his head. "No. Can't say that I have."

Danny said, "Have you got a haematology department here, or immunology?"

David nodded.

"Then run some tests on Michael's blood. You won't believe what you find. Come on, you can at least do that."

David looked at Albert. "Are you really seventy years old?"

Albert said, "Sixty-nine, actually. Mr Lane, sir, what Danny here is saying is true. My boy Michael has worked on this all his life – it was his dream – and by God he achieved what he set out to do. What you heard about the Secret Service – that's all true too. We're all risking our lives by being here talking to you, but I guess it'll all be worth it if we save the lives of everyone on the planet, won't it? Danny tells us you've got the wherewithal to help us. You might be the only one who has. Don't think we're crazy – we're not. We need your help. The whole world needs your help. Just run the tests like Danny said and you'll see we're not... normal."

"That I already believe. All right. You've got me intrigued. Don't think I believe your story, but I have to admit I can't see what you've got to gain from this if it's all a lie. You better stay here. I'll find rooms for you."

"Can I use your phone?" Tara said.

"Sure."

David left the room and Tara called Graham to tell him they were okay and that he could fly back home. They wouldn't be needing him for a while.

David made his way to Helen's office. Of course the idea was crazy. Reversing the aging process? Sure, it would be the most amazing thing if it could be done, but he didn't see how it could be – not yet anyway. One day in the future, perhaps – but the far-off future. His own laboratories were working on face creams to help reduce wrinkles, with some success too, but what this Michael Richards guy was talking about was much more than that. If that young looking man really was seventy years old... David began to imagine the implications of such a discovery, and a shiver ran up and down his spine. It was... unimaginable, fantastic – there weren't words to describe it.

He entered Helen's office and placed a plastic bag containing Michael's bloodied handkerchief on the desk in front of her.

"What's this?" she asked. David didn't answer. "David? What are you up to?"

"Let's just say I need you to help with an investigation. I want you to check out the blood on the handkerchief and tell me what you think."

"What do you mean, 'what I think'?"

"I mean, run every test you can think of on it. Tell me what you can about the DNA of this person – everything. Whatever tests are possible for us to do – do them. We need to build up a total picture."

"What is this, are we working for the police now?"

"No. I'm doing my own investigation. Don't want to tell you what I'm investigating yet; it might prejudice the results you get. I want it to be like a blind test. When can you do it?"

"Is it urgent?"

"Very."

"I'll get someone on it as soon as I can."

He smiled at her, turned and walked towards the door, then said, "By the way. Don't let anyone talk about what you find. No matter what it is, okay? Strictly confidential."

He stepped through the doorway, turned right and heard Helen call after him, "David, what are you up to?"

Joss entered Cleaver's office.

"Morning Alistair."

Cleaver stood up. "Morning Joss. Thanks for dropping by."

"No problem. Now then, what did you want to talk about?"

"I wanted you to see something." He held up the two photographs of Michael Richards. "The scanned image is a picture of Richards at college."

Joss looked carefully at the photos. "Looks like the same person to me."

"It is. I've had some of our chaps look at it. They've taken measurements of his bone structure. They're sure it's the same man."

Joss slumped down on a chair, looking for a moment like a beaten man. The blood seemed to drain from his flesh. He stared out into space, immobile, except for the flaring of his nostrils when he breathed in. "Then he's done it. I don't know how, but the bastard managed to string us along, and then… this. He's got to be stopped."

"I know. Do we have any idea where he might have gone after Croatia?"

Joss's chest began to heave and the blood flowed back into the capillaries of his face, its reddish hue returning, a menacing look in his eyes. Then he said in a chilling whisper, "Find him Alistair. Find him."

Chapter 5

David had come home early. He wanted some time away from the distractions of his office so he could go over the budget for the new hospital. He was sipping his third cup of coffee when Helen arrived. She put her arm around his shoulders and kissed him on the side of his cheek.

"How's it looking?"

"Fine."

"When can we get building it? We've got more on than we can cope with, almost at full capacity. We need more beds. We're missing out on a hell of a lot of turnover."

David looked up at her. How had she got to be so money-motivated? When he first met her she had been a doctor, disenchanted with the National Health Service. She had even written a medical thriller, which had become a best seller and had highlighted the problems within the health system. Back then she had always wanted to save people, to help the sick – money had never been important to her. But now she never talked about the patients, just how much profit they were making. The change in her was disturbing.

"Did you get any tests done on that blood sample?"

"Immunology and Haematology did some. Come on, David. What was it you gave me to test?"

"Just some blood."

"Yeah, but it wasn't like any blood sample they'd ever seen before. Are you working on some new drug?"

"What makes you say that?"

"Because they said it seemed to eat up any viruses they introduced to it, as if it had been treated in some way. They haven't worked out what you added to it yet. Whatever it is it seems to be undetectable, so why don't you save us the trouble and tell us what it was?"

"It's strengthened the immune system?"

"From what I heard that's an understatement. Come on, you can tell me – what is it?"

"Wait a while. It'll be a nice surprise for you."

They had each been given their own room, but they all sat together in Michael's now. Danny and Tara were playing cards; Albert was watching a film on TV. Michael was sitting up on his bed, a flat screen computer monitor on an arm positioned in front of him.

Michael said, "This hospital is amazing. It's like a five-star hotel. You should see this computer system. I've got Internet access, VOIP telephone calls – all free of charge, games – all sorts of things. There's even an in-house virtual meeting room. I've been chatting with a woman who's just had a baby and a man with a broken leg. Incredible. He must be busy – I mean who'd want to go to any other hospital?"

Danny said, "He's caused a stir. The government hates him – he makes the National Health Service look stupid and inefficient. Compared to this it is, of course."

"How does he do it?"

"I read an interview with him once. He said it's all down to applying business practice to health care. He said something about his costs being low because he runs it in an efficient way – free of bureaucracy. Insurance companies love him because he charges less than the other private hospitals and he always leaves the patients happy. Half of them don't want to go home."

Tara said, "Was he a doctor before?"

"No he was a billionaire – probably a good thing to be if you want to start a hospital. He made his money buying up ailing companies turning them around and selling them on. I think he wanted to prove a point when he went into healthcare. It's not just hospitals – it's pharmaceuticals, old folks homes – he's got a huge chain of those. I guess he realised the population was getting older."

The door opened and David walked in.

"Hi. Hope you're all comfortable."

Albert said, "Yeah. I'm thinking of moving in. What's for lunch?"

"Get Michael to bring up the menu on the computer. You can order what you want online and it'll be brought to you."

"Room service. Just like a hotel," Danny said.

"That's the way I like to think of it. A five-star hotel with operations thrown in."

"Novel approach."

"I like to do things differently. But… that's not what I'm here to talk about right now."

"You've run some tests?"

David nodded.

"Well?" Danny said.

"He's got a strong immune system."

"That's all you've got to say?"

Michael said, "Easy, Danny. That's all he's going to see at first."

Danny pointed at Michael's head. "Go and take a look."

David walked over to Michael and looked at his forehead. There wasn't a mark on him – no trace of where the gash had been.

"See anything?"

"No."

"You think it's just an immune system that did that?"

David looked puzzled. "No – I, er… I've never seen anything like that. There's no scar. It's … strange."

"I told you what the High Priest said. He told us he was The Second Coming and it was because he healed like this that he hadn't got any scars on his hands from when he was nailed to the cross."

"Yeah, but you don't believe that do you?"

"No, of course not. The guy was a fake, as far as being The Second Coming was concerned, but there was no trickery when it came to healing scars. You know that yourself now, you've just seen it."

"Doesn't prove that Albert is seventy years old though, does it?"

"No, but…" Danny scratched his head. He looked at Michael. "You know, I think we're wasting our time here. We're not going to convince him."

Michael said, "Patience, Danny. In the end all he's got to go on is that I look young and healthy and I'm not an alien with a different kind of body. I'm a human with a body that's normal in every way except that it won't get ill and it'll never grow old. He needs to do a lot of work studying my DNA to see where the difference lies. No one's just going to believe what we say."

David said, "Not unless…"

"What?"

"Not unless you turn someone young."

"Oh yeah, sure. Just wheel 'em out and we'll make 'em young," Danny said sarcastically. "I suppose you've got someone in mind."

"Yes, as a matter of fact I have."

Chapter 6

The old man lay on his back, an oxygen mask on his face. His arms lay on top of the bedcover, his gnarled hands protruding from the sleeves of his striped pyjamas. Electrodes were stuck on his chest and a line on a monitor jumped up and down when his heart beat. David stood beside him.

"Uncle John."

The old man stirred. "Ah, David," he said in a weak voice. He tried to sit up.

"Don't try to get up. There's something we have to talk about."

John smiled. "You want to listen to more ramblings from an old man? I've already told you all about your father and mother, God rest them, and how things were in the old days."

"They were good times, yes?"

"Hah! They were the best!" He coughed. "It's funny – I can't remember yesterday, but the old days – ah, yes… I can run those movies over and over again in this old head. I can even smell the sea and feel the sun beating down on my body back in Italy when I met your Aunt Maria. She was so beautiful! When I first saw her it was like a sledgehammer had hit my chest. I swear I couldn't breath for five minutes. It was so long ago, but... life passes so fast."

"Would you go back there if you could?"

"What a question! You ask me this as I lie here dying? What answer do you think I would give you?"

"What if you really could go back there?"

"I've lived with your Aunt Maria for fifty-five years and I've loved her all that time with all my heart. Soon death is going to separate us. I'm not a religious man, David. You think I want to end up rotting in a box six-feet under the earth? There is nothing I wouldn't do to stay with her. There's no fun in growing old. Wise – yes, but old... no. Age creeps up on you. You wake up one day and find things don't work the way they once did – and you know they never will again. Would I go back to those days... when we were both young, full of hope, brimming over with the joy of living? If you know what love is you don't need to ask. Of course I would!" He started to cough again, his body convulsing, and then he put the oxygen mask over his face and took deep rasping breaths until the coughing fit subsided.

David said, "What if I told you that you really could go back there?"

"I'd say you're an incurable romantic – just like your father was."

"Uncle John. There's something... some new medical breakthrough... that might be able to make you young. I want to give it to you."

"Hah! Go and get the pills!"

"I'm not joking."

The old man looked into David's eyes and they held each other's gaze for a few seconds.

"My God... you're serious aren't you?"

David entered Michael's room.

"You sure this is going to work?" Michael nodded. "And it's safe?"

Michael hesitated for a moment, then said, "There can be no guarantees. I haven't had an opportunity to test it much on humans, but then I never will, will I?"

"What are you going to do, inject him with your blood?"

"Yes."

"Is that it? I mean is that all you did to become young, inject yourself with some blood from The High Priest?"

"No, it wasn't that easy. The High Priest provided me the basis for this, but I had to do some engineering. He wasn't quite the finished article – he was getting older."

"But it just seems so easy."

"It is now. But I had to change my own DNA by infecting it with a version of the AIDS virus that had been crossed with genetic material from The High Priest. It altered the makeup of every cell in my body and I became young and free from aging. My blood contains the virus now and it's extremely virulent, rabid almost. Once it enters the body of your uncle it will make him forever young too. He will be immune from the aging disease, as I call it."

"You better know that, although the man you're going to be giving this to is my uncle, I regard him as my father. He brought me up, along with my aunt Maria. My parents were killed when I was very young."

"Sorry to hear that."

"Wasn't looking for sympathy. What I'm trying to say to you is that you better make damned sure you've got this right before you go ahead. This man is precious to me."

"I understand. But I'll say it again – there are no guarantees. People die, sometimes undergoing minor operations. Mistakes happen."

"Just be sure of what you are doing, okay?"

"If you don't want me to do this, I won't."

"I didn't say that."

Michael met David's gaze for a second. "You see we both know what *is* guaranteed. If we don't do something your uncle is going to die. Very soon. Looking at it like that, safety becomes less of an issue, don't you think?"

"Maybe. I don't want to do anything that speeds up the process."

"You don't want to be responsible for it. But you're not. Time, the aging process, whatever you want to call it, is responsible, not you. You are responsible for trying to save him – no matter what happens."

David looked at the floor for a few seconds. Then he lifted his head and said, "He's weak. We can't wait any longer. Let's do it tomorrow."

Chapter 7

They made their way to John's room, David in front, Danny, Tara, Michael and Albert following. When he reached the door David paused for a moment, getting his thoughts straight, coming to terms with what he was about to do. He glanced behind at the others, took a deep breath, turned the door handle and stepped into the room.

Beside the bed, holding John's hand, was a woman, five foot four inches tall, dark hair flecked with grey, pulled back in a bun, emphasising her high cheekbones.

"Aunt Maria, we're ready now. It's better if you leave us for a while," David said.

"I'm not going anywhere. You need to know that we've been talking and we've reached a decision."

David sighed, then got agitated. "But we don't have a choice. Uncle John doesn't have much time. We have to at least try this!"

"David, calm down. We don't want to stop what you're going to do, but we'll only agree to it on one condition."

"What?"

"That you give us *both* the treatment, together."

"What? No! Look... Aunt Maria, Uncle John has no choice, he's going to die if we do nothing. But you... you're not ill, you're not dying. There are risks involved here. We can't take the chance of giving it to you – it might not be safe."

"You think I care? Do you think I want to live without him? If he dies... then I'll be dead anyway."

"But if it doesn't work and you both die, I'll be responsible!"

"You are not responsible for my life – I am. It's my – OUR decision.

In a weak whispery voice, John said, "David, you're missing the point. I don't want to live forever and be separated from her."

"But you won't be separated from her. She'll be here!"

Maria said, "If he goes back to being twenty-five years old, what use will I be to him? I'm sixty-eight years old. We'd be separated by two generations! We've made our decision."

"Listen to her, David. We want to live together or die together," John said.

They were as stubborn now as they had always been. Realising he would never win the argument, David turned to Michael and said, "Have you got enough blood for two people?"

Michael nodded.

"Then I guess I better get another bed in here."

An hour later Maria was sitting on the edge of her bed next to John's, holding her husband's hand, gazing at him as he lay asleep, still with the oxygen mask covering his face. David entered the room and Maria turned to look at him.

"Everything is ready," David said.

Maria nodded. "Just... give us a moment, would you?"

He left the room, closing the door behind him. Maria bent over her husband and kissed his forehead, waking him up.

"John... they're ready." She smiled at him and smoothed his hair. "Suddenly I don't know if I should be saying goodbye, or..."

John pulled the oxygen mask away from his face and said, "Are you sure you want to do this?"

"Of course I do, my love. You know I'd give anything to live another fifty years with you."

John smiled and said, "You remember that first summer we spent in Sicily?"

"Like it was yesterday.'

"Maybe we can do it again tomorrow?'

Maria laughed softly. "Promise me you'll take me there and dance with me at the Grand Hotel?"

"I promise. Kiss me one more time."

She kissed him on the lips, made her way over to the door, opened it and beckoned them in. Then she returned to her bed and lay on it, taking John's hand in hers once more. She closed her eyes and a serene smile played on her lips.

Five minutes later Michael filled a syringe, found a vein in John's arm and injected him. He took another syringe and did the same to Maria.

They stood behind Michael, their faces full of apprehension, wondering what would happen. And then David's eyes widened with surprise, his mouth fell open and he watched in awe as his uncle's and aunt's facial lines began to soften and their skin tone changed.

"My God!" he said. "It's working!" He stood with the fingers of his hands interlocked, like hooks. "It's... it's a miracle!"

Twelve hours later he sat in a chair opposite the beds, his mind racing with thoughts about the world turning young – thoughts that only a few hours earlier he would have dismissed as those of a madman. But now...

Michael sat on the chair beside him, keeping watch, making sure his patients were going to be all right.

"You know... this is just... I give up trying to describe it – there aren't words, are there?"

"No. I guess there aren't," Michael said.

Suddenly John and Maria began to shake violently.

David leapt to his feet. "Something's going wrong!"

Michael grabbed his arm. "Take it easy. It's okay. Same thing happened when I gave it to my father. It's normal."

John and Maria continued shaking as if an electric current was pulsing through them.

"Why do they do that?"

"I'm not actually sure," Michael said. "It's like their bodies are getting charged up in some way."

"Charged up?"

"With life. I can't explain it any other way."

The convulsions stopped.

"They look half their age already. I... I can't thank you enough."

"You don't need to thank me. Eradicating death is what I set out to do – it's my life's work."

David smiled. "There's nothing like thinking big, eh?" Michael smiled back. "Do you know what this means – what is going to happen to mankind, the world?"

Quietly, Michael said, "Yes... I do."

Chapter 8

At 9.00am Danny, Tara and Albert entered John and Maria's room. David and Michael were dozing in their chairs, but they woke up when they heard the door open.

Danny walked over to John and Maria.

"Jesus… You've done it. My God, it's just… amazing."

They all gathered at the end of the beds, looking down at two people who looked like fit, healthy twenty-five-year-olds. John stirred. He yawned, stretched his arms above his head and then rubbed his eyes. Suddenly he became aware of the faces gawping at him.

"David? What are you all looking at?"

John sat up. He looked to his left and saw Maria lying there, twenty-five years old again. For a few seconds he stared at her, transfixed, mouth open, trying to come to terms with what was before his eyes. He reached out and touched her face. Then he noticed his own hand and how young it looked. He looked at David.

"Am I…?"

Michael held up a mirror.

John saw himself newly young for the first time and traced the contours of his face with his fingertips, feeling his taught skin.

"I… I don't know what to say. Thank you… thank you…"

Maria awoke. She sat up and saw her husband looking just as he had when he was twenty-five years old.

"John? John… is that you? It is! My God it's really you!"

They both leapt out of bed and hugged each other.

John said, "Show her the mirror!"

Michael handed it to her and she looked at herself, eyes wide open in shock, her lips parted. Then she turned to the side and examined her profile. Tears ran down her cheek. John put his arm around her and together they looked at their reflection.

"It's us. It really is us," John said. "Just like we were when we-"

He cut short his sentence, ran over to the wardrobe and took out a photograph from inside his wallet.

"Here, look! It's us on our wedding day. We're the same!"

David hugged him and then hugged Maria. "How do you feel?"

"How do I feel? Like I could take on Joe Louis and Muhammad Ali at the same time – with one hand tied behind my back. That's how I feel!" He turned to Maria. "We could start up the old act! We could play the London Palladium again, like the old days!"

Maria said, "Great idea, but I'm not sure they want stage hypnotist acts these days. We'll have to learn something else."

Danny said, "You were in show business?"

"You bet we were. We were the best – played to full houses everywhere!"

John grabbed Maria and kissed her neck. She giggled girlishly and then David said, "I think we better give you some time alone. Just… don't leave the room, okay? I'm going to lock you in."

They stepped out into the corridor and David closed the door. He told a nurse not to let anyone enter the room or go in herself and then said to Michael, "I think we better talk."

Danny sat down in the boardroom. The others joined him, David sitting at the head of the table. Danny looked at David's face, trying to work out what was going on in his head. He had seen him in the newspapers and occasionally on TV, always looking cool and confident, like any other billionaire. But not now, of course – he'd just witnessed his uncle and aunt being saved from death, made young, immortal, resistant to illness, full of life and vibrant. David shifted around on his seat, as if a thousand thoughts were fighting for prominence in his consciousness. Finally he put his elbows on the table, rubbed his eyes and looked at Danny.

"Sorry I doubted you," he said.

Danny remembered how he had felt back in France when he had first realised what Michael had been working on. He knew what David was going through. "I would have in your position. It was a crazy story."

"Was it *all* true? I mean, I know now the bit about making people young was true, but the High Priest… ?"

"Every word was true."

"So, the British Secret Service blew up the convent?"

Danny nodded. "As soon as they found out I was onto the story. They backed off from trying to kill us when they heard I'd sent the story to five lawyers in different countries with instructions to send it to the newspapers if anything happened to either Tara or me. If you think the government is full of nice, happy, well-meaning people, you're mistaken."

"I'm under no illusions about that. But they don't know what you were really working on do they? Didn't they think you were developing some kind of gas for them?"

"Yes. A really nasty gas, capable of wiping out a country in two weeks – and they wanted it bad. Nice people. David, you're aware of what this discovery means, aren't you?"

"I'm trying to grasp it."

Michael said, "It takes a while for it to sink in, but let me put it this way. Every social structure man has ever created has been built within the context of there being a thing called death. Which means that if you eradicate death, the way society is constructed is no longer relevant. Everything we know will change."

"A lot of people aren't going to like that."

"Power structures will be ripped apart. If you don't get old and ill, we won't need so many doctors, hospitals, or chemists. Pharmaceutical companies will collapse. Old people's homes will be a thing of the past."

"What you're telling me is that I'm going to go out of business."

"Think what would happen to pension funds. They won't exist as we know them. No one's going to get to retirement age, which is just as well because if they did the pension funds would have to pay out forever. But it goes deeper than that because the biggest investors in stock markets *are* the pension funds, and they won't be there anymore. Everything – the way we live – it will all change. Everyone will have time to do anything or learn anything they want to. The old will be prized for their knowledge and experience; youth will be a given – everyone will have it."

Danny said, "You have to think about religions too. There would be no point in preaching about salvation in the afterlife if there was no death. But it's the politicians who are going to freak out most about this. Imagine a world of healthy happy people – no sickness, no death, no pensions to worry about. What are they going to ask you to vote for come election time? They're going to lose their power over us and that's why they will do anything to stop it. What they did at the convent in France is nothing compared to what they would do if they knew what we are really doing."

David sat back in his swivel chair, folded his arms and swung gently from side to side, seemingly deep in thought. "My God, it's impossible. How can you keep something like this quiet? I've got an aunt and an uncle who are twenty-five years old again, and they look like they want to jump up and down and shout about it. If they see any of their friends… They *can't* keep it quiet – it's the biggest thing that's ever happened to them – it's the biggest thing that's ever happened to mankind."

For a moment no one said anything. Danny eventually broke the silence. "We were hoping you could help us."

"How did you think I was going to do that?"

"I don't know."

"I'm a businessman, not God. You said it yourself – the moment they get wind of anyone turning young they're going to stop it. Someone is going to have an accident. Jesus Christ – I thought I was saving my uncle and aunt; I might have just signed their own death warrants! They are going to have to move to another country – somewhere where nobody knows them. I just don't know what can be done to help you, I really don't."

Tara said, "But we can't do nothing, can we? I don't want to sound melodramatic, but the truth is that if we don't do something we are condemning six and a half billion people to a needless death."

"So… no pressure then?" David said.

With no clue as to the whereabouts of Michael Richards, Cleaver flew to America, thinking the scientist might return to his roots. He entered a bar – the third one he had visited that night in the small Ohio town. Not wanting to stick out like a Jamaican at a Klu Klux Klan reunion, he had forsaken his usual pinstriped suit and breast pocket handkerchief, but his navy blue blazer with the gold buttons didn't make him blend in with the locals either. He might just as well have put a neon light on his head saying, I'm a foreigner.

He sat on a barstool next to a stocky man who wore a dirty red baseball cap and stained overalls.

The man turned to Cleaver and said, "You ain't from around these parts are ya?"

How astute.

Cleaver examined the man's craggy face with its ruddy complexion and squinty eyes and concluded he was probably the end product of a long line of inbreeding.

Cleaver forced a smile. "No, I'm not. I suppose it's obvious."

"Hey, that accent. You're foreign, right? What are ya? Let me guess – Australian? Yeah, that's it."

"British."

"British. That's great. What are ya, on holiday?"

"Well, yes, sort of. I, er, I was in New York, you know, seeing the sights and all that. Then I remembered someone I met once in London many years ago and I thought I'd try to look him up."

"Where're they from?"

"Here. Obviously."

"Right. You found the guy?"

"No, not yet. Just arrived here, you see. Not sure where to look."

"Well it's a small town. Lived and loved here all my life. Maybe I can point you in the right direction."

"I'm trying to find Albert Richards."

The man let out a guffaw and Cleaver raised a quizzical eye.

"You and the rest of us!"

Cleaver cleared his throat. "You and the rest of us? What does that mean exactly?"

"Means no one round here knows where he is. He just up and left about three years ago. Never said goodbye or nothing. Don't know why he left or if he's coming back. No one does. Mind you, some of us have our suspicions."

"Meaning you, I take it?"

"Yeah… I got a hunch."

"Care to share it with me?"

"How badly do you want to find him?" Cleaver took out his wallet and extracted a $50 note. "Don't know who you are mister, but you're no friend of his."

"What makes you so sure?"

"Not sure you'd be so quick to give me your money if you were just a friend. Don't think you want to pay him a social call. Apart from that… Albert ain't never been to England. Lived here all his life. Never left the place; never went to England – unless that's where he is now. But you said you'd seen him there many years ago, didn't you. You didn't. That I do know."

The man swigged the last of his beer from its bottle and stood up to go, leaving the $50 bill on the bar.

"Wait." Cleaver took out a $100 bill and put it beside the $50 one.

"You sure do want to find him, don't you?"

"Let's just say I'm intrigued to hear your theory."

The man picked up the money.

"I got a hunch Albert found religion."

"Why do you say that?"

"Well… couple of things. Albert had a son called Michael. He was real smart. Didn't get his brains from Albert, but he got them, that's for sure. He went to college and got a good education – something biological or medical, I don't know which. Thing is, the boy got religious and got himself mixed up with some kinda cult led by a long haired guy who looked like Jesus Christ himself. They took off somewhere. Don't know where. But Albert loved his son – that I do know. He worked his butt off to get him through college and he was none too happy when he upped and left. Michael was all he had after his wife died and it looked to a lot of us that when Michael left here something died inside of Albert. He always said his son would come back someday and that he was busy doing important work. Don't know if that was true or just a proud father talking. Far as I know Michael never did come back. But I reckon wherever he is is where you'll find Albert."

"You say he just disappeared three years ago?"

"Yep."

"How do you know something bad didn't happen to him? He might have had an accident or something."

"Because he cancelled the newspapers before he went. He didn't say he'd be back in two weeks. He just cancelled them period. To me that sounds like someone who *knows* they aren't coming back. But then you'll know that – you're the private dick, right?"

Chapter 9

David turned the key in the lock and entered the apartment. He wondered what he was going to tell Helen. Before leaving the hospital he had gone to see John and Maria again and had told them they were to stay in their room, which was difficult for them, because they wanted to go outside and breath the air, run up a mountain, dance in a fountain, or do something a little crazy just to celebrate life. Still... it seemed like they were having a great time in bed together.

On the journey back home he had thought about the conversation in the boardroom and the implications of turning the world young. Whenever he felt he'd grasped it something else came into his mind and he realised this thing was so indefinably big that he would have to change the whole context of his thinking if he was ever going to really 'get' it. His mind kept telling him it was science fantasy, but John and Maria were there in the hospital – living, breathing proof that it wasn't.

Helen was sitting at the table, tapping away on a calculator, running her finger down a column of figures again.

"Hi," she said without looking up.

"You had a good day?" he asked.

"Just a minute... almost finished." She tapped in the last figure then looked at the total. "Yes! This is great! We're going to make a fortune! I've got the prices down. You're not the only one who can negotiate!"

David tried to muster some enthusiasm. "That's great."

"I've screwed them hard. We're going to come in under budget, way under – I'm sure of it. And that means millions in our pocket."

"Well done."

"I'm going to look at that site near Leeds. We can push on with the next hospital, keep rolling them out, one after the other!"

"You haven't... screwed them too hard, have you?"

"What do you mean by that?"

"Just that we need them to work with us and care about keeping our business. If they can't make a profit from us we won't get any service from them."

"Make enough money from *us?* Are you kidding? They're greedy, all of them. They need cutting down to size. Anyway I'm more concerned about what *we* make than I am about them."

"You have to take care of your suppliers too."

"It's okay for you, you've made your money, built your empire. I'm building mine and I'm not letting anything get in my way. I'm going to grow this business fast. We're in the right sector – hospitals, pharmaceuticals, geriatrics – all growing – we're untouchable!"

David sat down. "Nothing's untouchable. Things change."

"People get ill, they get old, they die – can't change that. We're in the right market. Can't see a limit to how big we can grow. Just make sure your pharmaceutical companies don't make anything too effective."

"What? You're joking, I hope."

She laughed nervously. "Well… yes, of course."

A shiver ran down his spine.

She said, "It was you who taught me about making money."

"I taught you that if you concentrated on giving more value you couldn't help but make more money. If you only think about making more money and forget to keep increasing the value… eventually it will end in tears."

"Don't worry, David. There'll be no tears here. We're going to grow and grow!"

Danny and the others were sitting around the boardroom table again, waiting for David to arrive. Eventually the door opened and he walked in looking perturbed by something. He sat down on his chair, making no eye contact with anyone. They waited for him to speak. Finally he broke the silence.

"You know… I can't thank you enough for what you did for my uncle…" Danny sensed there was a 'but' coming. "You saved his life…"

"I think we did more than that." Danny said. "He got his youth and his health back too – and his young wife. We turned the clock back –

gave him the chance to run it again, only this time he can do things better because he'll have a lifetime's experience to draw on. Not a bad situation, huh? They won't ever grow old. They are just going to grow, together, for all time."

"I know," David said. "I can't get my head around it. I think I've got it, but then I realise I haven't – there's always more – bigger implications. What Michael said about everything man has created, everything we know, being based on the assumption that we die, is true. Living *and* dying has always been the way of things. Living and living, without death or aging... that's just..."

Michael said, "I want to bring it to everyone, give everyone the chance to live forever, if they choose to. It's the greatest gift anyone can have."

"I know, I realise that," David said. "But for the life of me I can't see how it can be brought to everyone. One sniff of this and you're right, governments will be falling over themselves to stop it. If they understand the implications of it they'll know that once it's out of the bag they'll lose power and control over people. I can picture the Prime Minister right now thinking about it. They say power is addictive, right? Once you have it, the thought of losing it... well, I'd say a lot of people would do anything to cling on to it... anything."

Danny said, "Does that include you?"

"What do you mean by that?"

"I mean it hasn't escaped my notice that you make a lot of money out of illness, what with your hospitals, drug companies – to say nothing of your old people's homes."

"Danny!" Tara said.

"Well, it has to be said. I think David has the power to do something to help us, but his power is built on the wealth he created from illness and aging. This is going to put him out of business." Tara, Michael and Albert looked uneasy, as if they sensed Danny was about to seriously piss off the man who was their only hope. "Well, it's true." He looked directly at David. "Are you willing to give up everything to save the world from death? It would be kind of like the ultimate sacrifice for you, wouldn't it?"

David paused for a moment before answering. "You know, Danny, you're no different to most people. You think that all entrepreneurs are only interested in making money. You can't see past the pound or dollar signs, can you? Oddly enough it's that that stops you making much yourself. I'm not stupid, Danny. You can give me credit for that, can't you? But I would be if I kept on doing what I do just to make more money. I can already buy more than I can conceive of spending, so I'd be wasting my time, wouldn't I? People like me get successful because we want to make a difference to something. If you've done your homework you'll know that I was a billionaire before I even went into healthcare. I got into it because in this country the government has a virtual monopoly on medical care, and when did you see a government provide anything efficiently or well? Ever see a nationalised industry provide its customers with good service? Why should it be any different with health care? Yet for some reason people see this as an area where business ideas are not welcome or appropriate – and of course, profit is a no-no. Odd thing is, every nurse and doctor comes to work for profit. They trade their time and skill for money, which they use to pay their bills. If their pay didn't exceed their bills – i.e. they didn't make a profit from their work – they couldn't carry on doing the job. Why should it be any different for the owner of the hospital? Why shouldn't he make a profit too? Danny, believe it or not, I came into this to make things better, not to make money. I just don't think it's an either or situation. But don't worry. I'd give up all this in an instant if I could help make people forever young and healthy. I just don't know how I can do it and stay alive. It's a paradox, isn't it? The secret to life will get you killed."

The room stayed silent for a while, then David continued, "I can't even let my aunt and uncle go home."

"What are you going to do about them?" Tara asked.

"I've got an apartment in Monaco. I'm going to put them in it until I come up with a better solution."

"But we can't just do nothing!" Danny said, banging the table.

"You want to get killed?"

"This is something worth dying for! We all agreed that before we came here. We can't keep it to ourselves, we have to get it out to people!"

"Danny, it's no use saying that – you've got to come up with an idea! As soon as someone is turned young and they get wind of it – that's it – we'll be silenced, for sure."

"There must be a way," Michael said.

"There is no way – there just isn't – I've thought about it," David said. "You can't turn people young without anyone noticing, can you? My God, it would create waves like nothing on earth has *ever* done!"

"But we can't let this go. Everyone is going to die, for nothing, if we don't do something," Tara said.

"Look, like I said, as soon as they know what we're doing we'll be killed."

"Well... then we'll just have to find a way to turn people young without them knowing what we're doing," Tara said.

"But there isn't a way of doing that, is there? You're old, and then you're young. You can't hide that – you just can't."

Danny sat looking at the table. It had all been a waste of time. They had put their lives at risk and come to England for nothing. Not that it was David's fault. Danny could hardly blame him for not coming up with a solution – *they* hadn't come up with one either, and they had had longer to think about it. Michael and Albert and John and Maria had benefited from Michael's aging cure. When the time came, Danny and Tara would benefit from it too. But they would have to watch while the people they knew and loved grew old and died around them. They wouldn't be able to stay friends with people for long, because they'd be unable to explain why they weren't getting older whilst everyone else withered away. It was a sickening thought.

And then David spoke.

"Wait a minute. There might be a way after all."

Cleaver sat at his desk looking at the picture taken of the two young men in Croatia. He heard someone open the door and felt the rush of air as the person entered without knocking. Cleaver didn't need to look up to know who it was.

"Ah, Alistair. You're back. Fruitful trip I hope?"

"Hello Joss. Would you like to sit down?"

"No time. Just give me an update – short and to the point."

Cleaver let out a sigh and then said, "It seems it's as bad as we thought."

"Go on."

"I found myself in a bar in the town where Richards was brought up. It's a nasty little place. I asked around trying to find out more about our young scientist and his father. Apparently the father disappeared three years ago. Didn't tell anyone where he was going, just that he was going away. No one knows where to, and no one's heard from him since."

"Three years ago, eh...?"

Cleaver continued, "I don't think I need to remind you that three years ago was about the time of the, er... situation down in France. We know one of the twins in this picture is Michael Richards – his college yearbook confirms it."

Joss's eyebrows drew closer together on his forehead. "What you're going to tell me is that the other character is actually Richards's father?" Cleaver nodded. Joss picked up the photograph and stared at it. "My God. Two genetic freaks running around, doing... heaven knows what. It beggars belief..."

"I don't suppose there's any hope he might just... I don't know, use it for himself and his father and leave it at that, is there?"

"Not likely. Anyone mad enough to tinker like this with nature must have an ego the size of Everest. No... he'll try to spread it, or sell somehow."

"I don't see how he's going to do that without us spotting it straight away."

"Just you bloody well make sure we do! I want this stopped permanently – you know what I mean? What about that reporter chappie?"

"Danny Avery. Like I said before, I don't think he knows about all this."

"Make sure he doesn't."

"I've got someone checking it out right now."

Chapter 10

David had given them the outline of his plan, stunning them into silence, but ten minutes later they were all for it – it was all they had. Danny glanced around the room wondering what the others were thinking. Michael seemed uneasy about something.

"You look troubled," Danny said.

Michael paused for a moment and then said to David, "You need to be sure about this." David met his gaze but said nothing. "Look, we've got you involved in this and obviously you didn't know what you were getting into when we barged our way in here."

Danny said, "Michael, what are you saying? We fly over here to persuade him to join us and when he's on board you try to talk him out of it… ?"

"He has to *really* want to do this – of his own free will."

Michael looked at David and continued, "The rest of us knew we were putting out lives at risk, but it was our choice. What I'm trying to say is that Danny thought you could help us, and I think he was right, you can. But that doesn't mean you have to. We're asking you to do something that'll put your life at risk, and, if the plan works, will destroy what you've built here. What I'm trying to say is that you don't have to do it if you don't want to."

David steepled his fingers as if in prayer and tapped his fingertips on his forehead. Eventually he said, "I appreciate what you're saying. Thanks. But it's not something I can walk away from or ignore, now is it? As for what I'll be losing – I'm proud of what I've achieved here, but trying to compare it to what you've done would be like holding up a grain of sand against the Sahara Desert. Truth is I'd give it up in a minute to cure the world of death. Anyway, you've heard the plan. You can't do it without me, and you haven't got a better one, have you?"

Danny watched the exchange sensing that David was feeling just as he had when talking in bed with Tara about whether they should help Michael and Albert or just get on with their lives. It wasn't possible. Once you *knew* this existed your life was no longer the same – you *were* involved, and you *had* to do what you could to bring it to others. This was the moment of commitment, the moment from which there would be no turning back. What would follow really would be a life or death struggle, and he knew they might be killed by a government or someone with a vested interest in things staying as they were. But what difference would it make? If they couldn't get Michael's discovery out to the world, in a few decades they'd all be dead anyway.

David said, "Okay, let's do it."

The Preparations began.

David told Helen she was now in complete charge of running the hospitals.

"That's great. You wait and see what I'll do to the profits! What are you going to do?"

"I'm, er… I'm going to be working on a few ideas. Something on geriatrics. And I'm going to try to push along the development of some new drugs. I'll be spending some time away, I'm afraid."

She didn't look up from the spreadsheet she was working on. "Okay. Don't worry about me, I'll be fine."

And somehow he knew she would be. He packed a suitcase and left her to her figures.

The crucial element of the plan was the involvement of John and Maria. Without them there was no way forward. When David told them what he wanted them to do they were as excited as two five-year-olds on Christmas morning and couldn't wait to get started, but for now he needed them to stay away from people who knew them, and so he checked them into a hotel, told them to keep out of trouble, and said he would contact them when everything was set and ready to go.

Next he flew to Buenos Aries in his private jet, taking with him some samples of Michael's blood. He met with Jorge, the manager of his Argentinean pharmaceutical company, and instructed him to get on with breeding transgenic pigs. They would look like any other pig, but with one crucial difference: Their blood would be human, with the same anti-aging properties that Michael, Albert, and now John and

Maria shared. If it worked they would eventually have a constant supply of age-reversing blood.

He told Jorge, "This is top secret. You have to keep this to yourself. I want you to get a small team together and keep everyone else away from the project."

"Of course, Mr Lane. Can I ask what it is you are working on?"

"No. But it's something big. There'll be a bonus for you of $1,000,000 if it works."

"A million dollars! Are you serious?"

"Deadly. And there's another million to be divided up amongst the rest of the team you put together. The smaller the team the more each person will get, you understand?"

"I see, yes. You don't want many people to know about this."

"No one is to know about what we are doing unless they have to."

"And that includes me?"

"For now, yes. But it will soon become apparent."

David left Jorge and flew to his pharmaceutical plant in the Czech Republic, where he dropped off a sample of Michael's blood and told his plant manager to turn it into pills.

"But it's just blood. You want me to make blood pills?" The manager said.

"Just do it. Amuse me. But be careful. The blood has been treated in a special way. It's highly infectious. Make sure no one comes into contact with it. Treat it as if the sample is HIV positive."

David checked into a hotel. Two days later he collected the blood pills in sealed containers and then took off in his jet on the return journey to England. By the time he landed his luxury yacht, called *Karen,* had docked in Southampton on the south coast of England. Michael installed some medical equipment in one of the cabins and then supervised the upgrading of the satellite communication systems and the installation of a bank of TV screens.

Danny, Tara and Albert constructed the props to make a spoof film. They built a circular wooden platform and attached stage lights all around its circumference. Armed with a generator, some ropes and pulleys and a dry ice machine, they set off with the platform to find some woodland. At dusk they began recording a short film on Danny's mobile phone. Through the foliage the platform spun around, the coloured lights flashed and clouds of dry ice billowed. Then Albert pulled on the rope and the platform rose into the air.

"Cut!" Danny shouted. "That's a wrap!"

They giggled to themselves and gathered around the mobile phone to watch the shaky, amateur movie being played back.

"Perfect." Danny said. "You know what? I could be the next Stephen Spielberg."

Before leaving the woods they shot it again in three different locations using different angles.

The next day Danny wrote an article about aliens visiting Earth and posted it on his news website. Then he uploaded one of the films to the *YouTube.com* video sharing website. Over the next few days the word spread and the number of hits grew. They uploaded the second film and before long a national newspaper carried the story and their thirty-second movie was shown at the end of the BBC News. They uploaded the rest of the films, each posted with a different username, and soon the cyber-world was awash with gossip about visiting aliens. Just as they predicted, other people sent in reports to newspapers about UFOs, and news gatherers around the world interviewed ever increasing numbers of people who claimed to have seen aliens. *Sixty Minutes* ran a program entitled: *Are We Being Invaded?* Suddenly it seemed that half the planet was out at night gazing up at the sky for any streak of light that might be a spaceship.

The seed had been sown.

Everything was set.

The phone rang.

"Cleaver here… What?" His face turned white. "Are you sure?" He listened for a few moments, chewing his lip, and then said, "No, I'll let you know." He replaced the phone and looked up at Joss. "It seems he's left the island, along with the girl."

"Where've they gone?"

"He didn't know. Apparently they left in a hurry. The girl sings in a local bar. She didn't turn up one night and hasn't been seen since. The bar owner wasn't pleased. Why leave now?"

"Don't be so bloody naïve – you know exactly why. If you can't find Richards, find Avery. Find one you find them both, I'll bet my life on it."

Joss stormed out of the office.

Danny Avery mixed up in this? Poking his nose in to things he shouldn't again? The man was more irritating than a horse fly.

Images of the events of three years earlier in that grotty hotel on The Isle of Man flashed before Cleaver's eyes. He remembered the indignity of it all and the mental anguish he had suffered later when undergoing therapy. Therapy? His cheeks flushed with shame and anger at the very idea of it. He had been unable to wreak his revenge on the nasty little reporter thanks to that damned story lodged with the solicitors. But this anti-aging thing superseded everything. Now was his chance for redress! Wonderful!

He licked his lips like a cat about to be fed a fishy meal.

Danny walked up the gangplank of David's yacht. He paused before jumping aboard, looking along the length of the gleaming white status symbol, trying to guess how long it was. It had to be at least 150 feet, maybe more. For a moment he was lost for words; he'd seen yachts like this before but never imagined he would ever actually go on one. The captain, dressed in a white uniform with all the gold braiding, saluted him and welcomed him aboard, and then a crew member showed him to his cabin.

Danny entered the room with its ornate furnishings and lacquered wood, and flopped down on the bed, testing the feel of it.

The door opened and Tara entered.

"So, this is it," she said.

"Yeah. Big isn't it?"

"No, I'm not talking about the boat, silly. I mean *this is it*. We're ready to go – ready to change the world."

"Come here," Danny said. She lay beside him, her head on his chest, her leg draped over his and he played with her hair. "What must Michael be feeling right now?"

"What are *you* thinking?" she asked.

He let out a sigh. "I don't know, I really don't. It's all so crazy and wonderful and terrifying. If we pull this off we're going to end up in a place... in a world that's just impossible to imagine. If we mess it up... well, I don't know."

"Any regrets?"

"About getting involved in all this? No. I'm not a great believer in fate, but... you going into that convent and then the sanatorium, and me ending up in that hotel on the very day Virginie Lavelle turned up and died... Funny how unrelated events can become connected, a part of some bigger whole, almost as if some invisible force was intent on bringing them together – for a purpose."

"Spooky."

The internal phone rang. Tara picked it up. "Sure. We'll be there in a minute." She replaced the receiver. "That was David. He wants to meet with everyone. It seems this thing is ready to roll."

They gathered in the main saloon and stood in a circle, glancing at each other, aware of the poignancy of the occasion, and then they raised their champagne glasses and drank a toast to immortality.

David said, "It starts tomorrow."

Chapter 11

Two shadowy figures were looking at the shabby-bricked, semi-detached council house. The dark blue paint was peeling off the front door and the scrappy little patch of ground that was an excuse for a front garden was heavily overgrown. A light shone through the gap in the curtains of one of the downstairs windows.

Someone was in.

Slowly they made their way up the drive, past the rusty old car that stood decaying, its tyres flat, indicating that it hadn't moved for years, and when they reached the front door they paused for a moment to grin at each other, impishly. And then the one on the left said, "Let's do it!"

Harry Lewis sat in his favourite winged chair, his head tilted to one side. A line of dribble ran from his mouth and dangled from his chin. The TV was on; some comedy re-run, and every now and then he let out a laugh followed by a cough. His thick-fingered hands rested on the arms of the chair, the left one shaking involuntarily, and a blanket with a tartan pattern covered his knees.

His wife, Emily, a dumpy woman dressed in a green cardigan and grey woollen skirt, silently shuffled towards him on slippered feet. She was carrying a cup of tea. By the time she reached his chair half of the rusty coloured liquid was in the saucer.

"Here you are," she said, stretching out her hand. Harry went to take the cup from her, but before he could get a grip on it the doorbell rang, startling them both, and the cup crashed to the floor. For a moment they looked at each other, with fear in their eyes.

"Leave it." Harry said, gruffly.

"I can't just leave it."

"I mean the door!"

Emily sighed and slowly stooped down to retrieve the cup, but before she got to it the doorbell sounded again.

They looked at each other, and then Harry said, "Damned kids!" He coughed up some phlegm and wiped the back of his hand across his mouth. "There's no respect anymore. It's near midnight – who lets their kids out at this time of night?"

The bell sounded again, and then whoever it was started knocking.

"You think it's someone else?" Emily asked.

"Like who? Can't remember the last time anyone called on us."

The sound of more banging, and then a voice calling, "Harry, Emily, open up!"

"You hear that?" Emily said. "They know our names!"

"Cheeky young buggers!" Harry moved to get up.

"Don't. Sit down, for heaven's sake!"

"I'm not too old to-"

"Yes you damned well are, Harry Lewis! You're much too old to do anything about it at all, so don't even try."

He glared at her, and then the voice again, "Harry, Emily. Come on, I know you're in there!"

Harry pushed hard on the arms of his chair, struggling to get to his feet. "Right, that's it," he said. "I've had enough!"

"Harry, please! You know what happened last time! All we got was a brick through the front window!"

"I don't care. I've had it, Emily. You think this is any kind of life, living here like prisoners in our own home, terrorised by little thugs who haven't started to shave yet? In my day I'd have let 'em have it – you know I would! I'll not stand by and let this happen, I damned well won't!"

"No Harry, you'll get hurt!"

"Hurt? When was I afraid of that? You saw me in the ring, you saw me win the middleweight title! Was I afraid? No I bloody well wasn't – and I'm not now!" He made his way to the front door, lurching from side to side with each step, his arthritic hips hampering his movement.

Emily followed him. "No, Harry. Leave it." But Harry wasn't listening. In his mind he was back in his twenties, leanly muscled with fast feet and hands. He flung the door open and confronted the two youngsters on his step.

"You bloody well clear off, you hear! I mean it! Clear off!"

The young man, who looked like he was in his mid-twenties, folded his arms and grinned at Harry, seemingly unmoved by his protestations. At his side was a young smiling woman.

"Harry, you are a feisty one, aren't you?" said the young man.

Cheeky little bugger, thought Harry. "Feisty? In my day I'd have shown you what feisty is! Now, like I say, bugger off and leave us alone!"

Harry went to slam the door, but the young man was too quick for him, jamming his foot between the door and the doorframe.

"Leave us alone!" Harry cried.

"Oh my God, no!" Emily shouted. "Get out! Leave us be!"

"It's all right," the young man said. "You don't have anything to worry about." Slowly he increased the pressure on the door. It was too much for Harry; he couldn't hold it any longer.

"Get out! Emily, call the police!"

The young woman said, "Emily, you don't need to do that. Just calm down a minute. We're not going to hurt you."

Emily said, "We've got nothing to rob, honestly. There's nothing here!"

The young man stepped inside the house, followed by the young woman. They closed the door behind them. For a moment the four of them looked at each other, saying nothing, Emily cowering, Harry remaining defiant, standing as straight as his old spine would allow. And then the young man said. "Don't you recognize me?"

Harry said, "Of course I don't recognise you. Why should I? You little thugs all look alike to me."

The young man grinned. "Same old Harry. You don't change, do you?"

"When I was your age I called my elders, 'Mr'. I'm *Mr Lewis* to you."

"When you were young you were quick with your fists."

"Too right I was!" Harry looked intently at him. "Just who are you, exactly?"

"Do I remind you of anyone?"

"I can't say."

"Yes you can. Think harder."

Harry glanced at Emily who looked puzzled. Then the young man said, "I meant it when I said we mean you no harm. We want to talk to you. I think we all need to sit down, because what I'm going to tell you will be a shock."

Two minutes later Emily had turned off the TV and they had all sat down in the living room.

The young man said, "Look at us again. Think where you've seen us before. You know us both. Very well."

Eventually Harry said, "We don't know you. But... you remind me of someone I used to know. Both of you do."

The young man took out a photo from his back pocket and held it up. It was a picture of two young men and two young women on a beach somewhere, all of them in swimming costumes.

Harry peered at it, his eyes straining to see it clearly. The young man held it closer for him.

"You recognise it?"

"Yes. It's me and Emily, on holiday with two friends of ours."

"Look at us and then look at your friends."

Harry moved his gaze between the photograph and the two people who had invaded his house. "There's a likeness, I can see that."

"More than a likeness."

"Emily, can you see?" Harry asked.

She nodded her head. "That's us with John and Maria. Must be all of fifty years ago. I think I've got a copy of it somewhere."

Harry said, "You look like them. Are you... are you... relatives of theirs?"

"No, we're not related to them." The young man grinned at Harry. "You see... we *are* them."

Harry and Emily stared at them, their mouths open, looking confused.

"What? What are you talking about?"

"We *are* them, Harry. It was *us* with you at Brighton fifty years ago. It's *us* in the photograph. Look." He held it up again for them to see.

"You can't be them. This is some joke. I saw John and Maria only two years ago, and I'm telling you they didn't look like you two. They say John is near the end, at death's door, that's what I heard. So come on, who are you really?"

The girl said, "Harry it *really* is us. Don't you remember that holiday? You got locked out of your room, you lost your key and they tried to make you pay for another one, but you argued until they gave in."

"Who told you that?"

"No one told me that. I was there. John and I… we calmed you down, remember?"

Emily said, "And where was I while this was going on?"

"You were in our room. You weren't feeling well, which is why you were going back to your room and then found you had lost your key. We took you to our room while we tried to sort out a new key."

Emily put her hand to her face.

"Am I right?" the young girl said.

Emily nodded.

"Ask me anything you like," said the young man.

Harry looked at his wife and then turned to the young man. "Where did you two meet?"

"That's easy. Sicily. The Grand Hotel. We both had jobs there during the summer."

Harry said, "What make of car did I have when we went to Brighton?"

"Harry, you old fox! You didn't have a car. We went on the train! We got there at 4.00pm and had to look around for a hotel because we hadn't booked. Ask me another."

Harry shook his head.

"It's me, Harry, it really is."

"But… it's not possible. How…"

"You're not going to believe me when I tell you."

John began to tell him their pre-prepared story about how they were abducted by alien beings from another world, far more advanced than ours, where people never grew old and never died. He said they had watched us on Earth from afar and had decided to share their secret with the earthlings.

"You expect me to believe that?"

"You must have heard the talk in the newspapers, or on the TV about aliens and flying saucers."

"Well, yes, I've heard about it. Bunch of lunatics, I thought…"

"The reports you read were all true. They really did come to this planet. It's not a hoax."

"But… why you?"

"It's because of the act."

"The act?"

"Our stage act – the hypnotherapy act. I'm The Great Mandini, remember?"

"What does that have to do with anything? Don't tell me you're hypnotising people young."

"No of course not. But they want me to hypnotise anyone who wants to become young before they meet them. It's part of it – they have to be put in the right mental state."

"This is… this is all too much. You expect me to believe this?"

"Harry, think! You know it's me, John, don't you?"

"Well, yes, I guess so."

"I'm over seventy years old! Look at me. How the hell do you think I got to look like this?"

"I… I, er… I don't know."

"But I *am* young again, aren't I? How else could I have lost fifty years? The proof is right here before your eyes. I am telling you the truth. Why would I lie about a thing like this?"

"I don't know. You wouldn't, I suppose. It's just… For heaven's sake, this takes some getting used to. I can't get my head around it… Who else knows about this?"

"No one. Just us. It's not something you can shout about, is it? Not unless you want to get locked up."

"You're not wrong there."

"Aren't you wondering why we're here? You think we might be telling you this for a reason?"

"What?"

"We want you to join us."

"Join you? What do you… you don't mean…?"

John nodded. "We do. The people that did this for us… they said we can arrange for it to be done to someone else too. That's why we're here."

"You're joking."

"We want you to become young too. It's not just *become* young. You see we're never going to age – not ever. We're going to stay young forever."

"How come?"

"Harry, don't ask silly questions. I don't know how come, but I'm sure as hell glad they can do it." John held up his thumb and forefinger, looking as if he was about to pinch something. "I was that far away from death. I'm not joking. I thought it was all over for me… and then this. Harry, it's like living the best years of your life all over again, only better, because I'm not so stupid now as I was when I was twenty-five the first time around. You know what I mean? How many times have you said 'I wish I knew then what I know now?' It's like that, it really is! All the best years… but knowing what you know now… it's a dream come true. Except…"

"Except what?"

He sighed. "We're alone. We can't tell anyone how old we are – they'd freak out, or lock us up. We look twenty-five, but we're not. We can't spend our time with twenty-five year olds and we can't spend our time with old crocks like we were only a few weeks ago. We're stuck in the middle somewhere, and… we want to share it with you. We're going to live forever; we want all of our friends to live forever with us. You see, lifelong friendships kind of have a new meaning for us now, because we're going to have one hell of a long life."

Harry looked at Emily. "Am I dreaming? Have I died already and gone to heaven?"

Emily grinned and shook her head. "No, Harry, we're still alive – just."

Harry looked at John again. "I don't know…"

"You don't know! What's not to know? What's the alternative? Death? You want to die? One of you is going to die first. You want to bury the person you love – the person you've lived with all these years? You want to stare down that hole at the coffin lying at the bottom and know that you're never going to hold your loved one again? Jesus, Harry, come on!"

Harry paused for a moment and then said, "What about heaven – the afterlife?"

"You believe in that?"

"Not really. Gives me some comfort thinking maybe this isn't it, and there's something more."

"I don't know about all that, but I tell you something – I like it down here! I don't want to go to the next life, even if there is one. Now I'm young again, here is just fine. You want to take a chance on there being a life after death? What if it's all been a hoax? What if there's nothing more – just a hole in the ground, or getting burned up in an oven?"

"When you put it like that..."

"That's the way it is! Think what you could do! You could get back in the ring – you always said the fighters these days aren't a patch on what you guys were back then – you *fifteen-rounders* – remember?"

Harry grinned. "You always were a persuasive son of a gun." He turned to Emily. "You want to live forever?"

"I don't know... to be young again... to dance one more time..." She smiled to herself. "Oh, my... . that would be... just ... wonderful. Yes, I'd like that."

"It beats spending the rest of your days cooped up here afraid of the doorbell, doesn't it?" John said.

Harry said, "What do we have to do?"

Now they appeared to be twenty-five years old, John and Maria looked out of place driving along in the Austin Allegro they had bought in 1974. He said anyone seeing them would think they were a couple of youngsters with an appreciation of classic cars. Maria wasn't sure about the use of the word 'classic'. The car hadn't been used at all for three years and John had enjoyed tinkering with the engine to get it to work. He still hadn't patched up the bodywork so the white paint was peppered with rust spots.

Sitting in the back were Harry and Emily, Harry with a blanket around his shoulders, Emily wearing an old grey trench-coat, slippers on her feet, surgical support stockings on her legs. They could have been John or Maria's grandparents. Harry was nodding off, as he usually did, from the motion of a car. Emily looked apprehensive, her hands clasped together on her lap, fingers interlocked.

When they were close to Southampton John pulled over. Now was the time when he would find out if his old skills were intact. He had hypnotised people thousands of times on stage, but that had all been a long time ago.

Harry stirred. "Are we there yet?"

"No. But I have to put you under for a moment – get you prepared. You ready?"

Harry looked at Emily, a smile playing on his lips. "You ready to get young again?"

Emily grinned back, nodded and held Harry's hand. "I guess we better join these two kids in… a whole new life."

Harry said, "Okay, we're ready. Just do it, John."

"You two sit back, close your eyes, and relax. I'm going to start counting down and when I get to zero you will be in a deep, deep sleep…"

A minute later Harry and Emily had their eyes shut and were taking deep steady breaths. John told them he was going to stick a needle in the back of their hands and they wouldn't feel any pain whatsoever. He pinched the skin on the back of Emily's hand and pushed a needle straight through the flesh. She didn't flinch.

"Did you feel any pain?" he asked.

"No," she said.

John did the same to Harry and then he told them both they were going to be taken on a boat where they would be given the age reversing treatment. He said that the memory of everything that was going to happen to them was to be kept in an imaginary box deep inside their consciousness, and that they would not be able to access the box until they were given the key. John would let them know what the key was later. He told them he would plant in their minds an alternative story of what had happened to them, and that it would seem perfectly normal and very real to them. He asked them if they had understood what he had told them and they both confirmed they had. Then John told them they were to remember nothing of the conversation.

"On the count of three I am going to click my fingers and you'll be wide awake. One, two, three," He clicked his fingers and they both opened their eyes and sat up.

"Are we there yet?" Harry said.

"Almost."

They struggled to get Harry and Emily up the gangplank, but they made it eventually. John put them in one of the double cabins.

"Who the hell owns this boat?" Harry asked.

"As far as you are concerned this is a spaceship, full of little guys from outer space."

"What?"

John laughed. "Don't worry about it. You'll understand everything one day."

An hour later David, Michael, Albert, Tara and Danny arrived. Michael gave Harry and Emily an injection and they both lay back and drifted off to sleep.

Soon John said, "Look! Look at his face. I swear he's looking younger. His complexion's changing, the lines – they're fading from around his eyes!" Michael grinned at him. "Is that what it was like when we... ?"

"Just the same," Michael said.

Hours passed by with John and Maria gazing at their two friends watching them become more and more like they used to look fifty years ago. And then in the middle of the night, almost simultaneously, they began to shake, gently at first, then violently, as if they were in the middle of a fit.

John ran over to them, an expression of horror on his face. "Quick! For Christ's sake, do something! It's going wrong!"

Michael took his arm and pulled him away. "It's all right. It's what happens – you did the same."

"I did?"

"It's just their bodies being... charged up, as it were – with life."

In the morning they all stood at the foot of Harry and Emily's beds, gazing at two young people, quietly sleeping.

"This is just the most... amazing thing there ever was." John said. They're just the way they were when we first knew each other." He hugged Maria and kissed her. Then he turned to Michael. "Thank you. I can't tell you what this means to Maria and me." He shook Michael's hand.

"You're welcome. Are you sure your hypnotherapy is going to work?"

"Piece of cake. They aren't going to remember any of this. They'll only know what we planned."

The rest of the team left John and Maria in the cabin to wait for

Harry and Emily to wake up. When they did, the four friends shared a moment of intense joy, all of them with tears streaming down their faces. They gathered in a group around the mirror, beaming at their regained youth. Then Harry and Emily danced around the cabin trying out their bodies, getting the feel of what it's like to be young again.

Harry said, "I can't believe it. It's like the last fifty years, nearly everything that's happened to me… most of my life… it's all been a dream… and I've just woken up twenty-five again!"

"Emily said, "Is this it? We don't change from this – ever?"

"That's what they tell us. We've got forever to do whatever we want."

"Shit! Let's go somewhere!" Harry said.

"Where?"

"I don't know. Let's go on a world cruise! Hey, I better get back in training." He shadowboxed in the mirror.

"Take it easy," John said. "We've got time – all the time in the world. But we've got a few things to sort out first."

"Like what?"

"We've got to make sure everyone gets this."

"You mean… turn the whole word young?"

"We can't keep it all to ourselves now can we? Thing is… it's going to take some doing?"

"We'll help. What do we have to do?"

"You're going to become quite a celebrity."

Three hours later John put Harry and Emily into a deep hypnotic trance. He instructed them to wrap up the memory of what they had just been through and place it in the imaginary safe deep in the recesses of their mind – a safe that would be opened upon them seeing a special 'key'. He made them open their eyes to look at a picture of a symbol.

"This is the key. When you see it your mind-safe will open and you will remember what has really happened to you here. Until then your memory will be of something entirely different." John told them the false story they were to relay to the world. "And this will be real to you. You will remember this story in minute detail and no matter how many times you are questioned about your new-found youth – this shall be the tale you tell, and it shall be clear and vivid in your mind."

In the middle of the night John and Maria drove Harry and Emily, still hypnotised, back home. They led them up the stairs and put them to bed and then John said, "You will sleep now, a deep relaxing sleep, and when you awake in the morning you will remember only the story I have told you."

John and Maria left them and made their way back to the boat, hoping their two friends would cope with what was going to happen to them.

"You think we've done the right thing?" Maria asked.

"I don't know. I really don't."

"My God, I hope they get through it."

"They better," John said. "But whatever happens to them, it's got to be better than dying, hasn't it?"

Chapter 12

Jerry Dickinson was sitting on the sofa, waiting for his breakfast. "Miranda! Where is it for Christ's sake? Been waiting here ages, I'm getting cold."

"Well you should've put your dressing gown on then, shouldn't you? Anyway, it's disgusting sitting there with all your bits sticking out."

"What do you mean, *sticking out?* I've got me pants on."

"Yeah. Same ones you've had on for two weeks."

"I changed them last Thursday if you must know."

Miranda entered the room carrying a plate of fried eggs, bacon and beans.

"Where's the toast?"

"You're not having any."

"What?"

"Too much white bread's not good for you. You're having too many carbs anyway. I read it in a magazine. It's that what makes you fat."

"Bollocks."

"It's true, I read it."

"And that means it's true, does it? If I write *you're a stupid cow* on a piece of paper, that means you are one then, does it?"

"Shut up and eat what I've given you."

Jerry turned up the TV.

Miranda pulled back the net curtain and looked out across the front garden of the house next door. A young couple were out there looking at Harry and Emily's car.

"Come here, quick!"

"What is it, woman?"

"There's someone out there."

"Bloody hell! People out there! Whatever bloody next! I'm having my breakfast."

Miranda rushed over and snatched the plate away from him. "Go and look now! They're after Harry's car."

"What? That heap of old rubbish? That thing won't be going anywhere. Anyway, it *wants* nicking, does that. Messes the place up."

"*You* want nicking then, 'cos *you* mess up the place. Come and look!"

Jerry heaved himself off the sofa and shuffled over to the window, scratching his stomach and rearranging his testicles on the way. He peered out of the window.

"Look!" Miranda said.

"Yeah, well…"

"Who are they?"

"I don't bloody know."

"Well why don't you go and see?"

"I'm not dressed, woman!"

"So what?"

"Anyway, you don't know these days, he might have a gun."

"He doesn't look the type."

"Nor did Archie Newman's kid and he got sent down for holding up the corner Paki shop, didn't he? It's probably all nothing anyway. Now give me my breakfast, all right?" He snatched the plate away from Miranda and sat down on the sofa again.

Miranda said, "I've never seen any youngsters around their place. Never seen anyone around there, come to think of it. Something's going on. They might have turned the house over. They might have… tied them up or something! I'm calling the police."

"Bollocks. They'll be long gone before the police get here."

"No they won't. We're in the neighbourhood watch scheme. They'll come quickly to us."

Twenty minutes later a police car drew up outside the Dickinson's house. PCs Ellis Raymond and Mary Shaw got out. Miranda pulled back the net curtains.

"They're here. Told you. That was only twenty minutes."

"Must be a bloody record."

"For God's sake get your trousers on."

Miranda opened the front door. PC Raymond approached with PC Shaw in tow.

"Are you Mrs Dickinson?"

"Yes. They're in the house – I'm sure of it," she said excitedly, a gleeful glint in her eye. "They went in and no one's come out."

"Okay. Calm down. You know the owners?"

"Of course I do. Harry and Emily. Nice old couple. He's near to croaking it. Get in there for God's sake. Anything could have happened to them."

"You stay here."

PCs Raymond and Shaw trotted over to the house next door.

"Stay here? Not bloody likely," Miranda said. Jerry appeared behind her wearing his trousers, still barefoot. "Come on. I don't want to miss this."

Harry was in the living room sifting through his toolbox. Emily was in the kitchen making a pot of tea.

"You want one?" she shouted.

"I've got to get some more tools. I don't know where they've all gone."

"Can't you fix the car with what you've got?"

"If I could we'd be on our way to Brighton by now, wouldn't we?"

"What about your tea? Do you want one?"

The doorbell rang.

"I'll get it," Harry said. "It's probably someone selling something. I'll get rid of them. If it's kids causing trouble they're in for a shock, right?" Harry grinned and set off for the door, Emily following behind. When he opened it he was surprised to find a policeman standing in front of him.

"Morning officer," Harry said.

"Good morning, sir. Can I ask your name?"

"Harry Lewis."

A voice shouted, "He's lying!" Miranda and Jerry came into view.

Miranda said, "What have you done with them? You liar!"

PC Raymond took her arm. "Calm down, Mrs Dickinson, please."

"But he's not Harry Lewis! Tell him Jerry! Harry is an old man."

PC Raymond said, "Is there some misunderstanding? Can you clear this up for us, sir?"

Harry said, "Miranda, it's me, Harry."

Looking shocked, Miranda put her hand to her throat and then said, "How the hell does he know my name?"

Emily said, "Jerry, it's me, Emily."

Jerry's mouth fell open and he looked at PC Raymond. "I swear I've never seen her before in my life."

"Yes you have," Emily said. "I saw you in the supermarket a week ago, remember? You reached up and got that packet of biscuits down for me."

Jerry looked as if he had been hit in the face with a large wet salmon.

PC Raymond said, "Is this true?"

"Well, I... I helped her, yes. But this isn't her! Emily's an old woman. That's why I had to help her with the bloody biscuits! This woman is more like her bleeding granddaughter!"

"Are you Mrs Lewis's granddaughter?" PC Raymond asked.

"I *am* Emily Lewis. I don't have any children."

"She's lying, for Christ's sake! Lock them up. They've done something to Harry and Emily!"

PC Raymond said, "All right, calm down. Look, I think you and Mr Dickinson should go home and leave this to us to sort out."

"Are you going to lock them up?"

"I'm going to talk to them."

Harry said, "We don't have anything to hide. Why don't you come in? All of you."

"The bloody cheek of him!" Miranda said.

PC Raymond called PC Shaw who had been at the back of the house in case anyone tried to make a run for it by climbing out of a rear window. They all entered the house.

"What've you done with them?" Jerry said.

"There's no one else, just us."

"They've murdered them, they must have!" Miranda shouted.

PC Raymond said, "Mr and Mrs Dickinson seem to think you aren't Harry and Emily Lewis. They say their neighbours are an elderly couple and you are not them. Would you know why they might say this?"

"Of course."

"Of course? Would you mind enlightening me, sir?"

"No problem. We are Harry and Emily Dickinson and we used to be old. But now we're not."

"Now you're not old?"

"Yes. You see we were visited by aliens, and they made us young."

After PC Raymond had calmed Miranda down and stopped her screaming, he told Harry and Emily they were coming with him to the police station for questioning.

Harry told PC Raymond that would be fine, but he wanted to take his photograph album with him. Jerry and Miranda Dickinson stood side-by-side on the pavement scowling at them as they set off in the police car.

At the police station they were put in separate cells and made to wait three hours before they were questioned. Harry was first to be taken to the interview room. PC Raymond and PC Shaw sat side by side and told him he was not under arrest – just helping them clear up a few things. PC Raymond asked him to confirm his name, address and then asked for his date of birth. Harry told him.

"Well, by my calculations that would make you over seventy years old."

"Correct," Harry said.

PC Raymond sat forward placed his elbows on the table and supported his chin on his clasped hands. "Son, do me a favour. Tell me the truth, or give me the make of the face cream you use."

"I am telling you the truth."

"Yeah, right. You're Harry Lewis, seventy-five years old… and I'm The Pope. I'll ask you again, who are you?"

"Like I said, Harry Lewis. I can prove it. Get me that photo album you took off me when we arrived."

PC Raymond did as Harry asked and a few minutes later Harry showed the police officers pictures of his wedding and some of him wearing boxing gear, standing in a pugilistic pose.

"You see? That's me. I was middle-weight champ."

"Oh really. When was this exactly?"

"Forty-eight years ago."

PC Raymond shook his head. "And you haven't changed a bit."

"I told you. We were visited by aliens and they made us young."

"Fascinating. And when was this?"

"Last night."

"Not sure if I should lock you up for wasting police time, obstructing justice… or because you're a nut case."

"It's true, I tell you."

PC Raymond looked at PC Shaw, sighed and then said, "Amuse me. Tell me what happened. Start at the beginning."

Harry told him how they had been awakened in the middle of the night by flashing lights outside. Emily got out of bed, pulled back the curtains and saw a spaceship hovering. Before long a beam of light shot out from it, penetrating the bedroom wall and they were sucked along it towards the alien craft. Once inside they were surrounded by a group of beings from another planet with red scaly skin and huge black eyes. One of them said they had come to Earth to save everyone from death. They had been watching from afar and were sorry to see that we hadn't managed to overcome it yet. They said they were going to give us the secret of everlasting life. Harry and Emily lay on metal tables and an intense white light shone down at them. Then pulses of energy shot into their bodies, causing them to jolt up in the air. It seemed to go on for about ten minutes, though it was impossible to be sure, because time felt different on the spaceship. When they sat up they looked just as they had done when they got married. They thanked the aliens, who told them to lie down again and then sent them back along the beam of light to their bedroom, where they slept until dawn before waking up and finding that they really were young again, and it had not been a dream.

"That's a great story. You should write science fiction novels."

In a calm voice Harry said, "It's true. How else do you suppose I got to be young again?"

"Great answer, but come on…"

Harry scratched his head for a moment and then said, "I can prove it."

"Oh really?"

"Take my fingerprints. You already have them on file. You see I wasn't always a good citizen. When times were hard for us I fell in with the wrong crowd and got involved in a little pick-pocketing. You arrested me a long time ago."

PC Raymond thought for a while, then said, "The way things are going we'd get around to taking your fingerprints soon enough, so I suppose we may as well do it now."

When they had a full set of prints from Harry they put him back in his cell and interviewed Emily. She gave them exactly the same story. After they had put her back in her cell, PC Raymond said to PC Shaw, "I don't know what we've got here. Are these two just a couple of nutcases, or is it their neighbours who've been sniffing something they shouldn't have?"

"I can't work it out. If that house is owned by an old couple, where are they?"

"Those pictures he showed us. It's him alright, and she's his wife, you can see from the wedding photo."

PC Shaw said, "And his boxing photos look genuine enough – definitely him – but who takes photos in sepia these days?"

"An artistic photographer, perhaps – trying for that nostalgic look?"

"I'll check a few things out."

Two hours later PC Shaw and PC Raymond met up again.

"I... er, I can't explain this," PC Shaw said.

"Try."

"The house is registered to Harry and Emily Lewis. It's in joint names."

"And?"

"It has been for thirty years."

PC Raymond scratched his chin. "Go on."

"I, er... I checked the prints. They match the Harry Lewis we have on file. Only... the Harry Lewis we have on file is in his seventies. Like he said, he was caught pick-pocketing, or rather he was acting as a decoy for one, over forty years ago. He got a suspended sentence."

"And you're sure about the prints?"

"Absolutely. There's a full set on file and they're a perfect match – no room for error."

"So what do you make of it?"

"I don't know."

PC Raymond paced the room. "So... we know he's Harry Lewis, and he's the registered owner of the house, which means he hasn't broken in. And he looks about fifty years younger than he is. The neighbours say he's not their neighbour, he can't be because he isn't old enough."

"That's about it."

"Anything on the neighbours, Jerry and Miranda Dickinson, right?"

"Yes. Nothing on them."

"Well that's it then."

"What?"

"Obviously they were abducted by aliens and turned young."

"You believe that?"

"No, of course I bloody don't! Look, I've had enough of this. The only crime he might have committed here is looking young for his age and I can't lock him up for that."

"But fifty years younger?"

"Don't ask me – I don't really care. Let them go. They can argue it out with the Dickinsons. As long as they don't create a disturbance it's all right with me."

Two days later a man wearing brown corduroy trousers and a dark green woollen jacket knocked on Harry and Emily Lewis's door.

"Morning. Mr Lewis?"

"Yes," said Harry.

"Name's Bob Morris from the *South Eastern Times*. Wonder if I might have a word?"

"What about?"

Bob forced himself to keep a straight face, and said in a calm, even tone, "Well, I've heard that you, er... had an encounter with some aliens."

"Oh that. Yes, I expect you've been talking to someone at the police station haven't you? You want to come in?"

Bob spent a surreal couple of hours, chatting away to a couple who recounted the story of their alleged encounter with aliens with all the matter-of-factness of someone describing how they had filled in an application for a new driving licence.

The next day the paper ran the story on the front page: *Alien Invasion. Local couple made young!* The article included some pictures of the couple now and as they were fifty years ago. It wasn't long before a small crowd of locals gathered at the bottom of the Lewis's drive to gawp at the pair of newly-youngs, followed by reporters and photographers from the national press. Hours later a van with a satellite dish on its roof pulled up opposite the house and a TV news reporter spoke into a camera whilst a technician held up a big fluffy microphone, keeping it just out of camera shot.

Harry and Emily pulled back the curtains and gazed out at the throng.

"Well I never. Looks like we've caused quite a stir," Harry said.

"Hmmm. We're going to be on the television, I think," Emily said.

At first the story was treated as a joke, the reporters telling it with their tongues lodged in their cheeks. It was just a couple of hoaxers having fun at the public's expense, but it was mildly amusing all the same. The item was tacked on the end of the nightly news bulletin to leave the viewers on a lighter note.

But there was one person who didn't find the story funny at all.

Joss burst in with a copy of the newspaper.

"Have you read this?" Cleaver nodded. "He's started it, I knew he would! Little red spacemen – where the hell did he come up with that? Have you found Avery yet?"

"No. There's nothing yet. He wasn't booked onto any of the flights out of the Turcs and Caicos. Of course he may have left by boat, but he has one of his own, a forty-five footer. Apparently it's still in the harbour."

"He'd have used it if he was going to leave by sea – much easier."

"Unless he didn't want us to get suspicious."

"He didn't know we were watching him. We *weren't* watching him, for heavens sake! Why would he leave secretly like that? There'd be no reason to unless he was up to something. What about over here? Has he got a house in the UK?"

"No. He had one in Leyton-Middleton, but he sold it three years ago."

"Well we know he's damned well here now, don't we?" Cleaver nodded. "Anything else to tell me?"

Cleaver looked down at his desk for a moment, and then said, "There is one more thing. You remember I said I was sure Avery knew nothing about all this and that he had been duped by Richards just as we had?"

"Go on."

"Well… that might not be the case."

"What makes you say that?"

"Well, I suppose it might be a coincidence, but… It's just that the name of his boat – it's a little strange under the circumstances and I-"

"Spit it out man!"

"The boat's called *Immortality*. It could just be-"

"A coincidence? You fool! He's been rubbing our noses in it!"

"Yes quite. I'm on to it."

"Well you'd better hurry up before it gets out of hand!"

Chapter 13

David put down his copy of *The South Eastern Times*. "Well, we've started it. This thing is going to gather its own momentum. I've got an idea for the next one. There's a man in one of my nursing homes called Leonard McGuire, and I think he's perfect."

"How come?" Tara asked.

"Not long to live, never gets any visitors, and I know he has his own house to go back to. You see, we have a scheme for old people who want to come into our nursing homes but don't have enough money. They use the equity in their house to pay us. We take a charge on the property, they move in and we recoup the money when they die by selling the property."

"You had it all worked out, didn't you?" Danny said. David glared at him. "Sorry, I didn't mean it like that. I meant it was… all worked out – a good scheme – everyone's a winner."

David went on, "Anyway, he's ideal for it."

"You sure he'll want to live forever?"

"Yes."

"How come?"

"He may be dying, but if ever there was a man who loved living it's this guy. When you talk to him he's full of stories about when he was young. He was a hit with the ladies – a man with real spirit – a glint in his eye. Yeah, I'm sure he's not had enough of life just yet."

An officer said to PC Raymond, "You're wanted."

"Who by?"

"Some stick insect in a suit. Says he needs to talk to you. He's got the boss with him."

"Parker?"

The officer nodded. "Better get your skates on."

When PC Raymond entered Chief Superintendent Parker's office he was introduced to Alistair Cleaver and told to take a seat next to him.

"Mr Cleaver wants to ask you a few questions," said Parker. "Mr Cleaver works for the government."

Cleaver said, "You were the one who interviewed the couple who…" Cleaver grinned sarcastically, "Were turned young by the aliens."

PC Raymond took his cue and chuckled. "Oh, yes, sir – that was me."

"Amazing what the mind can do, eh? Coming up with stories like that."

"Yes, it's, uh… very strange."

"You interviewed them separately I take it?"

PC Raymond did his best to hide his irritation at Cleaver questioning his competence. "Yes, of course."

"There must have been some discrepancies in their stories?"

"No. I'm afraid there weren't. Their stories tallied."

"You took this seriously I hope? By that I mean you questioned them rigorously?"

"I would say I took it as seriously as I would take any story about little red men from space turning people young."

"Raymond, this is serious," Parker said.

"Yes sir."

Cleaver said, "So you questioned them and just let them go?"

"Can you tell me what I might have charged them with?"

"Wasting police time?"

"I thought about that. Trouble was they weren't doing anything wrong when we brought them in. It was their neighbours who said an offence had been committed, but if there was I don't know what. You see, the man appears to be who he says he is – we've got his prints on file – and he was just trying to get his car to work."

"You didn't think the story about aliens was wasting police time?"

"Difficult to say, isn't it sir? You see, I'm sure there are lots of people who believe in UFOs, and as you know there's been a lot of talk about them in the press recently. Not sure that being… a little eccentric, for want of a better word, is an offence. They look younger than their age, of course. But I can't lock them up for that, can I?"

"So how would you explain the way they look?"

"I don't know. Plastic surgery?"

David went to see Leonard McGuire, the next candidate for rejuvenation, who preferred to be called Lenny. He told him there was a revolutionary new treatment that could reverse the aging process. He said it was top secret and if Lenny wanted it he was to say nothing to anyone – not even the staff in the nursing home.

"What does it cost?" Lenny asked.

"Nothing. It's on me," David said.

"So I'd be a kind of guinea pig?"

"Yes. But I think it's quite safe."

Lenny laughed. "Safer than dying, eh?"

David told Lenny the plan and two days later Lenny told the staff at the nursing home that he wanted to die at home. They looked concerned, but David said Lenny had a right to die where he wanted and that Lenny could easily afford to pay for care at home from the equity in his house. David would arrange for a nurse to live in with the old man until the moment came. Lenny was taken home in an ambulance, a nurse was installed in the spare bedroom and a week later, when she was fast asleep, John and Danny got Lenny out of the house, into the car and onto the boat where Michael made him young again. They took some of his new genetically altered blood to use on other people, and then John hypnotised him and planted the alien abduction story in his memory. They got him back home and in bed by 06.00am, and when the nurse entered his bedroom that morning she screamed.

"Who are you! Where's... where's Mr McGuire?"

Lenny yawned, stretched and said, "You're looking at him." He rubbed his eyeballs. "Hey, you're pretty cute." He pulled back the bedclothes. "You want to get in here and keep me warm?"

The nurse ran out of the house. A hundred yards down the road she took out her mobile and called the police. At the station Lenny gave them the story about little red aliens and the police, who of course had heard the story before on the TV news, didn't know what to believe, but they couldn't find anything to charge Lenny with, so they had to let him go. The next day Lenny's house was besieged with news reporters and he basked in the limelight, grinning at the camera and the cute blonde reporter from Sky News.

A week later Harry and Emily stood in the wings waiting to be called onto the Herman Miller show. Herman was finishing his usual introductory routine, cracking jokes about politicians and things that had been in the news the previous week – the usual chat show opening. And then he said, "Ladies and gentlemen, let's meet our first guest – a couple of newly-youngs – Harry and Emily Lewis!"

Harry and Emily ran onto the stage holding hands, all smiles and grins. The audience cheered and Harry and Emily took their seats. Herman began to ask about the little red men that had taken them away and made them young. Every now and then he would wink at the audience, half of whom seemed to think they were watching a couple of jokers, the other half staring straight faced, as if both puzzled and intrigued, not knowing if they believed the story or not, but wanting to all the same.

Then Herman said, "Now Harry, we know that you're seventy-five years old, but when you were in your twenties you were middleweight boxing champion, isn't the right?" Herman winked at the audience again and before Harry could answer he said, "Let's hear it for the ex-middleweight champ!" The crowd cheered and clapped like trained seals. "Now ladies and gentlemen, we've got something set up here to let Harry show us some of his old skills from fifty years ago. Come over here with me, Harry."

In the corner of the stage was a punch bag dangling on a chain. Herman gave Harry some gloves to put on and said, "Okay Harry, show us what you can do."

Harry danced around the bag, jabbing and crossing, then he let go a flurry of body shots, his hands a blur, the air filled with the thwacking sound of his heavy blows striking the punch bag. Loving the moment, Harry turned away from the bag and danced around Herman, throwing out punches, stopping an inch away from the presenter's face.

"Whoa! Hold on champ!" shouted Herman. "I'm not going to go twelve rounds with you, no sir!" Herman turned to the audience. "Lets hear it for the champ, Harry Lewis! And his wife, Emily!"

Harry and Emily walked off stage waving and smiling as the audience cheered.

Joss watched the spectacle at home, seething. He made a couple of phone calls, then called Cleaver.

"Alistair, I'll be along to pick you up in the morning. This is getting out of hand. There's someone we're going to have to share this with."

"But I thought you said-"

"I'm afraid we've no choice."

"Who is it?"

"The Prime Minister."

Chapter 14

Cleaver sat with Joss on the back of the black Jaguar on their way to Downing Street. "I've not met him before. What's your take on him?"

"The Prime Minister? He's a vote junkie. Our illustrious leader is a buffoon – a complete idiot. Behind those flashing teeth there's… precisely nothing. He's a vacuum. We're here to save the public from politicians like him. Never underestimate the stupidity of the public, Cleaver. They were stupid enough to vote him into Number Ten, and now look at them – clamouring for aliens to come and save them."

"I wasn't sure he was quite such an intellectual lightweight. Thought it was all an act, you know. Appeal to the masses."

"It's no act."

The car pulled up outside the door to Number 10 and the chauffeur opened the door for them. Five minutes later they were inside, waiting for the Prime Minister to arrive.

"If he's that stupid… I mean, it makes you wonder if we really ought to tell him all this," Cleaver said.

"If I had my way I'd rather not, but if it all gets out of hand and we haven't told him… Well, it could prove a little awkward."

"Yes, I see. We can't say we didn't know – we'd have egg on our faces. And if we say we *did* know, then why didn't we tell him."

"Indeed."

The door opened and in came the Prime Minister, who gave them his piano-key grin and shook their hands.

"Nice to see you. Look, I'm afraid I haven't got long. Need to keep this short. Got a press conference this afternoon. You know, a country to run and all that."

Joss bristled. "We'll try to keep it as brief as possible, to let you get back to… more important things."

"Yes, right. So what's this all about?"

"Little red men from space," Joss said dryly. He then went on to tell the Prime Minister how it had come to their attention that a geneticist had developed an age-reversal potion of some kind and was turning people young.

"Oh. So the alien thing is all made up then?"

"Er, yes Prime Minister."

"So this chap who's invented the potion – is he British?"

"No, Prime Minister."

"Where's he from?"

"America. I'm not sure this is relevant."

"Damn it. Would have been a first for Britain, you know. Medical breakthrough by one of our top scientists. Would have been good for the country's morale. National pride, and all that. So why the alien story and why are you chaps on the case?"

The man was away with the fairies.

Joss said, "I don't think you've grasped the seriousness of the situation."

"Really?"

"This lunatic is playing God. He's interfering with the very nature of existence – the order of things. Let me put it in more simple terms. There is a deficit in the country's pension funds, is there not?"

"Well... I would never admit to that, of course."

"No, you wouldn't. But just between us, there is a slight... funding problem, shall we say?"

"Well these things go in cycles, of course. Sometimes they're up, sometimes they're down. When they're down they correct themselves. Economic cycles and all that. The Chancellor is well briefed on everything."

"Quite. Now imagine if the pensioners were to take a pill that made them live forever. How would the pension funds sort themselves out then? Isn't one of the problems the fact that people are living longer these days? You pump more money into the Health Service to keep people alive, which costs the taxpayers billions, and then you have to pay out again because they draw their pension for longer."

"Oh, yes, of course I see what you mean. And you're absolutely right."

"Indeed. You're on a very sticky wicket, aren't you? No chance of scoring a winning run with that kind of set up is there? The only way for the pension funds to ever get straight is for people to die. In fact, and I'm saying this off the record, what you really need is an epidemic of Spanish Flu to… clear out the dead wood and give the ship a chance to right itself, wouldn't you agree?"

"Yes… yes, I suppose you are right. My God, I hope you're not recording this. You're not are you?" He laughed nervously.

"I take it you are a believer, Prime Minister?"

"In what?'

"God."

"Oh yes, of course, absolutely."

"Then you will appreciate that He has given us a finite time on this earth. It is His plan that when our time is up we depart to another world. It would be arrogance of the highest order to think we can alter His great design, don't you agree?"

"Of course."

"Trouble is, there might be some people who have crazy ideas about challenging the design of life, and if they were to encourage others… well… things could get out of hand. Expectations could rise. And if they did and people started demanding treatment to live forever you could end up having to fund it, along with the countless billions you would have to put into the pension funds."

"My God, that would be a disaster."

"Today's workforce would be forever in hock to the pensioners, taxed till their pips are squeaking, as someone once said, unable to make up the shortfall. How do you think that would play with the voters, Prime Minister?"

"It would be a catastrophe, of course. To say nothing of the population explosion."

"Precisely. Now you're getting the picture."

"This could be a complete disaster. It would upset things hugely. What do you need me to do, exactly?"

Michael turned three more couples young and the world's press went wild, especially when Arnold Linnet and his wife Gladys, now looking like a fit couple of twenty-five year olds, posed with their son and daughter who looked twenty years older than their parents.

"I… I can't explain it, but he *is* my dad… really he is," said the son. "He knows things that only he can know." He held up a photo album showing his father as a fighter pilot, looking the same as he did now.

"How does it feel having a dad who's younger than you?" asked a reporter holding a microphone in front of the bewildered son's face.

"A little weird. But we thought he was going to die soon and… well, this is better than losing him, of course. I just hope the aliens come back for me when I'm his age."

By now the south of England was awash with satellite dishes on the top of news vans, and the newly-young were followed around as if they were rock stars.

Chapter 15

David, Danny and Tara were watching the news on the television in David's master cabin aboard *Karen*.

"We need to broaden this out a little," he said.

"What do you mean?" Danny asked.

"We need to get people's attention away from here – make someone young somewhere else – it'll be safer."

"Like?"

"I've got a healthcare company in America."

"I didn't know that."

"I bought it two years ago. We've got fifteen old folks communities."

"You want to sail over there?"

"No, it would take too long. This thing is picking up momentum fast. We could fly over and do it. I have my plane, we could get in and out pretty fast."

Michael, said, "I can't see any reason why not. It's all working out better than I thought it would. I gave the last two the blood pills instead of injecting them and they seem to work just as well. Let's take things up a gear."

That night Tara and Danny were alone in their cabin. Tara was having difficulty keeping still. She felt energised and excited. She said, "This is incredible. What we've started here… there aren't words to describe it. And it's happening so fast. We're going to be there in no time, Danny. We will have done it – we'll have changed the world forever in only… I'm not sure how long, but it could be just months."

"Maybe."

"You don't sound so sure."

"We've been lucky so far. Cleaver and his crew, they haven't rumbled us yet – but they might. If they do… You know they'll stop at nothing to kill us."

"I know. But they aren't going to rumble us, are they?" Danny didn't answer, and his silence worried her. For the first time she contemplated the possibility and the consequences of being killed, and it scared her.

"You know… if we're going to America, I think I'd like to see my mom… just in case… I mean, what if I don't get the chance again?"

David flew them to Miami where he dropped them off and refuelled on his way over to California. He had a few candidates in mind for age reversal over there. Danny and Tara hired a car and drove out to Tara's mother's house, Danny remembering the first time he had made the trip there three years before. The same guard saluted when they entered the driveway and Danny wondered what sort of reception he was going to get from Isobel this time. They had only visited her twice since setting up home on the Turcs and Caicos islands. Once she had been pleasant and the other time indifferent.

They parked the car in the usual spot, but this time Isobel didn't come out to greet them, so they went inside to find her.

They entered the conservatory, where they had drunk tea three years before, and found her reclining on a wicker sofa, looking thinner than usual, her skin saggy and lined, and her dark hair, which had been glossy and luxuriant, was now dull and lifeless. Tara immediately sensed something was wrong.

"Mother, what is it? What's going on?"

"You never said you were coming. Trying to surprise me, were you?"

"You don't look well. What's wrong?"

She tried to sit up. "Here, help me," she said, stretching out an arm. Tara helped her adjust her position. "Comes to us all in the end, I suppose."

"What does? Mother, you're scaring me!"

Isobel let out a laugh. "Takes this to scare you, huh? I knew something would one day."

"If you're ill, why didn't you contact me?"

"I'd have got round to it a little later. Bit early at the moment – I've got a little more time, I think."

"Have you seen a doctor?"

"Tara, there's not much point in that. I've got cancer." Tara gasped and put her hand to her mouth. "It's okay. I've got used to the idea."

"Well I haven't!"

"But you will."

Tara sat beside her and held her hand. "You can't give up. There must be something. What did the doctors say?"

"They said six months. That was four months ago. Think I might outlive their predictions, though."

"You can't die!"

"We all have to someday. Not that those idiots going on about little red men from space would accept that. Lunatics. The world's gone crazy. You must have read about it. You do have newspapers on that island of yours, don't you?"

"We've heard about it, yes."

"Was it just a visit, or are you here for some other reason? Some other reason – it has to be. You don't do visits, do you? What is it this time?"

"It was just a visit."

"Well, it's nice of you to drop by."

"When were you going to tell me about this, mother?"

"Oh I don't know. A little nearer the end, I expect."

"Mother, I don't want you to die."

"I'm touched, of course, but it can't be helped."

"You're taking this a little lightly aren't you?"

"Lightly?" She chuckled to herself. "*Lightly* she says... *lightly!* You have no idea, absolutely no idea." The bitterness grew in her voice. "The hours I've spent sitting here since I found out I was going to die... running over things in my head, wishing to God I'd done things differently. There's so much I wish I could put right, but I don't have time, not now. Tara, if there's one thing I can tell you it's don't make the same mistakes as me. Of course, you *know* a lot of my mistakes – that business with your father. I wish I'd have told you sooner, but there you go. What's done is done, and the comfort I have is that, however bitter I feel about the past, I won't have to suffer it for long. Another couple of months and I'll be put in the family crypt to rot away with all our ancestors. A comforting thought, isn't it? Escape by death. Could be the name of a film, couldn't it?"

"I need to talk to Danny," Tara said.

"I hope he's good with money. Someone has to look after your inheritance."

"Shut up mother!"

Tara grabbed Danny's arm and led him outside.

"We've got to get Michael to turn her young. I can't stand by and watch her die."

"Of course we must. It won't be a problem, I'm sure. They can do it when they fly back for us."

"Do I have to get her hypnotised? She's my mother, I don't want her to be on the news telling a crazy story."

"Tara, it's risky not to."

"Is it? John's going to wake them up from all this before long. I don't want her on chat shows, drawing attention to herself."

"Just think about it for a while. I can't see any way out. I don't think David would agree to anything else."

"Fuck David! What about what I want?"

"Take it easy, okay? I'm on your side, remember?"

"We brought Michael and Albert to David. Without us none of this would be happening. They owe me this!"

Isobel tried to eat dinner, but it was almost impossible for her to get anything down.

"Sorry. Don't have an appetite for food anymore." She put down her fork.

"Don't worry, mother. It doesn't matter."

Isobel said to Danny, "You know how much Tara is going to inherit, I trust?"

Danny shook his head. "Are you any good with money?"

"Mother, for Christ's sake, shut up! You're not going to die!"

"My dear, you'll come to accept it, you'll see."

"I won't have to. Now stop talking like this, I can't stand it!"

"Can't put your head in the sand, Tara. You must never do that. I wish I hadn't. Remember this when I'm gone, okay?"

"You aren't going anywhere!"

Isobel patted Tara's hand. "It'll be all right, I promise."

Tara dropped her fork. "Mother, get all thoughts of death out of your head. You're going to live a lot longer than you think."

Isobel laughed. "Been talking to little red aliens, have you?"

"Maybe."

"Just what *have* you two been doing lately? You went to Europe again didn't you? Has Danny been working on another story?"

"Look, what if the doctors had got it wrong and you weren't going to die?"

"If you knew how hard it is for me to shuffle a few steps these days… I haven't done any yoga for ages. It makes you so weak. The doctors aren't wrong. I wish they were. I think, having been so close to death, if by some miracle I wasn't to die, I would certainly live differently. Yes… I'm sure of that. Sometimes life is cruel, an absolute bastard. But, you know, overall… life is wonderful. It really is. Don't ever forget that, Tara. Life is so enormously precious – a real gift. A wonderful gift, given to us all, and then it's snatched away… just like that."

Tara wiped a tear away from her face. "Get thoughts of dying out of your head, mother. It's not going to happen, I promise you."

In California Arnold and Violet Muller were made young and woke up in an old folk's home looking twenty-five years old, telling the tale of how they were sucked along a beam of light to a spaceship full of little red men. By the time the world's press heard about it David, John and Maria, along with Michael and Albert had landed at Miami International Airport and had entered the terminal to meet up with Danny and Tara.

Danny said, "David, we need Michael to make someone else young before we leave here."

"Who?"

Danny told the group about Isobel's illness. Tara said, "It *will* cure the cancer, won't it?"

Michael said, "I haven't used it to cure anyone of cancer before, but yes… I'm sure it will work. The cellular rejuvenation will turn the cells back to how they were before the cancer took hold. Let's go and do it."

"There's one more thing," Tara said. "I don't want her hypnotised."

David asked why.

"I'm not having her on the TV talking about little red spacemen!"

"But we have to. It's the only way we can explain it. We've done this with everyone."

"No you haven't. What about John and Maria, we didn't do it with them?"

"We couldn't – John's the hypnotist! Anyway they're part of the team."

"What difference will it make? The world's going crazy for this. CNN this morning were reporting non-stop on Arnold and Violet Muller. The rest of the old folks there are saying they wished they had been visited too. They're going to be up all night looking up at the skies for spaceships. Come on, David! We're going to be able to brake the spell soon and tell the world what's really happened, so we don't need her to be hypnotised and part of this… circus."

Danny said, "She doesn't go anywhere. She lives in a big house in the middle of nowhere. She won't bump into anyone."

"No, we can't do this," David said. "We could blow the whole thing. Do you want to risk that?"

Tara screamed, "This is my mother you're talking about. I'm not having her be part of this hoax! She'll keep away from everyone for as long as it takes. This is only happening because of us, David. You owe me this!"

David said nothing.

Danny said, "You know, it wouldn't hurt to come and meet her – see for yourself."

For a few moments David switched his gaze back and forth between Tara and Danny, then said, "I guess not. The pilot could use a rest. Okay, let's go and meet your mother."

David had to hire a minivan to get everyone in. They followed Danny and Tara who were in their hired Ford, heading west towards Naples, turning off a few miles short of the town, following the road until they turned right into the driveway of Tara's mother's house. The guard saluted and Danny parked the car in front of the house, the minibus pulling up behind. They got out and Albert said, "Nice place." John whistled in appreciation.

Tara led them inside. Isobel was reclining on the wicker sofa.

"Hi mom."

Isobel looked up. "What the..? What are you doing bringing these people in here? What is this, a peep show? Have you all come to watch someone die?"

"Take it easy, mom. These are friends of mine. They've come to help."

"Tara, you've got to face it. I'm beyond help."

Tara said, "This is-"

"Don't bother telling me their names. I'll never remember. Won't live long enough to get to know them anyway. Take them out, for Christ's sake. I don't want to be gawped at by a bunch of strangers."

Tara looked at Danny who said, "Come on guys. Let's leave them to talk a while." He shut the door behind them.

"I don't expect my own daughter to turn me into some kind of freak show."

"Mother, for God's sake, for once in your life, will you listen to me? You still talk to me like I'm some stupid kid who knows nothing. I'm not a teenager any more; I'm a grown woman. Take a look – I'm getting older. These people I've brought here, they're friends, but not *just* friends. One of them can help you."

"I don't want help – it would just prolong the inevitable. Unless he can cure me I'd rather speed things up."

"But that's just it. He *can* cure you."

"What is he, some healer or something? I was into that in the past, but I don't have faith in anything anymore."

"He's not a healer, mom. He's a scientist. Did you see the two young guys who looked like they could be twins?"

"I don't know – maybe. I didn't really look at them, but yes there were two that looked alike."

They're not what they seem, Michael and Albert. Albert is Michael's father. He's over seventy years old. And Michael is forty something."

"Rubbish."

"It's true."

"You're going to tell me these two have been visited by the little red men from space, aren't you?"

"No."

"What then?"

"There are no little red men from space. It's all a hoax."

"Well I thought so. I never believed-"

"Listen! We started it."

Isobel looked puzzled. "But why?"

Tara explained about Michael's age-reversal treatment and how she and Danny had stumbled across it three years earlier.

"Is this what you got mixed up in when you were in Europe?"

"Yes."

"The thing that was dangerous? You were in danger, I remember. Jim had to help you out."

"He got us out of a tight scrape, yes."

"So he knows about this?"

"No, mom. He thinks we were mixed up in something else, but it doesn't matter. The only thing that's important is that right now there is a man outside who can cure you."

"And you really believe this?"

"I *know* this. The people on the news – they really *are* young again. It has really happened – I've watched it happen."

"And this pill, or whatever you expect me to take. It will make me young, right?"

"Yes!"

"Not sure I want to be young."

"Oh right. So you want to die some agonising death, wasting away to sixty pounds? You want me to stand by and watch the cancer eat away at you until your body gives out and you die? What kind of a warped idea is that? You want to put me through that for nothing, when there's a man who can save you? Wake up mother!"

"But I'm not sure I want to go back to being twenty-five again. And you say, though I can't believe I'm entertaining the idea of something so fanciful, that these people who are turned young will never grow old?"

"Never."

"They'll live forever? I don't know that I want to do that."

"Great! So, at some point in the future you can commit suicide. Soon as you get bored you can shoot yourself. There you are, end of problem. But not now – I don't want you to die now, do you hear? I love you, for Christ's sake, and I don't want to lose you!"

Isobel looked shocked. "I, uh… I don't think you've ever said that before."

"So we aren't the most expressive of families. So what? We need to spend some more time together – I need to spend some more time with you. I don't want you to go yet."

Isobel's gaze fell on the floor for a few seconds.

"I take it he's brought some of those pills with him?"

Tara explained that she would have to stay in the house and that no one was to see her or know what had happened – not yet. The time would soon come. She told the servants that they were all to leave for a while and that she wanted to spend time alone with her mother until nearer Isobel's death. She would call them back before she died so they could say their goodbyes. When the last of them had gone Michael administered the aging cure and twenty-four hours later Isobel emerged from her bedroom, her long dark hair lustrous and thick, her slim body and flawless skin making her look like a younger version of the singer, Cher.

Tara and Isobel hugged, tears running down their faces.

"How are you feeling?" Tara asked.

"I… I can't describe it. It's like… an electric charge has been put through every cell of my body. I feel… light… I feel… alive – *really* alive! My God, this is amazing! What are you going to do with this… this cure?"

"We're going to make it available for everyone. But you have to realise that there are forces out there that'll do anything to stop this."

"But why?"

"You haven't thought it through yet. This is not just some anti-aging treatment. Sure it is that – but think about what it means. Like Michael said once, everything man has ever created has been made within the context that there is life and death. Remove death and everything changes – and that's the problem. Many powerful people are doing well in a world where people die. They won't want everyone to live forever. That's why this is dangerous. It's why we've had to use this hoax about little red spacemen. There are people out there who want to kill us, mom, and they'll want to kill you too."

"I can't hide forever, Tara."

"You won't have to. This thing is moving fast. Soon we're going to let the world know what's really going on, but not just yet."

"Tara, I'm worried about you!"

"Don't be. We'll make it. We have to."

"Promise me you'll stay in touch."

"I promise."

David drove the team back to Miami International Airport in the minibus. He said to Michael, "I hope we've done the right thing."

"You mean giving her the cure?"

"I mean not hypnotising her."

Chapter 16

President Bill McGovern sat in the Oval Office, twiddling a pen nervously. The Head of National Security, Henry Banks, knocked and entered.

"Henry, what the hell is going on here?"

"We don't know, Bill, but we're on to it."

"How are you on to it, Henry, how exactly?"

"I've sent two agents to interview them. We should have something soon."

"We've got to stop this. You damned well find me who's doing this, you hear? We're ahead in the polls, the economy's ticking along, the religious right are calm and under control, oil price is stable... and now this! Half the country thinks the world's being invaded by aliens! First England and now here. There'll be panic in the streets if you don't get to the bottom of it."

"We're doing what we can. We'll have answers soon I promise-"

"Henry, level with me. Do you know something?"

"No, not yet. I-"

"Henry! I mean, *do you know something*?"

"Sorry? I don't follow you."

"Yes you damned well do! All that stuff about aliens in the desert, the National Security Service hushing stuff up – you know what I mean. There's been rumours about all that stuff for years. Now you tell me – and I don't want you making a decision here about what I need to know and what I don't need to know. I want you to tell me exactly what you know about flying saucers and all that sci-fi crap. Is any of it true?"

"No, Mr President."

"No Mr President you won't tell me, or No Mr President there's nothing in any of that stuff and you never did any experiments on a bug eyed alien who dropped in to see how we do things down here on earth?"

"I mean no there's never been anything in any of those rumours. Just some faker playing tricks on the public, that's all."

"Then you find me who's doing this, and you find them fast, you hear?

"Yes sir."

"Have you spoken to the Brits yet?"

"I'm expecting a call from some guy called Alistair Cleaver. He's running the show over there."

The Happy Times Retirement Community was under siege from the world's journalists. Arnold and Violet Muller were in their bungalow, Arnold looking at some old photograph albums then holding up a mirror to gaze at his face, trying to see if there was a difference. Violet was standing with her leg on the back of a chair stretching forwards, grabbing her foot and pulling herself lower until her head was almost on her knee.

"Arnie, look at me! I haven't been able to bend like this for thirty years! You wait until I do aqua-aerobics next time. I'm going to show that Lauren Wheeler a thing or two. She's always going on about how far she can bend over and how she did ballet until she was fifty."

"Honey, you can forget about aqua-aerobics. You won't be going there again."

"Why not?"

"Because, honey, that class is for old folks, and we ain't old no more."

"Oh! But I'm gonna miss it. They'll let me go won't they?"

"Vi, you ain't old! You can't go. You think Lauren Wheeler and that cabal of witches she hangs out with are going to let you show them up? Anyway, we've got bigger things to think about."

"What are you saying?"

"We've got to decide where we're going to live."

"But I don't want to move. Our friends are here!"

"I know they are, honey. But this is for old folks, and like I keep telling you – we ain't old no more. We can't stay here."

"They never said when they was turning us young that we'd lose all our friends."

"We aren't going to lose them. We can come visit."

Violet looked out of the window at the TV cameras and the reporters talking into microphones. "Look! There's Lauren Wheeler. Someone's interviewing her! Trust her to get herself on TV!"

"Shut up about Lauren Wheeler, for Christ's sake!"

"There's two men coming to the door. Smart looking guys in suits – kinda nice looking."

Violet opened the front door, a volley of flashlights went off and the two men held up their identity cards for her to see, saying they wanted to ask her a few questions. Violet let them in.

"Arnie, these two gentlemen are here to see us."

"Come on in and take a seat," Arnold said.

The men introduced themselves as Gerry Mason and Tom Drew, working for the government.

"How can we help you guys?" Arnold asked.

The two men explained that they just wanted to clear a few things up and were anxious to hear how they had been turned young. Arnold and Violet told them the tale of the little red men from space and the beam they had been transported on and how the aliens had turned them young, saying they had come to Earth to stop people from dying. Gerry and Tom listened intently to the two newly-young inhabitants of the Happy Times Retirement Community, who both talked as if what had happened to them was perfectly normal – just an everyday occurrence in California. Gerry and Tom left the happy couple and reported what they had found, or rather had *not* found, to Henry Banks.

"You mean these two wackos are telling the truth?" Henry said.

"I… I don't know," Gerry said. "But they aren't old anymore. They showed us pictures of when they were young and … it's them in the pictures. And the old folks at the community all say it's them – the same Arnold and Violet – just fifty years younger. I don't know how to explain it."

"Gerry, there aren't little red men in spaceships visiting earth. If there were we'd have spotted them on our air defence systems."

"I guess so. But if they can turn people young, maybe they can get around our defences?"

"Jesus, you *believe* these two, don't you?"

"They were pretty convincing. They just told us what happened as if they were describing going on a picnic by the river. It was eerie."

Henry said, "But what they are saying, it's just so far-fetched…"

"But it's the same story as the ones in England came out with. If it isn't true, how did whoever did this get people from half way around the world to come up with the same story?"

"They could have read about it in the newspapers and just copied it," Henry said.

"But they really *are* young. In fact Violet is quite a looker. I tell you Tom's eyes were popping out when she bent over in her leotard to touch her toes. No seventy-year-old I've ever seen has a neat high little ass like that. Jesus, I wish my wife's looked that good."

After his conversation with the two agents, Gerry and Tom, (he made a point of never referring to them in reverse order) Henry tried to get his thoughts together. Just what in God's name was he going to tell the President? The whole thing was surreal. When he eventually returned to the Oval office he found the President staring at CNN on television.

"Henry have you been watching this? The goddamned world's going crazy. Seems like half the people actually want us to be invaded by little red men. What's the news? I saw your guys going in there. They were on the TV just a while ago."

"I, er… I'm not sure there is any news as such."

"What do you mean? They talked to them, I saw it."

"Yes they did."

"So who's doing this shit?"

"There… there doesn't seem to be anyone doing it. It… all appears to be… as they say."

"Henry, are you telling me we ARE being invaded by aliens?"

"Yes, er, no… not exactly. I… I just mean that… what they say, about the aliens… there's nothing to deny it."

"Bullshit! Unless… Henry, you *do* know something, don't you? Talk to me, goddamit!"

"I don't know anything, except that it appears these two people really have been turned young. How… I… . I can't explain it. The story they gave, as ludicrous as it sounds… there isn't any other explanation, not that we can come up with."

"What? Then… for Christ sakes, Henry! We've got to alert the military, The National Guard… Jesus Christ! I've got to address the nation. This isn't a movie, is it? Tell me I'm not dreaming…"

"You're not dreaming, Mr President."

The phone rang. Bill grabbed it. "Henry? Yes he's here." The President handed the phone to Henry. "It's a Brit called Cleaver."

Cleaver had seen the footage on CNN. Damn it, the Americans will be all over this now! Earlier he had received a call from none other than Henry Banks, that American National Security man who seemed to be on TV more often than the President himself. Cleaver had been reluctant to call him back, sensing the American would try to take over the operation. Oh they would make all the right sounds about working together, and teamwork – all that rubbish, but they would insist on taking control and treating the British as bit players, just as they had in Iraq and Afghanistan. Now that the 'aliens' had apparently been operating in California, Cleaver had no choice but to return Henry's call, but he would make sure the Americans didn't take over the show this time.

He picked up the phone. "Get me Henry Banks in America."

Five minutes later his phone rang and a voice told him he was through.

"Mr Banks?"

"Yeah. Is this Cleaver?"

"Indeed."

"What the hell is going on with this alien crap?"

"This… *alien crap*, as you put it, is under control. Have no fear."

"No fear, eh? You know what's happening over here? We've got people out on the streets calling for little red men in spaceships to come down to earth. You know how serious this is?"

"I can assure you everything is under control."

"It doesn't feel like it."

"Mr Banks-"

"You can call me Henry. No need for us to be stuffed shirts, is there?"

"Er, no. None at all… Henry. As I was saying, it's all under control. Just a few people messing about playing some kind of hoax."

"So these people on the TV aren't really young again?"

"Well… it seems that they have undergone a treatment which has… rejuvenated them, yes. But the alien story – that's all nonsense."

"If it's nonsense then how do you explain these folks looking like they're twenty-five years old all of a sudden?"

"There's a rogue scientist who's been messing about with some genetic engineering project. All unauthorised, of course. He's, er… he's had some success, so it seems, and-"

"My God. Have you people understood the implications of this?"

"Yes we have, I can assure you."

"Good. Well how come they're operating over here now?"

"We're working on it. They'll be stopped very soon, I promise."

"You better. We can't have this thing going on on American soil, you follow? We're going to have to jump in and see to things ourselves if you don't deal with it real soon, you understand?"

"Henry… rest assured, we are dealing with it-"

"I've got men I can put on it right away and-"

"No, you don't need to do that. Look, we've been on to this for the last three or four years, ever since they were working on developing a gas down in France. You can-"

"Three or four years?"

"Yes. We have been monitoring these people. They will be stopped very soon, as I have repeated several times."

"Okay. But do it quick, before the genie is really out of the bottle."

"Yes, Henry. You can… I think the current American expression is… *chill out*."

"Hell, you really are up to speed on things aren't you Cleaver?"

"The name's *Alistair*. No need to be stuffed shirts, right?"

"You're a real funny guy. I'll fill the President in with all this."

"Henry… you must be careful who finds out about this – I mean about what is *really* going on. If it gets out… it would be more difficult to handle than this alien story. Do you get my drift?"

"Yeah, I do. Don't worry. Only those who have to know will know."

"Right now I take it that's just you and the President?"

"Agreed. But to keep it that way you have to work fast, you hear?"

Before returning to England the team stirred things up a little more by flying to New York where they turned Johnny and Eileen O'Shea young in David's Good Hope Home For The Elderly. Just as in California, the TV crews descended and soon the newly-young couple became household names after appearing on The Letterman Show.

The President was watching the show with Henry.

"Good God, Henry. The audience – look at them. They've all gone mad. They really think it's aliens doing this. Look, if we know it's not aliens from outer space, why don't I just go on TV and tell everyone that it's this scientist guy – tell them what's really going on?"

"I, uh… I wouldn't advise that, Bill."

"Why not?"

"You might have an even bigger problem on your hands."

"Henry for Christ's sake stop talking in riddles. What are you saying?"

"What I mean is that right now the people think it's little red men from space that are doing this. The world is going crazy to get young again. It might be better they keep believing it's little red aliens that are responsible."

"Why?"

"Because if we can eliminate this scientist guy, we can just pretend that the aliens aren't coming back. Over time people would forget about it and things would get back to normal. We'd have a few genetic freaks to contend with who could make a living on the chat show circuit, but that would be all. If you tell the world it's not little red men and it's some half-crazed scientist who's developed an anti-aging drug… Well, people are going to want it. I mean half the population would have plastic surgery if they could. How are you going to tell them they have to die and living forever isn't an option?"

"I see what you mean. You're right. We don't have a choice. My God, we better catch these bastards soon or it's going to be hard to manage this. This Cleaver guy – you heard from him again?"

"No, not yet."

"Then you better make contingency plans, Henry. We can't risk waiting much longer."

Chapter 17

Jim Reynolds sat around the table with six other agents, awaiting the arrival of Henry Banks. One of the agents, a man named Neil Drover, asked Jim, "You know what this is about?"

"Well, no I don't. I guess if I did we wouldn't have to have the meeting, would we?"

"Tetchy this morning aren't you Jim?"

"'Bout the same as every other morning."

"Yep. That's true."

Henry entered the room and the agents sat up.

"Okay. You're all wondering why I've called you here, no doubt. I'll get straight to it. By the way – what's said here stays between these four walls, okay? For now, at least. You will all have heard about these old folks in California and New York, who used to be old, but aren't anymore. The ones that got a visit from the little red men?"

"Same as the ones in Europe," Neil said.

"Yes, just like those folks in Europe."

"You, er… you don't believe that stuff about aliens, though do you?"

"Don't be so damned stupid. There are no aliens. Not on this side of the damned universe anyway. I hope none of you were naïve enough to fall for this nonsense."

"No of course not, but it seems half the planet has," Neil said. "Jesus Christ. Elvis will be turning up next."

With a straight face and a quiet voice Henry said, "Elvis turned up a long time ago. You know he was working for us in the CIA? He needed to get out of the limelight and we hid him in a bunker under the Pentagon for two years until the fuss died down. Then we set him up with a little plastic surgery and new passport and a gastric bypass to stop him eating himself to death. He's in Hawaii now with a young Brazilian girl who looks after him, tends to his needs, if you get my meaning."

Neil Drover said, "My God... Tell me you're kidding..."

Henry kept his heavy-duty expression, stepped closer and bent down until his face was eighteen inches away from Neil's. "Yes, I'm kidding," he said.

The agents laughed, albeit a little uneasily, and Henry returned to his place at the head of the table. "None of you would be stupid enough to fall for that alien crap, now would you? But it's amazing what people will believe once you ply them with a little detail, isn't it?"

"So, who's behind all this?" Neil asked.

"I don't know yet. But I hope we're about to find out before the joke goes too far. There's an agent on the case – a Brit called Cleaver."

Jim sat up in his chair at the mention of Cleaver's name.

Henry said, "He's a cocky son of a bitch. Tells me he knows what it's all about. Says there's some rogue scientist he was watching in France who's developed some crazy potion that makes people young again."

Neil said, "Hey, can I get some for my wife?"

"You think this is funny?"

"Er, no."

"Good. Because people can't get to live forever. You get you three score and ten and that's it – you're out of here. People live any longer and we get a population explosion – we can't feed them. Be under no illusion, gentlemen, this living forever fantasy is dangerous – half the goddamned country's gone crazy for it. This is a threat to national security. Potentially more so than the cold war."

"So... who's this Cleaver, guy?" Jim asked.

"Like I said, some jumped up Brit who says he's on the case. He's tracking down the scientist guy and the people he's working with. Shouldn't take him long – they sound like a bunch of starry-eyed kids with big ideas."

Jim shifted around in his seat.

"Something bothering you, Jim?" Henry asked.

"Er, no – nothing at all. So, uh... what do you want us to do?"

"Nothing. Not yet. We're giving this Cleaver guy a little leeway to sort things out. But I'm telling you this because I want you ready, in case the Brit screws up. If he does we might have to move fast. Like I said, this could get out of hand very quickly."

Jim left the meeting with memories playing around in his mind of Cleaver sitting trussed up in a hotel room in the Isle of Man wearing purple boxer shorts. What Henry had said about Cleaver watching someone in France – it could only mean one thing. It had to have something to do with that business Tara had got herself mixed up in.

He had to go somewhere private and call Isobel.

Chapter 18

Isobel was dancing around in the conservatory. She had on her Indian music – sitars and bells clanging – and she was doing her hippy, expressive stuff, arms flailing, legs swinging up high, rapturous expression. She revelled in the feel of her body – the sheer joy of living in it. To be young again, to be energised like this… it was everything!

The phone rang. She ignored it. Let it ring, who cares, she thought, twirling to the music. But it didn't stop ringing.

"Okay, Okay!" she said, turning off the music.

She picked it up.

"Hello!" she said, her voice light and airy. Then she remembered she was supposed to be dying.

"Isobel, is that you?"

She recognized her brother's voice immediately and quickly changed her tone, making it sound flat and lifeless. "Oh… Hi Jim," she said weakly.

"How are you feeling?"

"Oh, you know. As well as can be expected."

"Are you managing to eat?"

"I'm eating… yes."

"Good. You have to at least keep your strength up. Your body needs nourishment." Isobel didn't answer. "Isobel? Do you hear?"

"Yes. I hear you Jim. Were you calling to check up on my diet?"

"No, of course not. I wanted to know how you were, that's all."

"Well, now you know."

"Yes. I need to ask you something. Have you heard from Tara?"

"Why do you ask?"

"I… I'm worried about her."

"Why?"

"Is she still with Danny?"

"Yes, of course. They're in love, Jim. You remember what that's like, don't you?" Jim didn't answer. "You never did like him did you?"

"I thought he might lead her into trouble."

"And?"

"I think I was right."

"Jim, what are you talking about?"

"There's only so much I can tell you. Let's just say that… Look, you remember when Tara met this Danny guy? They were mixed up in something."

"Yes Jim, I remember."

"I had to get them out of a tight scrape – and before you ask – no, I won't tell you about it."

"But that was three years ago."

"Yeah, I know."

"So… ?"

"I was called into a meeting earlier on. Something's going on, and I have a feeling it's connected to what Tara got mixed up in back then. Actually, it's more than a feeling. I *know* it's what she was mixed up in. I don't want to worry you, Isobel, but what she's involved with…"

"How much danger do you think she's in?"

"A lot. She's messing with something she shouldn't be. She's going to cause a lot of people a lot of problems and they aren't going to be happy about it. They are going to want to stop her. We've got to contact her. I'll try her number on that damned island she lives on."

"She won't be there."

"You know that?" Isobel didn't answer. "Come on Isobel, you know something don't you? You know where she is?"

"No, no, Jim, I, er… I tried her house – there was no reply."

"So, she was out. Maybe she was doing some shopping. But you *know* she wasn't doing any shopping, don't you?"

"I don't know. Try her. Maybe you're right."

"You can't lie to me, Isobel. I know when you're lying, I always did. You never could bullshit me."

"No, I… Look, you know, I'm feeling a little tired. Got to go. Bye." She put down the receiver.

Oh, hell! Now he was suspicious!

Chapter 19

Joss burst into Cleaver's office. "What's the progress? I pray to God there is some."

"Yes, there is. I was going to call you."

"Well I'm here, so what is it?"

"As you know Michael Richards and his father have been off the radar, so to speak. And we didn't know where the journalist and his girlfriend were."

"But you do now?"

"Er, no."

"Well what have you got then? Come on, spit it out."

"These people that have been turning young. There's a link between them."

"What?"

"Almost all of them are in, or were in, nursing homes."

"Yes, well a lot of old people are."

"There's more. All the nursing homes were owned by companies that belonged to the same person. Do you know a man called David Lane?"

"The billionaire chap whose into hospitals and pharmaceuticals? Yes, of course."

"He's the missing link. And he's got the means to stage something like this."

"Have you tracked him down?"

"Not yet. But I called his office and they told me he hasn't been seen there for some time. Not since around the time of the first … 'alien visitation.' They say he's taking time off to work on a special project."

"Then he's our man. Find him. And make it fast!"

"I'm going to pay a visit to one of his hospitals. What do you want me to do with him when I locate him?"

"You kill him, of course. And the rest of them. Kill them all."

Chapter 20

Jim had to find Tara fast if he was to save her from the mess she was in. He knew Isobel had been lying to him on the phone and so he flew down to Florida to find out what she was hiding. He would have to prize it out of her gently – she was in no fit state to be put under pressure.

He pulled up at the house in a car he had hired at the airport, got out and approached the door. Five yards away from it he heard music: it was Led Zeppelin playing *Whole Lotta Love,* and it was on very loud. What the hell was this? Whoever was playing it wasn't doing Isobel any favours. She needed rest, not this noise. He turned his key in the lock, opened the door and was hit by a wall of sound.

"Jesus Christ!" he shouted, though he could hardly hear his own voice. It was coming for the music room. He hurried over to the door, flung it open, stepped inside and saw a tall, slim, dark-haired girl, swirling herself around to the music, bending over at the waist, shaking her head from side to side, her hair flying out in all directions. Jim ran over to the woman, grabbed her arm and yanked her around to face him. For a moment they stared into each other's eyes, Robert Plant's voice cutting through the air, assaulting his ears, and then… he recognised her… and he stepped back, his eyes looking as if they were about to pop, his jaw hanging slack.

"Isobel?"

She walked over to the side of the room, switched off the music and turned to face him.

"My God… it's… it's really you, isn't it?" She nodded. "I… I can't believe it."

"Believe it, Jim. It's me."

"You're… just as you were… when… you were… twenty-five years old! I…"

"I guess you know it wasn't little red men from space."

"Are you… *well*, now?"

"The cancer? Gone. I'm young, fit and healthy, Jim. I've never felt so good!"

He stepped towards her and hugged her. "I… I don't know what to say…"

"Say… I don't know… congratulations or something!"

"Congratulations? I don't think that does it."

"Nothing does it, Jim. This is life… living… this is… joy!"

"How did it happen?"

"I'm not supposed to tell you. And you're not supposed to be here. No one's to know about this. Not now. They're going to tell everyone how it happens soon, but not yet. It's some kind of hoax they're playing, but only for a little while."

"Isobel, I don't know if I agree with all this, but-"

"You don't *agree* with it? You want me to die?"

"No, of course not. But… if everyone got hold of this…"

"Then everyone would be young!"

"I know but…"

"What's wrong with that?"

"It would mean… everything would get turned upside down – the balance of things…"

"Things getting turned upside down? Balance of things? For God's sake, Jim! We are talking about people's lives! This is about getting rid of death! And you're worried about the balance of things?"

"I know… I don't know what I mean – I have to get my head around it."

"Well get your head around this! I am young, I am alive and I am well. And I am your sister, goddamit!"

"I know. Isobel, I'm grateful, I'm over the moon with you being… young and healthy again. You look amazing!" He took her hands in his, feeling her taught fresh skin.

"I feel amazing! Jim, this is good. It's a *good* thing. People *don't* have to die. Can't you see what they've done here, or are you so contaminated with the shit the government's been pumping into you that you've lost the point of everything? You are supposed to protect the people – save people's lives! What do you think these people are doing?"

"It's easy for you to say that, but we have to think of other things – of the bigger picture. Look, I... all of us, the government, we have to think about what's best for *everyone*. If everyone thinks they can live forever, there'd be a population explosion, we couldn't feed everyone, the world would... I don't know, run out of space!"

"Jim, wake up! Listen to the crap you are coming out with!"

"Well how *would* we feed ourselves?"

"Do I look like a give a flying fuck? I'm alive! I'm young and healthy and I'll never get old! Let the world have this gift that's been given to me! As for how we'll make enough food – that's for the farmers and the scientists to work out. Make them all young and they'll have enough time to sort it out – what do I care? Life, Jim – it's the most precious thing. Get your soul back! They took it from you when you joined up and started talking like some goddamned government spokesman. Wouldn't you like to be young again, Jim?"

"I don't know... I-"

"You don't know because you haven't been close to death in the way I have. I don't mean what you do with your job. You wave a gun about from time to time, but you have some control over what happens, and you have a choice about it – you can give it up and do a regular job if you want. I'm talking about having something you can't control eating away at your insides, creeping up on you, draining you of life, one day at a time, and all the time you know you're just a few days away from your last, and you'll never feel the sun on your face or see the ones you love again. If you'd have been through that, maybe then you'd want to get young again."

Jim hugged her and kissed her head. "I don't pretend to know what it's been like for you, and I'm the happiest man alive now that you're not ill any more. Maybe you're right and I have lost the plot somewhere, I don't know. But I still have my soul, Isobel. I'm not like you, but I do have that."

"I know. I'm sorry. I shouldn't have said that."

They gazed into each other's eyes and then Jim said. "Shit! Looking at you is like going back in time, it really is. There's one thing I do know. They have to stay hidden. They don't know what they are up against. There are people out there who are going to want to kill them, and I don't know how to stop it."

Chapter 21

Helen had taken over David's office in the hospital. Well, why not? She was running the show now. Every day she arrived just a little earlier, not wanting to waste a second of the day. Ideas popped up from nowhere and flew around in her head and she scribbled them down quickly before she lost them. Each idea seemed to spark off another in a never-ending chain reaction. God, she never knew business could be such fun!

Someone knocked the door and opened it. Without looking up Helen said, "Yes?"

The familiar voice of her secretary said, "There's someone here to see David."

Still looking down at the papers on her desk, Helen said, "Well tell them he's not here."

"I already have, but he's most insistent."

"He can be as insistent as he likes, I don't know where he is or where-"

"Just a minute! You can't go in!" the secretary shouted.

Helen looked up and saw a tall thin man push past the secretary wearing a pinstriped suit with a flamboyant silk handkerchief in his breast pocket.

The man said, "I'm sure I can. This won't take long."

The secretary looked at Helen apologetically.

Helen eyed the man. Whoever he was he was a cocky son of a bitch. He stood there with a supercilious grin on his face. Eventually curiosity got the better of her and she said, "It's all right. Leave this to me."

The man seemed to take that as an invitation to sit down and he took a seat on the chair in front of Helen's desk. Helen nodded to the secretary, who then left them, closing the door behind her.

"I don't know who you are, but-"

"Cleaver, Alistair Cleaver."

"Mr Cleaver, if you want to talk to David I'm afraid you're out of luck. I don't know where he is."

"And you are in charge here, right?"

"Yes."

"All on your own?"

"Yes, Mr Cleaver… all on my own. What a clever girl I must be, wouldn't you say? Heaven knows what they'll be letting us women do next."

Cleaver grinned and then said, "Seems odd that Mr Lane would disappear and not be in contact with you from time to time… to check up on things. Not that you aren't a very capable woman, I'm sure. But he is still the owner of the company isn't he?"

"Let's get to the point. Why don't you tell me who you are and what you want. Maybe I can help you."

"I work for a branch of the government."

"Oh, I see. I should have realised. You *do* look like a tax inspector."

Any sign of levity fell from Cleaver's face. "Not that side of government. I'm more of…. a security advisor."

"Go on…"

"We would like to talk to Mr Lane."

"Why?" Helen looked worried. "Is he in some kind of danger?"

"Quite possibly."

"What's going on?"

"Nothing I can talk about – not yet. I mean until we are *sure* it would be silly to alarm you unnecessarily, wouldn't it?"

"You come here and tell me he might be in danger? Of course I'm alarmed."

"Well, we just need to locate him, to be certain."

Helen thought for a moment. "I meant what I said. I really don't know where he is."

"Did he say why he was leaving?"

"Just that he was going to work on some project, some new development. I don't know what, exactly. But it's not out of the ordinary, he's a creative man."

"Quite. So you don't know where he is, what he's doing, and he hasn't been in touch – not once?"

"No."

"Astonishing. He must trust you… implicitly."

"Of course he does. Our relationship is more than professional."

"You must be the love of his life. I'm sure he must tell you everything."

"What are you insinuating, exactly?"

"I'm just wondering how it is that the love of your life can bear to be away from you for any time at all, especially without contacting you, or telling you where he's gone."

Helen looked flustered. "Our relationship is *our* business, Mr Cleaver. What's going on here? Why is he in danger?"

Cleaver fixed his gaze on her for a few seconds, as if he was trying to read her mind. Then he stood up, took a card from his inside pocket and tossed it onto Helen's desk. "If he contacts you call me on this number." He turned and began to walk to the door. Helen ran after him.

"Just a minute! You can't just go like that!" She got between Cleaver and the door, blocking his way.

Cleaver looked unmoved. "If you want to keep him safe, find out where he is and call me. But I wouldn't tell him about our conversation. Not yet. It may… compromise his safety."

"Tell me!"

Cleaver grabbed her arm and gently pulled her away from the door, Helen feeling the quiet strength in his grip. Cleaver opened the door and as he left the room said, "Like I said, call me."

A few seconds later, the secretary came hurrying into the room.

"I'm sorry. I couldn't stop him."

"Don't worry. It's not a problem… .I… I've dealt with it."

The secretary left the room and Helen sat at her desk.

Who the hell was that guy? She replayed the meeting in her head. There was something about him that unnerved her, as if she sensed something of his essence, and it was rotten, sinister… violent even. Could he really be with the government? She picked up the card he had given her. There was nothing on it except a telephone number. Why did he think David was in danger? Was it a kidnap plot? A man of David's wealth would always be a target for criminals. But if it were that wouldn't this Cleaver guy have said so? What would be the point in *not* saying it? She went over the events just before David had left. Nothing unusual had happened. Life had been going on pretty much as normal. Nothing unusual... except for that blood sample...

Chapter 22

David and the team made one more couple young, this time in a suburb of Nice in the South of France. Eddy and Tessa Harris had retired to the Mediterranean after David had bought their small chain of nursing homes in Yorkshire. They had stayed in touch and three months ago Tessa had let David know in an email that Eddy's heart was weak and that she feared he didn't have long to live.

David gave them both a blood pill, John worked his hypnosis, and then the team flew back to Southampton leaving Eddy and Tessa to the French, and later, the world's press, who speculated on which country the aliens might visit next.

When they got back to the boat David turned on a bank of TV screens, which were tuned into the international news channels. CNN had positioned their cameras on the Hollywood hills and were beaming pictures around the world of a mass gathering of the hopeful, who looked up to the heavens, sang songs and, with arms outstretched, beckoned the aliens to come back to earth to make their elderly relatives young. The images were biblical, save for the baggy trousers, sneakers and baseball caps worn by some of the people – although there were enough bearded hippy types to make up for it. Similar scenes were broadcast from around the world. Millions of people had stopped going to work. It was as though they sensed the coming of an epiphany. Why bother going to work when the world was about to be saved by some advanced alien civilization? Perhaps nobody would have to work anymore.

Danny's website was ready to go. He clicked on the icon and uploaded it to the server. An hour later the first of newspapers displaying the full-page advertisements Danny had designed hit the streets. The advert said:

Let-the-aliens-know.com is for you to register the names and addresses of your elderly sick relatives. Alien beings will have the power to connect with cyberspace. Register here and let them know where to find your loved ones!

By noon the web traffic had picked up fast. Thousands of people were logging on to register names and addresses of people they knew who were in need of a visit from the little red men. Over the next twenty-four hours the ads appeared in newspapers in New York, Los Angeles, Sydney and New Delhi, and soon over one million people had registered on the site.

David opened his inbox and saw an email from someone called Doctor Lamont. He opened it and read:

Doctor Lamont from Florida would like to discuss the medical condition of the husband of one her former patients, which she believes to be life threatening. Dr Lamont believes it would be convenient to meet where you first met in London and hopes that it won't be raining this time. He will be there on the same day at the same time. Due to the critical condition of this person Dr Lamont insists on your UTMOST discretion.

David read it again and then leant back in his chair staring at the screen, blank expression on his face. Danny entered the room.

"You okay?" he asked. "You look like you've seen a ghost."

"I, er… I've got an email."

"And?"

"Something's wrong."

Danny walked around behind David, looked over his shoulder and read the email.

"I don't get it. What's wrong?" Danny said.

"It's a code."

"Who from?"

"Helen."

"Who?"

"She's my partner."

"Business or otherwise?"

"Both."

"So Dr Lamont is Helen?"

"She wrote a medical thriller and Dr Lamont was the main character. The rendezvous point she is talking about is the book store in London where she did a book signing and I turned up to surprise her."

"And it was raining?"

"Like a tropical storm."

"And you know the date?"

"It's tomorrow. But what worries me is why she's had to write an email in code and this bit about utmost discretion. Why didn't she just contact me? For some reason she must think she's being watched."

"I take it you're going?"

"I have to. We can't risk continuing without knowing what's going on."

"Does she know about all this?" David shook his head. "She's your partner and you didn't tell her?"

"I know it sounds strange, but no I didn't."

"How come?"

"I don't want to get into that."

Cleaver called Joss.

"We're getting somewhere."

"What have you found?"

"David Lane has a private jet, as you might expect. I've tracked its movements. Seems he recently took a trip to The States."

"I expect he goes there quite often. These business types do, you know."

"Yes, quite. However, he happened to go the day before that couple were turned young in California. Seems he flew to New York afterwards where another couple of old dears were turned into fresh young things. Then he made a trip to Nice and back."

"Good God! But we want to know where he is now…"

"The plane returned to the UK. Landed at Southampton."

"And it hasn't moved from there?"

"No."

"We've got him!"

"Not exactly. We know where his plane is, but we don't know where *he* is."

"Well, find him. And get someone watching that damn plane."

"I've got two men watching it. If he tries to use it again we'll have him."

Chapter 23

Henry had called another meeting. Jim sat with his head bowed, hands clasped together on the table, deep in thought. He knew what was coming but didn't know how he was going to deal with it. The door burst open and Henry strode in purposefully.

"Gentlemen, you don't need me to tell you why you're here, I'm sure. We are in crisis – deep shit. The country's gone mad. Make that the *world* has gone mad. People are up on the hills calling up to the stars for little red spacemen to come down and turn them young, for Christ sakes! Half the people aren't turning up for work and the economy is in danger of meltdown. I'm sure I don't need to tell you how serious this shit is – you've been watching the goddamned news, right?"

All the agents nodded. Then Neil Drover said, "I thought the Brits were handling it."

"They were. But we can't wait around any longer. This guy Cleaver is an asshole. We've got to track these people down and put a stop to it. But, gentlemen, take heed of what I am going to say to you. This is strictly between us. We can't, I repeat, *can't* allow anyone to know what is really going on here. Do I make myself clear?" The agents all nodded. Jim shifted around uneasily in his chair. "From now on I want you to make this a priority. Seek and destroy. Do you follow?" More nodding. "Well what the fuck are you all doing sitting here? Get to it!"

As soon as he got out of the meeting, Jim phoned Isobel.

"Isobel, Tara's in a lot of trouble."

"Why?"

Jim gave her the gist of the meeting with Henry. "Make no mistake, Isobel. When they find her..."

"Are you serious?"

"I'd hardly joke about something like this, would I?"

"What are we going to do? You've got to stop them!"

"Stop them? How the hell do I stop the combined might of the Secret Service, for fuck's sake? I don't see what I can do. Isobel, can't you see how out of control this has got? The security of the world as we know it... it's all going to shit. This is so big, I can't tell you."

"I know."

"You don't sound worried."

"About people not dying? About people like me getting cured of cancer? You're damned right I'm not worried about *that*. What do you expect me to do, feel guilty for being young, healthy and alive?"

"No, I-"

"Good. Because I don't. What I'm worried about is Tara."

"Me too, but I don't know what to do. You can't contact her, and we don't know where she is. She'll be found, that's for sure, and when she is, they're going to-"

"Wait. Okay, there's *one* person who *can* help her. I'm coming to Washington."

The phone went dead.

David arrived outside the bookshop wearing old jeans, a dark anorak and a balaclava with a baseball cap on top of it. Not the usual attire of a billionaire. He was unrecognizable. He looked in the window at the books on display, which was suspicious in itself, because he didn't look like someone who could read. On the other side of the road a woman wearing a raincoat, dark glasses and a pink scarf stood on the curb waiting to cross. David saw her reflection in the shop window but didn't recognise her until she stepped out into the road. That gait of hers, and the way she held her head, it could only be Helen. She reached the shop and looked up and down the pavement. Then David turned, walked towards her and said, "Follow me inside." He made his way between the rows of books, stopping at the psychology section, and when Helen approached him he said, "Dr Lambton, I presume."

She glanced behind her to check they weren't being watched then hugged him, burying her face in his neck for a few seconds before kissing him hard on the lips.

"David, what the hell is going on?"

"I was hoping you were going to tell me. Nice message by the way. You've not lost your touch with the creative writing."

"Is that all you're going to say? You've been off somewhere for days and you haven't once contacted me. I was worried about you."

"Were you?"

"Yes. Why do you say that?"

"You seemed to have only one thing on your mind, and it wasn't me."

"I have to do my work, you understand that, surely. But come on, David, tell me what's going on. We both know something's not right."

"Nothing's going on, I'm just working on something, that's all."

"Bullshit! If nothing's going on why are you dressed like you live on a park bench?"

"Look, tell me why you sent me the cryptic message."

"Because I had a visit. Some guy called Cleaver came to see me. Says he works for the government and he wants to find you. Do you know him?"

"I've heard of him."

"Tall guy. Something about him I really didn't like. He barged his way into the office and asked for you. He wouldn't tell me anything, but I got the impression he wasn't a friend of yours. More like the opposite in fact. I sent you the message because… I don't know, maybe I'm imagining it, but I thought if he was something to do with the government he could have bugged the office or something. David, have you pissed some people off you shouldn't have?"

"If I have it's hardly news, is it?"

Helen sighed. "What's happened to us? What's made you keep things from me? How did it get like this?"

"What else did this Cleaver guy say?"

"Nothing specific. He didn't believe you'd disappeared without me knowing where you were. He acted as if it wasn't believable, and you know what? I thought about it and he was right – it isn't believable. How come you went off like that without telling me where you're going and what you're doing? What are you up to?"

"Nothing."

"Stop saying that!"

"Look, it's better that you don't know at the moment."

"Why? It has something to do with this Cleaver guy, right? You disappeared off the face of the Earth. I thought you'd been taken away by these little red spacemen that are supposed to be turning people young."

"Did Cleaver say that?"

"No. Why would he? David? Why did you ask me that?"

"Did he say he was coming back?"

"No. But that doesn't mean he won't. What's going on? Why did you ask if Cleaver said something about these spacemen and UFOs that are supposed to be visiting us? Are you… ? Yes, that's it! You *are* involved in all this aren't you? That blood sample you got me to check – I went and took another look at it. Have you developed something – some new drug? There was something strange about the sample – it had properties I'd never seen before. Is it something to do with this, David? David! Talk to me, for Christ's sake!"

"Helen, don't ask so many questions, okay."

"Don't ask so many questions? This isn't fair, you know. I do *love* you. I worry about you. And I've got Secret Service men barging into my office and you won't tell me why? Why don't you talk to me?"

"Because… I don't know how you'd feel about what I'm doing, that's why."

"Well try me! For God's sake, we're practically married – you're supposed to be able to trust me, talk to me!"

"But what if it is something dangerous, and I'm protecting you from it?"

She looked up at him a concerned expression on her face. "You know… we *really* do have to talk. You have no idea do you… ?"

"About what?" he asked.

"Lets go somewhere else. I can't do this here."

She grabbed his hand, led him outside and then along the street to the park, which was five minutes away on foot. They entered it through a gate in the railings and began to walk along the perimeter path.

Helen said, "David, you don't know how much I love you, you really don't. You've made my life an adventure. I've learned so much from you, and I love running the business, being a part of everything. It's exciting, it stimulates me like nothing ever has before. But as much as I love it, I would give it up in an instant, without a moment's hesitation, if I were asked to choose between it and you. My God, I realise now how distant we have become. I got too wrapped up in the new hospital and I was wrong to let that happen. But David, don't for one moment think that the most important thing in my life is anything other than you. You are my *partner* – for life. You *are* my life. You say things like you did earlier about not telling me something to protect me from danger... do I care? I want to be with you to share everything... to share *life* with you. And if that includes danger – so be it. I would rather risk my life *with* you than to have no life by being separated from you. Do you understand? I want to be part of everything. Just let me in, okay?"

He looked into her eyes for a moment, then grabbed her and hugged her.

"What if I was involved in something that was going to take away everything we have? What would you say to that?"

"I'd say that you must have your reasons for doing what you're doing. I trust you, and I trust your motives. In any event, it's all yours to do with whatever you feel and believe to be right. I didn't create it, you did."

"You were the inspiration behind it. It was your ideas and your experiences that went into creating it the way we did."

"It was mostly your business sense and your money. But let's not argue about that. That's the past. I want to know about now."

"Can you imagine a world free of disease and death?"

"Only in my dreams."

"That would have been my answer until recently."

"And now? It's that blood sample isn't it?"

"Someone came to me and showed me something incredible..."

He told her what had happened when the team had first arrived at the hospital and how Michael's wound had miraculously healed and the story of how the cure for aging had been discovered.

"So this stuff in the news about little red spacemen was put about by you?"

He told her why they had come up with the idea and how desperate the government was to stop them.

"They want to stop this? But... why? It's the most amazing thing I've ever heard."

"It's going to upset a lot of people. Think about the pharmaceutical companies – mine too. We're going to put them all out of business. My retirement homes will become obsolete – the hospitals will probably close."

"And that's why you didn't tell me all this?"

"I, er… I didn't think you'd be too pleased. You were enjoying making money and…"

"But this is much more important than money! You're talking about saving the lives of… *Everyone!* The population of the planet! You thought I'd… *mind?* What the hell do you take me for?"

David looked at the ground. "I'm sorry."

"David, we mustn't ever let things get like this again, okay?"

"No, you're right. And we won't."

"I can hardly believe this. It really *does* turn people young?"

"What you saw on the news – those people – they've been turned young, yes."

"So… what happens now?"

"We keep on with the plan and hope that it all works out."

"Can I help?"

"There's nothing you can do. It's almost over. I don't want you to be put in any danger."

"But there must be something!"

"Helen… really, there's nothing. We're almost at the tipping point. There's only one more thing to do and then… it will all be over, one way or another."

"By that you mean… whether you're going to stay alive or be killed?"

Chapter 24

They had selected one hundred people from those who had registered on *let-the-aliens-know.com* and had sent them each a package containing one of the blood pills and a note, which said:

> *The little red men send you the gift of life. Give this pill to whoever is near death and they shall be turned forever young.*

Three days later the TV stations went crazy. There was 24-hour coverage from around the world of newly-young people who seemed to be popping up all over the place, this time with a different story. They all said they'd received a-pill-in-the- post from the aliens! It was the weirdest, wackiest story ever reported. But there was no denying that dozens of people really had been made young again.

In the Vatican the Pope and his advisors did not know how to respond. An aid told The Holy Father that he had to say something. Whatever or whoever it was that was turning people young was capturing the imagination of the world. Congregations were dwindling. The Pope was confused. Should he proclaim that the newly-young had been saved by God, or should he denounce it as the work of the devil? A Cardinal asked him, "Holy Father, if this continues, if there is no death… what does this mean for us?" The Pope shooed the Cardinal away.

CNN showed a priest in France who had denounced Catholicism and set up his own church, worshipping the planets. He said that what the world was witnessing were *real* miracles, and that it was a sign from God that we were not the only creatures He had created. He looked at the camera and implored the viewers to join him. "This is where our real salvation lies!" he cried, trembling with emotion.

The team gathered together in the main saloon on the boat, their faces twitchy with a mixture of excitement, fear, apprehension, and a sense of wonder at what they'd done.

"It's unstoppable," Danny said.

"It was unstoppable a long time ago," David said. "I think it's time we broke cover."

"Are you sure?" asked Tara.

"No I'm not," David said. "Once we do this we'll be exposed, but we can't make the whole world young in secret. We were always going to have to expose ourselves in the end."

"But they can't kill us – they daren't!"

"They might try," David said. "Desperate, short-sighted men are going to feel they are losing everything. There's no telling what they might do." He looked at the floor for a moment, then he added, "But, as we discussed in the beginning, once the secret is out and the people see we have the power to make everyone young… we might reach the tipping point. Can they afford to kill us when the desire for what we have to offer the world is so great?"

He turned to Danny, "Okay, this is it. Let's get those emails out."

Danny left the room to send the emails with the added attachment that he had composed earlier. David picked up the internal phone and called the captain on the bridge.

"Okay, it's time to take a cruise."

Karen slipped out of port and into The Solent. They turned to starboard and began to make their way into the English Channel.

Down in what had become the communications room, Danny clicked on the icon that sent the emails to the world's newsrooms. The attachment showed an image of a strange looking symbol. The email said the symbol was a secret sign sent to Earth by the aliens. Danny and the team knew that the TV stations, desperate for a new angle on the spacemen story, would include the image in every report for the next day or so, and when Harry, Emily and the other newly-youngs saw it they would instantly remember what had really happened to them and that the story about the little red men had been a hoax.

Now the cat really was out of the bag.

Danny joined Tara at the bow of the boat, the wind streaming Tara's hair out behind her. For a long time they said nothing, both deep in thought, trying to imagine what sort of a world they were going to live in. They held hands, their heads spun with jumbled thoughts, and their bodies tingled with excitement. A new epoch was dawning and Tara thought of her newly-young mother, saved from death, free of cancer, and suddenly she had the desire to share the moment with her. She took out her pay-as-you-go cell phone and said, "I want to call my mom, what do you think?"

"It won't be a problem. In an hour or two the whole world's going to know everything about all this."

Tara grinned and punched in the number of her mother's cell phone.

Joss barged into Cleaver's office, huffing and puffing, too wound up to sit down.

"Come on Alistair! This is taking an inordinate amount of time."

"If my hunch is right it'll all be over in a very short while."

"Hunch? What hunch is this? You haven't said anything."

"I've got Ronald Simmons checking something out."

"Well, don't be so evasive. What the hell are you working on? Come on, tell me."

"I wasn't going to say anything until I was sure-"

"Alistair, your reticence is tiring. Speak!"

"Well, it was the plane you see."

"What about it?"

"It's more to do with where it is, really. You see, I tracked its movements, as you know, and we established which countries it had flown to. But for some reason when it returned to the UK it landed at Southampton. I asked myself why. It's normally based at Farnborough, so why land at a different airport? Southampton is hardly the favoured landing place for most of these billionaire types. I pondered on this and thought about David Lane's disappearance and what Southampton is most noted for. Then I sent Simmons down there to check something out. If I'm right I-"

The phone rang and Cleaver picked it up.

"Ah, Simmons…" Cleaver nodded at Joss and then listened intently to the agent on the phone. "He has… .? Where is it… ? When..? Are you sure… ? Right. Do it now and then get back to me!"

He slammed the phone down, a deranged grin on his face, but said nothing. Joss looked at him intensely. Finally he could wait no longer.

"Well, what the hell is it? Don't just sit there looking like a pig on a shit farm — tell me!"

"We've got him!"

"Where?"

"He landed in Southampton because he's got a *boat* there, called *Karen*. Some great big vulgar gin palace apparently."

"And it's docked there?"

"It was. Not now though."

"Well where in God's name is it?"

"It left a short time ago."

"Going where?"

"I don't know, but it hasn't got far. Simmons is contacting the coastguard now. We'll have its position in a few minutes."

"Excellent!"

Jim met Isobel at the airport. She threw her overnight bag into the back of his car and got in beside him.

"Jesus, the airports are in a mess," she said.

"The whole *country's* in a mess, Isobel. I told you."

"There's chaos in there. The passengers are fighting each other, almost."

"They can't get their baggage. The handlers — most of them haven't come to work. They're up on the hills calling for spacemen to come and visit Earth."

Isobel smiled and said, "Come on let's get out of here — drive." Jim pulled away. "To think that all this… it's being caused by Tara…"

"Excites you, doesn't it?" Isobel nodded, a smile playing on her lips. "Always were the revolutionary weren't you."

"Nothing wrong with being unconventional, Jim."

"Is that what you call it?"

"You're still a square," Isobel said.

"Yeah. That's me. A government man, aren't I? Except here I am, complicit in something that's going to…"

"Change the world. That's what this is doing. I'm alive and well, thanks to Tara and her friends. This is a good thing, Jim. A very good thing."

"Where do you want me to take you?"

"The White House, of course. The President and I are going to have a little chat."

"What?"

London was at a standstill. Hyde Park was a mass of people sitting in circles on the ground, drinking beer and wine from the bottle, hugging and kissing each other. The Prime Minister watched the news reports.

"I haven't seen anything like this since… the sixties. It's incredible! We've got to do something."

His wife, Theresa, said, "You should send in the troops. You have to restore public order. You're entitled to use force."

"Well, yes I know, but… against our own people, I'm not sure I can do that… not yet."

The news camera in the helicopter looked down at the crowds.

Theresa said, "Look! It's growing! There's thousands of them coming along the streets to join in. The police can't stop them. You have to do something!"

"But I can't shoot them, can I? They're waiting for spacemen to come down and save their relatives."

"All this nonsense about wanting to live forever! They're selfish, that's what they are. You don't have to pander to them."

"I'm not pandering to them. I just don't want to have a Tiananmen Square incident on our doorstep. The political fallout would be impossible to control. The opposition would have a field day."

The protest continued through the night. No one cared about going to work the next day. Buses and trains had ceased to function, the banks were closed and it was impossible for MPs to get to the House of Commons through the blocked streets.

Theresa said, "It's a state of national emergency. Anarchy, that's what it is! You have the right, you have the *duty* to get the troops out to get the country moving again!"

The Prime Minister mopped his brow and stared at the television. And then the phone rang. He grabbed it and pressed it to his ear.

"Yes?"

A voice told him there was a Joss Whelan on the phone.

"Well, put him through." Joss came on the line. "Have you got something?"

Joss said, "We've located the people responsible for this."

"Thank heavens for that. Do whatever you have to do and for Christ's sake do it fast! "And Joss, you'll be rewarded for this."

"Thank you, Prime Minister."

Henry Banks called Cleaver.

"Look, I'm sorry, Cleaver, but in case you haven't got the full picture, the goddamned world is going crazy and we can't hang around any longer. I've got a small team on the job. They're going to-"

"Henry, you can call your men off."

"Don't get so defensive, Cleaver."

"I'm not being defensive. You Americans have so little faith in your allies. It's appalling really. We've located them. They won't give us any more trouble. In fact, as we speak a plane is on its way to... finish the job."

"Oh, I see. Excellent. If you need a plane I take it they're not in England. So where are they?"

"At sea. They've been operating from a boat. Fortunate really. One missile and they'll sink leaving no trace – nothing to explain. Boats sink all the time. It's a fact of life."

"Good work. I'll relay this to the President. It's going to put his mind at rest."

Before going to the Oval office Henry decided to called his agents personally to tell them to stand down. First on the list was Neil Drover. As usual he asked some stupid questions, which put Henry in a mood and by the time he got around to calling Jim Reynolds Henry was feeling irritated as hell and wondered what he was doing acting like a goddamned secretary to these guys.

Jim and Isobel were making their way to Pennsylvania Avenue when Henry called. Jim flicked open his cell phone.

"Yes?"

"It's Henry."

"Oh, right."

"You can stand down."

"Stand down? What do you mean?"

"I mean you can *stand down! That's* what I mean."

"Sure, okay. But why?"

"Because the Brit came through, that's why."

"How? What do you mean, came through?"

"Hey! How come you're asking the fucking questions! He's found them – it's over. He's dealing with it so you don't have to – so stand the fuck down, okay?"

"Right, okay."

"Just wait for my instructions."

The line went dead.

Jim told Isobel what Henry had said.

"Are you sure, Jim? Is he certain? There's no mistake?"

"Isobel, this is one son of a bitch who doesn't make mistakes."

"Just get me in to see the President – he's our only hope – Tara's only hope. Step on it, Jim!"

Jim weaved the car through the crowds. Most of the people had rapturous expressions on their faces, convinced salvation was at hand and the world was about to change. A man carrying a placard, which said: *Live Forever, Love Forever,* stepped out in front of the car and Jim screeched to a halt.

"Jesus! That guy ain't going to live forever. Watch where you're going!"

"Come on, hurry, Jim!"

"I'm doing it for Christ's sake! If I kill someone it ain't gonna help us get there any quicker!"

By the side of the road a circle of hippy types wearing white robes and flowers around their necks, held hands and sang, *We Are The World,* swaying from side to side, gazing at the sky.

Isobel couldn't help but chuckle. "Wow. It's fantastic, isn't it?"

When they were close to the White House they abandoned the car and made their way on foot, pushing through the throng, until they made it to the entrance. Jim flashed his identity card and told the man he had to see the President and that it was a matter of life and death. It was ten minutes before Jim had been sufficiently checked out for the guards to feel comfortable letting him into a security office. Jim banged the table to get people to listen, telling them he wasn't fucking joking and that someone had to get to the President and tell him Jim and Isobel Reynolds were waiting to see him with some news about this spacemen crap that was for his ears only. They sat in a side room waiting for the guard to get back to them.

Isobel's cell phone rang.

A voice said, "Hi mom, it's me."

"Tara! Where are you?"

"Now come on, you know I can't tell you that, but stop worrying, okay?"

"For God's sake Tara, you don't know how much danger you are in."

"Why?"

"Because they know about you and-"

Uncle Jim snatched the phone from Isobel.

"Tara!"

"Uncle Jim. What are you doing there with-"

"There's no time for any of that. Look, they know all about you, I'm sure of it."

"Did mom tell you about how she got young?"

"She didn't have to. I got called into a meeting in Washington. I was briefed about you before I found out what you had done to your mother. It's that guy Cleaver. He's been talking to Henry Banks. Don't ask me how, but they know everything."

"Shit! Are you sure?"

"Absolutely. They're going to do something to stop you pretty soon. We were going to be mounting an operation to find you, and then Cleaver calls and says we can stand down because they've located you. What kind of phone are you calling on?"

"It's okay, its one of these pay-as-you-go mobiles, it's registered to no one and this is the first time I've used it."

"Well don't use it again, you hear? And wherever you are, just get the hell away from there."

"I can't."

"Why the hell not? You have to!"

"I'm on a boat. Are you sure Cleaver knows we're at sea?"

Jim let out a sigh of exasperation. "I don't know. For God's sake be careful. We're going to try something here. Tara... keep safe, please!"

"I'll do what I can."

Five minutes later a guard with a stunned look entered the room and told them that the President would see them and that he was to arrange for their safe and speedy passage to the Oval Office.

In the White House a female aide, dressed in a smart navy blue business suit, hair immaculate, took them the last twenty yards. She knocked on the door, opened it and announced to the President that Jim and Isobel Reynolds were here to see him.

"Show them in," he said.

Jim entered first. "Mr President," he said.

"Hello Jim. Been a long time."

Isobel entered the room behind Jim. The aide closed the door behind them and Isobel stepped out from behind her brother so she was in view.

"What the... ?" the President said. "I... I'm amazed. You don't look any different to when..."

"When we last saw each other thirty years ago." Isobel said.

"No... How come you..." His words trailed off and he sat there, jaw hanging lose like a barn door with a broken hinge, eyes like a bullfrog's, forehead creased in puzzlement. "Isobel... I..."

"Take your time. Takes a little getting used to."

"I didn't know you'd... been... that this had happened to *you*."

"You wouldn't have. I haven't been in the news. Publicity was never my thing."

The President swallowed hard. "You... you look amazing... beautiful."

"Thanks. Always were the charmer, weren't you."

"When I heard that Jim wanted to see me, and you... I thought you might have some information about all this. Obviously you have..."

"Oh, yes. I know all about it."

"Well, good. You want to help stop this, right?"

"My God, you really think that, don't you?"

"It has to be stopped, Isobel. You have no idea what this is doing to the world. It's-"

"It's screwing things up a little for you – that I do know. Do you know why I look like this?"

"I guess you've been..."

"Visited by little red spacemen?" She laughed. "Something like that." She took a step towards him. "You don't know it, but I was riddled with cancer not long ago, with only a few weeks to live. I was on the point of calling my daughter – *our daughter* – to see her for the last time. Putting your affairs in order, some people call it. The cancer was gnawing away at me. I was so weak I could hardly eat, didn't want to eat – what would have been the point? It would have been a waste of good food. You hear what I'm saying? There was no hope for me – none. There wasn't a doctor in the world that could have done a thing to save me. And then I was offered this. The chance to… wind back the clock and stop it – to become young again and stay that way. I'll admit I wasn't crazy about the idea. I was conditioned to die, like all of us on this planet. A part of me realises I'd been subconsciously preparing to die since I was about thirty. And, strangely, taking away the prospect of death was a little scary at first. Stupid thoughts entered my head, such as, if I was going to live forever what the hell would I do with my time – stuff like that. But I guess having too much of something is less of a problem than not having enough, right? Anyway, what I wanted was to get rid of the cancer and be well again. So I took the cure and guess what? They threw in everlasting life as a bonus. I think I'm a very lucky woman. And you want to *stop* all this?"

"Isobel, for Christ's sake! I'm happy you have been cured of the cancer, of course I am. And… I have to say, I'm happy you're young again. Like I said, you look amazing – you haven't changed a bit since I last saw you. But I have to look at the wider picture here. I'm the President and I have to do what's best for the world as a whole."

"Listen to yourself. You know this is bullshit. You must do."

"This… this threatens everything, don't you see?"

"Of course it does. It tears it all down. But that's what you have to do if you want a better world."

"Look outside, for God's sake! You think chaos is a better world? This is not some tune-in-turn-on-drop-out hippy thing going on here. This is killing the world."

"As we know it – yes! I admit I had some weird ideas about all this at first. But hang on a minute. You are the President. You're supposed to be the leader of the free world. The *free* world!"

"It's not that way. This is real life. You can't have freedom like that. What you're talking about is anarchy."

"No! What I'm talking about is what we believed in all those years ago. Government of the people, by the people, for the people! What we got was more of the same old crap – comply or die! You used to be a fresh-faced idealist like the rest of us. What happened?"

"I grew up."

"Bullshit. You sold out. You became one of them. Look at you now, trembling with fear in case someone brings down your own personal edifice."

"That's not true, Isobel. I have to think of *everyone!*"

"And by thinking of everyone, you have to let everyone die, right? Is that some kind of inverted logic? My God, your thinking is so muddled pretty soon you'll be wiping your teeth and brushing your ass."

"You can't say that to me!"

"Because it's true, or because you're the President?"

"This is pointless. Are you going to tell me who these people are, or not?"

"Yes. I'll tell you who one of them is, anyway."

"Good. Let's have a name."

"Her name is Tara. And in case you've forgotten, she's your daughter. The one I kept secret all these years so I didn't upset your political career. Now what are you going to do, have your own daughter killed so you can cling on to your presidency?"

The President slumped back in his chair, folded his arms and looked down at the desk. "Oh, shit. How did she get mixed up in all this?"

"What matters is that she *is* mixed up in it."

"And you let her?"

"What? You dare to criticize me as a parent when you've never once met your own daughter?"

"I didn't mean it like that."

"I'm damned proud of her and what she's doing! She's trying to save the life of everyone on the planet. She has her values sorted out – though she sure as hell didn't inherit them from you!"

"But if… if this thing goes on… if it's allowed to continue… what's going to happen?"

"The walls of Jericho will come tumbling down. We'll have a new world. What we always wanted."

"The walls of Jericho have served us well over the years."

"Really? What's so precious about disease and death? You would sacrifice the life of everyone on the planet just to keep things the way they were. Lives for what – a bunch of structures and institutions? They were meant to serve *us*, not the other way around! Don't you have faith in humankind to evolve, to create new structures and ideals to live by – things that will serve the people better – people who are forever free of disease and death? Can't you see that you might have lost the plot somewhere?" He didn't answer. She went over to him, grabbed his arm and said, "Come here. Take a look." She led him over to the window. "Look at the people out there. They don't want to die. They don't want their parents and loved ones to die. All they want is to be free of death and disease. Isn't that the most basic thing? They are *your* people – you are there to serve them. Remember your oath? How can you deny them life? In any case… it's too late to stop it now. Too many people want it."

The President paced up and down, scratching his chin. "If we let it go on, what would happen?"

"Who knows? Do you care? Curing death is all that matters, isn't it? You will go down in history as the man who enabled the world to live. You will have granted them life forever. You will always be remembered for that!"

The President looked up. "All right Isobel. You don't have to oversell it. I've got it, okay? So what do we do next?"

The door burst open and Henry rushed in.

"Mr Pres- Oh! I didn't know you had… Jim? Didn't know you were here. Nor you, Miss..?"

"What is it Henry?" the President barked. Henry glanced at Isobel. "It's okay. You can talk in front of her."

"Right. As I already informed Jim here, I got a call from the Brit, Cleaver. He's located them."

"Is that all he said?"

"Yes. And that everything's under control. They're on a boat. Apparently there's a fighter jet on its way to deal with it right now."

Chapter 25

The President was put through to the Prime Minister. "Listen, you've got to call off this attack on the boat," he said.

"What boat?"

"The goddamned boat your plane is about to blow up and sink. Don't you know what's going on?"

"No – I mean, what are you talking about exactly?"

"Your guy, Cleaver! The spacemen thing. He's got a plane about to destroy a boat. A boat with my daughter on board!"

"You're daughter? I didn't know you had one."

"I don't give a fuck if you know that or not. I'm not here to discuss my family situation with you! Call off the damn attack, you hear?"

"You say it's Cleaver?"

"Yes! You've got to tell him. And you need to know that I've scrambled one of our fighters from one of our bases in Germany and they've got orders to intercept your fighter. Do you understand?"

"Of course. I'll call Cleaver right away. But why is he trying to blow up this boat?"

"The people on the boat are the ones responsible for this age reversal thing."

"Oh. Cleaver never mentioned a boat."

"It's too late to stop it now. Take a look on TV. The world is going mad for this. We *can't* stop it now."

"But we have to! Haven't you realised what will happen if it goes ahead? The world is going to turn upside down. The pension funds – we won't be able to provide enough for people. They'll have a pension forever!"

"Listen. Get this clear. It's too damn late! Didn't you catch CNN about half an hour ago? These newly-young folks – they've told the world that the spacemen thing was a hoax they had to play on everyone so they didn't get killed – by us! They were hypnotised to say it was aliens! The ones who've invented this, they've sent out pills to people around the world. People are turning young. Their relatives are dancing in the streets! The truth is out. They've let the world know they are responsible and we are trying to kill them. What are you going to tell the folks in England when they realise you've killed the people who have been trying to save them from dying? How the hell are you going to explain that? We've gone past the tipping point. The game is up."

"Oh my God! What do we do?"

"You better embrace it. Tell the country they are mistaken and that you support what they are doing. Go with the flow. There's nothing else to be done."

"How the hell are we going to cope with… people's expectations?"

"I don't know. We're in new territory. Where this will end up, I don't have a clue. What the hell am I doing talking to you! Make that call, goddamit!"

Cleaver got the call from the Prime Minister. Afterwards he immediately called Joss.

"What? Why the hell is he asking for the plane to be stood down?"

"He says the President's daughter is on the boat."

"He doesn't have a daughter."

"That's what I thought."

"You haven't called it off have you?"

"No, not yet."

"Good. Then don't."

"Just ignore the Prime Minister?"

"Alistair, in the fog of war, as it were, there is ample scope for… miscommunication – or no communication. People panic. Split second decisions are made – some of them wrong. You get my meaning?"

"It's going to be difficult to explain to him that he's made a wrong decision."

"No, no, no! We don't have to do that. We just don't tell the plane to stand down. We were too late. It's that simple."

David was up on the bridge when Tara and Danny burst in. Tara told him what her uncle Jim had said.

"Did he tell you exactly what Cleaver knows?" David asked.

"No, he just said they'd located us and were going to stop us.

Danny said, "What do we do?"

"What I'm wondering is why we're still alive. If he knows where we are I'm sure he'd have done something about it straight away. You two go down and monitor the TV screens. Look out for something… some sign, a report that insinuates they know where we are."

"Okay."

They left David on the bridge.

The captain looked up at the sky, then he picked up his binoculars.

"What is it?" David asked.

"Looks like a fighter jet. Probably on some kind of exercise."

"Let me see." David took the binoculars and trained them on the fast moving dot on the horizon. Suddenly it turned towards them. Closing rapidly, the dot growing in size, until he could make out the wings and the tailfin. Suddenly a quiver of fear ran up and down his spine.

Had they been discovered? Was this it – the end of the road?

The plane shot overhead, silent, until the thunderous roar of the engine caught up with it, filling David's ears with decibels of pain.

"Whatever kind of exercise he's on he's flying too bloody low!" the captain said.

David pressed his binoculars against the starboard side window and saw the plane streak across the sky and then shoot up vertically like a freshly launched rocket. It pierced some clouds and went out of sight. He tried to make sense of it all. If it was what he feared, how come the plane had not shot at them? Could it be that the pilot had merely been checking them out and had radioed their position to a nearby warship? For a moment David felt like a mouse in a shoebox with a hungry cat peering down at him, able to snuff out his life with a swish of its paw.

Suddenly there it was again on the horizon, speeding towards them. And then he saw another dot behind it. Now there were two planes – as if more than one were needed! The second one seemed to be catching up the first one quickly. It was higher by a thousand feet or so. Then from the first one came a flash of light and a streak of something. In a fraction of a second David knew it was a missile and they were doomed. He gripped the binoculars for an instant and then he relaxed, resigned to his fate, sensing his life was all but over. And then he saw a flash of blinding light, like a streak of condensed lightning, shoot out of the second plane and hit a point in space about one kilometre from the boat. An orange and yellow fireball exploded and then the first plane climbed rapidly, chased by the second.

"What the hell was that?" the captain said.

In a voice that was calm but conveyed a sense of bewilderment, David said, "I… don't know. I really don't."

Danny returned to the bridge.

"Guess what? Harry and Emily are on TV telling the reporter it was all a hoax and they were turned young by us on this boat!"

David was unmoved, still looking up at the skies.

"Danny, go back down and email all the newsrooms. Tell them who we are and where we are."

"Are you sure?"

"It might be our only hope."

Cleaver called the air force base.

"Is it done? Have you sunk it?"

"No. We fired a missile but it was taken out by a US fighter with an anti-missile defence laser. Our man had been shadowed by a US fighter from Germany. We thought he was just on a training exercise but he shot our missile out of the sky."

"What? There must have been some mistake. Didn't you go back and try again? You were given an order!"

"You're damned right I was. I was ordered to have our plane leave the area and abandon the mission."

"Who the hell told you that?"

"The Prime Minister."

"What? Hang on."

Cleaver put his hand over the mouthpiece and said to Joss, "The Prime Minister told them to turn back!"

Joss screamed, "That stupid little pipsqueak! The man's a complete fool! He hasn't got the balls of a mouse!"

Cleaver told the man on the phone to forget it; he would call him back.

"I don't see what we can do," he said to Joss.

"The idiot has no idea what this means. He can't foresee what he'll be having for breakfast, never mind what'll happen to the world if we don't stop this."

"But we can't override him. They won't listen to us if he's called them personally."

"There's only one thing for it. You're going to have to take care of it. Take a couple of our own men and a helicopter. Kill them all. But make it seem like an accident. Boats sink all the time."

Chapter 26

They were still cruising along the English Channel on their way to the Bay of Biscay. Danny gripped the binoculars and scanned the horizon looking for an approaching battleship, knowing that if he saw one there was nothing they could do. Perhaps it was better not to know when your life was about to be snuffed out. He lowered the binoculars, took Tara's hand and felt a rush of love for her. If these were to be his last minutes on earth he was glad that-

Out of nowhere, a green helicopter appeared in front of them. It hovered over the bow of the ship.

"What the fuck is that!" David said.

Danny remembered the last time he had seen a green helicopter appearing from nowhere and a chill ran up and down his spine.

"Cleaver? No, it can't be…"

The helicopter descended and through its open door Danny saw three figures carrying weapons. One of them seemed to be getting ready to jump down onto the boat.

"Turn! Shake them off!" David shouted.

The captain turned the wheel first to the left, then to the right and the helicopter stopped descending, the pilot trying to follow the movement of the boat. The bow bobbed and weaved, making it impossible for anyone to jump down, and then the helicopter climbed twenty feet in the air.

"It's working!" David said.

Danny saw one of the men take aim with his assault rifle. "Look out!"

A spray of bullets hit the window of the bridge leaving a line of spidery holes. One hit the captain knocking him backwards. He lay on the floor with blood seeping into his white shirt from the hole in his chest.

"Oh, shit!" David said. He jumped up and ran over to him. "He's dead." He grabbed the wheel and took control of the boat.

The figure on board the helicopter gestured with his arm for the boat to slow down.

"What the hell do we do?" Danny said.

For a moment they looked at each other with panic-stricken faces and then David said, "We've got to stop. We're unarmed. They can sink us if they want to."

He pulled back the throttle and the boat immediately began to slow.

Michael, Albert, John and Maria entered the bridge.

John said, "What the fuck is going on?"

"We've been discovered," David said. "Danny thinks it's Cleaver on the chopper. Guess we'll know soon enough."

The helicopter descended and when it was hovering four feet above the bow, three men jumped down dressed in black combat gear, carrying assault rifles. The helicopter arose into the air taking up a position a hundred feet above the sea.

John said, "Have we got any weapons?" David shook his head. "We can't just wait for these guys to kill us! That's what they're going to do aren't they?"

Danny said, "I don't doubt it."

Tara said, "But it's too late for them. They can't stop this!"

Danny said, "You remember Cleaver. You think he gives a shit? He's going to want to squeeze the trigger anyway."

The three men in black were running along the port side of the boat making their way towards the forward cabin.

"I'm not going to wait to get shot," John said. He turned and ran towards the steps leading down from the bridge.

"Wait!" Maria said. She tried to grab him but he shook her free and hurried towards the steps.

"Hold it!" David shouted. John stopped. "Get back here. Look after Maria. Danny and I'll do it."

David and Danny hurried down the steps and pressed themselves against the wall, laying in wait for the men to enter through the side door. A few seconds later the door opened and the first man in black burst inside. It was Ronald Simmons. David grabbed the end of his rifle and yanked it out of his hand. He swung the butt down hard his head, then began to turn, but before he could take aim the second man stuck his rifle in David's ribs and shouted, "Don't move!" David froze. "Back up! Slowly!" Danny recognised the voice – it was Cleaver. David stepped backwards, Cleaver following, the gun still against David's body. As Cleaver entered, Danny kicked the barrel of the gun away and shoved him sideways into the wall. The third man outside began to take aim, but David was too quick for him. He levelled his gun and fired a shot, blasting a hole in the man, sending him toppling backwards over the side rail and into the sea. Simmons was still on the floor and he grabbed David's legs. As David tried to shake him off, Cleaver regained his balance and cracked David on the side of the face with his rifle. David dropped his gun, Danny grabbed it, but it was too late. Cleaver already had his rifle pointing at him.

"Drop it Avery!"

Danny realised there was nothing he could do. He let the gun slip through his fingers and clatter to the floor.

"You know, it feels like we've been here before," Cleaver said. "But Mr Reynolds isn't here to save you this time. What a shame." He said to David, "Who've you got on board? I want an accurate answer, or I'll shoot someone."

David rubbed his neck. "Just us, a handful of crew and four others."

"Are you sure?"

David nodded.

Simmons got to his feet, picked up his gun and hit David on the side of the head with it.

"I think he owed you that one," Cleaver said. "Right. Well... all hands on deck, as they say. Get your crew assembled and fast."

Wincing, David held his head. "We need to go to the bridge for that."

"Then lead the way."

On the bridge Tara, Maria, John, Michael and Albert took a step backwards as the others entered.

"Well, I never," Cleaver said. "It's the scientist fellow. One of you is anyway. Which one of you is Michael Richards?"

"I am," Michael said.

"You, er... you've caused quite a stir, haven't you." Cleaver shook his head disapprovingly. He turned to David. "Call the others."

David used the intercom to summon the crew. A few minutes later they arrived.

Cleaver turned to one of the crew. "Is this it?" The man nodded. "You see what happened to your captain?" He pointed to the bloodstained corpse lying on the floor. "If you are lying you will join him. You understand?" The young man nodded again, looking terrified. "I am going to check the boat – you realise this, don't you?"

The man said, "It's just us – honest."

Cleaver turned to the rest of the crew. "I don't want any heroics, you understand? If you try to escape or suddenly feel the need to do anything desperate, I promise you I will shoot your boss, Mr Lane. Nod if you understand." They all nodded. "Good." He asked the young crew member, "Do you know your way to the engine room?" He nodded but looked puzzled, as if wondering why he was being asked such an obvious question. "I want you and your shipmates to go there, escorted by Mr Simmons here. He'll lock you in for a while, okay?" The man nodded. "Remember, I'll be here with a gun pointed at Mr Lane. Now off you go, and… ." He turned to face Albert and the others. "Take these with you, everyone except for Michael, Danny and David. Hope you don't mind me using your first names, but… well, we can afford to be a little informal don't you think?"

He gestured to Simmons who put the strap of his rifle over his neck, took out his pistol and jabbed it into the back of the young crewman, whilst slipping his left arm around his neck.

They began to make their way to the engine room and Cleaver said, "And Ronald… find out where the sea cocks are, will you?" Simmons nodded. "Hurry up back."

Cleaver turned to Michael. "All that stuff about a gas. You had us fooled for a while. Pity really. It would have been a useful weapon."

"I think developing the means to save lives rather than destroy them is much more important. You know… it's too late to stop this," Michael said.

"He's right," Danny said. "The world wants to be made young. In any case, everyone knows how it was done. We've emailed the newsrooms with what really happened and who we are. You're political masters are finished now, Cleaver."

"You really are stupid aren't you? You think we can afford to let you upset the apple cart like this? We are not going to let the world descend into anarchy."

"The people will not allow you to stop this. They-"

"The people are idiots! They don't know what they want – they need to be protected from themselves!"

"How will you explain killing us? We're the ones that brought immortality to the world."

"Simple. You were lost at sea. Happens all the time. A tragic accident. Or maybe we'll tell them you were taken away by little red spacemen. Yes, that would do. We could say the email you sent was all rubbish. You were a bunch of jokers trying to take credit for what the aliens had done, and now the aliens have got angry with you. They've taken you off to their planet, vowing never to return here to save the naughty earthlings! Yes, I like that!"

"There are too many people out there now who are newly-young. It's unstoppable. You won't get away with it."

"I don't see that as a problem. They might be resistant to illness and aging, but it doesn't mean they can't be killed."

"You are one sick, son of a bitch!"

"Yes. You see, there are poisons we've had for a long time that are undetectable. Even if they didn't work, I suppose a bullet in the brain would suffice. It worked for The High Priest. Mind you I like the undetectable poison idea. We could tell the world that they weren't immortal after all, that they had been made young, but unfortunately their systems couldn't cope with it and they were doomed to die. We could finish them off one by one, nice and slowly. Yes… I'm pretty sure that after a while people would go right off the idea of becoming newly-young."

"Sick!"

"Rather ingenious, I would have said. Anyway, don't worry about it. In just a short while you won't have to worry about anything ever again. There, I'm sure that's a comfort to you."

Simmons returned.

Danny racked his brains trying to come up with an idea, something to distract him, to buy some more time. But how did you reason with someone who was hell-bent on killing you? Was there something Cleaver wanted more – something they could trade for their lives? "So get on with it," he said. "Shoot us if you have to. But let the others go. They're not really part of it."

Cleaver grinned. "Noble to the end. Touching – really it is. But I think shooting you is too merciful and quick. I have something else in mind. Imagine the water rising up and up, soon to pass over your head, and as you watch it you breathe ever more heavily, faster and faster, and your poor little heart's thumping away on your ribcage, knowing that soon you will be taking your last breath. And then you're under water, and as you slowly expel the last cubic centimetre of air from your lungs and you know there won't be any more to replace it – you have breathed your last. Your lungs ache for more air, and you fight against your diaphragm, desperate to stop it drawing in… . seawater, nothing but seawater… Then your head becomes light, and the urge to gasp in something – anything – into your empty lungs overwhelms you, and you do what you know you mustn't – you open you mouth and breath in the cold, choking, salty water, and then you realise that you are not a fish, you cannot live as they do, you cannot live at all! Ah yes… . I can see it now!"

"Why don't you stay with us and see it all close at hand?" Danny said.

"Amusing. But though the temptation is strong, I shall resist," Cleaver said.

And then Danny had an idea. "What if I traded something for our lives?"

"Your lives I do not value, but your death… now, that I value highly. You have nothing to trade."

"But I do."

"Really? Such as?"

"The gas."

"Don't be ridiculous."

"You don't want it?"

"It doesn't exist!"

"Of course it does. Tell him, Michael."

Danny sensed that Michael knew what he was trying to do. Michael said, "You think I'm really capable of fooling you guys like that? Nice idea but I'm afraid I couldn't. Olivia was really smart. She rumbled the gas a long time ago. I had to develop it to keep you guys on side whilst I developed my anti-aging potion"."

"You're lying."

"I'm not."

"All right. Amuse me. Tell me what you did with it."

"I sold it."

"You *sold* it? To whom?"

"The highest bidders."

"Who?"

"The, er… the Chinese of course. They wanted a quick way to jump ahead of the Americans in the arms race. It was easy. Anyway I needed the money to fund my research on this."

"You're lying."

"I'm not. You guys in the west are living under an illusion. They have the gas. They can wipe you out any time. You don't have the means to respond to that, so they hold the balance of power. Of course I could swing it back to you."

"If you are not lying and you give it to us, we'd all just be equal."

"Except I didn't give them the *antidote*. I *could* give it to you. You could drop the gas on them and they could drop it on you, but you would all be immune to it. The antidote is the key to the whole thing."

"You're lying."

"You think so? You want to risk it?"

Danny said, "You are stupid Cleaver. He's offering you the chance to get what you always wanted – your name in lights. This is your opportunity to get hold of the biggest breakthrough in weapons technology that's ever been made, and you can't see it. You were stupid enough to be fooled by him all this time, and now you're too stupid to see the opportunity that awaits you. You are a one-dimensional thinker Cleaver, you really are!"

"How do I know you are not stalling for time?"

"I can show you," Michael said.

"Show me? You have it here?"

"Of course not – you don't carry stuff around like that. But I have the formula on my computer. You can see it and the calculations I made for how quickly it would kill off a whole nation."

"Where's your computer?"

"In my room."

Cleaver stared at him as if trying to read his mind. Then a voice crackled on the radio communication device clipped to Cleaver's shoulder strap. "You need to hurry up in there. Fuel's getting low. We need to fly back soon or we won't make it."

Cleaver pushed a button and spoke into the microphone. "We won't be long in here." Then he turned to Simmons and said, "Escort him to his cabin and bring his computer here."

Outside Cleaver's field of vision, Michael managed to throw Danny an anxious look before he left with Simmons, and Danny knew Michael had nothing to show Cleaver. If he and David were going to try anything they had to do it now.

Cleaver wore a smug grin. "You two put your hands on your heads." He brandished the assault rifle at them and they raised their hands. Danny looked at the matt black metal killing device with its intricate nooks and crannies, and then at Cleaver's face. He realised that Cleaver was replaying the scene from three years ago in The Sunshine Hotel on the Isle of Man, only this time the roles were reversed. This was the re-match and Cleaver could determine the outcome – settle the score.

"Your scientist friend had better be telling the truth."

"I wonder which you would prefer, that he's lying and you get to sink the boat with us in it, or he's telling the truth and you get your killer gas?"

"It's a toss up, isn't it? I'm not sure."

"You need the gas. I don't see how you can get the approval of your superiors without it. I can't believe they think much of you. Can't believe they still pay you for whatever you do. How did you explain being found three years ago covered in sick with your trousers around your ankles? Must have taken some living down. So embarrassing. Simmons was on the floor laughing at you, you know? You wouldn't have seen it, but I did. I think he was having trouble containing himself."

Cleaver stepped forwards and swung the butt of the rifle, cracking Danny in the face, breaking his cheekbone, opening up a gash.

"*I've* got the gun this time, Avery."

Danny held his head with both hands, a dull ache spreading behind his ear, his vision distorting, things out of focus, and a nauseous feeling in his stomach. David inched closer to Cleaver, who spotted it, swung the barrel of the rifle in his direction and said, "I wouldn't."

David inched back, giving him a look that said, *fair enough*.

Cleaver said, "Just tell me something, Avery. Did you know about this anti-aging thing back then when we were in the hotel?"

"Of course."

"You didn't put it in that story you wrote."

"It's been our little secret all this time."

"But there was a gas?"

"Yes… yes, there was always the gas. I don't think we would have been clever enough to fool you that there was a gas when there wasn't. Michael had to make it – he didn't really want to, I'll grant you. Let's just say it was the price he had to pay for the opportunity to make his youth potion."

Cleaver grinned. "I knew it. I knew there was a gas."

"Your superiors are going to be happy with you aren't they? Especially when you tell them the Chinese have had it for a while and you have got the antidote."

Cleaver's eyes seemed to sparkle and Danny noticed him relax. Then Cleaver said, "You know, I'm glad we've met up here. Strange circumstances, I'll grant you, but… well… things just might turn out the way they were meant to. You've made things very difficult, but the situation is not impossible to salvage."

Simmons and Michael appeared, Michael holding his laptop.

"I'll, er… I'll boot it up now and show you the formulae."

He walked over to where Danny and David were standing and put the laptop on the chart table behind them. He pushed the power-on button. Danny and David turned towards the screen and had their backs to Cleaver for a moment. Michael mouthed the words: *Do it now!*

Cleaver's curiosity got the better of him and he approached the laptop, letting the barrel of the assault riffle point down to the ground. Simmons stood two paces away, his rifle cradled in his arms resting across his chest. Thick-necked and red-faced, he looked bored – a man who had no time for computers or formulae. Now Cleaver was standing close enough for Danny to smell his aftershave. He bent over the computer and Danny steeled himself for the fight. He inched closer, praying that Cleaver wouldn't notice. Just an inch or two more and he could make a move on the lanky British Secret Service man. Just an inch…

Cleaver stood up straight. "Just what am I supposed to be looking at?" he asked. "I can't see any formula. If this is supposed to be-"

But he didn't get time to finish his sentence. Michael picked up the laptop spun around and swung it hard into Cleaver's jaw, sending him staggering backwards. David launched himself at Simmons, tackling him to the ground, and then Danny leaped at Cleaver and raised his hands to grab his throat. Gripping his rifle, Cleaver swung it towards Danny, missing his head, but knocking his arms away from his neck. He whipped the rifle back round in the other direction and this time it crashed into Danny's skull sending him flying backwards against the chart table where he came to a stop beside Michael. Danny's blurry eyes quickly began to clear. He saw Simmons lying on the floor just a couple of steps away, out cold, with David standing over him.

Cleaver raised the barrel of his rifle "Hold it!" he shouted. David froze. "Step back!" He did as he was told. "Get over here with your two stupid friends." David stepped towards Danny and Michael, the three of them now in a line standing in front of the chart table, all of them breathing heavily.

"Three ducks in a row," Cleaver said. "Easy." He began to take aim at Michael.

Suddenly Danny realised what was happening. *No, it can't end like this. Cleaver cannot be allowed to win!* Danny lunged towards him but had only made half the distance when a streak of fire flashed from the end of the barrel, Danny's ears filled with a deafening percussive crack, and he felt something hit his body with the force of a juggernaut, knocking him to the ground. He lay on his stomach, the side of his face pressed against the carpeted floor, a tired, numb feeling spreading through his body. His ears filled with an echoey ringing, and then a rushing sound, as if he were in a giant seashell. Was he alive or dead? Would he see a bright light at the end of a tunnel and disappear along it like people said they did when they had a near death experience? Then he recognised the sound of his own breath, although it seemed to be amplified a hundred times, and felt a rhythmic throbbing in his temple, like a pulse. Yes, he was alive, he was sure of it now. After what seemed like minutes, but was only seconds, the rushing sounds faded, he opened his eyes and was able to focussed on the pile of the carpet. He heard he sound of a man talking. At first he thought the voice was distant, but then realised it was close.

The voice said, "You really are a fool, Richards. Immortality? You're ridiculous friend, Danny, doesn't seem to have attained such a lofty ideal. But then I suppose he hasn't been visited by aliens, has he?" The sound of that upper class, supercilious voice pulled Danny back into the present. "The games up for you too, Mr Lane. All you new-money types make your cash and then insist on spending it inappropriately, don't you? But really... messing with the rules of life... So arrogant and vulgar. Well, at least you didn't buy yourself a pink Rolls Royce."

Danny caught sight of Simmons's rifle. He stretched out a hand and pulled himself closer to it. Got to get there – got to get to it! He reached out again and dragged himself nearer, until he was able to touch it with his fingertips. He heard Cleaver say, "Okay, Richards. It's time to give your immortality drug the ultimate test. Can you survive a bullet in the brain? The High Priest couldn't. I wonder if you can? Let's see, shall we?"

Now Danny had it in his hands, his finger positioned on the trigger. All he had to do was turn and fire. In a split second his memory flashed back to The Sunshine Hotel when he had held a pistol pointing at Cleaver. He remembered the feeling of power he had felt then, and he felt it again now. Back then he'd had the chance to take Cleaver's life but had shunned it. He had known that he wasn't like Cleaver, but had sensed that the act of killing was an addictive drug and that he might *become* like him if he squeezed the trigger. Now he had no such qualms. He could definitely kill Cleaver. In fact he relished the idea.

Cleaver said, "Should I shoot you in the brain or the heart? Which would be the greater test I wonder? Difficult isn't it? Eenie meenie miney mo."

Danny had one chance. One heave, one twist of his body, using all the energy he could muster, every ounce. It had to be now! He took a deep breath gripped the gun and jerked himself around on his back. He trained the gun on Cleaver, heard him say, "Let's go for the heart," saw him press the stock of his rifle against his cheek, and then Danny fired three times, sending Cleaver across the room where he clattered to the floor, a limp, lifeless, ex-human being.

David ran over to Cleaver and grabbed his gun.

Michael rushed to Danny's side. "Danny, don't move," he said.

"Is he dead?" Danny asked.

Michael looked over at David who nodded.

"Yes, he's dead."

Cleaver's radio crackled into life. "Cleaver? Cleaver? Can't wait any longer. Going to refuel. Don't sink the boat yet."

The thwocking sound of the helicopter's rotors began to fade as it made its way back to base.

Michael examined the bullet hole in Danny's chest.

In a weak voice Danny asked, "How's it looking?" Then he coughed and a trickle of blood ran down the side of his mouth.

"Not good. You need a hospital." He looked at David. "How long will it take to get the boat to Southampton?"

"A few, hours. I'm not sure."

"We don't have time. He's bleeding internally."

"Am I going to die?" Danny asked.

Furrowing his brow, Michael looked intently at him, and then said, "Danny, there's only one solution to this. How do you feel about getting young?"

It was a no-brainer.

Michael filled a syringe with his own blood and injected it into the wound in Danny's chest, hoping it would infect him with anti-aging properties quickly enough to save him. Simmons began to stir. David tied him up and then released the others from the engine room. When Tara saw Danny lying unconscious on a sofa with Michael kneeling beside him pressing a folded towel against his chest, she let out a scream of anguish.

"Oh my God! Is he... ?"

"He's going to make it – I hope. But he's never going to look the same," Michael said.

Confused, Tara looked down at Danny's unmarked face (the bruising from Cleaver's rifle butt had already faded).

"What do you mean, he won't look the same?" Michael looked up at her and smiled and she said, "You've given it to him, haven't you?"

"I had no choice. I've got nothing else to stop the internal bleeding." He lifted the towel and looked down at the wound. "It's working. I think he's going to make it."

They wrapped Cleaver's body in a sheet and mopped up the blood from the carpet as best they could. Then they sat watching the TV screens. The world's newsrooms were going mad. Presenters were interviewing so called 'experts' who were trying to shed more light on how the cure for aging could have been developed. Other channels flashed up pictures of David Lane, the billionaire industrialist and then Sky News showed images from their helicopter of *Karen*, two hundred feet below, sailing towards Southampton. Then the BBC showed an interview with the Prime Minister who said:

"We must be proud of this wonderful achievement, which is a real breakthrough for the health of our nation, and indeed for the world. I am proud to say that there has been a strong British involvement in its development, and we shall of course do everything we can to ensure it is made available to as many people as possible – after stringent testing and the necessary licensing procedures have been complied with, of course. It is the government's responsibility to do whatever is necessary to make sure it is safe before it is made more widely available."

The interviewer said, "It appears it's only been given to people who were on the verge of death. Surely the government could license it for people in such circumstances? Safety is hardly an issue for the dying is it, Prime Minister?"

"Er, well… no, I suppose not in those circumstances. We'll be conducting a thorough review of all this, of course. And I'll be appointing an independent committee to review all options and procedures. We must wait to hear their recommendations before rushing in to things…"

David said, "I think that's it. We've done it."

"Why do you say that?"

"He's going with it. We've passed the tipping point. He's embracing what we've done. It's in his interests to keep us alive now and do what he can to cream off some of the credit for what happens next."

Michael said, "Then he hasn't got it has he? He can't see what's going to happen. He's not going to be able to control this."

"We know that, but it's good that he doesn't. As long as he thinks he might be able to ride the wave and control it, we'll be safe. And he *will* think he can get something out of this – there's no underestimating his arrogance."

"Then it's over. It really is. We've done it."

David instructed the crew to turn the boat around and head for Southampton. Danny grew young before their eyes. It was quicker for him than the others, he was younger and had less age-related damage to his cells. Halfway back to port he began to shake, and two hours later he looked twenty-five again. Scar tissue had formed over his wound and he had regained consciousness, Tara hugged him and laughed with joy, telling Danny he was her toy-boy now.

The Prime Minister really did want to ride the moment. When they arrived at Southampton he was on the quay along with several thousand people who had got wind of the arrival of the team who had saved the world from death. The Prime Minister stood on a chair and spoke through a loudhailer, but he was drowned out by the cheers. Then the crowd surged forwards and the TV cameras recorded him being knocked off his chair, disappearing under the stampeding mass of people. The images were broadcast around the world. No one realised then just how prophetic they were.

David began the process of distributing Michael's pills, made from the blood of the transgenic pigs in Argentina. Amazingly, several politicians who remained detached from the mood of the people called for David's arrest, saying there had been no clinical trials of the drug and that David was acting recklessly and illegally. But they soon shut up – such was the strength of public feeling and demand for immortality. Initially only the sick and elderly wanted to take the pills, but soon normal healthy people took them – people who wanted to retain their youth and vigour and live life as it should be lived. Eventually the pharmaceutical companies realised the game was up for them and in an attempt to retain some goodwill they offered to manufacture Michael's blood pills and give them away for free to whoever wanted them. Searching for new things to sell they turned their attention to developing drugs and treatments which genetically enhanced intelligence and human performance – products that could assist mankind's evolution.

At last people were really free, not because of some abstract political ideal, but because the reality of everlasting youth released people's spirits, allowing them to soar, encouraging them to reach new heights. A psychological switch had been thrown. Now people knew they really *could* realise their dreams – they had forever to do it, and a wave of true joy, creativity and love swept the planet. Religion and politics lost their appeal – people were too busy *living* to pontificate on things that had lost their usefulness. Short of voters and congregations, politicians and priests became redundant and were forced to seek out alternative employment.

But there were those who refused to be made young. They said they didn't want to 'interfere with nature', and became known as *The Diehards*. One of them was Joss.

A year after the team had returned to Southampton, Joss's wife, died. He stood at her graveside watching as they lowered her coffin into the ground, the vicar muttering away. It was a grey, rainy day and a trickle of water ran down his head and fell onto his clasped hands. He looked up at the sky and for a moment he was puzzled by what he had always believed to be a part of the Lord's design for humanity – death. He saw its ugliness, its finality, and its sheer pointlessness. For an instant his resolve flickered and he wondered if, just by some remote chance, it really could be part of the Lord's plan for us to discover the secret to eternal life. In giving us freewill had He deliberately furnished us with the ability to discover the means to eradicate death? But Joss had lived too long with his beliefs to let them go now. He shook his head and told himself, No, it couldn't be. Surely God would have made us immortal from the beginning if He had wanted us to be that way? Soon He would send His wrath to earth to punish us, to teach us not to get above ourselves – to restore order. The day would come… the day would come…

Six months later Joss died.

Part III

12th July, 2062

The young man had dark hair, was slim and fit, and was wearing a strange all in one white garment made of some Lycra-like material that formed a skin over his body, showing off his lightly muscled frame. In his hand he held a sphere that appeared to be made of chrome. Beside him sat a boy, similarly dressed, who looked about five years old. They were both looking at giant TV screen on the wall. An image of David Lane's boat, *Karen*, faded away. Then the man put down the sphere and the TV screen vanished, leaving a plain white wall with a smooth matt surface.

The man said, "Adam, this is a great thought projector. Glad we got you the latest model."

"I know, dad. I'm going to make some movies. Do you think I can sell them on the global net?"

"There's always a market for good stories, Adam."

"That was a great one you just showed me dad. Did you think it up, or was it a real one you had in your memory?"

"That was a real story, son. It was the story of..."

"Mankind," said the blonde woman who had just entered the room. "It's *the* most important story – the story of how we conquered disease and death."

"What's disease, mom?"

"It's something that used to kill people a long time ago – before you were born. People used to get ill, as we used to call it. That meant they would feel bad and sometimes they would die because of disease."

"What does disease look like?"

"You can't see it, Adam. It's something too small to see."

"Wow! You mean things you can't see can creep up on you and kill you? That sounds weird. It sounds like the world used to be a scary place!"

"It was, Adam. It was."

"But that story you thought-projected for me. There were people in it that looked different, not nice. They had strange skin, with cracks in it. You had some too dad. Not mom though."

The woman laughed. "Danny, do you want to explain that or shall I?"

"A long time ago people died not just from accidents, like today. They died of disease or something called aging."

"Aging? How did that kill you?"

"Times were different. Getting older didn't mean getting more experience and knowledge, as it does now. People had bodies that used to… sort of wear out. And part of that meant getting lines on your face, your hair going grey, and your muscles wasting away."

"Yuk! That sounds terrible! Who was that guy they called the Pope, or something?"

"He was a religious leader."

"What's religion?"

"Something people believed in a long time ago. People thought it was necessary to have religion to keep things in order, but they were wrong. There was a man who wrote a song called *Imagine*. In it he talks about a world where there was no religion, no wars, just people living in harmony, like we have now. Trouble was, back then everyone wanted a world like that, but no one knew how to get it. People kept looking in the wrong direction."

"Was your thought-projection about that, dad?"

"It was. What you saw on the screen was how we finally got to stop our bodies wearing out and cracks forming in our skin, as you put it. When we stopped dying, our minds changed too and we began to live differently. It's not easy for you to appreciate how things were, I know. But I'll thought-project it again for you one day and it might become clearer. Anyway, enough of that. We're taking you to the concert tonight."

"Yes! Great dad!"

"Michael and Albert who you saw in my thought-projection are coming too. So are David and Helen."

"Great! Have you seen the band before, dad?"

Danny and Tara looked at each other, smiling. "Many times,

Adam. But we want to see them again. They seem to get better and better. It's going to be fun." Danny stood up and looked out of the window. "I think I'll turn up the sunlight a little." He touched a pad on the wall, slid his finger down it and the light outside grew more intense. "You know, when I was your age we didn't have sunlight reflectors in space."

"How did you turn up the sunlight?"

"We didn't. We had lots of grey days with almost no sunlight."

"Didn't that make you unhappy?"

Danny chuckled. "Yes it did. We used to go on holidays to get some sun."

"What's a holiday?"

"It was when we used to stop working for maybe a couple of weeks and go to a part of the planet where there was some sunshine."

"You know dad, I'm glad I wasn't alive then. I don't think I would have liked the way things were when you were my age."

Tara said, "Are we going to eat before the concert or afterwards?"

"I'm hungry now, mom."

Tara took three small green pills from a cupboard and put each of them on a separate plate. She put the plates under a metallic canopy, pushed a button and the pills began to vibrate and expand. Two minutes later, three roast chicken and vegetables dinners were piping hot and ready to eat.

After they had eaten, Michael and Albert arrived at the house.

"Hey, are you ready for the concert?" Michael asked Adam.

"You bet. Dad says they're pretty good."

"The best there ever was. They're beaming the concert by hologram all over the world, but there's nothing like the real thing, huh?"

Adam said, "I don't know. I've seen lots of hologram concerts. I'm not sure; I can't tell the difference."

Danny said, "Young people today, huh?" and gave Michael a high-five.

"What is that thing you and Michael do, dad? Slapping each other's hands like that. You're always doing it."

"Just something we used to do a long time ago, son."

They got into the travel pod, Danny tapped their destination into the trip computer and the pod rose into the air and set off, joining the line of travel pods on their way to the Amphitheatre, where it came to rest in the pod-stack. They met up with David and Helen and made their way to their seats. The Amphitheatre was full of people all wearing the same kind of one-piece clothing made of stretchy, clinging material. Everyone seemed to be the same age – around twenty-five, except for a few children like Adam.

"It's a full house, dad," Adam said.

"It's not surprising. They haven't played here for six years. But that's not the only reason. This is a special concert – an anniversary concert. That's why they're hologramming it all over the world." A man walked onto the stage. "Here we go, Adam."

The crowd cheered in readiness, and then the man said, "Ladies and Gentlemen. I give you The Rolling Stones!"

The crowd roared, the curtain began to rise and then the Amphitheatre was filled with the sound of Keith Richards playing the familiar opening chords of *Brown Sugar*. Mick strutted onto the stage, Ronnie grinned at Keith, Charlie played drums, wearing his usual deadpan expression, and Bill's fingers tweaked the bass strings, a hint of a smile playing on his face, indicating he was glad to be playing with the band for the first time in decades.

The crowd were up on their feet, rocking to the music of the greatest rock and roll band of all time. When they finished *Brown Sugar*, Mick spoke to the crowd, welcoming them to their 100th anniversary gig. "Ladies and Gentlemen, it was a hundred years ago today that we played our first gig at the Marquee club in London." He pointed to a giant screen. "There we were!" On the screen the band members looked just the same as they did today.

"Where's Ronnie, dad?" Adam said.

"He wasn't in the band back then," Danny said.

Mick said, "Hey, we were pretty good even then, right!" The crowd cheered and clapped. Then Mick said, "All right. We're going to do a number we did about eighty years ago." He pointed to the screen at the footage of the band looking old, craggy-faced and wrinkled. "That's how we looked when we were younger!" he shouted. Then Keith struck the chords to *Start Me Up*, and the crowd stood up and rocked to the music.

Adam looked up at Danny and shouted, "They used to have cracks in their faces, dad. Like some of those people in your thought-projection."

"Yeah, They look like they *should* look now though. You enjoying it?"

"It's great, dad. Is it the same as when you first saw them?"

"Yeah, you bet! No different at all, Adam. But then there are some things you never want to change."

The end.

Also by Peter Kitson

Another fast-paced page-turner

Human Shield

When David Lane watches his wife die before his eyes, he promises he will finish what they set out to achieve – it will be his monument to her.

Driven and focussed, he creates an empire, but overstretches himself. In desperation he flies to Florida to meet with a trusted friend but is flagged down by a mysterious, stranded motorist.

Suddenly his world is turned upside down, and he is pitched into a battle to save not just his empire, but also his life!

Order now from www.peterkitson.com